A Bowers Thriller

Island of Bones

MARTA SPROUT

PRAISE FOR ISLAND OF BONES

"Fabulous — I love main character Kate Bowers... she's one for the ages."

— LEE CHILD, INTERNATIONAL BESTSELLING
AUTHOR OF THE JACK REACHER SERIES

"Hard-edged and gripping, brimming with reality, intensity and passion. This one packs a powerful punch."

— STEVE BERRY, INTERNATIONAL
BESTSELLING AUTHOR

"*Island of Bones* is a breathtaking, action-packed thrill-ride. Kate Bowers' strength, compassion, and a fierce streak honed in combat, makes this story a must read."

— ROBERT DUGONI, INTERNATIONAL
BESTSELLING AUTHOR OF THE TRACY
CROSSWHITE SERIES

"Set in colorful Key West, her plot is filled with twists and turns coming at the reader from all angles... Kate Bowers is a terrific blend of brains, strength of character, and pure guts...Those who enjoy suspenseful stories will be glad they decided to read this spellbinding thriller."

— GARY W. NOESNER, CHIEF, FBI CRISIS
NEGOTIATION UNIT (RETIRED)

"There are a lot of fine thriller writers, but few are as thrilling as Marta Sprout. Her stories can be by turns terrifying, classy, heartwarming, quirky or hilarious. One thing is certain, she'll keep you eagerly turning pages--if you dare! World-class."

— DAVID FARLAND, BESTSELLING AUTHOR
AND HOLLYWOOD GREENLIGHTER

Island
of Bones

COPYRIGHTS

Published 2021 by Deep Blue Press
www.deepbluepress.com

Cover Design by Books Covered

ISBN: 978-0-9857973-7-9
First Edition

*For the Men and Women in Uniform
who go to work each day and
put their lives on the line
to protect others.*

FIRST RULE: NEVER PANIC

S WIMMING IN THE OCEAN WASN'T THE PROBLEM: the big hands holding her underwater were the issue.

With her back pinned to the bottom in the shallow waters near shore, Kate Bowers struggled against the weight of the man on top of her. Her mask and snorkel were torn from her face. Inches away, a shimmering sheet of light danced above her. Beyond that—air. Barely out of reach.

If only she could break the surface.

The mindset she knew from combat kicked in.

Straddling her, the man rammed his knees into either side of her torso. She caught a blurry glimpse of a pale face ringed in short dark hair looming above her as he unbuckled his belt.

Son of a bitch.

When she felt his calloused fingers glide over her bare skin and slip inside her bikini bottom, she bit down hard on the large hand over her mouth. He yanked both hands away. From underwater, his yelp sounded muffled and distorted, like a recording played at half speed. The tang of saltwater and blood filled her mouth.

Bowers deflected his blows, which came in punishing waves. Water churned each time he slammed her against the shells, rocks, and broken pieces of rebar and concrete on the bottom. Grappling for leverage, she wished she'd worn a wetsuit and dive knife instead of this stupid bikini.

Second Rule: NEVER GIVE IN.

The man, who outweighed her by a good eighty pounds, shoved down harder, causing bubbles to escape from her nose and race toward the surface. In the turbulence, wisps of her brown hair swirled in front of her eyes.

As he tugged at her bikini bottom, his barrel chest cast a shadow over her face. She landed a few solid punches, but they only dialed up his aggression.

While her lungs ached for air, he kept his chin and shoulders above water.

Critical seconds ticked away. Her blows grew more frantic as he pulled her bikini bottom to her ankles and slipped it off.

The rumbling of a boat motor distracted him long enough for her to poke her head up for a quick gasp of air.

He shoved her down again, driving the bottom's jagged debris into her bare flesh.

Enough of this crap.

Lack of oxygen sapped her strength, as he clamped both hands around the base of her neck and smiled down at her.

He thrust his knees between her thighs. With her wide open and vulnerable, he unzipped his fly and exposed himself.

Oh, hell no.

The vision of obliterating his junk with a 12-gauge shotgun spurred her resolve.

She braced her heels against the seabed's rubble for balance and felt for anything sharp. She found a short section of rebar with a jagged point.

Using her remaining strength, she jabbed the sharp end at his exposed crotch. His screams rose to a squeal as he used both hands to cover himself. When he pulled away, she thrust her hips up, throwing him off.

Bowers rolled up onto one knee and gasped when she broke the surface.

"Say your prayers," said the tall man as he swung his arms wildly. Something fell from his wrist as he slipped on the algae-covered stones and tumbled to her right with a splash.

"Shit," he howled, as he cupped his bleeding crotch with one hand and reached out with his other to grab her.

She snatched a softball-sized rock from the bottom and stood ready with it in one hand and the rebar in the other.

"Back off," she ordered in a hoarse voice, "or I will end this."

He lunged. Anticipating the attack, she drove her fist forward with all the force she could marshal. The rock protruding from her fist landed in the middle of the man's face. That knocked him on his ass. Dazed and wincing in pain, he struggled to stand.

Bowers sucked in more air.

Blood poured from his nose. Pure rage blazed in his dark eyes as he dropped to his knees.

He waved her off with one hand, but then tried to grab her again. She went at him with both fists, bludgeoning him with the rock and stabbing him with the rebar until she'd pummeled every trace of fury from his face.

He lurched away and fell.

Bowers watched his faltering attempt to steady himself. Mission one had been to get him off her long enough to escape. Now the soldier in her wanted to finish it.

Still on guard, every flicker of movement captured her attention as she watched him grimacing. Her ragged breathing rumbled like jet engines in her ears. The churned water smelled of rotting sea grass.

Her muscles quivered as the man rolled away and lumbered to his feet. Blood-tinted water dripped from his blue T-shirt. While pulling up his shorts, he stumbled a few steps, reminding her of a boxer on the ropes.

He hunched over and winced. They were both clearly spent.

Beyond the swim platform, a narrow strip of beach lay between her and the hotel where a woman stood on the second-floor landing. When she raised her phone, Bowers crouched to conceal her naked hips below the surface.

The woman shouted at the attacker, "Hey asshole, I took your picture and called the cops." The man's neck flushed, as he fumbled to stuff his joystick back into his pants.

At the sound of a barking dog, he did an about-face. A sleek white fishing boat glided into view in the cobalt waters of the channel.

The boat driver pointed at her attacker. "Hey, you!"

The golden retriever onboard danced in circles. His bark rose to a frenzied pitch.

Her attacker screamed, "Mind your own business, asshole." He then sloshed his way toward a gray skiff nestled in the shadows of the dark-green mangroves where the roots dipped into the water like huge red straws. As bystanders gathered, a cluster of egrets screeched. Their white wings beat the air as they retreated to higher branches.

Under a clear blue sky, the white hull of the fishing boat gleamed in Key West's early morning sun. The occupants appeared to be a dark-haired man with a short ponytail and his dog. As if attached by an invisible thread, their heads oscillated in unison between her and her assailant who hurried to make his getaway.

Her attacker hoisted himself onboard his skiff. After a few tries, the engine sputtered and he fled toward deeper waters. As he headed west, Bowers' fingers let go of the rock and rebar. The rock hit the water with a *ker-plop*.

Four feet to her left, Bowers spotted her blue bikini bottom floating on the surface. She nabbed the suit and slipped it on while keeping a wary eye on her surroundings.

On shore, people from the hotel gathered on the beach only a few yards from a row of white lounge chairs where she'd left a towel and her bag. The scene had every element of a tropical postcard with the additional novelty of Key West's free-roaming chickens.

The man in the boat called out in a stilted voice. "Hey, the driver of this here rig wants to know if you're okay?"

Bowers paused to consider his odd speech pattern. She waved him off. "I'll be all right. Thanks."

The air tasted sweet, but the adrenaline dump left her drained.

The ingested saltwater made her queasy. Like clashing cymbals, a cascade of relief and regret collided in her thoughts.

Part of her wished she'd crushed her attacker's skull with the rock or driven the rebar through a femoral artery.

Goosebumps rose on her arms as a breeze swept over her wet skin. This was her first time in Key West and a long way from Washington, D.C. and the killers she'd put in jail.

She couldn't help but wonder: Was this a chance encounter with a local rapist or someone she'd arrested who'd hired a hitman to send her a message?

The last faint whine from her attacker's outboard faded into the distance and was replaced by the chatter of the bystanders. Being the object of their gawking left her feeling starkly alone. Even the strange man in the fishing boat hadn't taken his eyes off her.

HENRY EDGED HIS BOAT forward and hesitated like a cat circling a snake.

The woman in the bikini had walloped that boy pretty good. Mindful of the shallow depth, he eased in as close as he dared.

"Lady, you all right?" He grunted a few times and dropped the engines into reverse to back-up a bit.

"Yeah. Thanks." She nodded west. "You know that guy?"

He thought for a second as the *blub-blub* of his finely tuned engines burbled. "Don't rightly think he's familiar."

His eyes went wide when the woman stood and stared right at him. She was pretty, all right. Real tall. It fascinated him how her wet brown hair flowed so smoothly over her neck and the top of her shoulders. If it weren't for her staring at him, he'd still be checking her out.

He quickly glanced away. "No ma'am. Don't reckon the driver of this here boat knows him at all."

Henry thought about the skiff. "Buddy, I wonder if that fella had something to do with them missing girls?"

KILLER SMILE

T HE SHOCK OF THE ASSAULT clung to Bowers, as the gentle aqua-green sea swirled around her hips. The water felt cool against her fingertips.

Her assailant's behavior haunted her. The way he had smiled when he tried to strangle her confirmed one grim reality: he took pleasure in causing pain. No doubt, he'd done this before.

As a homicide detective, she knew people like him were the most dangerous of all.

She remembered the tear-drop tattoo he wore under his left eye. Such tattoos were worn to boast of killing and warn others that he wouldn't hesitate to do it again.

The assault had caused more than bruises. Her wounds stung. There wasn't anything she could do about being alone and injured but being vulnerable and unarmed was something she wouldn't tolerate for long.

At the weathered dock that extended from the beach into the water, she slogged up the aluminum swim ladder. Her legs felt heavy as she hurried past her swim fins lying in the sun.

Ignoring the pain and her waterlogged ears, she stepped down onto dry sand and strode toward her lounge chair, trying to ignore the murmuring crowd.

Bowers glanced up at the lady on the second-floor landing, then took a seat. She pulled her navy-blue beach tote within easy reach.

To her left, bystanders continued to gather in the shade at the back of the hotel. Some appeared anxious, while three or four took to the beach as if oblivious to what had just happened. A little boy squealed with delight. His blond hair glinted in the sunlight as he ran for a beach ball before being scooped up by his concerned father.

Despite the welcomed warmth from the sun, the coldness of her skin seemed to penetrate her marrow. She scanned the secluded area surrounded by the mangroves where she'd been attacked. To her left a beautiful ribbon of beach stretched along the coast. The sight of sunbathers enjoying a normal day made the reality of nearly drowning hit home.

It seemed ironic that she'd come here to take a break from police work and the violence inflicted on the innocent.

She shivered. Goosebumps rose over her torso.

Down the beach, teenagers played in the surf. To the sound of their giggling and shouts, Bowers assessed the stinging scrapes and bruises on her forearms. She wrapped her arms around her sides where a fibrous scar splattered like dried paint over the ribs on her left side. She brushed sand off her hip where a fresh scar from a gunshot wound was still an angry red. Until recently, she'd hidden her scars and rarely spoke of them.

Her new bikini symbolized a shift. Maybe not full acceptance of the scars, but close enough. This morning's assault slapped that sideways. The aqua-blue bikini with the tiny palm tree on the hip no longer flew like a banner of victory over her past. Instead, it left her feeling cold and exposed.

Bowers wrapped the towel around her shoulders and pulled out her cellphone. The time read 8:25 a.m. Riggs—the person she trusted most —would understand, but she hesitated to call. He wouldn't take the news of her assault well.

She buried her head in her hands and her feet in the coarse sand.

Saltwater dripped from her hair and pooled around her toes, mingling with the bright-red blood from the cut on her foot.

She glanced up at the channel where the man in the skiff had disappeared. Bowers smirked. "You think you've escaped. You have no idea what is coming for you, asshole."

ROUGH DAY

F BI SPECIAL AGENT STEVEN B. RIGGS took a sip of his coffee and scrolled through his phone, wishing for some sleep, wishing Bowers would call, and wishing their informant would bring in a new lead. Anyone of those would do.

Riggs knew he would never forget their last case together and that moment when he'd taken a bullet for Bowers. He'd do it again in a heartbeat. Life without her wasn't nearly as interesting.

Riggs exhaled loudly. Perhaps when she returned to D.C., he could talk her into joining the FBI. They needed people like her.

He leaned back into the worn cushions of his desk chair, where yesterday had bled into today.

His phone buzzed. The caller ID read: Kory. His friend in the Secret Service rarely called this early. They typically met after work with other law enforcement types at a local landmark known as The Old Ebbitt Grill.

"Hey Kory, what's shaking?" asked Riggs.

Kory's tone had the raw sound of a guy who'd recently been in a jam. "Can you meet me later?" Riggs exhaled loudly.

"Sure," said Riggs. "Rough day?"

"Last night, Roadrunner went off-grid."

"Again?" asked Riggs.

The president's headstrong daughter Lauren, a.k.a. Roadrunner, had developed a habit of ditching her security detail to hang out with her high school buddies. It wasn't the first time her shenanigans had put Kory under the gun.

Riggs checked the time. "You find her?"

"Yeah, but Redwood wasn't pleased."

Riggs understood the codename for the president. "What do you need?"

"Cold beer. Chew the fat. Your place?" he asked with a sarcastic snicker. "And maybe a ride home or a place on your couch, if I get too fucked-up to drive."

Riggs didn't completely buy Kory's story. He still sounded as if he had more on his mind than last night's kid-recovery mission.

"No problem," said Riggs. "Come over when you get off. It's my turn to get the pizza."

A few minutes later, Riggs flipped through a pile of reports on his desk until his phone buzzed with a call from Bowers.

The instant he heard her voice his relief did a nosedive. "What's wrong?"

"Been through worse," she said.

A prickle ran up his neck. "What happened?"

He heard only breathing.

"Talk to me," he said, trying his damnedest to avoid making it sound like an order.

"The drive down went okay. It's been uneventful until I was assaulted."

Shit. "When?"

"Ten minutes ago. On the beach."

He pulled out a notepad. "You okay? What the hell happened?"

Horrible images careened through his mind along with a grim checklist: *How badly is she hurt? Who's the scumbag who did this?* Most of all he wanted to know if she were still in danger.

"Riggs, he tried to rape me."

His hand clenched into a fist around his Zebra pen. Everything in him hated asking, "Did he—"

"No. I played skewer-the-sausage with a broken piece of rebar. That shocked the hell out of him."

Riggs bit his lip. At some point, they'd probably laugh about her vigorous response but not today.

It didn't surprise him that Bowers would be that resourceful. He'd witnessed her uncanny ability to fight back with startling force.

"I should've seen him coming."

Riggs heard the exasperation in her voice. "Who is this bastard?"

"Don't know." She sounded spent. Whenever Kate Bowers put aside her cop voice and allowed her softer side to show, it always caught his attention. "You sure you're not hurt?"

"I'm a little sore."

His mouth went dry.

"And a little cut up, but I'm okay. You know me. I'll be all right."

For the next few seconds he heard only a faint siren in the background.

"Riggs?"

"Yeah?"

"I miss you," she said in that voice that turned his insides to mush.

He glanced at his car keys laying on the corner of his desk. He chose his words carefully, knowing anything that smacked of handling her wouldn't fly.

"Listen, why don't you come back?"

Silence.

"Or," he said, "do you know anyone there you can stay with?"

She coughed. "An Army buddy used to live here, but I haven't talked to him since leaving Iraq."

The sound of sirens grew louder.

"Listen, the cops have arrived. I've gotta go."

"Wait." He'd seen her like this before. "What's your plan?"

"Rent a jet ski and blow off some steam."

He didn't buy it. The Bowers he knew wouldn't go sightseeing after an event like that. He knew exactly what she would do. "You're going after him. Aren't you?"

"What? You want pictures of the body?"

AMPED UP

E VEN ARMED WITH A KNIFE, Bowers felt naked as the warbling sirens raced closer.

The two-story hotel with its sunny yellow color and cottage-like design seemed at odds with the horror she'd just experienced. The ads had touted its secluded beach and sparkling blue pool as a peaceful, private place to unwind.

A couple had joined the woman on the second-floor landing. Together they continued gawking.

So much for privacy.

Five bystanders had moved closer to the pale-green fence around the pool. An older fellow in a Key West ballcap approached her. "My name's Jeb. I saw what happened. I hope you're all right." He handed her a bottle of water. "Is there someone I can call for you, miss?"

"No, sir, but thank you."

The sirens were cut. Moments later, a patrol officer in a rumpled uniform marched toward her. He kicked sand at a reddish-brown hen who cackled and scampered away.

"Is this the incident they called about?" he asked Jeb without giving him a chance to answer. "Stand over there. Now."

Bowers frowned at the young cop. Jeb glanced at her with obvious concern and backed away.

She studied the young officer. His shoulders tensed. Beads of sweat dotted his hairline. The soldier in her mistrusted anyone in unpolished boots.

Maybe a rookie, trying too hard? *All swag and no experience. Lovely.*

Right behind him came another patrol officer, who strolled over the sand with purpose, all six-foot-five of him. With biceps the size of a man's thighs, he still managed to graciously step aside for a young mother with two small boys.

Once again, the edgy cop yelled at the older man. "I said, go over there!"

Bowers put both hands on her knees and rose slowly to her feet.

The cop's head snapped around to glare at her. "Did I give you permission to stand?"

She calmly folded her arms and stared back. When she reached for her bottle of water, the officer flipped out his baton and smacked the lounge chair's blue cushion, narrowly missing her fingers. She heard and felt the *thwack* and pulled her hand away.

Pal, you missed the classes on de-escalation.

"Hands up," he shouted, ready to strike again.

She straightened to her full height, knowing that she had at least three to four inches on this clown.

"What's your name?" he demanded.

"Bowers."

He gripped the baton so tightly his knuckles blanched.

"You always threaten victims?" she asked in a deliberately calm voice. "Sounds pretty back-ass-wards to me." Bowers held her arms out and her palms open, hoping he'd see the defensive wounds.

"I said, hands up and keep your mouth shut." He brought one leg back. Classic stance of a man ready for a fight.

Bowers slowly raised her arms in compliance. *You need to dial it down, son.*

Bystanders murmured among themselves. The woman on the landing took pictures with her phone. *Great. That'll end up on social media.*

The twitchy cop held his baton ready.

"Vega. Take it easy," said the other officer. "Ma'am, do you need medical assistance? You look pretty banged up."

At least one of them paid attention at the academy.

"I'm just swell, officer," she said. "Since arriving here twelve hours ago I've been attacked by a scumbag who tried to rape and drown me and then—as if that wasn't bad enough—one of Key West's finest shows up and threatens me with his baton. I'm surprised he didn't pull out his 9mm Glock." Bowers put her hands on her hips. "It's shaping up to be a great vacation so far, don't you think?"

The tall officer's mouth dropped open as if to speak, but only a sigh escaped.

Still keeping Vega's baton in her peripheral view, she confronted the short man with a direct, eye-to-eye challenge.

"Drop the towel," he ordered.

"What do you think I'm going to do? Snap you to death?"

Vega glared at her. "You armed?"

His coarse black hair glistened in the sun. Even freshly shaven, he appeared to have a five-o-clock shadow.

Bowers dropped the towel from her shoulders onto the lounge chair. "There's a pocketknife in my bag."

"Do you have a gun?" he yelled.

She glanced down at her bikini and bit back a smirk. "Sure," she said as she swiveled in a circle. "I've got a .308-suppressed sniper rifle in my bathing suit bottom and a couple of Uzis in my top." She stopped and stared down at Vega who took a step back.

"For real, man?" she said. "I couldn't hide a tampon in this suit."

Vega's smoldering expression darkened. Yet, something about him appeared desperate. Maybe even lost.

Time for a different strategy.

"Look, officer, I'm no threat to you. All I want is to cover up so pictures of me aren't all-over social media. Besides, I'm injured and cold. May I please have my towel?"

The tall cop with tightly cropped, blond hair, barked at his partner. "Put the baton away."

Now we know who's in charge.

"Ma'am, I'm Officer Brian Cooper," he said while eyeing her closely. "Everyone calls me Coop."

He handed her the towel. The man's confidence implied time on the job. "Your name, again?" he asked.

"Kate Bowers. Everyone calls me Bowers."

He watched her wrap the towel around her torso. "Tell me what happened."

"Sure," she said, reaching for the bottle of water. She stopped when Robocop twitched.

Coop stepped between them and handed her the water.

Bowers washed the taste of salt and blood out of her mouth and gulped down a few swallows.

"Thanks," she said. "I came out this morning to enjoy the sunrise and try out my new mask and snorkel."

Coop's eyes scanned her lounge chair and a small table where she'd left her sunglasses and a half-empty cup of coffee. He nodded to her bag on the sand.

"That's mine." Before he even asked, she said, "The knife is in the outer pocket and my Glock and Non-Resident Firearm License is in my room."

He set her bag out of reach and pulled a small notepad from his pocket. "Where's your gear?"

"Fins are on the dock. I lost my mask and snorkel in the scuffle." She gestured toward the water.

"Where did this happened?" asked Coop. He followed her along the shore. Vega remained behind, haphazardly hanging yellow tape between the palm trees.

She showed Coop the swim ladder. "I went in here." While he took photos of the streaks of smeared blood from her cut heel, she continued to explain what had happened.

"As I watched a baby barracuda, I heard splashing. When I felt a hand grab my ankle, I flipped onto my back and the fight was on."

She pointed at the dense mangroves. "His skiff was tied up over there."

Eighty feet away, boats big and small traveled the channel.

"You didn't hear him coming?" asked Coop.

"Officer," said Bowers, "if I had looked up every time I heard a boat, my mask would never have gotten wet."

Coop scanned the dock. "Why are your fins dry?"

"Too shallow to use them," she said, "I didn't want to stir up the bottom. Makes it impossible to see anything."

Coop continued taking notes. "You're a guest at this hotel?"

"Yes sir," she said. "My room is on the second floor."

A moment later, he appeared to be studying her.

Coop toyed with his pen. "How do you know the man who attacked you?"

"I don't." She rewrapped the towel around her hips and tucked a corner snuggly into place.

Coop glanced over the edge of his notebook at her bare belly and went back to taking notes.

"What did he look like?" asked Coop as he kept a respectable distance.

Bowers gave him a full description. "He also had a tear drop tattoo below his left eye."

Coop frowned as if the description bothered him.

Twenty-five feet from them, the hen herded her chicks well away from Vega as he wandered along the shoreline.

Before returning to his notes, Coop glanced at his partner. "No offense," said Coop, "but most of the women I know would be pretty emotional after an experience like that. You sound unusually calm."

Using a corner of the towel, she carefully brushed sand off the cuts on her arm. "Anyone who says they don't feel fear is either lying or a psychopath. But then you know that, don't you, officer?"

A flicker of a smile crossed his lips and his intense blue eyes homed in on her. "You know weapons and you have a few battle scars, one of which is recent. I don't run across that every day."

"I used to hunt down assholes for a living."

He glanced away and smirked. "Come on. Seriously?"

It wasn't the first time a guy had underestimated her. "I was a homicide detective," she said. "The job comes with risks."

"Where?"

"Metro PD in Washington, D.C. Army before that."

"What was your MOS?"

"31 Bravo."

"Military Police?" Coop's brows went up. "Wow."

Behind him, Vega squinted at the water.

Coop still seemed hung up on her job skills. "Why didn't you tell us you were a cop?"

"Wyatt Earp over there didn't exactly give me an opportunity."

Jeb, the older gentleman with the ballcap, marched toward them. "Officer."

"Can I help you, sir?" asked Coop.

Jeb cleared his throat and puffed up his narrow chest. The man pointed at Vega with a boney hand. "That young fella over there is your partner?"

Coop's head cocked slightly. "Yes, sir."

"Well," said Jeb. "I apologize for havin' to tell ya this, but your partner's a dick." The old man nodded as if to punctuate his point. "Thought you should know."

"Sir," said Coop, "I'm sorry to hear that. Can you tell me—"

Without another word, Jeb marched away with his head held high. Coop went back to his notepad.

Bowers chuckled. "The assailant wore a stainless-steel bracelet, but it wasn't on his wrist when he left."

Coop stopped writing. Like the tattoo, the bracelet also seemed to bother him.

"Coop. Get over here," shouted Vega. "I've got something."

Bowers followed Coop to where Vega pointed at the water.

"Check this out," he said with a smart-assed grin.

Bowers studied the lapping waves. Three feet from the beach, winks of sunlight sparkled on the surface. During a lull in the wave action, she saw what he'd found.

There among the rocks lay the remains of a partially skeletonized human hand.

FULL THROTTLE

THE STEERING WHEEL FELT smooth in Henry's rough hands as he backed off. It didn't surprise him to see Coop and that hot-headed cop interested in something in the waters along the shore.

Disturbing items had recently been washing up on their beaches. He'd found a wallet of a missing girl and a fisherman cleaning grouper claimed he found an ear in a big one's stomach with an earring still attached.

While they were distracted, Henry quietly drifted into the channel and out of sight.

As he cut through the gentle swells, he couldn't get that woman out of his head. She intrigued him.

Henry always talked to his dog, who didn't seem to mind. "Ya see, Buddy, in a fight, it all comes down to training and the right attitude."

The way that woman had faced violence meant she was no average civilian. "Buddy," he mumbled. "She's got military in her veins."

It had been quite the pleasure to watch her hand that jerk exactly what he deserved. Even so, Henry still took it personal when some yahoo messed with his corner of paradise.

After checking his watch, Henry headed toward the marina. His boss would be expecting him.

He stayed within the deeper waters of the channel where hotels lined the beaches on his left. The shallow area on his right, known as the Flats, was filled with prop-scarred rocks. The locals avoided the area unless they were drunk, inexperienced, or stupid. Henry had pulled plenty of boats off those rocks.

This morning's mist had burned off nicely and the sky held the promise of another blue-bird day. He steered through a narrow 300-foot canal between Key West and Fleming Key. Henry stood at the helm of their client's 26-foot Robalo as he piloted the boat under the Fleming Cut Bridge.

A few minutes later, he cleared the large Coast Guard Piers to his left, giving him full view of the colorful boats dotting the clear waters up ahead. Normally, Henry would have enjoyed such a festive sight, instead, he wondered where that shit-bag had gone to hide.

While Henry searched for the gray skiff, Buddy barked and wagged his tail at a pair of dolphins playing in their wake.

Henry had recently returned to The Rock—as the locals called it. At first, it had seemed unchanged until he'd noticed a few new faces had moved in, this fella in the skiff being one of them.

The scent of the sea eased Henry's mood. He scratched his dog's ears and enjoyed the satisfying rumble of the twin 250hp Yamahas. He'd tuned the engines himself and knew his boss, Clyde, would be happy to know the test-ride went well.

A buoy bell clanked in the distance. As Henry tested the steering, Buddy barked at the aerial acrobatics of seagulls as they squawked and squabbled over fish scraps tossed overboard by fishermen.

Henry had grown up in the Keys and knew the area like a father knew the face of his own kid.

As he picked up speed, he heard a distant knocking from an outboard. Henry lifted his sunglasses and squinted at a pontoon boat 300 feet off his bow. From behind it, the gray skiff careened into the channel and was running flat-out in front of a V-hulled fishing boat. Both were racing toward him like someone had rung the dinner bell.

On the bigger boat, Henry saw two men with something in their hands that made his hair go up. A flare of sunlight glanced off the lens of a rifle scope.

RIGGS RESTED HIS HAND on the grip of the Sig Sauer P226 seated in his hip holster. Normally, he enjoyed his small office with the coffee machine just down the hall. Today it felt like a holding cell.

He rolled his empty coffee mug between his big palms. Everything in him wanted to gear up and go find Bowers.

Last night, he'd slept on the worn recliner in the corner. With his caseload busting at the seams, that wasn't uncommon.

He and Willie were at a critical juncture in their investigation of an outlaw biker gang known as the Changós.

The bikers' expansion into Florida might help Riggs' Request-for-Travel to Miami, but it wouldn't be enough to persuade his supervising agent, SSA Patrick McDougall, to cut him loose. With a perfectly capable field office in Miami, Riggs couldn't blame him.

The clock said 9:07 a.m. While he waited for the latest reports to come in, Riggs wondered why Kory wanted to meet at his apartment instead of Ebbitt's.

Something's under that man's skin.

Riggs and Kory had weathered Washington's egos and the ups-and-downs of politics for years. It was unusual to see an experienced Secret Service agent squirm.

With his mug in hand, Riggs followed the scent of fresh-brewed coffee down the hall to the break room. On his way back to his office, Willie flagged him down.

"Got a minute?" he asked.

"What've ya got?" Riggs opened the door.

Willie entered and hung his black leather jacket on a coat hook next to Riggs's bulletproof vest.

Riggs felt a bit old school compared to Willie with his curly brown hair pulled into a man-bun and a shoulder holster worn over his blues-band T-shirt that said *Crank It*. Even though he'd earned a reputation for getting results, his attire often bought the guy some not-so-friendly razzing within the bureau.

"Check your inbox," said Willie. "Our biker boys were busy last night."

Riggs had been waiting for this report. "Any leads on the missing girl from Jacksonville?"

"Nope," said Willie. "But two men were murdered in Virginia just off the I-95 corridor."

"I heard," Riggs mumbled. "I hate these shitbags."

He wasn't worried about the typical riders' club. They were regular people who enjoyed the camaraderie of riding together. It was the one-percenters, committed violent outlaws, that got under his skin. He searched his computer for the report.

Riggs had traced the Changós to a Cuban cartel. These bad boys had evolved into a rolling crime wave. Drug trafficking, burglaries, home invasions, shootings, even buggering underage girls weren't out of their realm. Riggs' job had been finding the missing girls.

Riggs sipped his steaming cup of coffee. When the bikers had taken their criminal enterprise across state lines and began kidnapping, the FBI had become involved.

"I just discovered something," said Willie as he took a seat next to Riggs' desk, "the word *Changó* comes from the mythological god of thunder—the grand master of storms and destruction."

"How fitting," said Riggs.

Surveillance footage on his computer included clips of the Changós revving their engines. The thundering roar was intended to strike fear into the hearts of their enemies.

It took a lot more than noise to unnerve Riggs, but he found their weapon of choice, an ax, unsettling.

"Take a look at this," said Willie. He pointed to a file on the screen which held the FBI's Evidence Response Team's photos of the crime scene where the two men had died. The victims were identified as members of a rival gang known as the Latin Kings. Mug shots from last year showed the two men proudly displaying their jeweled crown tattoos.

"Their membership just got canceled," said Willie.

Unless the pending autopsies proved otherwise, the cause of death appeared to be near decapitation.

Riggs squinted at the screen. "Killing them wasn't enough."

"I know. It's freaky." Willie grimaced. "Their tattoos were sliced off while they were still alive."

Riggs nodded. "The bastards used an ax." Violence was common between all rival gangs, but the Changós took it to new extremes.

"Riggs, we've gotten more sightings of them in southern Florida."

He immediately thought of Bowers. "Access to Miami ports and waterways would be a prime asset for their drug network."

Riggs remembered the surveillance clip of the Changós robbing a liquor store in Jacksonville. The whole incident had taken seventy seconds.

A fourteen-year-old girl at a gas station next door had been kidnapped at the same time. It worried him that he hadn't found her yet.

Kidnapping with a motorcycle was impractical, which meant most of the missing girls had been seduced into coming willingly. Usually, they were raped and later found shaken but alive. Not this time. Something had changed.

Willie sounded tired. "Still no word from our asset, but the scuttle-butt is he skipped town. Last time I heard from him was a month ago. Went quiet after that."

Willie complained about losing an informant that had taken more than eight months to put in play. "The Changós' leader tasked our asset to go down to Miami with Gunner."

Gunner's name popping up was never good news nor a surprise.

Riggs tapped on his cellphone and pulled up a mugshot of Gunner, a.k.a. Gerome Angelo, taken at his last arrest for unlawful possession of a firearm by a felon. He'd been caught with an AR pistol loaded with a thirty-round magazine. His profile picture showing a tattoo of a revolver on the side of his shaved head hadn't bolstered his plea of innocence. Gunner, like most career criminals, started with petty robberies. Today, this guy's lengthy rap sheet spoke for itself. He and some of his crew were suspected in another gang rape. Riggs knew the

Metro PD detective investigating the case, who told him the vic was too scared to talk.

"My guess," said Riggs, "is that Gunner is looking for bigger payoffs both in terms of rank within the biker gang and money."

Willie rocked back in his chair. "Some have been arrested for shaking down game-rooms and casinos. Looks like they now have their hands in the sex and drug trades. Our asset might have provided serious intel on some of the missing girls, but Gunner apparently got greedy. Word on the street is that he wanted to make a hit on our guy and take over. I'm not surprised our asset took off."

"Any idea as to where?" asked Riggs.

"Maybe. Rumor is he had his eyes on getting even."

"Gunner's a fool," said Riggs. "Our asset can disappear into the wind. Gunner will never see him coming. Find Gunner and we'll find our asset."

TARGET

W ITH TROUBLE RUNNING straight for him, Henry spun his boat into an abrupt U-turn. An air horn sounded, but with the morning sun blaring into his eyes he couldn't tell where it had come from.

Wind and a fine mist of saltwater battered his face as he hit the throttle. A Tiki boat with a thatch roof drifted in front of him. Henry immediately changed course and steered around the floating party where a potbellied man tumbled into the clear tropical waters with a bottle of beer in hand. The group onboard cheered and lifted their Mimosas as Henry raced past.

Behind him, the gray skiff veered away from the Tiki boat and within fifteen feet of a young man on a jet ski, who flipped him off for getting too close.

Henry's shirt flapped in the salty air as he kept a close eye on the fishing boat. The 35-footer with triple Mercury 400s presented a far greater threat than the skiff.

Henry knew his boat could outrun the skiff, but his twin 250s were no match for the 35-footer's 1,200 horsepower. As it drew closer, fishing rods swayed in their holders and the armed men onboard hunkered down at the bow.

The vessel blew past the skiff and rocketed straight for Henry. They clearly weren't dropping by for a friendly chat.

Henry thrust the throttle forward. "Hold on Buddy."

He made a few sharp turns, sending rooster-tails of wash into the air. On the dashboard an orange flare gun rocked in a cupholder and his bottle of water tumbled to the deck.

"Down boy," shouted Henry, hoping his smaller boat would prove more maneuverable. He glanced over his shoulder as he took the agile Robalo through a series of zigzag turns, leaving the waters behind them tossed and turbulent. Saltwater sprayed the deck. His heart pounded.

The two boats lurched in his chop, giving him a few seconds to search for safety.

If he couldn't outrun them, he needed to disable them.

Henry grinned as a plan took shape. "It's gonna be okay, Buddy."

He pushed the throttle wide open and headed straight for the Flats. "Let's introduce that boat's props to the big ol' rocks waitin' for 'em."

Henry sped away from the menagerie of boaters and whipped around Trumbo Point. He pushed the Robalo to its limits. His jaw tightened as he flew under the bridge, missing the abutments by five feet.

Knowing his boss would lynch him if he brought a customer's boat back damaged, Henry wobbled left and right, trying to make himself a harder target.

He raced past the mooring field to his left and closed in on the Flats. The 35-footer came up on his tail.

Behind him, the two gunmen raised their rifles. Henry ducked.

The explosive *pop-pop* of gunfire filled his ears. He felt the whoosh of a slug barely miss his head.

Just before his bow entered the Flats, Henry spun the steering wheel to port. "Hold on, Buddy."

Water spray flew into the air. His boat tilted. He heard metallic clinks and clanks as his toolbox tumbled over. Buddy clawed at the deck, trying to hold on.

Henry grabbed the flare gun.

As the gunmen bobbled in the chop and attempted to re-align their sights, Henry pulled the trigger. The flare whooshed toward the big boat, trailed by an arc of reddish-orange smoke.

The 35-footer didn't make the turn. Just as the driver entered the Flats, the flare smacked into the center console and burst into a plume of orange. The big fishing boat hit the rocks hard, throwing the driver against the windshield and one gunman overboard.

Henry heard the scraping of the props grinding into stones. "Eat rocks, assholes. We got 'em, Buddy."

The flammable chemicals burst into a huge fireball. Henry flinched. Within seconds, black smoke billowed fifty feet into the air. The driver and the second gunmen screamed as they leapt into the water with their hair and clothing on fire.

Henry veered toward deeper waters, well away from the fire.

The shallow-draft skiff skimmed over the Flats and screamed toward Henry.

As he passed a Coast Guard boat heading toward the fire, the skiff's engine sputtered and went silent.

Henry slowed to an idle. His boat rocked in the gentle swells, as he watched the skiff bobbing in the waves like a pelican with a full belly. The outboard had given it up.

Henry grunted. "Ya shoulda taken care of yur boat. Yup, yup."

As the Coast Guard doused the fire, Henry knew this man was trouble. Having accomplices meant he wasn't working alone. Henry suspected this wouldn't be the last time he'd see this guy.

MONEY AND POWER

THE SOUND OF A FIST POUNDING on Riggs' front door echoed through his condo.

The second he opened the locks, Kory entered and hustled past. His silver-gray hair and leather jacket were damp from the drizzling mist outside. He went directly to Riggs' kitchen where he left his jacket hanging over the back of a barstool at the breakfast counter and grabbed a beer from his fridge.

Kory knocked back a few swallows.

"I can't stay long," he said while adjusting his shoulder holster. "I have to catch a plane in the morning. Christ, I'm getting too old for this crap."

Kory sat on the leather couch like a man trying to gather his thoughts. "I don't know where to start," he said.

"Yes, you do," said Riggs, tossing him a dishtowel. "You just don't want to say it."

Kory snorted. "You S.O.B. You know me too well." He sat forward and wiped his face. "We gotta problem."

That was obvious. "About what?" asked Riggs.

"We both know the D.C. two-step, but this time it's different. I wish you'd been there this morning and seen the exchange between POTUS and the Committee."

Riggs snagged the boxed pepperoni pizza from the oven and set it on the coffee table next to the plates and napkins.

Kory rolled up his sleeves and wolfed down a slice. "Thanks. I needed this. Haven't eaten all day."

His friend had observed Washington's bullshit for nearly two decades. It wasn't like him to be this riled up.

Kory chewed thoughtfully. "Something doesn't add up."

"In what way?" asked Riggs.

"A little company in Sri Lanka has made a move to buy E-Connect, the parent company of our biggest communications network. The Committee and the Department of Justice are being pressured to sign off on it."

The controversy over selling U.S. businesses to foreign investors had been hotly debated. The Committee on Foreign Investment in the United States, known as CFIUS, often dealt with congressmen who were more concerned about money for their next election than national security or the dangers downstream for the American people.

Riggs sat back in his recliner. "We've been warning the White House about this for decades. So far, our intel has fallen on deaf ears. Their sights are locked on the game of partisan politics."

"You got that right," said Kory between bites. "CFIUS had a pow-wow in the oval office this morning. Senator Larry Fowler was there. The only thing he saw was a goldmine for the Political Action Committee and his re-election campaign."

PAC remained one of the open secrets in Washington. Ambitious lawmakers often raised millions to fund it and buy their way into powerful chairmanships. Fowler would seize any opportunity to ingratiate himself to his party, guaranteeing party support at his next election.

"Sounds like something Fowler would do," said Riggs. "It's no secret that the guy is willing to be a paid puppet, if the price is right."

Kory finished his beer. "Senator Ron Hogan is trying to stop the sale. The man was pretty damn outspoken. The Committee got the picture and Fowler wasn't pleased about it."

Riggs knew Hogan had a reputation for speaking his mind. Riggs admired his integrity as a man who couldn't be bought or manipulated.

The implications of this deal had Riggs' worried. "It brings a whole new dimension to the issues of border security."

"Makes marijuana mules the least of our worries. Doesn't congress have any clue that turning our communications infrastructure over to foreign entities is incredibly stupid?" Kory threw down his napkin. "Riggs, what in hell's name are they thinking?"

"They aren't," said Riggs. "Money equals power. It's the traditional Kool-Aid in Washington."

"You got that right." Kory's cynical laugh underscored his frustration. "They've lulled each other into believing their own rhetoric. Hell Riggs, our enemies don't need wars, bombs, or spooks. All they have to do is buy us out, one business at a time."

It deeply worried Riggs that China was producing more than cheap consumer goods. "Have you noticed bullshit like hacking our major defense sites, forcing indebtedness in impoverished Caribbean countries within striking range to the U.S., taking over uninhabited islands owned by Japan, and producing toxic pharmaceuticals keep trailing back to China?"

THE DUVAL CRAWL

THE FUN-LOVING CHARACTERS cavorting around Coop on the busy sidewalks of Key West lightened his mood. Duval Street came alive after dark.

After yet another argument with his wife, he figured a walk downtown beat the hell out of flipping channels and staring at a TV screen while his wife stormed around their home, slamming cupboard doors.

Coming home to his wife and daughter had once provided a kind of stability that balanced out the shit-show he saw every day.

As he passed the colorful awnings and a trolley car, Coop tried to pinpoint when his homelife had gone sideways.

Even off duty, he couldn't help getting out of the house and checking out the action on his beat along Duval Street. The small shops, the sound of scooters, the chatter of friendly crowds and live music drew him back and made him wonder why he often felt more at home on these sidewalks than he did on his own couch.

The ocean breeze offered some relief after a day that had turned out to be even longer than usual. Following this morning's assault on Bowers, he had made a few traffic stops. All had been routine, except one.

He glanced down at his split knuckles. Crap always seemed to happen when he didn't expect it.

Today's close call could've cost him big. And yet, here he was standing on the very spot where it had happened. He felt like an addict going back for another fix. And yet, being on these streets made him feel alert and in sync with something important.

As he strolled down the sidewalk, a couple in matching Hawaiian shirts teetered by with fresh sunburns that marked them as tourists. He watched the couple's uneasy balance and chuckled to himself. *They never learn.* People often underestimated the impact alcohol had on folks not used to the heat and humidity. Coop kept watch over them until they hailed a cab.

Farther down the block, Key West's nightlife rolled on with the usual drumbeats and party atmosphere. The air smelled like fried seafood and alcohol from a bar, where a bouncer stood guard in a pair of boxer shorts.

Coop remembered being called there to break up a fight. He never took any of it personally. In the heat of the moment, sometimes people fueled by alcohol did stupid things they wouldn't normally do.

Coop couldn't see inside, but he heard the sassy voice of a singer and the warble of a country tune spilling out onto the sidewalk. On the street a pedicab rolled past. The sweaty driver peddled his squeaky, three-wheeled bike, towing a carriage that held wide-eyed tourists.

The air felt balmy at the intersection of Duval and Caroline where Coop stopped to survey the nightly party that had started somewhere in the late afternoon and would carry on until the bars closed at 4 a.m. Locals called the all-night bar hopping *the Duval Crawl.*

He couldn't help wondering how Bowers had fared after the assault. Despite taking a hell of a beating, it intrigued him how she had been able to fight back.

At the station Marc Ingram, their Chief of Police, had been impressed by the calls up to the Metro PD. Their glowing comple- ments had Coop wondering why she'd left.

Coop didn't expect her to be out partying tonight, but he doubted she would be locked up in her hotel room, either. She didn't seem the type. Her account of the suspect still bothered him. He knew a man who fit Bowers' description all too well, right down to the stainless-steel bracelet.

Movement up ahead captured his attention. He stopped in front of The Bull and Whistle where a petite woman stumbled into a row of parked bicycles. A clatter arose as they fell like a series of dominos. Coop watched her struggling to regain her tenuous balance and take a seat on the curb. Every patrol officer in town knew Lily.

Coop crossed the street.

He didn't know if Lily was her real name or not and didn't care. She wasn't a threat to anyone, except maybe herself.

Locals called her habit of getting toasted every night *Key Disease*, in which the Duval Crawl had evolved into a lifestyle. Coop figured life had already handed the poor woman enough hardship. He didn't need to add to it. Besides, Lily often told him about things no one else would notice.

"Lily, you doin' okay?" Coop asked in a gentle voice.

Standing next to her on the curb, he tried to assess how bad off she was this time. Her cough sounded like a bark. With matted blonde hair, her head lolled back as she gazed up at him with glassy eyes and a filthy face. At thirty, she appeared closer to forty. Her weathered face resulted from a hard life on the streets.

Coop knelt. "You got a place to stay tonight?"

She opened her hands, stared at the two quarters and bits of discarded food she'd collected from the trash bins, and shook her head.

"You want to come in for the night?" He could smell the booze.

She nodded and coughed again.

Coop stood and flagged down a fellow officer driving by. The cruiser pulled over. The officer leaned toward the open window on the passenger side. "Hey, Coop," he said. "I heard about what happened. You doin' okay?"

"I'm all right," said Coop as he looked through the open window. "Stay safe out there, brother."

The officer nodded toward the curb. "Looks like Lily is having a rough night."

"You should hear her cough. I'm worried about her."

"I'll take her in," said the officer. "The Doc can give her some medi-cine." He flipped on his strobes and stepped out of the vehicle.

Together Coop and the officer helped Lily to her feet. They sat her in the back of the cruiser. Coop clicked her seatbelt.

"Thank you," she said in a gravelly voice.

Coop wished he had some magic fix. "I hope tomorrow's better."

"Me too." She burped and seemed embarrassed.

As the cruiser headed toward the jail, Coop straightened the bikes and determined that no damage had been done. When he'd finished, he spotted Kate Bowers across the street.

He could see the cop in her. She appeared focused on the streets as if hunting.

Coop waved when she glanced his direction. She took a few steps forward.

THE HUNT

BOWERS SEARCHED THE SEA of faces on Duval Street for the man with a freshly broken nose.

With casual ease, she strolled through every bar. Each time, she either bought a bottle of water, asked for a map or directions, or used the restroom to conceal being on the hunt.

She'd purchased a Key West ballcap and a pair of yellow tinted sunglasses from a giftshop. When she found him, she didn't want him to recognize her too quickly.

As she strolled the sidewalk, she listened for feet scuffling. Bowers watched for any sudden movement and even smelled the air for any sign of danger.

To fit in with the local vibe, she wore a pair of wild pants she'd purchased in D.C. They were made from a gunmetal gray fabric with swirls of white and black, and maroon splatters. She could still hear Riggs teasing her and saying they looked like a crime scene photo. That made her chuckle.

The air vibrated with booming live music. As she left a bar, a tall man with short dreads followed her onto the sidewalk and threw his arms out wide. "Yo, mama. You gots it goin' on, girl."

Bowers gave the man a high-five and continued her search. A few minutes later, she sidestepped a *sidewalk inspector*, an inebriated long-haired man passed out on the walkway with an empty bottle still cradled in his arms. *Some things never change.*

Sunset seemed to have signaled the beginning of one hell of a party. The place reminded her of New Orleans and Miami Beach rolled into one. Under different circumstances this could have been a good time.

Just when Bowers thought the sights couldn't get any goofier, a potbellied man dressed as a chicken stood at the corner talking to a fellow wearing white tights and a silver cape embellished with feathers and tinsel. Her pants paled by comparison. As if their attire were perfectly normal, their relaxed mannerisms and the casual way in which they ate their ice cream cones made her laugh.

Key West certainly added a whole new dimension to people-watching.

Bowers passed a restaurant's patio where folks in pirate and Star Wars costumes gathered under blue umbrellas. Apparently, the Halloween spirit had hit.

A shadow and a shift in the crowd's movements caught Bowers' attention. The women in skimpy costumes posed no concern. Their outfits were too revealing to hide any serious weaponry. The men dressed as pirates and Greek warriors weren't any more modest.

Those wearing masks were harder to read. The feeling of being watched annoyed her.

Bowers doubled back on her route and blended into the crowd. Her instincts told her she was being followed, but none of her usual tricks had exposed anything useful. Bowers changed directions several times and watched for anything out of place.

Strands of hair stuck to her sweaty neck. Even in October, the Keys were warm. She pulled her hair up into a ponytail.

A few blocks later, she came to a stop at a curb where a dead pelican lay on its back. A clump of brown feathers showed where it had collided with a phone pole. This beautiful creature's splayed wings and sightless eyes tugged at the senseless deaths that she'd come here to forget.

Further down the block and across the street, blue-and-red lights drew her attention. A police cruiser had rolled up near a row of bicycles. A tall muscular man waved at her.

She immediately recognized him as Coop.

Bowers watched as he gently helped a disheveled woman into the backseat of a patrol unit. After the cruiser left, Coop glanced her direction. Their eyes met.

As soon as she nodded, he crossed the street and stopped.

"Hey," he said, as he leaned against the black wrought-iron fence behind her.

With the toe of her boot, she sent a bottle cap skittering into the gutter.

The light from the streetlamp cast deep shadows over Coop's features and made the curly blond hair on his massive forearms appear illuminated. She laughed to herself. *You could put this guy in a bunny costume and he'd still look like a cop.*

"You clean up nicely," she said.

"Speak for yourself. I hardly recognize you in clothes." Coop rubbed the back of his neck and grimaced. "Sorry. That came out weird. I didn't mean—"

"Don't worry about it," she said. Bowers nodded toward the bikes across the street. "What happened?"

"That was Lily." His head swiveled left and right as he kept an eye on the foot traffic. "She's a fixture around here and is usually pretty hammered by this hour."

"You arrested her for public intox?"

"We did."

A man wearing a thong and black top-hat rode by on a scooter decked out in flashing Christmas lights. Without any hint of surprise, Coop barely seemed to notice.

"At least she'll have a place to sleep and a meal in the morning, which is more than she'd get out here. When she's sober, we'll expunge her record and let her go."

"Just like that?" asked Bowers.

"This isn't the big city." Coop crossed his arms. "We try to have each other's backs. Besides, I feel bad for her. She doesn't have family or any friends that I know of."

Bowers wished more people had his attitude.

"No harm. No foul," said Coop. He stretched as if his shoulders and neck were tight.

She glanced across the intersection at the crowded bar. "That place is popular."

The second-floor balcony reminded her of New Orleans, but it was the rooftop bar that caught her attention. The perimeter was encircled by a railing and rows of potted bushes in an attempt to conceal a party unlike anything she'd ever seen.

In her peripheral, Bowers could see Coop studying her.

She lifted her yellow glasses. "What the hell?"

The plants offered some concealment, but not enough to hide a lot more than bare shoulders. A group of tanned men and women in their mid-twenties waved. Some not-so-shapely, over-sixty types began to dance.

"I can't unsee that," said Bowers.

Coop laughed. "Clothing is optional. As long as they stay up there and don't cause any problems, we're good."

"Damn." Never had she seen anything like this. "Booze and bare skin. I don't even want to think about policing that."

"You get used to it," said Coop. "Funny thing, the older folks are more willing to take it off than the young ones." He shrugged. "I'd rather see that than some gangbanger shooting up the place."

"Good point."

He grew quiet. "Listen, I'm sorry if this has put a wrinkle in your vacation. Key West is usually a friendly place."

"I see that." Bowers rubbed her sore arms. "Any word on the guy who attacked me?"

"We're working on it."

She kicked at another bottle cap. "Either you find him, or I will."

Coop folded his arms. "We may not have all the resources you're accustomed to up in D.C., but we do a damned good job."

"I don't doubt it," she said, "but I still had to ask."

"Bowers, we'll get him. Give us a chance."

"We have to find this guy before someone else is hurt."

Coop studied her expression but didn't reply.

She left him to his thoughts and watched customers coming and
going from the bar. None of them sported black eyes or a broken nose.
When she shifted toward Coop, she realized he was still staring at her.

"Hey," he said. "Let me buy you a beer?"

"I'm not going in there."

"Me neither," he said. "There's a place up off Whitehead." He
checked his watch. "It's ten o'clock. They have live music and good
beer. Besides, I owe you one after the way things went down this
morning."

Bowers scanned the street, knowing Coop waited for her reply.
Torn between some much-needed rest and the urge to continue her
search, her senses were still bristling. Coop could have some new information and she could use a break.

LOUD AND PROUD

BOWERS APPROACHED the Blue Coconut Bar and Grill with Coop at her side. A middle-aged woman with a leathery tanned face stood outside like a guard dog. She greeted most with a big smile. One man she chased away.

The woman greeted Coop by slapping a poster against his chest. "Hold this." Her cigarette bobbed up and down as she spoke.

With the back of her hand, she pushed a lock of graying blonde hair away from her tanned forehead. The booming bass and twang of guitars played in the background.

As Coop held the Fantasy Fest poster in place, the woman stapled it to the bar's parrot-green exterior.

The barn-style doors had been rolled wide open, leaving a clear view of the interior. Bowers spotted a huddle of tattooed men in leather vests mingling around a cluster of tables at the far wall.

The woman eyed Bowers as if curious. "Coop, we'll need extra security this year. You're gonna be around, right?" She nodded toward the bar. "The bikers are back. Gunner's inside."

To Bowers' left, a row of Harleys lined the curb.

Coop pulled a packet of gum from his pocket. "No worries. I'll be around," he told the woman.

She hugged Coop. "Who's your friend?"

Coop smiled. "This is—"

"I'm Bowers," she said as she shook the woman's hand. "I'm visiting from D.C."

The woman had a surprisingly firm grip. Her warm hand bore the callouses of someone who worked hard.

"Maggie's the name," she said. "Nice ta meetcha."

Maggie winked at Coop and went back to decorating with streamers and beads.

Coop popped a stick of gum in his mouth. "If you thought the Garden of Eden was something, wait until you get a load of Fantasy Fest."

"I'm hoping to be out of here by then," Bowers said as she surveyed the bar. The place sat on the corner of an intersection with much of the interior viewable from the sidewalks, which meant that most of the people at the big circular bar had their backs to the open doors. There wasn't a chance in hell that she would sit with her back exposed to the street.

She liked to see a fight coming, especially with one-percenters onsite.

Bowers entered the bar with Coop. They walked through a cloud of cigarette smoke.

Coop coughed. "Let's take a table in the back, under the fans."

As the band jammed on, a waitress waved at Coop and a few men at the bar tipped their sweat-stained ballcaps.

He scanned the bar. "I do security for them in my off hours. I'm surprised to see only one bartender. On such a busy night, Maggie usually has at least two."

The ceiling and rafters were packed with an array of posters, a bra, beads, and photos of Hemingway and the community coming together after a hurricane. A large sign caught Bowers attention. It read: *What defines us is how well we rise after falling.*

Across the room, one of the bikers wore a red beard and a tattoo of a revolver on the side of his shaved head. He jabbed the guy next to him and gave him a knowing nod. Within seconds the entire group had their eyes on Coop. Judging by the way the bikers paid close attention to Coop's presence, they knew him as more than a bouncer.

"Who's Gunner?" she asked.

"A cocky thug and general pain in my ass. He's the one with the red beard."

Bowers watched Gunner attempting to lure a waitress into his lap. "I take it that Maggie has had trouble with them in the past?"

"Last year," said Coop, "Gunner and a couple of his guys beat up one of Maggie's bouncers. That's when they hired me. These boys are here to raise hell."

One of the bikers threw his hands up and pretended to rev his machine. While doing so, he knocked over a glass of beer. Gunner spat on the floor and laughed. The bartender wasn't amused and made a beeline for the bikers.

"Excuse me," said Coop. He marched toward the ruckus. The music stopped mid-song and the band took a break. Gunner's head jerked left and right as his crew beat on the tables and hollered hoots and howls.

"Show some respect, man," said the bartender. "We just cleaned that floor."

Gunner flicked the ashes from his cigarette onto the deck. "Oops," he said with a wise-ass grin.

The bartender's temper flared.

"Lonnie, go back to the bar," ordered Coop. He faced Gunner. "Let's not repeat last year. I don't want to make you leave or trespass you from the property. So, how about you boys act like gentlemen?"

Gunner sat back as if he owned the whole damned town. "Tell Maggie that we'd never want to cause her any problems." His sarcasm and hardened glare said otherwise.

Coop pointed at Gunner. "You've been warned."

After returning to Bowers, Coop whispered, "Lying sack of shit."

A few minutes later, the band returned to the stage. Bowers glanced at the clean polished concrete floor and the tables and walls covered in handwritten scribblings in black marker.

A waitress hurried by with a tray filled with glasses of draft beer and baskets of sizzling wings. The sweet-tangy scent of buffalo sauce and blue cheese dressing made Bowers' stomach rumble.

Coop pointed to a table under a fan. They settled into the seats with their backs against the paneled wall and a small table in front of them.

Coop leaned over. "What would you like?"

"Dark beer and a burger. Thanks, but I can pay."

"So can I," said Coop. "But I get a discount, you don't."

He moseyed toward the bartender he called Lonnie. The intense black man seemed to be in his late twenties.

A Breaking News banner flashed across a TV screen above him. She recognized the two men in the report as Senator Larry Fowler and Senator Ron Hogan. It didn't surprise her to see them in a heated debate. During her time in D.C., they had rarely agreed on anything.

She went back to surveying the customers and didn't see anyone with two black eyes. Bowers fixed her attention on the people clustered around the stage.

A young man in a wheelchair played on his phone and bobbed his head in time with the band's music. She felt for the boy who appeared to be around twenty.

Four men, who had been watching football on the bigscreen, moved away from the bikers. Undaunted, Gunner and his gang remained loud and proud as they emptied several pitchers of beer. They all wore 1% patches on their vests. After scratching at his bushy beard, Gunner glanced her direction and winked.

A few minutes later, Coop returned with a bowl of pretzels, a bottle of beer, and a Coke. The bulge on Coop's right hip told her he was carrying.

"Why did you—" he started to ask, but the band's volume rose. After a hard guitar strum and the brassy clang of cymbals, the band went silent.

Coop waited until the lead singer put down his guitar. "What made you choose Key West?"

"I've been wondering that myself," she said with no attempt at hiding her annoyance.

"I'm sorry," he said.

"Not your fault." Bowers took a sip of her beer. "And you? What brought you here?"

Coop continued watching the crowd. "Like most folks, I came for island living. Small-town feel. Fishing. The water. It's hard not to love this place."

Bowers sipped her beer. "Key West is beautiful."

When one of the bikers swaggered toward the restroom, Coop stiffened and shifted his hand closer to the bulge on his right hip. "Even in Paradise, it's sometimes the same shit-show as everywhere else."

"I thought you liked it here," she said.

"I do." He took a sip of his Coke. "Some days more than others."

"And today?"

"Not one of my better days."

The abrasions on his knuckles confirmed that.

A server set a plate in front of Bowers piled high with fries and a burger. She also handed Coop a basket of wings, and no bill. Obviously, his part-time gig came with benefits.

Coop picked up a napkin and kept the bikers in his peripheral view.

Bowers waited until the server had left. "So, what happened?"

Coop dribbled a pile of ketchup on his plate. "I rolled up on a traffic stop this afternoon. A woman was at the wheel. Before I could ask for her license, she jumped out of the vehicle and started screaming at me. Then the baby in the backseat started wailin'. The woman went for the kid. I stopped her. Everything about her attitude didn't pass muster. Then this punk on the curb starts yelling and taking a video with his phone. I didn't care. My body and dash cams were on. Just then, the woman's boyfriend pops out of the trunk like a jack-in-the-box with a crowbar. It was hands on.

"It turned out that they both were wanted in Georgia on multiple felony warrants. After we had the couple in custody, I checked the baby. Poor little guy was dirty and had bruises you don't want to see on anyone, especially a kid."

Coop twirled his coaster and tapped it to a stop. "Motherly instincts were lost on that woman."

"Where was your backup?" Bowers scanned the exits, aware that Gunner still had his eyes on them.

"Wasn't expecting a problem with a female and a baby. I called in the plate number before making contact. Damn good thing I did. Dispatch realized the vehicle was stolen and automatically sent backup. Saved my bacon. While I had the boyfriend on the ground, the woman tried to pull a revolver from the baby's car seat. If it weren't for backup..." Coop shrugged, "it coulda been a real bad day." He stared at the table. "Hate seein' a baby and a 38 Special in the same seat."

Bowers nodded at his knuckles. "Looks like we're both beat up tonight."

He chuckled and clinked his Coke can to her beer bottle. "You got that right. I'm sore as hell."

"You saved that child."

He glanced at her. "Thanks." Coop sounded tired. "I hate when a baby gets caught up in all this."

Bowers could relate. "People have no idea how fast something can go lethal."

"Roger that," said Coop, as he dug into his pile of wings. "When I got home, the wife bitched at me about missing dinner. There I was all tore up and tired as hell and she wants me to paint the bathroom some color she called teal. What the hell is teal?"

"Blue-green."

He frowned at her and shook his head.

"It's tough," she said, "to make the transition from doing felony stops to doing the dishes." Bowers took a bite of her burger. "This is good. Thank you."

Coop nodded. "It's nice talking to someone who gets it."

Bowers swirled a long French fry through the red ketchup. "Any news on the hand you found on the beach?"

Coop was about to take a bite of his wings and stopped. He sighed and stared at her.

"Were you able to get prints?" she asked. "Was it disarticulated with a blade or sawed off? Have you checked missing persons?"

Coop grimaced and pushed his basket of wings away. "We've got this, okay? We're sending it up to Miami."

Bowers sipped her beer. "It was in that water before I even left D.C. The decomp says that much."

"I know," said Coop. He started to dip a fry into the ketchup and changed his mind. "Once a detective, always a detective?"

She nodded. "Sorry. Making sense out of a crime scene is habit."

Coop took a sip of his Coke and went back to his wings.

She watched him. "Your partner is in trouble. You know that."

"You don't miss much, do you?"

She'd obviously hit a nerve. An awkward minute passed, leaving Bowers eating her burger in silence.

The football enthusiasts jumped up and cheered at the overhead screen. Above them, lazy fan blades turned in a slow rotation. Coop seemed a man as torn and worn as the scuffed tactical boots on his feet.

He pushed away his empty Coke can. "We have our quirks. If I exceed the speed limit on a hot call, I get my ass chewed."

Bowers' eyebrows went up. "Seriously?"

He shrugged. "The chief is particular about gettin' things done right. Can't fault him for that."

Coop went back to wolfing down his wings.

Bowers smiled at the memory of squealing tires and the many high-speed chases she'd done in D.C. "Hot pursuit at thirty miles per hour," she said with a giggle that rolled into laughter.

Coop started to relax. "It makes sense once you see the crowds and how many people are on scooters." He sat back with a grin until his partner staggered in with a bottle of beer in hand, appearing as if he were well beyond the legal limit. The bartender stopped tending bar and glared at Vega.

"Aw, crap," said Coop.

BAR WARS

B OWERS COULD SMELL a fight coming.
The bartender set down a bottle of whiskey without taking his dark eyes off Vega.

Customers continued whooping it up, as Lonnie tracked every step Vega took.

She could feel the tension between these two.

After this morning's assault, another grappling match was the last thing she needed, but she wouldn't leave a fellow cop without backup.

When Coop rolled up onto his feet, she stood.

He extended one arm as if to protect her. She found the gesture noble, but unnecessary.

The bartender and Vega continued glaring at one another like a couple of young bulls waiting for the other to make the first move.

Coop kept his voice low. "There's bad blood between those two."

"I see that, but why?" she asked.

"Deon, the young man in the wheelchair, is Lonnie's brother." Coop grew tense. "Last year, Vega and Deon got into a tussle. Vega claimed the injuries were accidental and that Deon resisted."

Vega swaggered up to the bar where a man was about to sit down.

Complaints rose when Vega shouldered the man out of the way and took his seat.

As if deaf to the grumbling, Vega took one last swallow of beer, rolled his empty bottle across the bar, and snapped his fingers for service.

"This shit stops now," snarled Coop.

Bowers followed him as he pushed through the crowd toward the bar. As they dodged a group of young ladies, a bouncer in a Security T-Shirt moved in.

Lonnie gripped the edge of the bar. "You know better than to come in here."

"Gimme a Bud," said Vega. He wore the same wise-assed expression she'd seen this morning.

Lonnie chucked Vega's empty beer bottle into the recycling bin. "You've had enough. You've got blood-shot eyes and I can smell you from here."

To Bowers' right, the young man in the wheelchair rolled closer apparently to see what the commotion was about. "Hey," shrieked Deon, "you're the asshole who did this to me!"

Conversations fell to a hush. Even the customers watching the football game focused on the bar.

Lonnie signaled his brother to stay back. "Vega. Leave now. You aren't welcome here." The bouncer stepped forward.

Vega pointed at the tap. "I said, I want a Bud."

The stools emptied rapidly as people vacated the bar. Coop made quick work of moving in next to Vega.

Bowers stood by the bouncer and kept an eye on the bikers, knowing they would welcome any excuse for a brawl.

As Vega reached for a bowl of pretzels, the bartender snatched it away and pointed to the door. "Outside, now," he said.

Coop put his hand on Vega's shoulder. "Let's go."

Vega shoved it away. "Get outta my face, Coop."

Vega wore an Army-green jacket and a pair of black leather gloves. Without taking his eyes off Lonnie, Vega pulled a stack of brand-new bills from his pocket and slapped it on the polished wooden bar.

People jostled to see. Their eyes moved between Vega and the crisp stack of one-dollar bills that still had the bank's paper band around the middle. He slowly tugged one fresh bill off the top, crumpled it into a tight ball with his gloved fingers, and flicked it across the bar at Lonnie.

The curious had their eyes on Vega as he slowly did the same with the next four bills. "Get me the damned beer."

"That's sick, man," said a guy, who moved away.

"Enough," said Coop.

Vega stood and puffed up his chest.

Lonnie pointed at the bouncer. "Get him out of here."

The moment the bouncer's fist had a good grip on Vega's jacket, he shoved the bouncer backward.

Bowers tried to catch the falling man, but he stumbled into a knot of guys in fishing shirts. When their drinks hit the floor, the cursing and shoving began.

Vega pushed through the crowd toward the young man in the wheelchair. Coop snagged him by the sleeve, but he pulled his arm away and bumped into a waitress. Her tray of shots tumbled onto the table in front of Gunner.

Bowers took a deep breath and waded into the crush of bodies as the bearded biker tossed chairs aside and headed straight for Coop.

COOP FELT LIKE a salmon swimming upstream as he fought against the tide of customers streaming for the doors. The fight was on. More shoving broke out. Tables overturned. Glassware crashed to the floor.

A gaggle of customers encircled the chaos to gawk, taunt, and jeer.

Coop helped an older woman to her feet and pointed her toward an exit.

"Everyone, calm down," demanded the bouncer over the mic. Maggie blew a whistle, which only added to the uproar.

"Call 911 for backup," Coop shouted at Lonnie as he jumped into the sea of screaming red faces.

Seven feet ahead, Vega shoved and stumbled his way toward Deon, whose eyes went wide as he attempted to wheel away. Overturned chairs obstructed any hope of escaping.

Coop glanced to his left and realized Bowers had his back. Her hand rested near a bulge under her vest, which he presumed was her Glock.

He jogged around two young men in a verbal altercation and was about to tackle Vega when Gunner stepped in and blocked his path. Coop tried to skirt around him, but Gunner continued to jam-up the works. Public disturbance was this guy's middle name. The biker cracked his knuckles as if itching to jump into the fray.

"Back off," shouted Coop, "or face a night in jail."

Gunner's eyes narrowed as he spat out his toothpick.

Coop stepped forward. "I said—"

Bowers stepped between them so quickly, she startled Coop. While she engaged Gunner, the bouncer shoved a table sideways and tackled Vega. The two men hit the deck and slid into the wheelchair, tipping it over.

Like a ragdoll, Deon toppled onto the hard floor. His phone skidded across the polished concrete.

Coop shouldered closer. He heard Vega shrieking at Deon, "Get off your ass. I've seen enough of your bullshit."

The bouncer still had Vega by the collar, but that didn't stop him from kicking at the wheelchair and continuing to mouth off. "I know you're fakin' it, ya little shit."

As Coop muscled Vega away from Deon, he heard Bowers order the crowd back in a tone that meant business.

Seconds later, Vega pulled away and faced off with the bouncer. Vega started to swing a wooden chair up high until Coop ripped it out of his hands. "Knock it off," he shouted.

Vega responded by throwing a punch.

Coop's head snapped back. The smack against his jaw pissed him off.

Bowers intervened, standing only inches from Vega. His eyes went wild.

Coop tried to pull her back, but Bowers refused to backdown.

"You're losing your shit." She said. "Stop now."

Coop lurched forward to restrain Vega. He was too late. Vega's knuckles rocketed toward Bowers' face like a bullet leaving the chamber.

In a blur, she jerked to the side, clasped her hands, and drove all her weight into deflecting his fist. Before he could recover his stance, she planted a kick to the back of his knee, causing it to buckle. The final blow came as she slammed the heel of her right hand under Vega's chin.

He never saw it coming. Vega crumpled like a rockslide and landed on his back.

Coop immediately put Vega in a headlock and wished he could see that again. *Damn. That was slick.*

Vega shrieked, "I'll bust your face in, bitch!"

Bowers' calmly glanced down at him. "Call me anything you want, but I'm the one still standing."

"Enough!" said Coop. "It's time to go."

Vega started to resist, but Coop tightened his grip. "You want me to take this to the lieutenant or call Bowers back over here?"

Vega relaxed and gave up the fight.

Just when Coop thought this was over, six bikers wearing Changós vests lined up next to Gunner.

TWISTED FANTASY

"SAY YOUR PRAYERS," said Bo as he gazed up at the inky black sky, pointed his finger like a gun at the golden moon, and softly said, "Pshoo."

His truck sat in the shadows under a broken streetlamp. While smoking a cigarette, he continued watching the bar scene across the street at the Blue Coconut.

He'd been scheduled to bartend tonight. *Screw that.* He was in no mood to play nice with a bunch of drunken fools or deal with Maggie's bullshit.

Despite his aching face, watching the fight break out amused him. A departing server came over and leaned in his window.

Her V-necked shirt gave him an eyeful. "Hey, sweet thing," he said. After she bought his excuse about his messed-up face, he asked, "Who's that woman?"

The server glanced over her shoulder at the bar. "The tall one with brown hair? Oh, yeah. Coop called her Bowers." The server played with her necklace and offered him a sly grin. "They say she is a former cop."

Bo slipped her a ten and now knew the name of his prey. He also knew why he'd gotten the shit kicked out of him. Next time, she wouldn't be so lucky.

Through the bar's open doors, light shone like a beacon. As usual, Maggie ordered the staff around.

Bo hadn't read Maggie's text, but after not showing up for work this week, it didn't take a college boy to figure out what it said.

Bo settled back in his seat in the comfort of the darkness. Even as a kid, he'd found solace under his dad's workbench in the basement or in the darkest corner of the coat closet where he could be alone with his thoughts.

He toyed with his pocketknife. Fury smoldered as he watched Bowers.

On the beach the Urge had been strong. He'd come so close to achieving that intoxicating high he craved, but Bowers had ruined it. Even now, his pulse quickened as thoughts of exerting his power over her blossomed in his mind. Like a thirst he couldn't quench, he yearned to see her eyes wide with fear and witness her life slip away.

He wanted to feel her quiver as she died. Instead of nursing a busted nose, he should be riding high over his conquest and reliving each titillating moment.

Bo had lived with his cravings for so long he'd given them a name: The Urge. It had come to him in the summer after fifth grade when he'd killed the neighbor's dog. His dad had once asked him why he'd done it. "Just wanted to," he'd said. He never told the old man that he'd enjoyed it.

In the headlights of a passing cab, Bo glanced into the rearview mirror at his blackened eyes. A whopper of a headache throbbed in his skull.

As one of the cops on scene hurried out to his car, Bo pretended to be texting.

After the officer left, he eased his truck back a space for a better view of Bowers. It goaded him that she didn't look nearly as messed up as he did.

Seeing her again made him determined to finish this.

Bo continued to toy with his newly sharpened pocketknife and nicked his thumb. As he licked the tiny wound, the taste of blood and the fantasy of using that blade on Bowers aroused him.

He needed to conquer her.

Bo kept his eyes on Coop and the cops inside. The Urge didn't like waiting. It wanted what it wanted.

"We'll get her," he promised himself.

MAD DOG

BOWERS HAD SEEN BIKERS, beer, and brawls more times than she could count and had no patience for it tonight.

She let out an ear-splitting whistle. Everyone stopped.

All eyes focused on her, including the police officers who had arrived on scene.

"You." She pointed at the bikers. "Stand down," she ordered with the force of a drill-sergeant. "Vega is leaving. Isn't he, Coop?"

To her right, Coop stared at her for a split-second.

"Yes, ma'am," he said as he dragged Vega to his feet. "You all listen up and behave yourselves," said Coop, "unless you want these fine officers to babysit you for the entire evening."

"No way, dude," said a voice in the crowd.

The bikers grumbled but retreated.

As Coop escorted Vega toward the door, the crowd made a hole like a ball of bait fish who wanted no part of a bull shark in their midst.

Gunner strolled back to the cluster of tables in the corner and took a seat. The bikers who had been next to him sneered at the officers and followed. They assembled at their tables like a pack of wolves refusing to give up their turf.

For now, the chaos had ended.

Bowers helped Lonnie hoist Deon back into his wheelchair.

"Thanks," the young man said in a voice that was barely audible. Deon reached behind his boney back and pulled his shirt down over the large surgical scars along his spine. Bowers watched him adjust his lifeless legs. It was a sight she'd seen too many times. The battles in Iraq and Afghanistan had damaged the bodies of many young men and women.

Two young men involved in the brawl came to Deon's aid. Maggie handed Deon his phone. He briefly glanced at the people watching and seemed embarrassed by the attention.

After the crowd had settled, the police officers spoke with Maggie and went back to their beat. Bowers slipped into a seat at the bar, facing the streets. From the large mirror behind the row of liquor bottles she could watch her back without being obvious.

She heard a crisp pop as Lonnie opened a cold bottle of Guinness and slid it in front of her.

"On the house," he said. "Thanks for your help."

She raised the bottle in salute.

Outside on the sidewalk Coop pointed his finger in Vega's face and was giving him an earful. Bowers noticed a pickup truck across the street pull away and a guy on a scooter weave between pedestrians.

Meanwhile, Lonnie straightened a display of calendars next to the register and glanced over to check on his brother who still sat slouched in his wheelchair, poking at his phone.

As Maggie organized the cleanup effort, Bowers watched Lonnie juggle bottles and fill drink orders.

His hardened features gave him the aura of a man on a slow burn. He stood about her height, around six feet. He wore his curly black hair short and his sleeves rolled up to reveal a tattoo. The words *Duty, Honor,* and *Country* were inked over his biceps.

She took a moment to collect her thoughts until Gunner slipped onto the barstool to her left. Lonnie glanced up from filling a line of shot glasses with tequila.

Gunner slid a ten toward him. "I'd sure like to get me one of them."

Lonnie pushed a shot over to Gunner, who seemed more interested in sizing her up than his drink.

He stroked his red beard. "You are what I'd call a one-kicker. An engine that starts every time." He leaned in closer than she appreciated. The stench of his boozy breath and sweaty leather vest were revolting.

Lonnie set a bowl of pretzels in front of her. "You a cop?" he asked.

Gunner carefully lifted his shot glass to his lips with sausage-like fingers and stopped as if interested in her answer.

"Used to be." She nodded at Lonnie's tattoo. "Used to be Army too."

Gunner slammed back the tequila. His jaw tightened as he squinted at her in the mirror. Like Vega, he was another one with a short fuse. A bad temper fueled by alcohol spelled trouble.

The news that she had been a cop didn't seem to sit well with Lonnie.

"Why'd you help us?" he asked.

"Why wouldn't I?"

"Most cops wouldn't," he said.

Bowers knew where this conversation would go.

The pitch of Lonnie's voice went up. "I don't have any use for cops."

Gunner raised his beer glass. "I hear you, brother."

Tensions at the bar rose. The woman on Bowers' right picked up her wine glass and left.

"What about Coop?" Bowers asked. "He's a cop."

"He's different," said Lonnie. "My brother never hurt no one. He was unarmed. He didn't deserve what happened to him."

Lonnie explosively threw a bottle cap into the trash. "Next thing I know, I'm getting' a call to go to the ER." Lonnie's mouth tightened into a slit. "Until that night, my brother used to be really good at basketball, ya know? He had a shot at a scholarship. He had things he wanted to do in life."

Lonnie drove a metal scoop into the ice bin like a bayonet. *Chunk. Chunk.* He thrust it in harder. *Cha-chunk.*

"That weren't right," said Gunner as he pushed his empty shot glass toward Lonnie for a refill. "Vega needs to watch his back."

Bowers listened but said nothing.

"Vega robbed my brother of his future," said Lonnie. "Mama and I ain't never gotten over it. We're still paying medical bills. That asshole took everything away from all of us. You saw what Vega did here tonight. How can you defend that asshole?"

Bowers sipped her beer. "I don't. I'm the one who put him on his ass. Remember?"

Gunner snorted a laugh and pushed his empty beer glass toward the tap.

"Lonnie," said Bowers. "Most cops aren't your enemy. If some thug were to rob this place, those cops would be the first ones running in here to protect you."

Lonnie mumbled something inaudible and snatched up a wad of bills from a guy next to Gunner and went to the till.

Bowers had heard similar stories. No doubt, behind the badge there was a brotherhood, but what Lonnie didn't understand was that no one wanted a loose cannon in the family. When Lonnie returned, she said, "I am sorry for what happened to your brother and your family."

Lonnie glanced at her as if torn.

A few minutes later, he reached out and shook her hand with cold and slightly damp fingers. "Sorry. I get fired up about this stuff. I just hate seeing him stuck in that damned chair."

Gunner tapped his empty shot glass on the bar. When Lonnie ignored him, he turned his attention to Bowers. "That was some trick back there," he said as he leered at her with a tobacco-stained smile. "I like a woman who has some fire. You can be my back warmer anytime."

I'm out of here. She pulled out some bills to leave a tip.

"Hold on now," said Gunner as he put a hand on her arm.

Bowers glanced down at his hand and leveled a stare at him with a clear warning.

"Gunner," snapped Lonnie, "Behave yourself unless you want to be sittin' on the curb."

The biker withdrew his hand, but the coldness in his eyes spoke of a man not used to being rebuffed.

Bowers slid off the barstool and stood.

Gunner accepted another beer and used his lower lip to suck the froth from his mustache. "Before you go," he said. "Tell me one thing. What brings you all the way down here?"

"Scuba diving," she said.

His bushy brows went up. "Like underwater shit?"

"Yes." The exits were calling her.

"Hew, wee." Gunner slapped the man seated next to him. "She's a *scoo-baa* diver."

The man leaned forward. "Diving here is great."

"What do you see?" she asked as she tucked a tip under her beer bottle.

"Big barracuda," he said. "Tuna, grouper, snapper. We have our own way of dealing with them lionfish. Kill 'em and grill 'em. They're good eatin'."

The man pointed to the stack of calendars next to the register. "Lonnie, show this lady the calendar."

Lonnie snagged one of the glossy calendars and handed it to her. "The bartender who didn't show up tonight is the diver who took these pictures. We sell his calendars. Tourists love them and it shows what's in our waters."

Bowers thumbed through the pages and saw a huge barracuda and an amberjack that had to be close to a hundred pounds.

At the back of the calendar near a blurb about the island she noticed the portrait of the photographer.

The hair rose on her arms. She read his name, Bo Somers, and immediately knew why he hadn't shown up for work.

Even in profile and in a wetsuit, there was no doubt this was the man who'd attacked her.

Son of a bitch. Coop had to know this guy.

WITH VEGA ASLEEP in the passenger seat, Coop wondered if tonight had been the tipping point. His partner's path of self-destruction had gone too far.

At the eastern end of the island, near the airport, he pulled into a parking spot and helped Vega out of the car. The man reeked of beer as Coop escorted him up the stairs to his rented condo.

"Hey bro," said Vega. "Fun night, huh?" He stumbled on the steps. After dusting himself off, he said, "I'm okay."

His lack of balance and slurred speech said otherwise.

Coop waited as his partner fumbled for his keys and attempted to put his handcuff key into the deadbolt lock.

"Let me help," said Coop. After straightening out the keys, he opened the door and switched on a light. Like a homing pigeon, Vega went straight for his bedroom. He flopped on his bed and began to snore.

Coop flinched as a jet flew over. The roar of the engines rattled the windows and the dishes in the cupboards. *No wonder he got this place cheap.*

Vega showed no signs of hearing the thunderous racket.

Coop leaned on a folding chair. It seemed everything the guy had worn in the last month lay on the floor.

In Vega's small kitchen, Coop found a box of cereal on top of the fridge and half a case of beer inside. *Not exactly the breakfast of champions.*

When Vega had first graduated from the academy, he'd been solid. Two years later, things had begun to unravel.

Then came the altercation with Deon and the investigation by Internal Affairs. Vega was never the same.

He became edgy and confrontational. His wife left him. Policework wasn't for everyone. Coop had watched the system eat Vega up, one shift at a time.

Coop strolled through the meager 800 square-feet of living space where faded photos told a different story.

An image of him in uniform somewhere in Afghanistan and a letter of commendation from his superiors lay face down on the bookshelf. Coop studied a photo of Vega in a hospital bed with his legs and one arm bandaged. Coop found other snapshots of his wife pinning on his badge at his graduation from the police academy and him holding their newborn son.

Where had all that bravery and promise gone?

Coop had warned Vega. "With most jobs, the risks are predictable. A welder wears a face shield. An EMT puts on gloves. Boaters carried lifejackets in case of an emergency. Cops had little to no warning. The moment that could kill you could be at a traffic stop or around the next corner."

Survival required hyper-vigilance, but it came at a cost. When cops went home at night with the energy level of a dishtowel, it didn't always sit well with spouses.

As he glanced around the small room, it bothered him that Vega now seemed so different from the confident young officer he'd known just a few years ago.

Coop picked up Vega's uniform shirt from a recliner and ran a thumb over the KWPD patch on the sleeve. He listened to the snoring in the bedroom. "Ya don't walk away from a drowning man." *Especially when he's your partner.*

UNDER THE GUN

O N A GOOD DAY, BO HAD A BAD TEMPER, but tonight the pressure built like a volcano about to erupt. He strolled toward the pier where the 160-foot super-yacht, the *Leisure Lee*, had docked. Security crawled over the ship like a bunch of ants. One of them would surely whine about him being late.

After watching Bowers, the Urge coursed in his veins. He could almost feel his hands around her slender neck.

Bo stopped near his Boston Whaler where his wetsuit called to him. He loved night-diving. Alone. Sometimes he'd drift in the black waters to soothe his temper.

Tonight, he continued toward the big ship and began to laugh. Preston and the guards in their black shirts and vests thought they were badass. If they had any idea as to what he'd done and how much he'd enjoyed it, they'd quake in their boots.

Bo put aside the Urge and masked himself in his good-guy persona. For now, he intended to tolerate the skipper's BS as he rose through the ranks and finished getting his credentials. One day soon he'd be in command of his own ship—or possibly this one.

A loose board creaked under his feet.

Ahead at the gangway stood Jung Ji-something-or-other. Bo never could remember the guy's whole name, not that it mattered. Like always, Jung wore a black shirt and that smug expression. Bo didn't know whether Jung was Japanese, Korean, or Chinese and didn't care. The guy had way too much swag for a little punk.

Jung approached as if he'd been waiting for him. "Hey, asshole."

"Evening, Prick," said Bo. The guy got way too close. "Back off, man. I'm not your girlfriend."

Jung's face never showed expression, which bothered Bo. "The skipper wants to see you."

"Of course, he does," said Bo. He headed toward the gangway. As he trudged up the steps, he didn't care for the way Jung followed.

Sure enough, he found the skipper, Barrett Preston, on the bridge where he leaned over a table and pointed at navigation maps with that weird finger. The man's index finger was a gnarly stub. Preston had claimed a shark ate it, but Bo didn't buy it.

The skipper's neat, graying hair and beard made him appear distinguished and squared away, but Bo knew better. He was on the take like the rest of his crew.

"Skipper," said Bo, "You wanted—"

"Didn't I warn you to steer clear of the girls in town?"

Here we go again.

Preston stood inches away. "The last thing we need is the cops showing up with a search warrant."

As Preston yammered on, Bo studied the man's crisp white shirt. Someday those epaulets with gold braid would be his.

"Look at your face," said Preston, "do you really think that sets a professional image?"

"Tell 'em I took one for the team." Bo smirked.

The skipper opened his hand as if to slap him.

Bo held up his arm. "So, I'll fix it."

Preston lowered his hand.

Bo put on a smile. "Come on, Skipper. When have I ever let you down? She'll go away just like the others."

"She'd better," said Preston, "and quietly." He smoothed his beard with that finger that intrigued Bo and gave everyone else the creeps. "If not, I'll put Jung on it."

Ten feet away, Jung appeared to be listening.

Bo pointed to his face. "Skipper, she owes me for this. I need to make this right."

Preston gripped his shoulder. "Listen to me, you do solid work, but I can't allow you to become a liability. If you even look at another girl in town, I'm going to cut your dick off and feed it to the crabs."

Jung snickered at that. "Then you'd really have crabs."

Preston poked Bo in the chest with his stub of a finger. "We've got a special VIP trip scheduled. I can't have shit blowing up. We have to keep it cool."

"Nothing is going to blow up," said Bo.

"It already has!" said Preston. "I've got the Coast Guard breathing down my neck and a burned-out boat that's a total loss."

Bo hated it when Preston stuck his nose into his personal business. "I said I'll fix it."

"You better," said Preston. "Your neck is on the line."

Jung's smile widened. Bo glared at him, knowing he'd take it as a challenge.

Jung stepped forward.

"Back off, asshole," said Bo, as he balled his hand into a fist. "I could do him too, while I'm at it."

"Enough," shouted Preston. "Bo, just go take care of this."

Bo headed for the door. "I'll do it tonight."

TUNNEL VISION

A NAGGING SENSE OF UNEASE weighed on Riggs as he pushed through his morning workout.

By 7:00 a.m., he headed down the hall to the breakroom to fill his cup with the black stuff the Bureau called coffee.

Riggs took a seat at the round table where he kept his ears open for the latest scuttlebutt. Most agents grumbled "Morning," or nodded and went back to their desks.

Scuffling footsteps drew closer. Greg dropped into the seat next to him.

Riggs knew him from the counterterrorism unit. They'd worked together many times and had often spent hours kicking around thoughts on each other's cases and life within the Bureau.

Greg's unruly black hair and bloodshot eyes meant he had also endured a tough night. He yawned and stared into his cup as if it contained answers.

"Good Morning," said Riggs.

Greg nodded, but didn't look up. He wasn't a big man, but Riggs knew he was smarter than most and had a wicked ability to find that one detail that cracked a case.

"You look like a country song," said Riggs, "where a guy loses his job, lady, truck, and dog."

Greg glanced down at his crumpled shirt and chuckled. "That bad?"

"What's up, brother?"

Greg sipped at his steaming cup. "I used to think that providing reliable intel meant something. That congress would take the appropriate measures." He raised an open hand as if at a loss. "From what I see, you'd think protecting home and country were the last things on their minds."

Now Riggs understood. "You're referring to the bid for E-Connect?"

"Word travels," said Greg. "What does it say when a modest little Sri Lankan company like SriCom steps up to bid on the multi-billion-dollar sale of a U.S. company?"

"Tells me a government behind the scenes is involved."

"Bingo," said Greg as he brushed back his wavy-black hair.

"It could be Russia," said Riggs, "Venezuela, Iran, North Korea, or China."

Greg glanced over his shoulder and lowered his voice. "I was in a meeting at the White House yesterday that made me want to bitch-slap everyone in the room."

"Even Hogan?" asked Riggs.

Greg hesitated as if puzzled by Riggs' knowledge of Hogan's presence.

"A friend attended."

Greg nodded. "At least Hogan uses his brain, but there was no getting through to Fowler."

Larry Fowler had been in office for as long as Riggs could remember. "He's the poster boy for why we need term limits."

Greg laughed. "Good point."

He watched another agent come and go. "Fowler only cares about preserving his own seat in congress. National security isn't even on his radar."

"Let's hope CFIUS and the Justice Department don't sign-off on it."

"I don't think they will," said Greg, "but they're under a lot of pressure."

Greg toyed with a sugar packet. "With Midterms, Fowler is so busy making backroom deals with other congressmen that he has tunnel vision. It was like discussing calculus with a cocker spaniel."

"You know how it is," said Riggs. "There's always more at play than what's on the table."

"It's not just the money," said Greg. "Where are they going to find the resources to manage such a large company? They don't have it. Hell, most of the rural areas in Sri Lanka don't even have phone service yet, much less the internet."

Riggs refilled Greg's cup.

"Thanks, my friend," said Greg.

Riggs drummed a thumb on the table. "Even Fowler should understand that allowing an enemy to control our communications networks would be cutting our own throats."

Greg nodded. "Exactly."

He rubbed his eyes. "Look how dependent we all are on our phones and the internet. If this deal goes through, I'm afraid America will wake up one morning to dead cellphones and no internet."

"It would bring the entire nation to a halt," said Riggs. "All we can do is warn them. Give them the facts."

The deep circles under Greg's blue eyes spoke of more than one sleepless night.

"Greg," said Riggs, "you're overdue for some shuteye."

"I know," said Greg. "Appreciate your input."

Riggs started to stand.

"Wait," said Greg, "you've got the mind for this. I'll make a spot for you anytime you want to come over to counterterrorism. It's good experience and might lead to a promotion. Besides, we could use your skills."

Riggs considered his offer. "I have to admit that crimes against kids is wearing on me. It's brutal."

"Think about it," said Greg. He glanced up at a calendar on the wall. "At least we get a bit of a breather. Fowler is going on some kind of fancy fishing trip and dragging Hogan along with him. Word is they plan to negotiate. Maybe Hogan can knock some sense into him. POTUS will also be gone. He flew out this morning to Miami with his family to do some midterm campaigning and a little golfing in the Florida sunshine."

Riggs now understood why Kory had left town.

"Glad I'm not on that detail," said Riggs. "Roadrunner is trouble waiting to happen."

"You can say that again." Greg went silent when Riggs' supervisor, Patrick McDougall, shuffled past the door. His stooped shoulders and hulking frame were hard to miss. Wearing his usual scowl, he did an about-face and poked his head into the breakroom.

"Riggs," he said in his usual gruff tone, "I expect that report on my desk by tomorrow morning."

"Yes, sir," said Riggs. "Willie and I are working on it." Riggs listened to McDougall's footsteps fade as he walked away.

Greg lowered his voice. "Remember what I said, we need you."

Riggs heard heavy steps running up the hall. Willie burst into the room.

"Good morning. Come grab some coffee," said Riggs. "I was just—"

The car keys dangled from Willie's hand.

"Riggs, we found the Jacksonville girl. We've gotta go. Now!"

GRAVE WARNING

HENRY WAS GOOD AT SEEING things others didn't. He pulled open the dusty green curtains and peered out his window onto the docks, where fishermen cleaned their catches and pelicans and gulls vied for the scraps. He wondered where the guy in the gray skiff had gone.

Every morning since Henry had returned to the Rock, he would stand at his little window, watching the dock's ebb and flow during the early morning hours.

Best damned time of the day.

Today the docks were quiet. Water gently lapped at the boat hulls. Henry could tell the hour by watching the activity on the docks. Fishermen left before dawn. Tourists filled the afternoons. Partiers came out at dark. Such predictability provided a rare sense of security that had drawn him back to the Keys.

Henry thought about the guy in the skiff and watched the bright yellow sun sit on the eastern horizon like a sunny-side-up egg. His stomach grumbled. It was time for breakfast.

After a yawn, he closed the stiff green curtains. As part of his compensation, Clyde had allowed Henry to live in part of his storage space. It wasn't much to look at, but he happily put up with a kitchen that wasn't much more than a table, microwave, and small fridge. At least it had a good bed.

Henry appreciated that Clyde had always had a job and a place for him whenever he'd come back into town.

His curmudgeonly boss didn't go by the numbers on his watch. Rather, he judged starting and stopping times by the amount of work needing to be done and the amount of daylight on hand to do it in. The shorter days in October were easy compared to the long hot days of July.

Like water always finding its level, the world seemed to demand balance. Even assholes, like the man in the skiff, would eventually succumb to their own stupid decisions.

Buddy pawed at the door to go out.

Henry put on sunglasses and his favorite ballcap. He grabbed Buddy's leash—not that his dog needed one. He always stayed on Henry's heels like it was a sworn duty.

With only a few chores to do this afternoon, Henry looked forward to taking the morning off and checking on the whereabouts of that guy in the skiff.

He left his room without bothering to shave and took in the salty air of the docks. After ambling toward the parking lot of the marina, he reached Buddy's favorite patch of green grass. As his dog sniffed to find the perfect spot, a boat pulled up to the gas dock behind him.

Nearby, Clyde walked in circles with his phone to his ear. He frantically waved Henry over.

"Listen," said Clyde, holding his phone to his chest. "Can you fill up that guy's boat before you go? I'll be tied up here for a few minutes."

"Yup, yup," said Henry, "reckon we can do that. Come on, Buddy."

Henry jogged toward the dock and secured the lines of the cabin cruiser. Hinkley made good boats, but this one had seen better days.

As the bumpers on the dock protected the beat-to-hell fiberglass hull, he snickered at the irony until the fur on Buddy's back rose. His dog usually paid no mind to visiting boats unless there was a dog onboard.

Henry pulled the brim of his dark-green hat down low.

"Fill it," said a man with a nasally voice.

Henry set about doing the fill.

While listening to the thumping of the gas pump, Henry eyed the boat more closely. Seeing a Hinkley out of Miami around here wasn't unusual, but triple 350hp Mercs on a boat ready for the scrapyard caught his attention.

The boat's scraped-up hull wore peeling letters that read: *Off Grid*. A lot of rigs had funny names like *Beeracuda* and *She Got the House*.

Henry couldn't help wondering why they needed $100,000 worth of horses on that scrapheap. He wiped his hands on a rag and figured people were stupid.

A growl rumbled in Buddy's chest when the boat's driver stepped off his vessel onto the dock. In spite of his puffy, black eyes and swollen nose, Henry recognized him immediately as the man who'd attacked that woman.

He kept his cool. "Hey, brother. Someone messed you up pretty good."

"Nah," said the man. "I partied too hard. Tried to jump off my boat and tripped. Smacked my face on the dock. Should've known better."

Henry grunted. He liked people who lied even less than those who didn't take care of their boats.

"I reckon," said Henry, "we've all partied a time or two."

He had no use for this jerk before, and he surely didn't like him any better now.

The Hinkley's grimy deck, streaks of rust and ruin, and the stench showed he'd been hauling something nasty.

When the man handed Henry a credit card, Buddy stood.

The man's jacket and the card bore the name of a super-yacht Henry recognized. In any marina, the 160-foot *Leisure Lee* would be hard to miss.

He ran the card and watched the man polishing a handrail. Henry laughed to himself. *That's like polishing a turd.*

While this fella signed off using the name Bo Somers, Henry noted streaks of blood on the Hinkley's swim platform.

Bo glanced at the stern and back at Henry, who patted his leg to call his dog closer in case this went south.

Bo kept his head down. "Yeah. I've been fishing. Cleaning the catch is messy business."

Henry tidied up around the fuel pump and locked up the digital device for taking payments.

Meanwhile, Bo scrubbed away the red streaks by the swim platform and gunnel. When finished, he shoved the rags into a plastic bag, hopped off the boat, and came toward Henry.

"Hey, tell me something," said Bo.

Henry took a step back. Buddy immediately put himself between him and this Bo fella.

"Easy, boy," said Henry. "It's okay."

Buddy showed his teeth.

"He's just smiling. Don't worry about him," said Henry, knowing his dog would rip this guy apart if he made a wrong move.

The man stepped away from Buddy and snorted as he breathed through his nose. "That your trashcan, over there?"

"Yes, sir." Henry rubbed the soft fur of Buddy's ears and studied the man's face. He'd seen channel markers runover by a barge that had looked better.

Again, Bo shied away from the dog. "Does the city pick it up?"

Henry hesitated. "You mean the trash?"

"Yeah."

Henry had never seen anyone so interested in their trash bins. "That's our burn barrel."

Bo hadn't taken his eyes off the barrel. "How often do you light it up?"

Henry glanced at the clouds rolling in. "Fixin' to do it today unless it gets windy."

The man dropped his bag in the burn barrel, which annoyed Henry. Plastic had no place in there.

After pocketing the receipt for the gas, Bo cast off, and drifted away.

Henry watched until the boat was out of sight.

Before leaving, he had to do something with that plastic before he forgot about it. Melted plastic made a mess. He returned to the burn barrel where he removed the bag and was about to toss the whole mess into their city pickup bin where it belonged, but Buddy got in the way. The dog sniffed at the bag with intense interest.

Henry stopped and tore open the sack. Inside he found rags made from old beach towels. He expected to find bloodstains, but these were soaked in it. In a fold in one of the rags lay a fake fingernail that had been painted bright pink. Henry lifted his sunglasses for a closer look.

The blood-stained nail appeared to have been ripped off.

"Fishing my ass," he said to Buddy. "Fish don't have fingernails."

Henry grunted. "This boy is about to git his-self in a bad way."

HOT SEAT

A S BOWERS LIFTED WEIGHTS in the hotel's gym, her determination burned along with her muscles. With each biceps curl and pushup, she focused even harder on finding the man who'd attacked her.

By 8:00 a.m. Bowers passed the coffee stand and took a seat on a bench outside a giftshop next to a potted palm.

A rooster's shrill *cock-a-doodle-doo* startled her. *Pal, you're going to end up in a potpie.*

Cars streamed past. People stood in line for coffee. Tourists wandered the sidewalk. It seemed as if she and the palm were an island apart from the bustling paradise surrounding her.

A young woman's voice from the coffee stand called out to customers waiting in line for their morning brew.

Bowers checked her phone. Nothing from Riggs, yet. She'd given him the name *Bo Somers* and had little doubt he'd go after that with a vengeance. Bowers groaned when she discovered an article in the local news about her assault.

That's swell. A least she had her back turned in the photo.

Bowers glanced up at the squeaking of rubber soles against the concrete. The bench rocked as Coop took a seat next to her. Winks of sunlight glinted off his shiny gold badge and wedding ring. His uniform appeared fresh from the cleaners, except for a dried mustard stain.

He took a sip from the steaming cup in his hand. "You ever have Cuban coffee? Looks like you could use some."

The enticing aroma hung in the air. She swirled the cold brew in her paper cup from the gas station. "It has to be better than this crap."

"Cuban coffee got me through many long shifts." Coop tugged at his duty belt and rubbed his palms on his thighs.

"I'm sorry," he said, "Key West hasn't exactly offered you its usual warm welcome. You must think we're a bunch of thugs."

"Come on, now," said Bowers. "Everywhere has crime, alcohol, and people whose emotions get the better of them."

"You doing all right?"

Bowers nodded as a man zipped by on a skateboard being pulled by his setter. "Other than feeling like a piñata, I'm fine."

Coop seemed to be searching for words as he used his thumbnail to scrape off the bits of dried mustard on his trouser leg. "I hate seeing someone's hard-earned vacation screwed up."

"Not your fault." She took in a deep breath. "If I have to stay here, at least the scenery is good."

Coop stared at his coffee.

Bowers dumped the black sludge from her cup into the potted palm.

The leather in Coop's duty belt squeaked when he reached forward and set his cup on the concrete next to his boot. "Listen, I need to ask you to do something for me."

She listened.

"Stop playing cop," he said. "Let me do this. Don't try to investigate this on your own."

She held out her phone and showed him a photo of her in fatigues armed with a .308 sniper rifle.

"Coop, let me make this clear." Her voice hardened. "I've taken down terrorists and killers. I wasn't playing the role of an MP or a cop. I was a cop."

The word *was* pained her. Maybe taking a step back had been a mistake.

She pulled open her collar, revealing the dark purple handprints at the base of her neck. "This wasn't some pretend game, either. This is real."

Coop sat mute.

Bowers crushed her cup with the heel of her boot. "Bo Somers is a predator. He bartends at the Blue Coconut on the same nights you work security. Why didn't you tell me you knew him?"

COOP'S EARS BURNED like a schoolboy sitting on the hotseat. He didn't know what to say.

"You're right. I know Bo."

Coop reached down to pick up his coffee and thought better of it. "I should've told you, but..." *Shit.* He could feel Bowers studying him.

"And?" she asked. The calm, but undeniable tenacity in her voice made him wish he had come clean with her sooner.

"When you mentioned the tattoo and his stainless-steel bracelet, I had my suspicions, but as a victim you know I couldn't share that with you. All I'm saying is that the chief and especially the DA won't rock with a civilian doing her own investigating. We have methods of dealing with things. Just give it some time."

"What is this, Coop," she asked, "another small town steeped in good-ole-boy politics?"

Her words stung like having his ears boxed.

"It's not like that," he said. "It's just that everyone here knows everyone. If word gets out that Bo is on our radar, he'll head for the mainland faster than a Daytona race car."

"I can see that," said Bowers, "but—"

"As I said before, Chief Ingram is particular about how things get done. That's all."

He squinted against the bright sunlight and tried to appear more confident than he felt. Bowers appeared to read him like a roadmap. Despite being covered in scrapes and purple contusions, her legs crossed at the ankle and she showed no signs of being nervous or backing down. He couldn't help but admire her. "I promise, I'll do everything I can."

She wore a smirk. "So you want me to leave my flash-bangs and AR-15 under lock and key?"

Coop chuckled. "I'd appreciate it. Although, I wouldn't mind watching you put Gunner in his place."

She laughed.

He couldn't help but like this woman. Something about her reminded him of why he had become a cop.

"Listen," said Coop with a twinge of regret. "Thanks for having my six last night."

"No problem," said Bowers. Coop watched her focus on an older woman with a fancy purse picking through seashells at a little kiosk.

Bowers sat forward in her seat. "Lonnie told me the story about his brother."

"I'll bet he did. He tells everyone who will listen. First thing this morning, he lodged a complaint against Vega. Maggie called in too and chewed the chief's ear about it."

"Lonnie's reaction is understandable," said Bowers, "considering his view is skewed by a bad experience."

Coop gripped the edge of the bench.

Bowers seemed unflappable. "I still can't justify putting an unarmed teenager in a wheelchair."

Coop brushed at the mustard stain. "I'd love to know what really happened that night. Vega wasn't always like this."

Bowers stared straight ahead. "That doesn't excuse his behavior."

"I know." Coop sat back. "The chief was furious about the bar fight. Put him on leave, pending an investigation."

Just as she was about to say something, Coop heard footsteps coming closer. Sara, his sister, hurried toward him.

"You forgot sugar," she said with a playful grin. As she dropped the packets into his hand, he noticed her wearing the silver bracelet he'd given her for her twentieth birthday. Its three tiny sea turtle charms sparkled in the morning sun.

"Thanks, sis." Coop introduced Bowers.

In the distance, the man at the coffee stand's window hollered. "Sara! *Andale!* The line is backing up."

Sara hugged Coop. "Gotta go."

As she hurried away, she pulled her tawny hair into a ponytail.

Back at the window, Sara handed a dog biscuit to a lady with a little yapper that looked like a slipper on a leash. Adding to the illusion, the woman had dyed the pooch's white fur pink.

Thirty feet from them, a scruffy guy caught Coop's attention. "Sara's a good kid," he said. "I was wide-eyed and fearless like that once."

"Weren't we all?" said Bowers. She seemed to home in on the same shady dude inching closer to the lady with the big purse.

Coop could see the cop in Bowers. When the suspicious man moved toward the kiosk with his eyes on the purse, Bowers stood and marched toward him. He took off at a dead run. The lady with the purse was oblivious to the thwarted purse snatcher and continued shopping for trinkets.

Bowers returned to the bench. "Sara's a pretty girl and smart."

"Don't I know it," he said. "She's dating a new guy. I keep tellin' her to bring him around so I can meet him, but she's not keen on that idea."

"Like I said, smart girl." Bowers brushed a strand of brown hair from her face. "A big brother who's six-five and a cop would intimidate any prospective boyfriend."

Coop had to chuckle at that. "Protecting her is my brotherly duty. At least we don't usually get the serious stuff here in Key West." He wished he could've taken those words back the moment they flew from his mouth.

Bowers stared straight ahead.

"I didn't mean to imply the crime against you wasn't serious."

"Like I said, either you find him, or I will."

THEM BONES

BOWERS STOPPED A FEW FEET from a disheveled woman in a tattered gray sweatshirt, who mumbled to herself as she inspected discarded to-go bags in the trash.

When Bowers started to pour out Coop's cold coffee, the woman responded instantly. "Lady, wait," she said in a gravelly voice. "I could take that off your hands, if you don't want it."

Bowers studied the woman's weathered face. It seemed she had once been pretty, but living on the street had hardened her features. "You're Lily, aren't you?"

The woman hesitated. "Yes'um," she said, as she kept her focus on the cup. Clearly Lily wanted that coffee.

"Tell you what," said Bowers, "I have a better idea." She dropped Coop's cup in the bin.

Lily's brows furrowed as she stared into the trashcan.

"Come with me," said Bowers. "I'll buy you a fresh cup. At least it will be hot. Will that work for you?"

Lily studied her for moment, then nodded.

Seconds later, she followed Bowers to the coffee stand's window. While a man in a Naval flight suit picked up his order, Bowers asked her, "What kind of coffee do you like?"

She glanced nervously at those around them. "Anything hot, ma'am, would feel real good on my sore throat."

Sara took the order. The colorful hand-painted signs around the window boasted a variety of temping pastries and fresh sandwiches.

Sara handed a large steaming cup of coffee to Lily.

She held the cup as if it were made of gold. "Thank you."

"Wait," said Sara, who disappeared. A few seconds later she returned, holding a small white sack. "It's a sandwich. Someone ordered it, but never picked it up. I hope you like turkey." She handed the woman the sack and offered her cream and sugar.

Lily glanced between Sara and Bowers. "Bless you."

Moments later, they strolled the plaza. Lily's smile showed she hadn't seen a dentist in a while.

"Thank you," said Lily. "Thank you so much."

"Enjoy your breakfast." Bowers began to leave. She hadn't gone four feet before Lily blocked her path. She peered at the people passing by as if someone might hear.

Her smile had vanished. "They're watching."

Lily squinted at the footpath to the right of the shell shop that led to the marina. It seemed as if time on the streets had left the poor woman with a twisted view of reality until Lily nodded toward the water and said, "Be careful. Them bones you found ain't the only ones out there. You be mindful of that, missy."

LOST GIRL

R IGGS BRACED HIMSELF for another tragic scene. It was all part of the job, but it wasn't pretty.

As he and Willie raced to the site of the reported murder, October's fall foliage in full regalia seemed less about the colorful changing of seasons and more about withering leaves heralding the cold, dark days ahead.

Any crime involving a kid created a hellish rollercoaster ride for the victim, the families, and the officers involved in the case. Even if they successfully prosecuted the perpetrator, it would only be a token of justice. It didn't alter what had happened. At least getting the perpetrator off the streets would save someone else from the same fate.

Blustery cold winds hit Riggs' face. He rolled up the window. "Where we going?"

"Virginia. Head toward Colchester," said Willie as he eased back the passenger seat of their customized Ford Expedition. "It's twenty-two miles. Should be there in a half hour, if traffic doesn't screw us."

Riggs wove around eighteen-wheelers and the usual tie-ups. "If this is our missing girl from Jacksonville, how'd her body get all the way up to Virginia?"

"No clue." Willie flipped through his notes. "But Jacksonville and Colchester are both off I-95."

Riggs stomped on the brake and laid on the horn when a white pickup cut him off.

"Sad shit," said Willie, as he reviewed the file. "She was fourteen. I get two adults getting pissed off and into a mutual fight, but why hurt a kid?"

"Willie," said Riggs. "You're looking for reason where there is none. It will never make sense. The best we can do is to hunt down the asshole who did this and stop him."

They raced toward another scene he didn't want to see.

Forty minutes later, they exited onto 611 and Old Colchester Road where they passed fields, farmhouses, and a horse ranch. After crossing a stream, they entered a densely forested area of mostly pines until they came upon the flashing lights of a sheriff's vehicle and a Fairfax patrol car.

As an officer in a tan shirt approached, Riggs rolled down his window and noted the odor of pine and damp earth.

"Can I help you, sir?" she asked.

Riggs flashed his Bureau ID.

She leaned in closer.

"The scene," she said, "is down this dirt road." When she had spoken the word *scene*, she'd hesitated. "I'll move my vehicle, Agent Riggs, but be careful where you park. It's muddy and there is a parking area set up to your left."

"Thank you, Officer," said Riggs. Judging by the newness of her gear and her age, he suspected she had been out of the academy only a few months.

"How'd you find the body?" he asked.

She put a hand on her duty belt. "Beyond the smell, the road to the left runs to the river and the Fairfax Yacht Club. One of their members noticed a bunch of bikers out here. He went home, thought about it, and figured they were up to no good. This morning, he came back to look for himself. The guy alerted us to the body."

She squinted into the distance. "Agent Riggs?"

"Yes?"

The officer tugged down on the neck of her vest. "This one's ugly."

RIGGS RUMBLED DOWN the rough dirt road, hoping to find enough evidence to nail the suspects.

He parked off to his left in the area the officer had described. Fellow agent Willie Ranker clicked open his seatbelt and watched the activity in the woods with a bleak expression.

Riggs checked his phone where a message read: *Gunner. Changós. In Key West.*

"Let's get this over with," said Willie.

As they carefully trudged toward the yellow crime scene tape, Riggs felt his shoes dampen.

"I've got a sinking feeling," he said.

Willie glance at the mud engulfing their feet. "Not Funny."

"I'm serious. Our evidence has been laying exposed to the elements for days. We'll be lucky if any of it is still intact."

A sheriff in a big black hat emerged from the forest and approached Riggs. He reached out to shake hands. "We sure appreciate your help on this one."

The trees buffered the wind, but it was still cold. The sheriff's jaw tightened; his breath visible in the cold air. "Thought I was pretty tough. All them years on the force. Never did I see something such as this."

A haze hung in the evergreen boughs and cast a flat gray pall over the churned-up dirt. The birds were silent. A large raven perched on a branch above him.

Riggs found himself so moved by the sheriff's stoic resolve he barely felt the cold. "We'll take care of her. Our Evidence Response Team should be here any minute."

The sheriff gripped his duty belt. "Just find the bastards who did this. I'll help in any way I can."

The odor of decomp hung in the air.

Riggs and the sheriff locked eyes. Without saying a word both men understood their mutual disgust and the rage that came with it.

"Never gets any easier." The sheriff handed Riggs his card. "I have a granddaughter that age. Kills me to see this."

"I know, brother," said Riggs. "Appreciate your help."

Riggs avoided breathing deeply as he carefully studied the scene. Even before he saw the body, the number of animal tracks told him what he'd find.

Some elements were an eerie reminder of his last case with Bowers.

A minute later, he spotted the victim. The girl's naked body lay chest down in a gully at the side of the trail. Animals had found her. Riggs crouched on a tarp near her feet. Her toenails had been painted pink. A delicate string of tiny blue beads encircled one ankle.

He wanted to punch someone.

Around him a hushed, almost primal regard hung over the entire scene. Even the raven appeared to stand watch.

Determined to find the evil that had done this, Riggs stood and continued to search for answers in the details.

The FBI's forensic team arrived. Willie directed them to the scene where they immediately began to set up white canopies to protect the evidence from the elements.

Riggs watched as they filmed and processed the scene.

"I've already asked for dental records," said Willie. "With her braces, the X-rays should confirm her identity fairly soon."

"Judging by the volume of blood," said Riggs, "she was murdered right there."

Willie gazed up at the treetops as if he couldn't stomach any more. "Riggs, they used an ax."

"I know." The forlorn sound of the raven's caw echoed through the forest.

The girl's head lay five feet from the body. It struck Riggs as odd that Grace's light-brown ponytail was still neatly in place.

He ached for her parents and what she'd been through. "This has to be the work of the Changós. Even the Pagans wouldn't do this. Look at the tire tracks. There could have been six motorcycles or more back here."

Willie took notes as Riggs called over the photographer. He

pointed to an area off the side of the trail. "Log these tracks. Those weren't from a motorcycle."

A crime scene tech put down yellow markers.

"Looks like a truck," said Riggs, "or maybe a van."

That caught the sheriff's attention. "The witness said an older white van followed the bikers. The logo on the side had two crossed wrenches. He thought it was their mechanic's vehicle."

That made sense. If a bike broke down, it could be rolled inside the van and fixed without holding up the whole gang.

Riggs wrote down the info and the name of the witness. "I've got something else. Gunner and his crew are in Key West, which means the Changós are moving up and down the East Coast."

"Great," said Willie. "As soon as the Pagans get wind of that, there will be a war. There's no limit to what mayhem they'll do." He paused. "The amount of decomp fits with the witness's account about the bikers. They had plenty of time to skedaddle down to Key West."

"True," said Riggs. "Maybe they're lying low and don't think we're on to them."

A crime scene tech waved over Riggs. On the tarp at her feet lay a backpack. Crammed in a pocket she'd found a photo and a bunch of receipts.

"What do you make of these?" she asked.

With gloved hands, he examined the materials. "They read like a roadmap from Jacksonville to Fayetteville and finally to Richmond. Good find."

Riggs knelt and examined a photograph of a girl with light-brown hair, grinning at the camera with a puppy. He recognized her from a photo her parents had given them. He handed the picture back.

"It's Grace." Riggs pointed to the receipts. "She kept these to tell us where she'd been."

The sheriff approached Riggs. "When you find these bastards, I want to know about it."

"Yes, sir."

Like a promise, Riggs pulled out his pen and wrote *Grace* on his palm.

BARE FISTS

WITH HIS SIRENS SCREAMING, Coop's red and blue lights flared as he raced toward a call about a disturbance at a convenience store. The lack of information meant this could be anything from a full-blown hostage situation to a nothing-burger.

So much for a lunch break.

With the sun at high noon and the typical array of cars at the gas pumps and in the parking area, he saw no signs of trouble.

With his hand on his weapon, Coop peered through the glass door of the store. Inside, he spotted the store clerk, a dark-haired young man in a blue vest, engaged in an argument with a teed-off older gentleman.

"Good grief," said Coop. He ripped open the door. A bell chimed as he entered. The musty smell of refrigerators in need of a good cleaning and greasy hot dogs on a rolling rotisserie put a damper on his appetite.

The clerk shrieked, "Hey, old man. It's a dollar and seventy-nine cents, plus tax."

The paramount issue seemed to be a frozen cherry cola.

Coop wanted to knock both their heads together. One cola hardly merited this much fuss.

The white-haired gentleman wore a veteran's ballcap. He trembled with outrage and pounded a finger on the countertop. "Young man," he yelled, "I already paid you."

Coop stepped in. "Sir, take a step back."

A lady with heavy perfume dropped a ten-dollar bill on the counter. "I've got kids in the car." She held up a bag of chips and six-pack of ginger ale. "Keep the change."

"See, dude," screeched the clerk. "You have to pay."

"I'm not your dude," scolded the older man. His face flushed crimson. "Sonny, I've been paying since before you were born. I put my life on the line for this country."

As he plopped the drink on the counter, the lid popped open and a gush of slushy-red cola flooded the counter and splattered all over Coop's boots and trousers.

"Look what you did," yelled the clerk. "Pay up or get outta my store."

The old man's voice shook from age and anger. "Show some respect, young man. I gave you money. It's right there next to the register."

Coop put himself between the two. "That's enough."

As he began negotiating a truce, the rumble of motorcycle engines vibrated the walls.

Outside, a horde of outlaw bikers rolled in. The hair went up on Coop's arms.

He called for backup. "Over a dozen bikers are swarming the gas pumps. Their guys are blocking the exits. Looks like they're planning to hit the place. Send units."

"Stay on the line," said the dispatcher.

Coop watched the bikers dismount and leave their motorcycles blocking the gas pumps. "Step it up. They're coming toward the store. I've got eight civilians in here with me. We need help. Now."

As he ended the call, Gunner pointed at the store. Coop could tell by Gunner's body language that he'd spotted Coop's cruiser.

Bikers marched toward the entrance.

"Keys," shouted Coop to the clerk. "Give me your keys."

The reluctant clerk tossed them over.

Coop locked the doors. As he and the bikers glared at each other through the glass, Coop flipped the safety off his holster with his thumb.

As an old Beach Boys tune played in the background, a biker tugged at the door handle. Another tapped on the glass.

If shit was going to happen, it would be now.

"Help us," pleaded a terrified woman. The little boy with her began to cry.

Coop directed the clerk and customers toward the back of the store.

The bikers shattered the store's double glass doors with their axes and streamed inside. One sprayed the lens of the security camera with paint. Another jacked bottles of No Doz from the counter.

Screams and shouting from bystanders added to the chaos.

While the bikers grabbed booze and beer, Coop hustled the clerk and customers into the back room. "Keep the door locked," he ordered.

All complied, except for the older man. He charged toward the front of the store. As a biker with a case of beer under one arm headed for the exit, the old man in the veteran's cap blocked his path.

When the biker balled his hand into a fist, the defiant old guy shouted, "Buzz off, asshole. You have no right to burglarize this store."

The biker shoved the elderly man into a display of nuts and potato chips.

Coop called in on his radio. "Step it up," he said, as he headed for the old man.

Another biker emerged from the far end of the store with two big bottles of Jim Beam. He hurled one at Coop and raced for the exit. Coop tackled the man. At the same time, glass shattered as the Jim Beam crashed into a shelf of wine bottles.

On the floor, Coop blocked the biker from whacking him with the remaining bottle of Jim Beam. The tussle flared into a bare-fisted boxing match.

"Knock his socks off," hollered the feisty old man, rooting for Coop.

Blows and blocks flew in rapid succession. Coop gained the upper hand until two more bikers entered the store.

Coop pulled his pistol. "Don't even think about it."

They backed away. The air smelled like a barrel of bar rags.

Coop felt movement and glanced down to find the whiskey thief groping for his ax. Coop aimed his pistol at the man's head. "Touch it and you're dead."

At the sound of sirens, Coop's detainee stretched his arms out like airplane wings. Coop secured his pistol. As he began to cuff the biker, the song *You're The One That I Want* from the movie Grease, played in the background.

The biker grinned up at Coop, as if he thought it funny.

"Turn off that damned music," Coop shouted at the clerk.

The biker elbowed Coop in the face and tried to escape.

"Shit," snorted Coop. This time, he pulled his Taser and aimed. "Last warning. Stop. Now."

The biker didn't listen. *What a shock.*

He charged toward the door where the old man grabbed a can off the shelf and blasted the biker in the face with bug spray.

The biker immediately began to spit, gasp, and try to wipe his eyes. "Damn that stings."

"Don't move," ordered Coop, "or I will tase you."

"You son of a bitch," shrieked the biker, as he lurched toward the old man.

Coop pulled the trigger. The barbs and coppery tentacles shot through the air. One embedded in the biker's butt and the other nailed him in the back. He keeled forward and hit the deck. The crisp repetitive snapping of the Taser punctuated his shrieks of pain. "Mother fucking. Goddamn. Son of a bitch."

"You want another hit?" asked Coop.

The biker shook his head. "No way, dude."

"On your knees. Hands on your head."

Dogs and Tasers had a remarkable way of gaining compliance.

Coop grabbed each wrist and slapped on the cuffs. "You're under arrest for burglary, damaging property, assaulting a police officer, resisting, and — if I could —I'd charge you with being a pain in my ass."

The biker's red eyes were still watering from the bug spray.

Coop called on his radio. "We need EMS."

Coop patted down the biker. As he took the man's ax and knife, the speakers in the ceiling began playing an old Bee Gees tune, *Stayin' Alive*. Coop envisioned using that damned speaker for target practice.

Leaving the barbs in place, Coop flushed the biker's eyes with a bottle of water.

The sirens were closing in. *About time.*

Coop ordered the cuffed biker to kneel on the floor with his face against the cooler.

The clerk continued to gripe. "I want my money."

Coop pulled him aside. "Seriously, you're still at this? Just give the guy his damned drink and be done with it."

"No," said the old man. "It's a point of honor. I'm a veteran and I pay my own way." His long boney finger pointed to a five-dollar bill on the gritty floor near the cash register. "See, that's the bill I gave you. I told you I paid."

"Enough," shouted Coop as he guarded the store's entrance. He still had a full mag in his pistol and two more on his belt.

The warble of sirens couldn't get here fast enough.

Out at the gas pumps, Gunner revved his engine. The others did the same. Hair rose on Coop's arms. The deafening sound drowned out the sirens as Coop maintained his position between the bikers and the bystanders.

"Don't mess with Gunner," shouted the cuffed biker. "He'll cut your nuts off."

Sure enough, Gunner showed no fear as he flashed Coop that wise-assed grin.

Gunner roared out onto the street. Others followed. Several burned rubber as they peeled out. The pitch of their engines rose with acceleration and they were gone.

The howl of police sirens sped through the intersection. Two units with lights and sirens blaring went after the bikers. Two more barreled into the parking area in front of the store.

Coop opened the door for a young officer, who asked, "What have you got?"

He handed the ax and the knife to the young officer. "Our biker here attempted to steal whiskey, he punched me in the face, and resisted arrest." Coop wiped blood off his forehead and one knuckle. "Have a medic check him out. I tased him and the man in the veterans cap sprayed him with insecticide."

The young officer's brows rose. "Roger that."

More units and a fire truck arrived with a paramedic who examined the biker and removed the barbs. While officers interviewed the customers in the backroom, Coop found the feisty old man sitting on an overturned plastic crate, dabbing at a cut on his arm with a napkin. He had that thin skin of an older person that bruised easily. "Are they going to charge me for the napkin too?"

"Absolutely not," said Coop. He returned to the register and nodded toward the older man. "He says he paid."

The clerk retrieved the bill from the floor.

Coop leaned on the counter. "Either accept that man's money or show me your security tapes."

The clerk wilted. "He can have his drink." He shrugged. "Sorry. He just pissed me off."

Coop took the change. "Thank you."

As he refilled the large plastic cup, the music stopped. The clerk pulled his hand away from a CD player.

"Thanks," said Coop.

The kid nodded.

Coop took a seat on another crate and handed the old man his change and cherry cola. He carefully set it down and straightened his ballcap. "Thank you, sir," he said. "This isn't about the drink. It's about honor."

Coop locked eyes with the man. "You remind me of my dad." After a moment of silence, he said, "You had me worried. I didn't want to see you hurt."

The old guy snickered. "Sonny, at my age, it doesn't matter."

"It does to me," said Coop. "Thank you for your service."

The old man dipped his cap. "We both know what it means to serve. Hopefully, that youngster behind the counter will learn to show some respect."

Coop chuckled and shook the man's hand. He left the store in time to see the biker being stuffed into the back of a cruiser.

The young officer approached him. "Coop, you need to see this."

Coop followed. He stopped and stared at his unit. "What the hell?"

The young officer stared wide-eyed at Coop. "The chief will be ripped about this."

Two of the windows in Coop's cruiser had been busted out. The word *pig* had been spray painted in hot pink on the trunk.

Coop glanced down at the red sticky stuff on his boots. "Gimme a break."

CHASING SHADOWS

FOR BOWERS, Key West seemed a place of extraordinary beauty laced with dark secrets lurking just beneath the surface.

Armed with a tourist map, Bowers passed smoke emporiums, surfing shops, and unique stores hidden down alleyways too narrow for anything but foot traffic and the local chickens that pecked at anything dropped by tourists.

Not far from where she'd had coffee this morning, she found a rustic, two-story shack that served as a home upstairs and a printshop, mail store, and gift boutique on the ground floor.

The merchandise spilling into the front yard reminded her of a Caribbean-style garage sale. A vintage motorcycle sported a price tag of $13,000. Hand-knitted caps in neon colors hung like Christmas ornaments from a banana tree.

A sign advertised key lime pie by the slice. If customers wanted a drink, there were vending machines across the street.

Under the tropical foliage, a handful of decoratively painted tables served as a gathering place for locals who sipped their sodas and shared neighborly chatter.

Bowers had almost given up on finding the publisher of Bo Somers' calendar until she spotted a stack of them piled on a surfboard that had been made into a table.

A cowbell dangling from the doorknob clanked as she ducked inside.

The store turned out to be much bigger than she'd anticipated. She pretended to browse the bins of shrink-wrapped photographs. Mostly she kept her ears open as she studied the interior and noted the exit at the rear.

In front of a passageway, a pile of posters for Fantasy Fest lay on a table next to a potted banana tree. The images depicted a raucous, Mardi-Gras-style party laced with fantasy costumes, parades in the streets, and a lot of bare skin covered by little more than artfully applied paint. Bundles of brochures and restaurant menus were stacked on shelves along the wall. The place obviously did a lot of printing jobs for the community.

She stepped around the crowded displays. The odd smell of coconut-scented air freshener and hot plastic came from a table behind the counter where the photographs were shrinkwrapped.

The wall in front of her displayed a dozen framed enlargements from Bo Somers' calendar.

A striking life-sized photograph of a bull shark and the enlargement of its steely eye staring at the camera were breathtaking.

A man with a round belly and a bright-blue apron asked, "Can I help you find something?"

"Nice photographs," said Bowers. "I've been diving for over a decade and haven't seen fish this large in years."

"Yeah, the kid who takes these has a knack for finding the big ones. You better grab them before he gets himself eaten and they all become limited editions."

Bowers pretended to be amused by the man's macabre humor.

A phone rang.

"Hon, can you grab that?" he called out to the woman behind the counter. "That's my wife. Don't know what I'd do without her."

The man straightened his apron. "We also carry his calendar," he said. "If you can hang on for another week or so, I'll have next year's printed and be able to make you a deal on both."

She thanked the storekeeper and bought a piece of pie as an excuse to hang around. She took a seat at a narrow eating bar and kept her ears open.

Back at his workbench, the storekeeper grumbled about needing more photos from Bo.

"Honey," said his wife, "Bo lives on his boat. Why don't you stop at the Marina and talk to him."

Well now, that's useful information.

Ten minutes later, Bowers walked toward the back and dropped the clear plastic box with the remains of the pie into the large trashcan.

As she wiped her hands on a napkin, the cowbell on the front door clanked. "Hey Bo, you're just the man I needed to see," said the shopkeeper.

Bowers' pulse went through the roof.

"Oh dear," said the shopkeeper's wife. "What happened to your face?"

Bowers kept her back to the door.

"It's my fault," said Bo.

Bowers smirked. *No shit, bucko.*

While Bo made up an excuse for his injuries, Bowers waited for an opportunity to slip away. If it weren't for the cowbell on the backdoor, she would've been gone.

A sign on the wall read *Restrooms* and pointed to her left. When a couple browsing through the photos moved between her and Bo, she slipped down the passageway where there were three doors. The one to her left read *Men's Room*. The one at the end of the hall read: *Staff ONLY*.

When Bowers heard Bo and the storekeeper coming closer, she took cover in the Women's Room.

Just as she locked the flimsy door with the hook-latch, she heard them in the hallway. Inches from where Bowers braced her foot against the painted-plywood door, Bo bragged to the shopkeeper about his new photographs. The jerk acted as if he were some kind of celebrity.

A moment later, the backroom door thumped shut. Their muffled voices were surprisingly audible due to the thin wall separating the two rooms.

The deeper voice of the shopkeeper carried better than Bo's nasally tone.

She pieced together the fragments from their conversation. It sounded as if Bo had brought in a thumb drive for the owner to download images.

"These are great," said the shop owner. "We only need two more. Get them to me as soon as possible."

Her assumptions were confirmed when the door to the backroom opened. "Thanks for bringing those in. I look forward to seein' the rest," said the shopkeeper. Footsteps faded as if he had gone back to work.

"Yes, sir," said Bo, standing only inches away in the hallway. She felt the thump of his boot bump against the door's kickplate. The rickety door would do little to protect her, if he really went at it.

"Asshole," mumbled Bo.

The hair rose on her arms. Bowers remained still and listened. She heard him struggling to breathe through his nose. Moments later he clomped away.

Bowers waited and let her bounding pulse settle.

After exiting the restroom, she peered around the corner into the main area of the shop. Bo stood near the front with his back to her. There he admired his artwork on the walls and carefully straightened one of the pictures.

"See y'all later," he said.

Bowers watched him from behind the potted plant.

She stayed back until Bo had left before dashing out the backdoor. The cowbell clanked, as she disappeared into a stand of banana trees and overgrown bushes.

Bo Somers blasted out of the backdoor. His head jerked left and right as he scanned the street and the sidewalk. She pulled her Glock and peered at him from deep within the shadows.

He searched the back of the shop and appeared more and more agitated. He tore open the lids of trashcans and kicked over a potted banana tree. He even stared up at the balcony.

As he approached her location, the shopkeeper appeared at the backdoor and shouted, "Hey, Bo, I got an idea for a picture."

Bo immediately returned to speak with the shopkeeper.

Bowers seized the moment, holstered her weapon, and sprinted out of the foliage and across the street. At the curb she glanced over her shoulder and caught a glimpse of Bo. His dark eyes glared at her.

The shopkeeper continued to talk with Bo, who hadn't taken his eyes off her. When the man checked his phone, Bo raised his hand like a gun, pointed at her, and pretended to shoot.

PAYBACK

WITH A KILLER ON HER TAIL, Bowers upped her game. Every block or so, she would hide behind a fence or weave into a clump of tourists to stop and check her surroundings.

Bowers ducked inside a laundromat. The glass storefront offered little cover, but it was better than being exposed on the sidewalk.

Inside, the rhythmic rumbling of dryers competed with the chatter on the over-head TV. Nearby, two women glanced up from their phones as Bowers darted out the backdoor.

Down the block, she blended into the crowd.

No doubt, Bo Somers was violent, but he was nothing compared with the insurgents she'd encountered in Iraq and Afghanistan.

From her first days in bootcamp, she'd quickly learned that mental toughness, adaptability, and thinking on your feet were key to survival. She had to outwit this guy.

Bowers passed a rusted-out, red pickup with a white door parked on the street. To her right stood a home surrounded by a masonry wall nearly concealed with overgrown bushes. The place appeared abandoned.

When steps came toward her at a fast clip, she ducked back into the leafy branches and pressed her back against the wall near a wrought-iron gate.

A couple jogged past. The moment of relief was brief.

Just as she started to step out onto the sidewalk, the gate creaked. To her horror, she felt her Glock lifted from its holster.

Bo pressed the barrel into her side. "I don't like people poking into my business."

He grasped her ponytail and jerked her head back as he moved in front of her. Pushing himself against her, he pressed the barrel against her ribcage.

Bowers stared straight ahead and refused to look him in the eye. With the business end of a .40-caliber pistol aimed at her, she made no aggressive moves.

Being shot with my own weapon would be a bitch.

Her best option was to wait for him to screw up. She let him think he had the upper hand as he forced her toward the two-toned truck.

While he held the pistol snug against her back, a couple with a small boy passed them. Bo tipped the bill of his ballcap and hid the gun.

"Open the door," he hissed, "and get in."

The old hinges groaned. Litter filled the passenger's floorboard with disposable cups, spilled onion rings, dirty rags, and a bottle of motor oil. A cupholder overflowed with cigarette butts. Bowers glanced at the missing door panel and altered dashboard. Beyond being a trash pit, Bowers spotted two alterations to create compartments of the type often used to conceal drugs.

She slid onto the vintage truck's bench seat. The vehicle reeked.

"Nice ride," she said.

"Shud-dup."

Bowers deliberately touched as many surfaces as possible. When Bo scanned the street, she tugged several strands of hair from her ponytail and left them where an investigator would find them.

Bo pushed in beside her. With her Glock, he forced her to slide over toward the steering wheel. "You drive."

He appeared to expect a fight. Showing any kind of fear would only enflame his fantasies and dial up his aggression.

"You owe me for this," he said, as he pointed at his swollen face. "It's payback time."

"Seriously? You're the one who attacked me. Remember?"

His body language showed no intention of backing down.

"Shut your mouth and drive."

She clicked on a seatbelt, which was an obvious addition for a vintage vehicle. His head jerked as she pulled out of the parking spot.

"Do you know how to drive a stick?" he asked. "Most girls don't know shit about driving."

You will eat those words, son.

She merged into the traffic.

He sat back and watched her every move.

"Don't do anything stupid," he demanded. Bo continued waving around her pistol and didn't click his seatbelt. *Fool.* He had just provided the opportunity she'd been waiting for.

He examined her Glock. "I think I'll keep this."

She ignored his prattling.

"Where to?" she asked, as if merely going to the grocery store.

"Go north toward Big Pine Key."

"Roger that." She had no intention of going anywhere with this clown.

"I know just the place," said Bo. "Only this time, we aren't going to be interrupted."

Don't count on it, asshole.

Bowers smoothly drove down Truman Avenue. Once on Roosevelt Boulevard, she picked up speed, a lot of speed.

Bo sat up in his seat and scowled. "Slow down. The police department is up ahead."

She floored it.

He jerked his head around, presumably to scan for cops.

As she approached the entrance to the police station, Bowers tightened her seatbelt.

"I said, slow the fuck down."

"Okay." Bowers stood on the brake, sending the truck into a controlled skid.

Tires squealed. Horns honked.

Bo flew forward. The *BAM* of a loud gunshot filled the cab as a hole blasted through the windshield. A fraction of a second later, his forehead slammed into the glass, followed by smacking his chin on the dash. He dropped her pistol, which clanked against something hard and landed somewhere under the clutter on the floor.

Bowers popped open her seatbelt with one hand and the door with the other. The smell of burnt rubber and hot brakes filled the cab.

Bo sat dazed and bloodied in the front seat. Before he could recover, she jumped out and peered through the open driver's window. "Was that fast enough for you, asshole?"

Bowers slammed the car door shut and jogged toward the police station. She'd been there after the assault and knew they kept the doors locked.

She now wondered if they would let her in before Bo recovered enough to come after her.

DEFIANCE

B OWERS DARTED AWAY FROM THE TRUCK, hoping that no one had been hurt by Bo's stray bullet.

Sprinting toward the Police Department's portico entrance, she found her path blocked by a cruiser and three police officers. No doubt they heard the shot and squealing brakes.

The officers had taken cover with their service pistols drawn. She couldn't blame them. The clump of trees standing between them and Bo's truck had blocked the officers from seeing what happened. She would've done the same.

Bowers stopped.

"Put down your weapon," commanded a dark-haired cop.

She lifted her shirt above her waistband and turned so they could see she was unarmed and raised her empty hands.

"I heard a gunshot," said the officer. "Where's the weapon?"

"In the truck." She pointed to the road. "Bo fired my Glock. Hurry, we need to make sure the bullet didn't strike anyone."

The officer with coarse brown hair pulled out his handcuffs. "Ma'am, put your hands behind your back. You're not under arrest, but you're being detained until we can figure this out."

His name badge read: NOLAN.

As Nolan snapped on the cuffs, Coop exited the building at a fast clip and did a doubletake.

"Bowers?" He hurried toward her. "What's going on?"

"Bo forced me into his truck at gunpoint. I got away and came here for help."

Coop frowned at the cuffs.

Nolan folded his arms. "Coop, we don't know what's going on here."

Bowers locked eyes with Coop. "After the assault, I cooperated fully. I gave you a statement and everything you asked for, including DNA. You told me not to leave the area. I'm stuck here like a hunk of bait dangling in front of a shark. This is the second assault in two days from this guy. I might as well have a neon target taped to my ass."

"Watch your mouth," said Nolan.

"I got this," said Coop. He removed the cuffs and waved at Nolan to backdown.

Bo's rust bucket lumbered up the driveway and stopped behind her.

Officers coming from the parking area joined the scene. Like most cops, they were curious as cats. The novelty of having the scene drive up to the PD's front door had caught their attention.

A huge captain exited the police station. His friendly demeanor quickly turned all business as he pulled aside one of the officers. More than his uniform commanded respect. The massive Samoan stood nearly seven-feet tall.

Bowers crouched behind the patrol car next to Coop and heard him mumble. "Dammit, Bo."

Coop's voice rose to an order. "Driver! Come out with your hands up."

After a tense few seconds, Bo stepped out and reached for his pockets.

COOP SHOUTED, "Show me your hands," as he approached the truck with caution.

"Come on, man," said Bo.

"Do it. We need to see your hands," ordered the captain, with his own weapon drawn.

Behind them, Coop heard the glass doors of the department swing open as Nolan escorted Bowers up to interrogation.

Bo leaned against the truck. He seemed nervous. Coop turn him to face the hood and cuffed Bo's hands behind his back. The guy twitched when Coop patted him down for weapons. Coop removed Bo's pocketknife and threw it onto the hood. "It's time you and I had a chat."

Bo's head jerked as he glared at the officers.

"Calm down," said Coop as two officers moved toward the truck with pistols drawn. They peered through the windows. "Clear."

One of the officers pointed at the shattered windshield. "Looks like a bullet hole."

Coop watched as they carefully searched the truck. "What a trash pit," said the tall one.

"Shut up, bitch," snorted Bo.

Seconds later, the officer shouted, "Gun."

They secured the large-caliber Glock. Moments later, a medic loped over from the fire department next door. After a quick exam and a few questions, the EMT taped a bandage over the wound on Bo's forehead. "You should see a doctor."

Bo pulled away. "Leave me alone, dude."

"Take him inside," said the captain. He waved over one of the officers. "Impound that truck and clear our driveway."

As Coop and the captain entered the elevator, they found a K-9 officer standing inside with his dog, Tanja. The Belgian Malinois was well-known for her exceptional ability to find narcotics. In the elevator, she immediately alerted on Bo.

Her handler said something to her in Dutch. Tanja responded by snapping her teeth and growling.

Bo went pale.

Coop locked eyes with him. "Good girl, Tanja."

The captain smirked. "The nose knows."

During the elevator ride, Tanja didn't take her eyes off Bo. Every time he moved a warning growl grumbled in her throat.

"I wouldn't argue with her," said her handler, "unless you want to be dog bit."

Bo's smart-ass comments ceased.

The elevator stopped and they entered the Criminal Investigation Division known as CID.

Tanja spotted Bowers and quietly sat next to her. The K-9 handler chuckled when his dog wagged her tail and leaned into Bowers' leg. She reached down and stroked the K-9's face. "I like you, too."

Coop spotted a detective he knew in one of the cubicles. Detective Rodgers hunched over his desk in a sweat-stained, blue shirt. Surrounding him were stacks of files and open boxes on a cart. An oscillating fan caused papers on his whiteboard to flutter in the breeze.

Coop put a firm hand on Bo's shoulder and ordered him to stop.

Bo rolled his eyes. "Coop. Jeez, man. Why you hassling me?"

"You reek of weed and you're accused of kidnapping at gunpoint. I have no choice but to investigate."

Coop scanned Bo's dirty jeans and T-shirt. "Anything in your pockets that I need to know about? Needles, grenades, dead bodies?"

Bo didn't respond.

Coop got in Bo's face. "Is there anything on your person that is going to hurt me?"

Bo glared at him for a few seconds. "No."

Coop stared at Bo's teardrop tattoo while checking his pockets. A few seconds later, Bo grimaced as Coop shook Bo's baggy jeans and underwear. With a gloved hand, Coop felt a lump in the man's drawers and retrieved a small plastic bag that contained approximately three grams of weed.

"What's this?" he asked.

Bo stood mute.

"Answer the question," ordered the captain.

Bo jerked his shoulders away from Coop. "It ain't mine. I borrowed these jeans from a friend."

"Right," said Coop. "Not my pants. Not my crotch."

Coop held up the plastic bag of weed.

"It's trash." Bo shrugged. "Saw it on the sidewalk. I was gonna throw it out."

Coop examined the weed and smirked. "Now you expect me to believe you walk around stuffing garbage into your underwear?"

"Get outta my face, bro."

"I'm not your bro," said Coop.

The captain used his sleeve to wipe the sweat off his brow.

"Sorry, sir," said Rodgers, "the A/C is out again. The interview rooms are all yours, but it's pretty stuffy in there."

The detective took the bag of weed from Coop. "I'll process it," he said and headed toward his cramped cubicle.

Meanwhile, Nolan had taken Bowers into an interview room.

A moment later, Coop held open the metal door to the other room that contained a battered table and three bucket chairs. Bo slumped into one of them. As promised, the space was stifling.

As Bo tugged at his crotch, Coop took a seat. Bowers' story about how she'd jabbed rebar at his tender parts explained the other reason the guy had flinched when Coop had yanked on his drawers. Coop wanted to strip him down to see if his wounds verified her account. Instead, he let the captain take the lead.

In a neutral almost friendly manner, the captain handed Bo a bottle of water. "Walk us through what happened."

Bo hesitated. "There was a dog in the road. I had to make a sudden stop."

That was bullshit. Coop took the direct approach. "If you were driving, how'd you end up on the passenger side with your face smashed against the windshield?"

"Umm..." Bo hesitated and stared at the floor. "My buddy was drivin' and hit the brakes too hard."

Coop thought of Bowers and bit his lip. *Buddy, my ass.*

The captain leaned forward. "Where's your friend?"

"I don't know, man. He took off."

"What's his name?" asked the captain.

Coop watched Bo squirming in his seat and staring at the water bottle. "Umm. Jerr... ah, Johnny."

The captain nodded. "This Jerr-ah-Johnny have a last name?"

As if a switch had flipped, Bo's expression turned to rage. "Fuck you," he hissed. The man seemed a different person as he grabbed the bottle of water, cracked it open, and gulped down a few swallows.

Coop felt the sweat under his bulletproof vest. "We have a witness who says you abducted her at gunpoint. Forensics is examining your truck right now. If she was in there, we will find the evidence verifying her story. It's in your best interest to tell us the truth. Now."

Bo glanced at the door.

The captain calmly asked, "How do you know her?"

"Never met her," said Bo. "Besides, Bowers is crazy. I never laid a hand on her or any other woman, this whole thing is bullshit."

"If you never met her," said Coop, "how is it you know her name?"

The captain never cracked a smile, but the crinkle at the corners of his eyes showed amusement.

Bo defiantly glared back and rubbed his wrist.

"Son," said the captain, "Just tell us what happened in the truck and on the beach with Bowers?"

Bo's entire expression changed again. This time, his eyes darted between Coop and the captain like a mouse trapped between a cat and a snake.

"It's not what you think," he said. "She attacked me."

Coop dropped his pen. "Hold on, you just said you'd never met her."

"Do you see my face?" Bo shouted. "She did this to me. She has to pay for this." His fury reverberated in the small room.

"Tell us your side of the story," said Coop.

Bo returned to rubbing his wrist. A week ago, Coop had seen him wearing his now-missing, stainless-steel bracelet.

"Okay," said Bo, rubbing his palms on his jeans. "I was at the beach." He paused as if thinking. "Yeah. I lost a fishing lure over there a few days ago and went back to look for it. Then outta nowhere, this crazy bitch attacked me. She smacked me in the face with a rock. She was all over me, man."

Bo jumped to his feet and showed them his swollen hand. "See? She bit me. This is all on her." When he pointed at them, his low-riding jeans nearly fell to his knees.

"Pull up your pants," ordered the captain. "And sit down. Now."

As Bo grabbed at his baggy jeans and defiantly kicked the chair. Coop intervened. He snagged Bo by the shirt and straightened the chair. In the tussle, he caught a glimpse of a graze across Bo's lower abdomen. Coop lifted the shirt for a closer look at the tip of the wound that started just below his navel and clearly extended under the waistband of his underwear.

Bo pulled down his shirt. "She did that too."

"So, you dropped your drawers on a public beach to look for your fishing lure and she attacked you for no reason at all, giving you that wound?"

"Screw you," said Bo as he wrestled his jeans back in place and took a seat.

The captain jotted down some notes. "You stated she attacked you. And what did you do?"

"I got the hell outta there, fast as I could."

"Did you hit her back?" asked Coop.

"No."

Coop stared at him. "So, you didn't hold her underwater?"

"I never touched her," said Bo. "I just tried to get away."

The handprints around Bowers' throat said otherwise.

Coop flipped his notebook shut. "So, you're telling me that she tried to strangle herself?"

Bo put his head down. "I didn't rape her."

Coop sat back. "No one said anything about rape." The attempted rape had been kept out of the press. Only the perpetrator would have known that information.

PROBABLE CAUSE

OUTSIDE THE ROOM, Coop studied the captain's expression. "Bo is lying his ass off."

"No doubt," said the captain, "but knowing is one thing. Proving it is another. You know what our DA is going to say."

Coop shook his head. "Unless we get the forensics, he'll take one look at Bo's injuries and dismiss the case."

The captain headed to the coffeepot, gave it a whiff, and grimaced. He poured himself a cup anyway.

"Captain," said Rodgers, "we found the slug in a phone pole."

"Good," said the captain. "Recover it. Do something else for me. Make sure forensics goes over that truck with a fine-tooth comb."

"Probable Cause?" asked the detective.

"Stolen tags, no insurance, no registration, used in a suspected aggravated kidnapping, and a bullet hole in the windshield. Hell, he doesn't even have a valid drivers' license. That ought to cover it, for now."

As Rodgers hurried back to his desk, Nolan came out of the other room, chuckling.

"Get this," he said. "According to Bowers, Bo kidnapped her at gunpoint and forced her to drive. He orders her to hurry up. She floors it right in front of the PD, then stomps on the brake, launching him face-first into the damned windshield." Nolan poured a cup of coffee, tasted it, and grabbed the sugar. "Resourceful use of the vehicle."

"Wish I'd seen that one," said Coop.

Nolan shrugged. "Maybe our cameras caught it."

The captain headed toward the other interrogation room. "I've got to meet this woman."

They found Bowers relaxing with her legs crossed, sipping a bottle of water.

Before they had a chance to take a seat, she asked, "Did you find my Glock?"

The captain nodded. "Yes, ma'am."

"What about the slug?"

The captain watched her closely. "It hit a phone pole. No one was injured."

"Good." She seemed relieved.

"The gun is yours?" asked Coop.

"Yes, sir. Bo took it. When I hit the brakes, I heard it fire. I thought he'd shot it at me." Bowers put the cap on her water bottle. "It used to be my service pistol."

"What's the caliber?" asked the captain.

".40 cal. You want the serial number?"

A knock at the door brought Coop to his feet. Rodgers motioned for him to come outside. They had a brief conversation.

"Thank you," said Coop, who returned to his seat.

Bowers watched as the captain turned his attention on Coop. "And?"

"Serial number confirms it's hers," said Coop, "and her license to carry is legit."

Bowers' demeanor fit with that of a person with nothing to hide. "If you want to know who shot my Glock, do a GSR swab of my hands and his."

"I appreciate your cooperation," said the captain.

A few minutes later, Rodgers swabbed her hands.

While waiting for the results, Bowers studied the captain. "Did you arrest him?"

The captain cleared his throat. "For now, we'll write him up for lack of registration, driving on a suspended license, and the weed we found on him."

"You have probable cause and yet you're cutting him loose?" asked Bowers.

The captain drummed his fingers on the table. "I get it. I wish I could change this, but we have a new DA who is picky."

The way Bowers glared at him spoke volumes.

"He's hesitant to press charges unless we have forensic proof. We had a domestic last year that backfired on us. We arrested the male. Turned out the female was the perp. It got us a lot of bad press. The DA knows a good defense attorney would claim Bo couldn't be the aggressor when he is the more seriously injured party."

She finished her water, crumpled the plastic bottle into a ball, and chucked it into the trash can.

"Bowers," said the captain. "I don't like this any more than you do."

Bowers glanced at Coop.

"I'll get divers," he said, "to go over the scene at the beach again and get forensics to put a rush on processing the truck."

Rodgers entered the room. "Her GSR is negative."

Bowers stood and stared down at the captain.

"We'll get him," he said, as he handed her his card. "Call me if you need anything. And watch your back."

Bowers smirked. "You can count on it."

The captain frowned.

She took the card. "Am I free to go?"

"Yes, ma'am. Rodgers will help you pick up your weapon on the way out."

Coop figured Bo was the one who needed to be worried.

COVERT

B OWERS LEFT THE PD with the grim reality that more than her future career options were at stake.

As much as it annoyed her to still be in Bo's crosshairs, Bowers had dealt with District Attorneys before, who didn't want their conviction rates marred by a case that could fall apart in court.

She and every cop she knew hated the politics that inevitably seeped into the job, but the captain did have a point. She couldn't deny that witnesses had seen her pummel Bo with the rock and rebar. With Bo's injuries and her background, a skilled defense attorney would twist the narrative, claiming that she attacked Bo unless that lady on the landing had a video showing otherwise.

Regardless of what the PD did, the time had come to corner this animal before he hurt anyone else.

Bowers returned to her hotel and quickly changed clothes. Over the next fifteen minutes, she packed up her things and filled her vest with essentials hidden in the hem and seams.

It was no longer safe to stay in the same room each night. She gathered her belongings and checked out.

Two hours later she found a storage unit to hide her car and rented a nondescript silver sedan with tinted windows.

Like the local iguana's that changed color to match their surroundings, she altered her appearance. With sunglasses and her brown hair and bangs pulled up under a ballcap, Bowers entered a store where she quickly purchased a couple of pre-paid phones and battery backups.

A few minutes later, she pulled into the marina parking area and sent Coop a text: *The stainless-steel bracelet is probably still on scene.*

Her phone buzzed with a reply: *Thank you. We'll get it. Watch your back.*

With Fantasy Fest opening that night, the PD would have their hands full. Even if they were committed to the investigation, nothing was likely to happen over the next few days.

Bowers hit the streets.

She painstakingly searched the town until she'd found Bo next to a big box store where he spoke with a man on a motorcycle, wearing a Changós patch on his vest.

After parking a few spaces away from a white van and the two men, Bowers glanced at the store's front entrance as if waiting for someone. With her hat pulled low and the window cracked open, she pretended to read a newspaper and listened.

The biker nodded toward the van and handed Bo a key. "We need it back by Friday," said the man.

Bo shook the biker's hand. "No problem, bro. Appreciate the help." He nodded and hopped into the white Nissan van with a bent license plate. Bowers wrote down the plate number and took a picture of the logo on the side.

She continued to watch her back as she followed Bo's new ride from a safe distance. A few times she turned down a side street or passed him only to circled back.

Fifteen minutes later, he parked up the block from where he'd abducted her.

What a dope. Most people who were lying low would change up their routine but not Bo. That spoke to his arrogance, sense of entitlement, or just plain stupidity.

Bowers turned onto a side street and waited. Before leaving her rented sedan, she added a locator app to both pre-paid phones.

As she strolled up the street toward the van, Bowers pulled a map out of her pocket and pretended to be searching for an address. Two men in basketball shorts strolled past.

Once the bystanders were out of sight, she slipped under the rear of Bo's van. With zip-ties and strips of duct tape, she secured the prepaid phone and a battery backup to the undercarriage.

Bowers started to stand until she heard Bo's voice and footsteps coming closer.

SECRET PATH

BOWERS QUICKLY SLIPPED under the Jeep parked behind the old white van. Just as she pulled her legs out of sight, Bo stepped off the curb and stood between the two vehicles.

"I told you. I'll find Bowers," he said to someone on the phone. "She's here somewhere."

Trapped between the tarry odor of the warm asphalt and the crackling sound of the cooling engine above, her pulse bumped when Bo leaned on the van and kicked the front bumper of the Jeep. She lay inches away from his feet and spotted dried blood on his athletic shoes.

His cigarette butt fell to the asphalt.

"Afternoon," said a voice she didn't know.

Her eyes widened when the Jeep's door opened. The vehicle rocked slightly. The drivers' door slammed shut.

Aw, crap.

Bo still leaned against the van.

When the Jeep's engine started, she had to move, fast.

After inching out from under the vehicle on the passenger side, she crouched low out of Bo's line of sight.

As the Jeep began to pull away from the curb, Bowers sprinted for a fence, raced around a corner, and dodged into an alley.

Behind her footsteps pounded the pavement. Bo yelled a stream of expletives.

Bowers ducked behind a dumpster. A moment later she heard water splashing and discovered Lily taking a drink from a garden hose.

Bo continued screaming. "You can't hide from me. I will find you."

Lily turned off the hose. "Come with me," she whispered.

Bowers followed her between a fence and a line of palm trees. At the sound of a sliding glass door, Lily held out her arm. They waited, as a woman draped a beach towel over a clothesline. Once the lady went inside, Lily continued on. She clearly knew this path that led from the alley to a drainage gully that wound between a maze of cottages.

A few minutes later, Lily stepped between overgrown bushes. She ducked under a tarp over hanging a weathered framework for an unfinished sunshade. The home's renovation project had obviously come to a halt.

Bowers peered inside through the dust-covered French doors. All signs of furniture or anyone living there were gone.

The small yard was little more than a concrete patio, bordered on two sides by an old wooden fence and one side by a hedge of overgrown bushes and a tree. A large blue ceramic pot sat in a corner, containing a dead plant.

Bowers took a seat on the cool concrete patio.

Lily shrugged. "It's not much, but we can stay here until he's gone."

Ten feet away, Bowers saw movement between the slats of the wooden fence to her right. She heard sniffing and a whine. A paw scratched at the fence and a small black nose poked between the slats.

Lily grinned. "That's Joey. He's the neighbor's dog." She dug in her pocket and pulled out a half of a hamburger patty wrapped in a napkin. As she peeled off the paper napkin, Bowers noticed scratches and bug bites on her arms.

"I got somethin' for ya," she said, as she poked the morsel through the opening. Joey gobbled down the treat and licked her fingers. "The folks next door don't take care of him like I do. They just leave him outside all day by himself."

With Lily sitting on one side of the fence and the pup who clearly liked her, sitting on the other, the rough fence and the dog seemed a metaphor for whatever had upended Lily's life and separated her from the things she loved.

Bowers studied Lily's face. "You come here often?"

She nodded. "I gotta make sure Joey has water." Lily gazed up at the torn blue tarp. "It's a good place to stay when it rains."

The woman took off her tattered gray sweatshirt and draped it over a branch. Her sleeveless blue shirt revealed painfully thin arms.

Lily took a seat on the concrete. She wore no bra and clearly needed a shower.

"You're a kind person," said Bowers.

Lily glanced away. "If people were kind, it'd be a different world." When a bird chirped overhead, her expression hardened. "Animals are nicer than people."

"What brought you here?" asked Bowers.

Lily's eyes held a vacant gaze. After a moment she said, "It was a lot of stuff."

As they sat in silence, Bowers waited patiently and continued to listen for Bo.

Lily picked at the dirt under her fingernails. "I been so scared for so long. People don't understand."

Bowers touched Lily's shoulder. "I want to understand."

Lily hunched forward. "I had a dog like Joey once," she whispered as if she didn't want the dog to hear. "But Daddy killed him with a hammer."

Bowers listened to the pain in Lily's voice.

"He was mean." Lily wiped her eyes on the hem of her blue shirt. "We had to get away."

Bowers studied her and wanted to know what she meant by *we*. "I hate mean people."

"Me too," said Lily. "That's why we came here."

Bowers knew alcohol had contributed to her situation. Was her reference to *we* a delusion?

Lily lived in the margins. Everything about her was complicated. Some of her story seemed a bit paranoid. At times she seemed like a lost child. At other moments, the woman had extraordinary clarity and could recall details most would miss.

"Lana, my twin sister..." Lily's stopped midsentence and shuddered. She pushed back her matted hair. "People don't understand what it's like to have a twin. We were like two sides of one coin. No matter what, we had each other." Lily stared at her empty hands. "She's gone and I don't know what to do."

As a radio played in the distance, Bowers cupped her arm around Lily's shoulders.

Lily's hands trembled. "It's my fault. I was the one that wanted to come here." Her voice grew thin and strained.

Bowers tilted her head and locked eyes with her. "Lily, it's not your fault."

Lily took off a necklace and handed the corroded piece of costume jewelry to Bowers. It was nothing expensive, but Lily handled it as if it were a priceless treasure. Obviously, it meant the world to her.

The tarnished pendant had been designed as half of a heart. *LANA* had been engraved on the back.

Lily stared at it. She then reached up to her neck and removed the other pendant.

The pendants were a matched set; each half of a heart that when put together spelled out *SISTERS*.

"I found Lana's necklace in the water at the beach." Her head dropped forward. She rocked as grief overtook her.

"I can't find her."

HELL'S HIGHWAY

AT 4:58 P.M. RIGGS ANSWERED his phone and received an earful of McDougall's gruff voice. "My office. Now."

His message held no greeting, no *good afternoon*, nor a *how are you?* Just his unequivocal order. Thank heaven he wasn't the secretary of state. We'd end up in a war.

A few minutes later, Riggs stood at the doorway of McDougall's office. Over the years, the big man had grown thick around the middle, giving his torso the appearance of a landslide.

His bushy black brows and perpetual scowl suited his gruff personality. Riggs didn't always agree with the man, but he respected him for doing his job and being fair about it. Most of the time.

McDougall called it as he saw it. No hidden agendas. Riggs had come to value that kind of terse honesty.

"Take a seat," said McDougall with his jaw set.

Riggs waited and let McDougall spill out whatever he needed to say.

"Where are we with the Changós case?" McDougall rested both elbows on his cluttered desk. Behind him, a large box of No. 2 pencils sat on a bank of gray metal file cabinets. Above them photographs of a younger, thinner McDougall posing with presidents and congressmen hung on the wall.

Riggs opened a manila folder and handed him a copy of the report. "In my report—"

"Give me the highlights."

"Yes, sir," said Riggs. "The Changós are using the I-95 corridor to run drugs between Florida and D.C. Historically, they've done petty crimes, but now they're evolving. We have reason to believe they are responsible for a recent spree of convenience-store holdups, a home invasion, kidnappings, and now murder."

McDougall tapped his yellow pencil on his legal pad. Old school to the core, he remained one of the last few who still used a classic No. 2 pencil. For as long as Riggs had known him, he habitually doodled during meetings and hated text messaging. He also had an uncanny ability to track down fugitives based on individual behavior patterns.

He pursed his thick lips and drew straight lines across the page of his legal pad. "Tell me how the fourteen-year-old you found this morning ties into this."

Riggs leaned back and crossed his legs. "We're investigating the disappearance of three girls between the ages of fourteen and nineteen, but we suspect that's only part of the picture. We're about ninety-five percent sure the body we found this morning is that of the girl who was abducted in Jacksonville. At the same time the Changós were looting a liquor store, this girl had the misfortune of being at the adjacent gas station. The Changós swarmed in with overwhelming numbers. One of them likely spotted her, all young and pretty, and snapped her up to service himself and the boys. She didn't have a chance against them."

Riggs heard the soft scratching of McDougall's pencil as he jotted down notes. "When will you know if this body is this girl?"

"She had braces," said Riggs, "As soon as we get our hands on her dental records, we'll know."

"Heard it was a bad one," said McDougall.

Riggs nodded. "It was, sir. They used an ax."

McDougall grimaced. "Poor kid. What a goddamn waste."

Just when Riggs thought his boss lacked all empathy, he would say or do something that showed otherwise.

"Is there human trafficking involved?" asked his boss.

"Yes," said Riggs. "The word on the street is they arrange for shipments of women from Cuba and sell to the highest bidder. We believe the missing local girls are likely ad hoc abductions to service their own. The girl we found this morning had been raped."

Riggs glanced at his hand where he'd written *GRACE* and couldn't get the images of the girl's ponytail out of his head.

McDougall scrubbed a hand across his mouth. "What port are they using to bring in the Cuban girls?"

"Miami would be a logical starting point but bringing them in there could expose them. It would be risky."

His boss' brows furrowed. He stopped scribbling and stared at Riggs.

"Considering that Cuba," said Riggs, "is closer than Miami, it might be safer and more expedient to transfer the girls at sea."

McDougall scowled at his pencil. "They're expanding their operations, no doubt. Any news on your missing informant? Hope he isn't in a ditch somewhere with his head missing, too. We used to get good intel from him."

Riggs hesitated. "Gunner is in Key West. My bet is our asset isn't far behind."

"How can you be so sure he didn't cut and run."

"I know him," said Riggs. "I could head down to Key West and get ahead of this."

McDougall's set jaw relayed nothing but disapproval.

Riggs wanted to argue but knew better.

"No." McDougall tossed his pencil aside and snatched up a perfectly sharpened one from his pencil cup. "Don't even think about it. You need something, punt it over to the field office in Miami. It's their turf."

That wasn't the response Riggs had hoped for.

After a few doodles, McDougall glared over the top of his glasses. "How in the hell are they kidnapping kicking, screaming girls on motorcycles and bringing them all the way up to Virginia?"

"We think they had a vehicle accompany them," said Riggs. "The tire tracks at the scene were identified as being from tires exclusively used on older Nissan vans."

McDougall shoved aside his notepad. "Go find that van."

HARD EVIDENCE

C OOP GRUNTED THROUGH his pre-dawn pushups and curls with 150 pounds. On the way to the shower, he pulled a new sheet of Ellie's favorite stickers out of his briefcase and slid it under her door.

Freshly showered, he hummed to himself and dropped a waffle into the toaster for his daughter. He looked forward to her birthday. Knowing that she was infatuated with princesses, he'd put aside a few dollars to buy her a princess doll that came with a matching dress and tiara just the right size for Ellie. The sales lady had promised everything needed to charm a six-year-old was in the box. Normally, he left gift-buying to his wife, especially the girly stuff, but this time he wanted to do something special for her.

The waffle popped up and he flipped it onto a plate and handed it off to his daughter who went back to playing with her new stickers and watching cartoons in the living room. Coop dropped two more waffles into the toaster, as his wife Linda hurried into the kitchen.

"Good morning," he said. "You want a waffle?"

Linda didn't answer.

Coop bit his lip and poured a cup of coffee. Instead of a *good morning* or *how'd you sleep*, he got another dose of the silent treatment.

He could almost feel Linda glaring at his back.

"She wants an iPad for her birthday," his wife said as she pulled out containers of protein powder and yogurt.

He slumped against the counter. "What's wrong with dolls and crayons? You know we can't afford an iPad."

Linda threw a frozen banana into the blender. "I'll tell you what's wrong," she said. Her brown hair sat high on her head in a messy tangle that bounced as she spoke. "I never see you. We never go out. When was the last time we went dancing or fishing or hit the town and enjoyed the nightlife?"

Coop held out his arms. "I've already bought her a—"

Linda turned on the blender. Apparently, she wasn't interested in what he had to say.

As she poured her smoothie into a glass, she said, "Hey, Linda," in a mocking voice, "let's move to Key West and live the island life. The least you could do is show some interest in your daughter's birthday."

"Linda, come on," said Coop as he reached out to hug her, but she pulled away.

Coop put his plate back in the cupboard. "Of course, I care about her birthday. I also care about fixing the fuel pump in your car, the shower head in our bathroom, and paying our rent on time."

Linda leaned against the counter, sipping her smoothie, and glaring at him.

Coop ignored the toaster as it popped. "What do you want from me? I'm already working two jobs to support us."

"Daddy?" His daughter's tiny voice put a halt to their argument. She peered around the doorway into the kitchen with stickers on her pink shirt and a pout that nearly tore his heart out.

He never did get his breakfast. On his way out of the door he said, "Linda, Ellie, I love you."

Coop drove to work with their latest tiff replaying in his mind.

He pulled into the PD parking lot and put aside his thoughts about this morning. Upstairs he strolled in and took his usual seat for the briefing. On the table by his chair, he spotted a bag of *Chicharrones*, fried pork rinds. The lieutenant entered and glanced at the table and the bag. The snickering started.

Coop got it. After the Changós had written *PIG* on his cruiser, he had faced a lot of razzing and no small amount of grief from the lieutenant, who tossed Coop the keys to the oldest piece of shit in the fleet.

The snickering turned to belly laughs.

THIS MORNING'S SUNRISE brought Henry more surprises than the occasional squall. Clyde had sent Henry over to Garrison Bight, a marina nearby, to install a new speedometer on a high-end cabin cruiser.

"Yup, yup," he mumbled to himself. "With a boat, ya never know what yur gettin' into." A simple thirty-minute job could turn into a four-hour pain in the keister.

Henry finished the job and gathered up the rest of his tools. "Time to git back and take Buddy out for his pee."

On a sailboat in the slip next to him, a shifty-looking man nervously puttered with the rigging.

As Henry prepared to leave, the owner of the cabin cruiser admired the new speedometer. "Say, Henry, can you take a look at my cleats? One of them is loose."

Henry put down his toolbox. "No problem."

While replacing a stripped screw, the rumble of a motorcycle engine caught his attention. Unlike the local scooters, this had the throaty growl of a Harley.

As much as he appreciated the sweet sound of a well-tuned engine, it surprised him to see the Changós in this part of town. Like roaches, those fellas normally hung out at the bars by night and slept it off by day.

Henry kept his head low and took his time rechecking and securing each screw. He watched the biker leave his motorcycle at the entrance. Like a poster boy for one-percenters, the man wore the vest, a do-rag, and of course the attitude. The heels of his black motorcycle boots thumped against the weathered wood as he marched up the dock with a package under his arm.

Henry caught a whiff of cigarette smoke and spotted a man with a ferocious red beard emerge from the sailboat next to him. Henry stifled a laugh. Gunner on a sailboat seemed like all kinds of wrong.

Henry could see that the two outlaws had arranged a hand-off. He suspected the box contained something other than a book from Amazon. He figured it had to be drugs.

Ten minutes later, Henry stood inside near the helm. As he waited for the owner to pay him, Bo Somers rode up to the sailboat on a jet ski and took the package.

RETRIBUTION

A S A GOLDEN SUN PEERED OVER the horizon, Bowers leaned on the rails of a balcony and watched an athletic woman jogging along the glistening beach below.

The ability to spot evil lurking under the surface often felt like a curse as she watched a man below trailing the woman jogging. When she stopped to take a sip from her water bottle, he hid in a clump of trees.

The hair rose on Bowers' arms, but she was too far away to intervene. As the man continued to follow the woman, Bowers considered calling 911 until two workers moved into the area to empty the trashcans.

Spooked, the man crossed the street and went the other direction.

Bowers relaxed and focused on the day ahead. Even with the serene sounds of the sea and shimmering light playing on the gentle swells, Bowers couldn't get Lily out of her thoughts.

After finishing a series of pushups and stretches, the shrill squawk of a seagull demanded her attention. Key West's birds were a vocal lot. A gull with an injured foot perched on one leg and repeated its demand.

Bowers tossed a peanut from her protein bar to the hungry gull, who snagged it in midair and flew away.

She showered, grabbed her backpack, and headed toward the marina to meet up with a dive boat.

Parking near the coffee stand, Bowers spotted Coop's sister helping an older gentleman wearing a Miami Dolphin's ballcap.

When she glanced up and spotted Bowers, her face brightened into a big smile. She waved goodbye to the gentleman and headed straight for Bowers.

"I have something for you."

Bowers followed Sara to the coffee stand. After ducking inside, she handed Bowers a crumpled article torn from an old newspaper.

"It's from Lily. She wanted you to have it."

"Thank you," said Bowers as she scanned the article about a missing girl named Lana. Now Bowers had a date and a photo to go with Lily's sad story. Bowers couldn't help aching for both of them.

"There's more," said Sara. "Lily had two quarters. She used them to buy you a coffee."

Sara set a large steaming cup on the small counter.

Bowers took the coffee. "If you see her, please tell her I said thank you." Stunned by the gesture, Bowers pulled out her wallet. "I can pay you the difference."

"No need," said Sara. "We let her pay what she could. It made her happy."

"You sure I can't—"

"Nope. I got it," said Sara. "Seeing Lily so proud over such a small thing was payment enough."

"You're amazing. Thank you," said Bowers. As she shook Sara's hand, her sea-turtle bracelet jingled.

Bowers watched Sara return to taking orders. She was still stunned that Lily had used her last two quarters on someone else and that Sara had allowed Lily the dignity of paying what she could. Bowers wrapped her hands around the warm cup, knowing she would never forget this one.

After waving to Sara, Bowers headed to the docks.

She entered the dive shop where two young men grunted as they loaded heavy scuba tanks onto a cart. The odor of damp wetsuits hung in the air.

"Do you need weights?" asked a tall fellow with short dreads.

Bowers signed the paperwork. "Yes. Twelve pounds, please."

"No problem." He handed her a blue belt. "Here's your weight belt. We have plenty of weights onboard. The boat will be ready to board in about thirty minutes." He pointed toward a coffee maker. "Help yourself."

The shelves of the dive shop were well stocked with an assortment of dive gear, T-shirts, and magazines on diving. She tried on several high-end masks, including a ScubaPro and a Cressi. Both were excellent, but after losing her high-end mask in the assault, she chose one in the mid-range that fit well.

After purchasing the mask and snorkel, she went outside and wandered the docks. As she waited for the dive boat, Bowers enjoyed the crisp morning air. She watched pelicans sitting atop pilings and fishermen heading out to sea.

Sipping her coffee, Bowers noticed a yacht, about a fifty-footer. At the end of the dock sat an impressive super-yacht that appeared to be three times longer. *Must be nice.*

A few moments later, she tossed her empty cup into a trashcan filled with beer cans, plastic bags, rags, and soda bottles.

To her left a man and a woman that appeared to be in their mid-thirties approached. Their clothing matched that of a young professional couple making use of a day off. They struggled to hoist an ice chest onboard and Bowers could see why. The red-haired woman's noticeably pregnant belly threw off her balance.

"Wait," shouted Bowers. "I can help." She took one of the handles. Together she and the man in the polo shirt swung the chest onto the deck of his fishing boat.

"Thank you so much," said the woman, with one hand guarding her expanded belly.

While waiting for the dive boat to finish preparations, Bowers leaned against a piling and spoke with the couple as the tall man washed out a bait bucket at the spigot. "It's a great day to be on the water and do some fishing," he said. "We don't get out here as much as we'd like."

Bowers glanced out at the water. Fifteen feet from the end of the dock, she spotted Bo coming in on a jet ski. As he tied up, Bowers pulled down her ballcap and casually adjusted her position so that the fisherman's body blocked her from Bo's view.

Bo finished tying up. As he tromped past, Bo talked to himself as if pissed off. He hesitated long enough to fling a plastic bag into the trashcan, then hurried toward the other dock. When he reached the super-yacht, he marched up the gangway and disappeared inside.

Once he'd left, Bowers continued to help load supplies aboard the couple's fishing boat. When the man slung a bag of trash and a faded rope on the dock, she asked, "Do you want me to toss this out?"

"That would be great," he said, "Thank you."

"The rope too?"

"Yeah, I don't need it," he said, as he started his engine. "Thanks again." The couple waved as they cast off.

Bowers dropped the bag of trash into the bin, then opened the sack Bo had discarded. Unfortunately, it held nothing more than used tissues and two empty water bottles.

The time had come to throw him off balance.

Still holding the rope, she thought about Bo's jet ski and smirked. *This will be fun.*

Bowers kept the rope and retrieved a handful of greasy rags.

The docks were quiet except for the dive operation busily loading up air tanks, weights, and cases of bottled water. People near the dive boat had their backs to her.

Bowers stripped down to her swimsuit and left her clothes on top of her backpack at the end of the dock. She tucked the rags under her shoulder strap, put on her fins and the new Cressi mask and snorkel. With the rope over her shoulder, she slipped into the water.

Bowers took a deep breath and swam below the surface where she strung the rope around the piling and secured it with a clove-hitch. After pulling the knot tight, she came up for air and worked her way to the stern of the jet ski where she tied the rope to a metal ring designed to hold a tow rope for pulling wakeboarders.

With her mask at sea level, the super-yacht loomed high above her.

This time she dove under the jet ski where she quickly stuffed the rags into the jet-drive's intake grill.

The rope sank well below the surface, leaving almost nothing above the waterline. *Perfect.*

After rechecking her knots, she hoisted herself onto the swim platform of a nearby bay cruiser and jumped back onto the dock. A horn sounded as the dive boat signaled *all aboard*. Bowers quickly threw on a shirt, grabbed her gear, and waited in line.

She spotted movement on the super-yacht, where Bo stood on deck, arguing with a small man in black, holding an AK-47.

Well now. That piqued her curiosity.

After the gunman stormed back inside, Bo leaned against the rails and scanned the docks until their eyes met.

She waved back just before boarding the dive boat. As they pulled away from the dock, Bo scrambled to exit the super-yacht. Once on the dock, he sprinted toward her, but the dive boat had already drifted away as it idled toward the marina's exit.

Bowers knew what he'd do next.

BOWERS SMIRKED as she sat back to enjoy the show.

With a furious scowl, Bo jumped on his jet ski and revved the engine. The Sea-Doo dug in and raced for their boat until the anchor rope snapped tight. The abrupt stop threw Bo over the handlebars where he splashed into the water.

The engine died.

While the dive boat gently accelerated toward the channel, Bo swam back to the jet ski. She suspected it wouldn't take long for him to figure out what had happened.

He found the problem even faster than she'd anticipated. The jet ski rocked as he swung his fists and the air. With his hair wet and face in a red knot, he screamed at her with such ferocity, he almost tipped over the jet ski and nearly fell back into the drink.

Bo grabbed the handgrip on the back of the seat to regain his balance. He cut loose the rope, tossed it aside, and pointed his knife at her before revving the engine. This time, he raced toward their boat at full speed. Forty feet from the dive boat, Bo's jet ski made a strange whine.

When the engine went dead in the water, Bowers chuckled.

WHAT LIES BENEATH

A S THE DIVE BOAT SURGED through the blue-green swells, Bowers watched a sealion pop to the surface. A few minutes later she took a seat and dared to close her eyes and relax in the warmth of the sun.

As they approached their dive spot, a dive master provided an overview of the Vandenberg wreck, which had been a warship during WWII and then had become a missile tracker. It now rested on the bottom in 140 feet of water.

"This noble ship," said the dive master, "now serves as an artificial reef."

After the usual pre-dive briefing, the fit, tanned dive master approached Bowers. "You're the one with the advanced dive card, right?"

"Yes, sir," she said. The big fellow next to her leaned in to listen. He wore his mask like a headband with his snorkel upside down.

The dive master looked up from his clipboard. "We'll keep the recreational divers on the upper deck, but feel free to explore the deeper sections. Bottom is at 140 feet. Do you have a partner?"

Bowers scanned the rookie divers fumbling with their equipment.

"I can do it," said the big man next to her.

"Okay," said the dive master. He scribbled something on his notepad and went to help the other divers.

In Bowers experience, every dive boat had rookies, a few great divers, and one clueless jerk. Bowers wondered which one her new partner would be.

His wetsuit and deconditioned body reflected decades of abuse.

"How long have you been diving?" she asked.

"Oh hell," said the big man with a square face and pale green eyes. "I've been doing this for twenty-five years. My name is George."

She shook his hand. "Bowers."

When it came time to enter the water, she did a giant stride into the sea, cleared her mask, and waited for George, who needed two men to escort him to the stern where he tripped over his fins and fell into the drink with a belly flop.

That was graceful.

As Bowers and George descended, she cleared her ears and watched him closely. Every diver carried a flashlight or a camera, but George resembled a dive store display. He wore everything from glow-sticks, to a dinged-up flashlight, spare air, a slate for writing, and a GoPro camera on a retractable cord, along with a host of other items.

Bowers descended into the watery world where everything faded to shades of blue. At least George remembered to clear his ears.

Judging from the amount of bubbles he blew out, George sucked up a lot of air. That could indicate fear, being out of shape, or both. His rapid consumption also meant he couldn't stay down as long. If she had to babysit him, her own dive would be cut short.

As their depth increased and they drew closer to the ship, the waters became colder and began to clear. The rhythmic rasp from her regulator and the burble of bubbles when she exhaled welcomed her back to the weightless realm of the sea.

Out of the darkness the haunting outline of the wreck emerged. The ship's huge body appeared black against the ocean's blue hues. The whine of a distant boat engine added to the creepy feel of the ship's lonely silhouette.

With a hull the length of two football fields, she couldn't see the other end of the vessel.

Bowers drifted down toward the upper deck where the distinctive radar dishes stood like sentinels. As if abandoned on a strange planet, this critical equipment—once the eyes and ears of the ship—had now been left in the depths to deteriorate. For some, these were cool relics from WWII; for others they stood as a somber monument to the lives lost in war.

Her partner stopped to take a selfie in front of the *Duval Street* sign mounted on the foremast.

As she waited, she remembered that Bo was a diver. Bowers kept an even closer eye on the waters around them.

As other divers gathered around the *Duval Street* sign, she signaled George to follow her as she descended along the hull.

Over its ten years entombed on the bottom, the ocean had slowly taken claim to what had once been a proud vessel. The sight reminded her of the pelican on Duval Street that had fallen from the sky and died. Both the bird with its broken wings and this great ship seemed out of place.

Movement caught her attention.

Above her, George whooshed his arms in a panic.

The source of his distress swam about twenty feet away where a young barracuda had been drawn in by the winks of light reflecting from the silver cross on George's necklace. Bowers swam to him and grabbed George by his buoyancy compensator. He frantically pointed to the fish with its unblinking stare and needle-sharp teeth.

Ever curious, barracuda were like underwater cats, attracted to anything shiny. Bowers scooped up the cross and tucked it inside the neck of his wetsuit.

The young barracuda quickly lost interest and swam away.

Over the next few minutes, Bowers motioned for him to follow her, hoping he wouldn't do anything stupid.

She drifted down without touching any of the sharp corals or sponges that adorned the ship's exterior. At eighty feet, she peered inside a cutout in the hull that opened into a cavernous space she suspected had once been a storage compartment. She clicked on her flashlight and immediately found herself eye to eye with a goliath grouper who had taken up residence within the hull of the ship. The yellow-eyed fish had to weigh 300 pounds.

George swam in for a look over her shoulder. The moment he saw its huge gaping mouth, George flailed his arms and legs to back away. He knocked her against the side of the ship. Bubbles and debris filled the water.

Spare me.

Part of her wanted to haul George back to the dive boat and leave him there. And yet, she'd noticed that his wetsuit and boots were tattered. Unlike the other divers with the latest equipment, his gear wore the dull patina of age and hand-me-downs.

Once George calmed down, he wrote *sorry* on his slate. She nodded and gave him the OK sign.

As George went back to filming, she noticed that his pencil had been attached to the slate with a shoestring and duct tape. His older-generation GoPro camera had a handle he'd cobbled together with rusted screws and PVC piping.

Bowers relaxed in the warm waters and watched George captivated by tiny banded shrimp. It had likely taken a long time for him to save up enough for this trip. Diving clearly meant something to him.

She took the time to show him a creature known as a Christmas tree and a needlefish. As she watched his green eyes light up with glee at the sight of a colorful soft-bodied mollusk known as a nudibranch, she realized he'd shown her something too.

At first glance, the only thing she'd noticed about the ship had been its desolate burial until George had drawn her attention to the cloak of sea life thriving thanks to this great vessel. This proud ship was still on duty, offering protection to sea life big and small.

Where she had seen only loss, George had found life.

A few minutes later, she patted his shoulder, checked his air and gave him another OK sign. George had already sucked up over half of his air. She still had 2,000 psi or two-thirds of a tank.

As George continued to follow her lead, he became more relaxed until he lost his grip on his GoPro camera. At first the retractable cord held, but in the current, it twisted and snapped. As the camera drifted away, he tried to go after it, but in his panic, he lost a flipper.

Bowers spotted the camera sinking toward the bottom and gestured for him to wait for her. She released some air from her BCD and swam after it.

On the bottom, she found the camera in 138 feet of water next to a discarded beer can. During her years of diving, she'd often found water bottles, abandoned fishing nets, and the occasional pair of sunglasses. However, finding a woman's sandal surprised her.

At first, she suspected it had fallen off a boat. Twelve feet away she saw another shoe. That caught her attention.

She checked her compass and surged forward. There on the edge of a gorge, a high-heeled shoe lay on its side. It glowed bright red under her flashlight. The satin fabric was too clean to have been there for much more than a day.

Bowers swam to the edge of the drop off. Within the underwater trough that went down another thirty feet or so, she saw more shoes and clothing scattered over the area along with what appeared to be bleached and broken shells.

After swimming down closer to the debris field, she hovered over the bottom. It quickly became apparent that the white shells were human bones.

DISTURBED

THE UNSETTLING SIGHT of the skulls' empty eye sockets staring up at her changed everything.

Bowers hovered in the water but couldn't safely remain at this depth for more than a few moments. With her phone protected by a waterproof pouch, Bowers quickly took pictures of the scattered ribs and skeletonized feet and hands that lay amid corroded jewelry, tattered clothing, and faded shoes. Bowers spotted movement amid the bones where an armada of crabs picked at the fresher remains.

Using her compass, she navigated back toward the ship and found George, who had recovered his flipper. His eyes were wide with worry until he spotted her.

When she handed the GoPro back, he eagerly wrote *thank you* on his slate.

She watched him swim off to film a ball of bait fish. His innocence and obvious joy over exploring sea life made what she'd just seen even more unsettling.

George and the others onboard didn't need to know what she had found.

Bowers directed his attention to a group of neon-blue tangs. As soon as the tangs drifted by, yellowtail amberjacks and king mackerel darted past them in a flurry.

George's eyes went wide. Bowers scanned the waters. Thirty feet away, a blue-gray missile of pure muscle chomped into a large mackerel. As the great fish swam directly toward them, blood trailed from its mouth. Bowers recognized the sleek creature as a large black-tip shark.

George panicked and swam as if his butt were on fire. As the shark glided past, it brushed against her leg like sandpaper.

She urgently needed to return to shore to report the mass gravesite. Bowers caught up with George. That his air supply was nearly exhausted gave her a solid reason to end the dive.

Once onboard the boat, she helped George with his equipment and began packing her gear.

The crew made sure everyone had been accounted for and the boat headed back to Key West. George thanked her again. "It was great being your partner," he said as he showed her his picture of the nudibranch.

After putting on dry clothes, Bowers sat in the sun and listened to George tell a swaggering tale of how he'd shooed away an aggressive lemon shark.

Bowers smiled to herself.

As the boat rode through the swells, Bowers thought about the dumpsite. That it hadn't been discovered didn't surprise her. It wasn't visible from the Vandenberg and it was much too deep for recreational divers.

Minutes later, she noticed something in the swells.

As their boat drove past, Bowers spotted a torn pink T-shirt floating with seaweed on the surface.

ARMOR PLATED

A T THE SOUND OF RAISED VOICES, Coop hurried inside the Blue Coconut Bar and Grill.

Maggie nodded hello and went to the backroom with her phone to her ear, leaving Vega and Lonnie to snipe at each other. The place smelled of beer, fresh paint, and disinfectant.

Lonnie glared at Vega who tossed aside a sheet of sandpaper and glared back at him.

"Lonnie," said Coop, "go back to work. I got this." He took a seat next to Vega. "Come on, man. Don't let this go sideways."

Vega gripped a can opener and kept his eyes on Lonnie. "I hate that bastard."

"Jeez bro," said Coop, "you started the fight. You busted up the place. Hell, you even slugged me. You're lucky you aren't facing charges."

Vega dragged a can of paint closer. "Everything I touch turns to shit."

Coop leaned on his elbows and noted Vega's cut ear and swollen right hand. "Listen," said Coop. "You've got to get your shit together. Talk with someone before it's too late."

Vega popped open a paint can. "Apparently, I'm too stupid to take care of my own problems."

"I didn't say that," said Coop. "Only that the job is tough enough, just don't go it alone."

He sat back. "Linda complains that I never tell her about my day." He rubbed his eyes and laughed. "I can just imagine sitting down to a nice dinner with the wife and telling her all about disarming a nutjob with a sawed-off shotgun who just blew the brains of his neighbor's dog all over the side of the guy's house, or the meth-head that came at me with a machete, or how a drunk puked in the back of my unit."

Vega chuckled. "That'd be a show-stopper. My wife used to say the same shit."

"See? Talking to someone who gets it helps." Coop hoped his words were getting through. He patted him on the shoulder and approached Lonnie.

"Hey man," said Coop. "How ya doin'?"

Lonnie glared at Vega. "He is supposed to be working, not flappin' his gums."

"Come on. Be glad he's here to make amends."

"It's a little late for that, don't you think?" Lonnie scowled at Vega. "Them tables ain't gonna paint themselves."

"What does it look like I'm doin'?" Vega continued stirring the can of paint. "Asshole."

Lonnie lurch forward. "You're the asshole who trashed the place."

Coop corralled him. "Stand down. Fists won't fix this."

Vega stood with his shoulders tense and the can opener held like a dagger.

"I said stand down. That means both of you," ordered Coop. He slid a few battered tables between the two men."

"You cops are all alike," snorted Lonnie. "You just like to hide behind your stupid badges and don't give a crap who gets hurt."

Coop jabbed a finger toward Vega. "You want to hold him accountable. Legally and in court. Do it. But get off my ass. I'm not your enemy."

Lonnie thumped his fist against his black T-shirt. "My life matters. So does my brother's."

"You think I don't know that?" shouted Coop, as he pointed to Maggie and a couple walking by. "Their lives matter too. So does everyone's. If I didn't believe that, I wouldn't be out there busting my ass and putting my life on the line every damned day."

Coop ripped off his bulletproof vest and shoved it into Lonnie's hands. "Wanna trade your T-shirt in for this? Want to see what it feels like to have to wear that every damned day, hoping you'll survive to go home at the end of your shift?"

Lonnie stood there mute, clutching the heavy armor-plated vest.

Coop wasn't done. "When did I ever screw with you? We know Bo's a fuck-up, but I never condemned you or other bartenders because of his crap. I've never given you any reason to come at me. In fact, if a guy with a shotgun were to walk in here right now, I'd be the dope who'd put myself between him and you."

"What's going on?" asked Maggie, as she hurried toward the ruckus.

Without taking his eyes off Lonnie, Coop signaled her to stay back. "If you think being a cop is so goddamned easy, why don't you come on a ride-along with me and see what it's like to have less than a fraction of a second to make a decision that could end your life or someone else's."

BAIT

AS THE SUN SETTLED toward the horizon, Bo rocked in his boat offshore, drinking his beer. Over the years, the ocean had become Bo's solace. A place of peace.

Last night Preston had ordered him to use his own boat to dump the used-up girls. The job didn't bother him, but the extra work of cleaning his boat afterward annoyed him.

What Preston and the others didn't know was that he enjoyed killing. Bo smiled as he relived the quiet hours before dawn where the one in a red dress had surprised him.

She'd swung his cooler at him. He remembered the feel of slapping her. The woman had stumbled overboard. He'd thrown his cooler at her head to make his point. He figured she had drowned and would sink soon enough.

He'd used his knife on the one in the pink shirt, who had been so stoned she never knew what hit her. He had flopped whatever was left of her body into the black waters like a dead fish.

The whole operation had only taken a few minutes, but it pissed him off that he'd lost his cooler.

Tonight, he used his GPS to locate his favorite sandbar, thirty feet under the surface where he glided into place, reversed engines, and dropped anchor.

As he tied off a floating diver-down flag, dusk faded to twilight. He donned his scuba gear, checked his camera and flashlight, and anticipated capturing some great shots. High-contrast photos taken after sunset were always more dramatic and powerful.

Normally, he loved diving, and yet the damage to his face made tonight's dive a royal pain. If it weren't for the printer's deadline, he wouldn't have done it.

Bo slapped his fins onto the deck and leaned forward to jam his wide feet inside. As he bent forward to snap his heel straps in place, the pressure on his face triggered another explosion of throbbing.

With his camera held close to his chest, he eased down onto the swim platform and into the sea. For a moment he relaxed in the cool waters and the relief it brought to his aching face.

Bo glanced up at the darkening sky, then followed his anchor line down. Clearing the growing pressure in his ears required clamping his broken nose shut to equalize the pressure. The pain made his eyes water.

He didn't mind the darkness, but wind had churned up the sea, making it murky. That wasn't his fault. The stupid deadline pissed him off. It wouldn't kill the printer to wait one more week.

Nearing the bottom, his flashlight lit up the outline of his home-made mooring.

Last night, Bo had stopped by and left fresh bait to draw the interest of the bigger fish.

With his camera ready, he hovered nearly motionless, but nothing bigger than a squirrel fish swam by. Black tips should be circling by now. Why weren't they?

Bo swam closer to the mooring. His bait was gone, except for part of a foot.

LONNIE'S ATTITUDE STILL annoyed Coop as he rested his elbows on the table at Pepe's and waited for his sister.

"If someone is going to be mad at you, it should at least be over something you actually did," he mumbled as he glanced through the menu. The aroma of blackened fish, sizzling steaks, and burgers made his stomach grumble.

Coop checked his watch and sent his sister a text: *Got a table. See you soon.*

While waiting for her to show up, he glanced up at the green canopy above him and the faces of people enjoying their meals.

His sights landed on a woman pointing at him. "You see that cop?" she said to her boy who looked to be about nine. "If you're not good, he's going to arrest you and throw you in jail where you'd never see me again."

The child nervously glanced at Coop.

He knew the woman meant well, but he didn't rock with this nonsense.

Coop stood and walked over to the table and pulled out a chair. The woman's eyes went wide. The boy drew his body into a ball and wrapped his arms around his legs. "I'm sorry, sir," said the kid. "I won't do it again."

His soft brown eyes teared up.

"Hey buddy—you and me—we're okay," said Coop. "I came over to show you something."

"Yes, sir." The kid appeared terrified. He pulled up his T-shirt to wipe his eyes.

"Check this out," said Coop. The boy brightened up a bit when Coop opened his wallet and pulled out a gold sticker printed to look like a police badge. He pointed at the words on the sticker. "It says right here—*To Serve and Protect.* Do you know what that means?"

The boy shook his head. "No, sir."

"It means I'm your friend. It's my duty to protect you. It says so right here. If you're ever scared or in trouble or lost, I want you to promise me that you'll look for me or an officer with a badge. We will help you."

The boy sat up. "Yes, sir."

Coop handed him the sticker and enjoyed watching a huge smile bust-out all over the kid's face.

"Thank you," said the boy as he held up the sticker.

Coop shook the boy's soft hand and nodded to his mother. "You have a nice day, ma'am."

As Coop returned to his seat, an older gentleman in a ballcap gave him a thumbs up.

People of all ages filled the tables around Coop. Oyster shells hung on hooks around the canopy at the entrance. The place was packed with an eclectic array of memorabilia from old newspaper articles to an ancient Evinrude outboard motor.

He had downed his fair share of beers at their bar, but what he liked most was the welcoming staff and open-air dining that felt like sitting out back at a friend's house.

He checked his phone. Where was Sara?

Coop ordered another Coke and waited.

At a table adjacent to his, a man in his thirties draped an arm around the slender dark-haired woman with him. She wore a slim-fitting sleeveless black dress. The man's right hand cupped around her bare upper arm. With the side of his thumb he gently caressed her tanned skin.

Sitting there by himself made Coop feel stupid. Memories of Linda's laughter floated through his mind. He had always loved the warmth of her skin when they had been close. He missed those days. There had been a time when they too had sat making eyes at each other until their dinners had grown cold.

He checked his phone again and waited. While finishing his drink, he tried to ignore the happy couple's laughter and the man's hand on her bare leg.

Time passed slowly. The couple left. Coop sent Sara another text: *Where are you?*

Even before tapping send, he knew something was wrong.

STRYKER

I N THE GLOW OF A SETTING SUN, too many unanswered questions nagged at Bowers. She leaned against the marina's worn wooden railing. As she watched a pelican gliding over the shimmering waters in search of a full belly, she wondered what had happened to Lily's sister.

With images of the dumpsite flashing through her mind, Bowers feared she already knew the answer.

Riggs' inquiry about who she knew in Key West had her thinking about Jay, whom she'd served with in Iraq. The Army had given him several nicknames, such as Dog Face and a few others that were much more derogatory. With her shooting skills, her moniker had been *Stryker*.

She and Jay had fought shoulder-to-shoulder. Memories enveloped her with the sounds of a soldier's final breaths and the anguished sobs of grown men weeping.

Confident young faces tugged at her emotions. Some didn't live long enough to legally buy a beer, while others left behind young wives with newborns they would never meet.

The boom and echo of incoming mortar shells, the smell of dust and death, water rationing, and endless sweating under the weight of her armored vest momentarily filled her senses as if it had all happened last week. Justifying the experiences as defending the greater good helped.

As much as she hated war, she didn't want to forget these remarkable souls who would never return home.

Bowers pulled her hair up under her ballcap and shoved the ugliness of battle into the most remote fissures of her mind.

From an inconspicuous spot on the docks, she watched the sun resting on the horizon where deepening hues of violet were backlit by bright golden yellows.

Maybe Jay still lived in Key West. She tapped his number. Considering what they'd been through together, this call should have happened a long time ago.

She listened to the ringing, having no idea what to say.

"Hello," said a male voice. She heard a football game playing in the background.

"Jay?" said Bowers. "Is that you?"

After a hesitant pause, he said, "Holy crap. Bowers! How are you?"

The sound of his voice brought back even more memories and a lump in her throat. "I'm sorry, I didn't call sooner."

"Hey," said Jay. "I should've called you."

She swallowed hard. "You can call me anytime."

Within seconds their excited chatter progressed to catching up on what they'd done since leaving the Army. They talked, laughed, teased the crap out of each other, and shared a pain few understood.

After their call ended, Bowers sat on a plastic crate with her back against a pole. A smile snuck up on her. Reconnecting with someone who understood had been long overdue.

Much to her relief, they had talked as if they'd just seen each other last week. He'd told her about the new study he'd participated in, which allowed him to do things most took for granted, like the ability to stand so he could brush his teeth at the sink, wash dishes, and reach his cabinets.

She still remembered him running through the desert with his rifle and gear on his back. It seemed so unjust for anyone like that to be confined to a wheelchair.

Lonnie had no idea how well she understood his grief over his brother's injuries.

Bowers hadn't told Jay about the assault but did agree to see him tomorrow.

As twilight enveloped the docks, she pulled her ballcap down low and strolled along the weathered gray slats for a closer inspection of the super-yacht Bo had boarded this morning.

Forty feet from her, the huge vessel's gleaming white exterior and helipad laid claim to extensive wealth. However, the sight of armed guards left an unsettling impression. The ship's sleek black windows on each of the three decks made her wonder what lay inside.

As she drew closer, she found the name of the ship emblazoned on the gunnel: *The Leisure Lee*.

For fear of drawing suspicion, she spent little time eyeing the ship.

To blend in, Bowers wore her Key West ballcap and pulled a tourist map out of her vest pocket.

Two men appeared on the gangway. Their pounding footsteps and harsh voices came closer. Keeping them in her peripheral vision, she casually spread the map over a deck box covered in fish scales that lit up like glitter under the pole lamp.

Bowers pretended to study the colorful tourist map.

The men ignored her.

Their harden features and the distinctive way they walked caught her attention. These were not typical security guards. These men cradled their rifles with the familiarity and comfort that came from the trenches of war. Bowers knew it well. Just the way they walked made the hair go up on her neck.

A few minutes later, she bought a cup of ceviche from a restaurant on an adjacent dock and took a seat on a bench near a charter service. A soothing breeze off the water came as a relief.

Surveillance and recon missions had taught her patience. As Bowers took a bite of the citrus-flavored fish, two eyes near the trashcan watched her. A skinny cat with a cut ear crept a little closer.

"How do you feel about lime on your fish?" she asked.

The striped tabby didn't take its eyes off her. Bowers tossed a hunk of fish to the cat, who snatched it up and scampered back into the shadows.

From 200 feet away, Bowers still had an unobstructed view of the *Leisure Lee* and the series of boat slips next to it where Bo usually tied up.

Keeping track of the super-yacht proved easy, but Bo's whereabouts were another matter. According to her app, his van had been near the marina, but his boat slip remained empty.

The wooden bench creaked as Bowers rocked back and listened to the hushed sounds of a distant radio from one of the boats.

A small man in black appeared on an upper deck of the *Leisure Lee*. From the shadows, Bowers pulled a monocular scope from her vest and watched as he strolled around the ship's railings and occasionally gazed down at the water. As he went back inside, Bowers wondered what Bo did on that ship.

The stars came out as she ate the rest of her dinner with a plastic spoon. Most of the returning fishing boats slowed in the no-wake zone, except for a cabin cruiser that came in at near full speed. The cruiser docked about fifteen feet from her.

The boat's frantic crew tied up and quickly off-loaded an agitated woman. Her damp black hair and wet red cocktail dress caught Bowers' curiosity, but her body language triggered alarm.

She guarded her torso with her arms and pulled away when the men tried to help her off the boat. Bowers had seen this reaction before in victims who'd been sexually assaulted.

The men seemed befuddled as to what to do with her. One offered her a towel, but she pushed his hand away.

Bowers moved under a pole lamp and pretended to be texting. When the woman backed away, as if she were afraid of them, Bowers thought about intervening until it seemed clear the men were genuinely trying to help.

"Lady," said one of them. "I can take you to a doctor or call the police. We'll make sure you are safe."

The woman's accent sounded Cuban.

"No! No *hos-pi-tal*," she argued. "No *policia*." The woman pulled away from the men. "I must go. Now." She began to sob.

Bowers noted the woman's deep bruises and the ligature marks on her wrists and ankles. "They promise me job," she screamed, "money for my family. They say they care for me."

Her face twisted into a knot of anguish. "They lie."

She spat on the dock. "*Hombres malos*. Bad men."

The woman's voice tapered off into the desperate shriek of a person whose world had been shattered.

Bowers hadn't spoken Spanish in years. Even so, it was clear that whatever the young woman had endured had left her terrified.

She stopped in front of Bowers. The petite woman stood about five-foot-one, slender, with long black hair.

"I tell *policia*," she said to Bowers, "he say, he to kill my family."

"What is your name?" asked Bowers.

"*Mi llama es* Maria. Like *mi mama*." The way the woman had cried *mama* reminded Bowers of the whimper of a child.

"I can give you a ride," said Bowers.

"No. *Gracias*." Maria held up her arms and backed away.

"*Dónde está tu familia?*" asked Bowers, hoping to learn if she had family nearby.

Maria's chin puckered. "*Mi casa en* Cuba."

The bone-deep despair in her voice hit Bowers hard. "I can help you."

"*Por favor*, I go now." Maria stumbled past Bowers, her bare wet feet made a soft slapping sound as she hurried away.

A man with a ponytail approached the boat. "Hey Jim, what the hell was that about?"

"It was weird, man," said one of the fishermen. "We found her in the waters way offshore, clinging to a cooler." As he off-loaded his gear, he tossed a woman's red satin shoe onto the deck.

Bowers recognized it immediately.

BODIES AND BONES

B O RACED INTO THE DARK marina and backed his boat into the slip between the *Leisure Lee* and the Hinkley until it thumped against the bumpers.

He kicked an old pizza box out of his way and tied up.

Dead tired and pissed off, Bo wanted to sleep on his own boat, but Preston insisted he move to the Hinkley. "Asshole."

Arguing with the skipper had been pointless. He took a load of his things over to the Hinkley where he locked up his camera and took the Styrofoam cooler and a case of beer. He knew they weren't his, but felt Preston owed him that much.

Back at his boat, he stepped down into the cramped cabin. Bo pushed aside rags and a wrench and took a seat on the bunk.

The first beer went down quickly.

While waiting to feel the numbing buzz of alcohol, he threw a few shirts and a pair of jeans into his duffel bag.

While guzzling down another beer, he admired some of his photos taped to the walls and cabinets. It irked him he hadn't gotten the shots he needed.

After crushing his second empty beer can, he tossed it toward the trashcan and missed, and opened a third.

Bowers hung in his thoughts. Bo laughed at the cops' stupid citations laying in a pile. If they'd had any idea what all he had done, they would've locked him up.

He pressed the cold can of beer against his throbbing forehead. It helped a little. Missing a night's sleep, mixed with the alcohol and the gentle rocking of the boat, left his eye lids heavy. For just a minute, he rested his head on a pillow to relax.

Bo jerked awake and had no clue how long he'd slept, but the hand on his throat got his undivided attention.

He swung at a blur of arms and hands until he found himself staring down the hurtful end of a pistol.

"Come with me," said Jung with the barrel pointed at Bo's face. The muzzle's round black opening seemed big enough to swallow him. "The captain wants to see you. Now."

"Shit man," said Bo. "What's with this bullshit? All ya had to do was tell me there was a meeting."

Behind Jung stood another one of Preston's hired guns. Known as Scarface, for obvious reasons, he was sketchy as hell and even the other guards avoided him.

The two men hauled Bo to his feet and dragged him off his boat.

"Get your hands off me." Bo didn't appreciate their heavy-handed tactics. "What's your problem, man?"

"You," said Jung.

"Fuck face," said Bo.

Jung tightened his grip. "Dickhead."

Bo stumbled as the two men shoved him up the gangway and onboard the *Leisure Lee*. As they marched down the passageway, a deckman tried to slip by. Scarface slammed the guy against the wall and left him gasping for air.

Bo hated how they hustled him toward the forward cabin, as if he didn't know how to get there himself.

Preston strolled over and stood eye to eye. His expression had all the warmth of an ice pick.

"Sir," said Bo. "These assholes—"

Preston landed a fist into Bo's gut.

The blow left him gasping, but no air filled his lungs. It hurt so much that Bo forgot about his broken nose.

Once he could breathe, he felt like puking. Jung stood by, expressionless. The guy had about as much empathy as a bullet.

Bo held his sides. Confusion clouded his thoughts. The next blow knocked him to the floor. Limp as a kitten, he felt steel-toed boots bludgeoning his butt, thighs, and back. They even stomped on his hand.

This is it.

The thought of them dumping him at sea filled Bo's head with images both ironic and horrifying. He envisioned his body drifting down on top of all the bodies and bones he'd dumped there. Maybe he would end up as bait for the big fish he liked to photograph.

His split lip opened up. He coughed up blood. The coppery taste filled his mouth.

"Why can't you follow orders?" asked Preston. The blade-like edge in his voice left Bo mute. He knew the man had a bad temper, but he'd never expected him to turn on him like this.

Bo remained in a fetal position with his arms wrapped around his head.

"Why are you doing this?" he grunted between gasps.

Jung and Scarface yanked Bo up off the floor and dropped him into a chair. They zip-tied his hands behind his back. Bo was too beat up to resist.

Preston pulled up a seat. His every move seemed calculated.

With the skipper's forehead glazed in sweat, he pointed that creepy finger in Bo's face. "I'm trying to run a discreet operation here. I tell you about the gig we've got that's going give us the most significant payday yet and how critical it is to keep things cool. And what do you do? You go off and make a ridiculous spectacle of yourself right in front of the goddamned police station."

Preston shoved a phone in Bo's face that showed a picture of his truck sideways in the street.

"It wasn't supposed to go like that," said Bo.

Preston stood over him. "You're damn right. You fucked up."

Bo caught a glimpse of a fist and braced for impact.

Searing pain plowed into his left temple. His head rocked sideways. He felt something running from his nose and down his throat.

Bo found himself adrift in a black, swirling pit of agony where a thousand daggers seemed to be jabbing at him.

The pain began to drift away. Even the yelling faded beyond his hearing. Maybe this was what it was like to die.

After a gasp, his ragged breathing rumbled in his ears along with muffled voices that were beyond comprehension.

It took tremendous effort to open his eyes. He jerked when startled by the harsh laughter. Through the open door, Preston sat at his desk studying his papers.

"The princess awakes," said Jung.

Bo's addled brain managed to form one thought: how much he hated that guy. If only he could live long enough to gut him like a fish.

The jolt of pain from a deep breath helped him wrangle in his scattered thoughts.

Preston peered over the top of his glasses at Jung and then at Bo. "Where's this Bowers?"

"I don't know," he croaked at a near whisper.

Once again, Preston rolled his chair back over in front of Bo and took a seat. "Why the hell not?" he asked.

Preston grabbed Bo by the hair and pulled his head back until Bo had no choice but to look him in the face. The skipper cocked his head and leered at him. "From now on, you'll do whatever the hell I tell you. And you will, under no circumstances, go into town. Is that clear?"

"Yes. Sir," said Bo. Getting his photos for the calendar just went out the window.

"Screw up again and you're done."

Bo flinched as Scarface cut off the wire ties. His fingertips tingled as he rubbed his wrists.

"Jung," said Preston. "Go find Bowers."

BOWERS HAD CALLED Coop to fill him in on the dumpsite. When he didn't answer, she left a message, hoping he would call back soon.

She'd called Riggs. He didn't answer either.

Bowers took a seat in a bar's outdoor patio. Fantasy Fest had opened with a bang. Despite the late hour, crowd noise on the streets raged on, as someone played a lively trumpet.

The docks were busier than usual. Fishermen washed down their boats, while other vessels hosted private parties and tourists swarmed the restaurants and bars.

After ordering a taco, she sent Riggs a text message. Within a few minutes her phone vibrated with an incoming call.

"Sorry," said Riggs, "I've been wrapped up in my cases. How are you?"

"It's been a soup sandwich down here."

"You okay?" He had that tired, gravelly sound in his voice that meant he'd been working late.

In a span of seconds, memories of D.C. flooded back. The times when they'd been battered and bruised after a hard day floated through her thoughts. The best of those days had ended back at his place where they would down a few beers and decompress. Sometimes they sat in silence. Often, they made love. Other times they took turns pummeling his punching bag.

More than once they'd bandaged each other's wounds. She still remembered the clean scent of the soap in his shower and how uncomplicated their relationship had been. Despite their crazy jobs and relentless schedules, it had worked. She missed him. She also missed the resources the FBI could marshal when they wanted to track down a perp.

"You still there?" he asked.

"Sorry. It's noisy here. How's my uncle doing?" The breeze off the water blew a strand of hair into her face as a waiter dropped off her taco and a tall glass of iced tea.

"Your uncle is the most stubborn man I've ever met. Reminds me of you."

She chuckled. "It runs in the family."

"Despite giving the nurses at the home grief, they absolutely love him. I took him lifesavers and a box of motorcycle magazines, just as you asked. He says you owe him lunch, when you get back."

"Riggs, I appreciate you doing that." Bowers studied the people mingling near the docks.

Riggs paused as he often did before a serious question. "You gonna tell me what's on your mind or are we going to dance around and talk about the weather?" He was about as subtle as a flash-bang.

Bowers took a bite of her taco. "I'm homing in on Somers."

"Kate, wait."

Riggs' response startled her enough to put down the taco. Rarely did he call her by her first name.

"This guy is on our radar."

"For what?" she asked.

"Murder one," said Riggs. "If he's who I think he is, he's a fugitive on the run. He's dangerous."

"I went one-on-one with him, remember? Trust me. I know. What have you got on him?"

"Within a few weeks of his release from jail, his father, who'd testified against him, was found in a freezer. In pieces. We know Bo as Bob Somerson. He's been using aliases and running from state to state ever since."

"Doesn't surprise me," she said.

"What's your sense of him?"

"He's arrogant, angry, and entitled," she said. "I'm not sure he likes anyone, but he especially hates women. He takes any slight—real or imagined—as a personal injustice."

Riggs listened. "And?"

"He's still after me." She braced herself for Riggs' reaction and told him about being forced into Bo's truck.

Riggs vented his concerns. "Bowers, this is suicide. We've got to get you out of there."

"I handled it." She explained how she'd stomped on the brake and launched Bo into the dashboard. Bowers heard a chuckle.

"He earned that one." Riggs paused; his tone softened. "Come back to D.C. Please."

"I want to," said Bowers, "but, I can't outrun this. I have to deal with it. Besides, the PD ordered me to stay in town."

After grumbling something inaudible, he asked, "How can I help?"

"I want you to look at something." Bowers sent Riggs the pictures from her dive. "Check your text messages."

She waited for his response.

"Mother of God," he said. "It's a dumpsite."

"The skeletons appear to be mostly female. Some had been there so long that small creatures were using them for shelter. Some of the bodies were fresh and still clothed. Something is going down here."

"Someone wanted them to disappear," said Riggs. "Have you noticed anything else?"

"Earlier tonight, I spotted a boat offloading a Cuban woman. They'd found her offshore, clinging to a cooler and scared out of her mind." Bowers told Riggs about the young woman and her red shoe. "This has the earmarks of a human trafficking operation. And I wouldn't be surprised if our Bo Somers is up to his sideburns in it."

"Have you told the PD about this?"

"They're strapped," she said, "with Fantasy Fest and they're still investigating the assault. I left a message for Coop."

"Shit," said Riggs. "I've got to get down there."

"I wouldn't mind," she said, "but my guess is that McDougall won't allow it.

"You don't know the half of it." He told her about his boss refusing to cut him loose and the latest on Fowler trying to entice Hogan into a fishing trip. It was like old times when she'd listened to him venting about his cases.

"It still doesn't make sense," she said, "why is Fowler so interested in a nearly bankrupt company?"

"That's my question," said Riggs. "Some powerful people want this deal to go through."

"You know Fowler," said Bowers, "there's always a hidden agenda. My guess is that someone waved big dollars in front of his nose. Hogan is a man of integrity. It's no wonder he and Fowler butt heads."

"True," said Riggs. "It's hard having them both in D.C. at the same time. Can you imagine being stuck on a boat with the two of them?"

Bowers kept an eye on a man ten feet away. The bulge at his ankle meant he was likely packing heat. "Maybe Hogan will persuade Fowler to give up on the deal."

"Anything is possible," said Riggs. "Hope he can do it before the Committee on Foreign Investments makes their decision. Intel community is going nuts about this one. NSA and even military brass are weighing in."

Bowers thought about CFIUS and the fishing trip. "Something is screwy."

"True," said Riggs.

"I'm meeting a friend tomorrow" she said. "He has his ear to the ground when it comes to the buzz on the internet."

"You mean your Army friend in the wheelchair?" asked Riggs. "From what I can tell, he's still active."

That Riggs had that much information and used the term *active* piqued her curiosity.

Bowers chuckled. "You checking up on me?"

"Maybe."

FRANTIC

S ARA HAD VANISHED. Coop's efforts to suppress his growing alarm became more futile by the minute. While covering his beat, he had stopped in at every one of his sister's hangouts. She wasn't there and no one had seen her.

He took a break from patrolling the crowded streets to check in with Maggie to make sure the bikers weren't acting up. The Blue Coconut was packed.

Just outside the bar, Coop stood at the corner and watched the crowd. A cacophony of sound filled the air. The clanking glassware and the driving beat of the band competed with the hoots of those downing shots. Being around people smiling and enjoying life felt like a much-needed break.

Once inside, Maggie waved at him from across the room as an exuberant patron waltzed in wearing a devilish set of black horns. From one of them hung a lacy pair of pink panties. Maggie laughed. She seemed to be enjoying the spectacle.

Coop understood her enthusiasm for the boost in revenues, but by this hour many of her patrons were sufficiently primed with enough alcohol to get themselves into mischief.

The two security guards she'd hired didn't exactly buoy Coop's confidence. Maggie had a habit of hiring cheap security, which meant their only experience with a gun had been minimal training, shooting at paper targets.

If things went sideways, Maggie would need help managing a throng of this size.

Lonnie approached him with a tall Coke. "It's on the house," he said. "Hey, I need to apologize."

"We're good," said Coop. "It's okay."

"No, it's not," said Lonnie. "I was out of line. A lot of crap gets under my skin, but that's not on you. You've been fair to me."

Coop shook his hand. "Thank you."

Lonnie put a bowl of pretzels on the bar within his reach.

Coop appreciated Lonnie's change of heart. "That offer for a ride-along still stands."

Lonnie grinned and tossed a bottle opener up in the air and caught it one-handed. "Maybe I will."

They both watched a woman with an uneven gait trip and spill her Bloody Mary.

"Here we go again," said Lonnie. He called the barback over and pointed to the spill. Across the room, Maggie helped the harried servers deliver food.

Coop spotted one of the security guards near the other door. The man's eyeballs nearly fell out of his head when a beautiful woman sauntered into the bar, wearing nothing more than a thong and elaborate body paint. Coop chuckled. *Ya gotta love this town.*

Coop's smile faded when he spotted a girl who reminded him of his sister. It wasn't like Sara to not answer his texts. He'd gone by her apartment earlier, but no one had been home.

He went outside and called her again. It went to voicemail. He scanned the streets, which were filled with food stands, body-painting tents, and musicians. Many of the revelers were covered in little more than artfully painted designs and strategically placed feathers. Bare butts and painted boobs were everywhere. A fellow with a giant beer belly walked in wearing a bright pink tutu, a feathered mask right out of a Vegas chorus line, and pasties with his plumber's crack on full display. The woman with him wore a colorful python painted around her torso and right leg.

Coop finished his Coke and caught Maggie's attention. "I'll be back in a little bit. Things are okay here."

She took a drag on her cigarette and squinted through the smoke. "Let's hope it stays that way." She coughed and glanced toward the cluster of bikers who'd taken over the same tables along the far wall.

As Maggie continued to bend his ear, he listened politely, despite his need to find his sister.

Coop remembered something Bowers had said about Sara's new boyfriend likely being intimidated by a big brother in law enforcement. He chided himself for being overly protective and tried to convince himself that Sara had probably been busy with her new man and had forgotten about their dinner.

Yet, the cop in him didn't buy it.

If he couldn't find her tonight, tomorrow morning he'd stop by the coffee stand. Sara never missed work.

Noise from the bikers ramped up when one of them grabbed a blonde waitress's butt. She didn't appreciate the gesture and said so loudly.

The security guard who'd been at the other door approached the tables. The exchange didn't go well. Swearing ensued.

Coop headed toward the commotion.

To his right, Lonnie shouldered through the crush of bodies with his arms wrapped around a case of beer and a bottle of bourbon from the backroom. As he passed the bikers, one of them snatched the bourbon from Lonnie's arms and dropped it like a fumbled pass.

The glass bottle shattered against the concrete floor. Bourbon and a starburst of glass shards splattered all directions.

The indignant waitress pointed to a cut on her leg. "Look what you did."

As Lonnie set down the case of beer, Coop shouldered through the crowd. Meanwhile, Gunner stroked his red beard and called out to Lonnie in a loud voice, "Hey *boy*, clean that up. Chop. Chop."

Lonnie stormed toward Gunner, who chewed on a toothpick and

grinned. "Come on *boy*," said Gunner, "you've been told what to do. Git to it."

Coop blocked Lonnie from getting any closer.

"This is how you wanna play? Okay," said Lonnie. He wrote something on a pad, tore it off, and slapped it on the table. "Sixty bucks is now on your tab for the bottle of bourbon you broke. Pay up now or I'll have you thrown out."

To the jeers of several bikers, Lonnie picked up their empty pitchers. "You're done for tonight."

Gunner stood and shoved a table sideways, knocking it over. The tab fluttered to the floor. "You don't be tellin' me what to do."

"That's enough," barked Coop.

The big biker stepped toward Lonnie. Customers backed away and conversations hushed.

When Gunner spat out his toothpick, a male voice said, "Oh, shit. I'm outta here."

Spit flew from Gunner's mouth as he snarled at Lonnie. "You're steppin' over the line, boy."

"Stand down," ordered Coop.

Gunner stared past him and grunted. He dug into his black leather vest and dropped two crumpled twenties on the floor. He signaled his crew with a whistle and marched toward the door.

The amount clearly wasn't enough to pay for the alcohol they'd consumed and the shattered bottle of bourbon.

"Asshole," said Lonnie as he picked up the liquor-soaked bills.

One-by-one, the bikers followed Gunner as if he were a motorcycle deity.

Coop started to go after them, but Maggie caught his arm. "Let 'em go. It's worth getting them out of here."

"Roger that," said Coop. He headed toward the door to make sure they'd gone. Outside he locked eyes with Gunner, who held his ax high as the bikers fired up their engines.

Threading their Harleys through the crowded cross street proved a challenge as they dodged acrobats, people dancing, and scores of scooters.

Like a swarm of bees, the bikers left by a less-populated side road.

The sounds of their engines were quickly obscured by the lively tunes from a steel pan drum and a corps of trumpets.

After they'd left, Coop wandered up and down the sidewalk, keeping an eye out for pickpockets, drunks, and disturbances. He stopped into an ice cream shop and an Italian restaurant Sara frequented, but no one had seen her since yesterday afternoon.

When he re-entered the Blue Coconut about forty minutes later, Lonnie sprinted toward him with his cellphone to his ear as he screamed at Maggie.

"I gotta go!" Lonnie dashed toward the door. Before Coop could ask why, Lonnie cried out in sheer panic, "My house is on fire. My brother's inside!"

FLASHOVER

COOP LAID ON HIS HORN. As soon as he found a clear path, he smashed the throttle against the floorboards and sped down a side street with his sirens screaming.

The flood of strobing blue lights danced off the hood of his cruiser. With Lonnie sitting in the passenger seat, Coop took a hard turn and made a call for backup.

Adrenaline bumped up his pulse. Having both Lonnie and dispatch yakking at him at the same time didn't help.

It was all Coop could do to keep from yelling into his radio. "Step it up, I need everyone out here. Fire. Ambulance. Backup."

While sweating a river under his bulletproof vest, Coop floored it. Speed limit be damned. The houses and palm trees on either side of them blurred as they flew past.

A few blocks from Lonnie's street, he called in to report the ominous red glow filling the sky above the rooftops and trees. His radio crackled with a message from dispatch for a second alarm, sending more engines to the scene.

He rolled down the window. The acrid smell of smoke filled the cruiser's cab.

"I'm gonna puke," said Lonnie.

"Not in my car."

Moments later, Coop screeched to a halt at the curb next door to the wood-framed home. Against the night sky, windows on the second floor glowed like yellow eyes, giving the house the appearance of a giant, steaming jack-o'-lantern.

"Oh God. Deon," whimpered Lonnie.

"Stay here," ordered Coop. He cracked his door open and ducked as a burning palm frond glanced off the roof of his cruiser and landed in the street.

Above him, swirling red cinders blew from the back and side of the house. Coop spotted Gunner straddling his motorcycle on the front lawn and howling to the heavens with a beer bottle in his hand.

Assuming the guy was drunk, Coop cut his sirens and stepped out of his vehicle. The unmistakable bellow of fire horns, police sirens, and even the thundering roar of dozens of motorcycles all seemed to be converging upon them.

As if mimicking the sirens, the biker howled again.

"Gunner," yelled Coop. "Come talk to me."

"Fuck you," screamed Gunner. He held his arms out wide. "It's the same shit every time I come here. You and your boy Lonnie can't resist disrespecting me in front of my crew."

The bearded biker flicked a lighter. To Coop's horror, the beer bottle had a fuse.

Coop sprinted toward him. "Stop."

Gunner lit the incendiary and chucked it at the house. It smacked against the porch railing and bounced into the flowerbed, where it erupted into flames.

"Hands where I can see 'em!" Coop pulled his pistol. Behind him, he heard his car door open.

"No," shrieked Lonnie. "You motherfucker."

"Get back in the vehicle," ordered Coop, without taking his eyes off the biker.

Gunner pointed at the cruiser. "Tell Lonnie he started this. You need to watch your back, too. It'd be a shame if something happened to your family."

Coop's jaw tightened.

A patrol car pulled up across the street with sirens and strobes flaring just as Gunner revved his engine and smirked. He lurched forward on the big Harley.

"Stop," shouted Coop.

Vega stepped out of his patrol car and ran across the street, barely dodging the throng of bikers rolling up. Not only was Coop outnumbered, his orders were lost in the loud rumble of their engines.

Gunner spun his tires, creating deep divots in the grass. As he whirled in a circle, the rear tire hurled hunks of sod and clods of earth into the air where they rained down on the porch and the flowerbed.

The moment the bike hit the asphalt, Gunner gave it full throttle and roared up the adjacent street where he disappeared into the pack of bikers.

With someone trapped inside the house, Coop wasn't about to waste precious time going after Gunner.

"Deon," shouted Lonnie. "Please, come out."

His unanswered calls came from the side yard. Lonnie dashed to the front door and instantly pulled his hand away as if he'd been burned. Meanwhile, a handful of bystanders had gathered on the street to watch.

Patrol officers arrived in force and immediately directed spectators away from the blaze and made room for the arriving emergency personnel.

Vega loped over to Coop's side. "What happened?"

"Deon is in there," said Coop. "We need to get him out."

Lonnie bent over and shrieked, "Do something."

Coop raced around the burning home, searching for the best entry point. The flames at the rear of the house gave off an otherworldly glow as they consumed the exterior walls and part of the roof. Ribbons of melted siding fluttered to the ground.

Coop's eyes watered. Inside, aerosol cans exploded like popcorn and the stench of smoldering plastic and chemicals burned his lungs.

The backdoor into the kitchen had been busted in. It appeared that the fire had been set in the corner of the kitchen and spread to the second floor.

Coop jogged back to the front lawn. So far, the front of the house appeared intact.

He scanned the steps leading up to the front door and wraparound porch. A wheelchair ramp had been built along the left side of the house.

Coop had been to Lonnie's home once and remembered the window to the right of the door was part of the living room. Being in a wheelchair meant Deon had to be on the first floor.

"Where's your brother's room?" Coop shouted.

Lonnie pointed to the window left of the front door.

The ground and even the air seemed to vibrate as the First Company arrived in a huge shiny engine. Their brakes sighed as they came to a halt. The engine moved forward, leaving room directly in front of the house for the Truck Company, which pulled in behind them with more men and rescue equipment.

"Anyone inside?" asked a firefighter.

"Yes," said Coop. "A man in a wheelchair."

The Truck Company immediately geared up for a search.

"This one is rockin' and rollin'," said a firefighter from the First Company as they connected a large hose to a fire hydrant and dragged lines toward the house.

Another returned from the side yard. "We got a working fire on the first and second floors in the rear."

"Enter through the front door," ordered the fire chief, "and knock it back."

The attack crew mounted the steps at the main entrance of the structure with fire hoses. As the lead firefighter kicked open the front door, they all fell flat on their bellies to avoid the searing blowback.

As they entered and began knocking down the blaze, firefighters from the truck followed to search the rooms, closets, and crawlspaces.

The heat intensified.

Vega smacked Coop's arm. "You'll see. That little shit is about to shag his sorry ass out of there any second now."

Coop shoved Vega backward. With a finger pointed in his face, Coop railed at him. "Look, moron, that kid could be burning to death right now."

He bit down hard to keep from belting the guy.

Vega appeared stunned. He stared wide-eyed at the blaze as if seeing it for the first time.

The roar of the flames grew louder. Something inside crashed to the floor. The roof became engulfed.

With horns blaring, the Second Company arrived and went to work. Red-hot cinders ignited palm trees and plumes of burning debris blew toward the house next door.

Coop called over two officers. "Evacuate the houses on the perimeter."

"Good call," said a firefighter. "This one's really cookin'."

The fire chief directed his men. "I want a master stream on sides Charlie and Delta and a water curtain on the adjacent structures."

The Second Company responded immediately and worked toward the back and side yard.

Deon did not come out. Nor did his dog.

Lonnie's gut-wrenching screams called out for his brother.

Coop couldn't wait any longer. He ran toward the front door. When Lonnie tried to follow, Coop pulled him back. "Let us do this."

"But—"

"Lonnie," shouted Coop. "I can help your brother or babysit you. Pick one."

Lonnie threw up his hands.

Vega skirted around Coop. "This one's on me."

In a flash, Vega sprinted up the steps and vanished into the smoky interior.

"Coop, stand back," ordered the fire chief. "I need you out here. We'll clear the rooms."

Coop heard the hiss of water colliding with hot flames. Gray smoke turned to a white fog of searing-hot steam.

He waited for the firefighters inside, hoping they'd find Deon before it was too late.

Smoke began seeping from the open doorway. Coop squinted inside with his eyes burning. Even as firefighters pushed flames back toward the kitchen, a thick layer of darker smoke built up under the ceiling in the front room. The heat became unbearable as the flames grew out of control.

The fire chief studied the blaze. "What are you thinking?" asked Coop.

"If you listen," said the chief, "a fire will tell you things."

Coop's ears and nose felt seared. He heard the crackling, pops, and creaking. "What's it saying?"

"This one is voracious. We may have no choice but to do a surround and drown."

That meant the house could be a total loss. Coop could not imagine what Lonnie must be feeling as the roaring blaze burned his home and belongings to ash.

"Please," said Lonnie. "I just want my brother."

Firefighters faced off with the inferno and fought the blaze with everything they had.

More patrol units arrived. The captain stepped out of an unmarked unit and ordered everyone to cut their sirens. As the number of spectators grew, a reporter from the local paper arrived with a cameraman.

The clatter intensified as the word spread about Vega running inside. With the house burning in the background, a reporter began to interview the captain.

A long minute later, Vega stumbled from the house. Over his shoulder, he carried a body covered in a scorched blanket. Voices fell silent until the blanket fell to the ground and an arm moved. Cheers rose from the crowd when Deon held up his head.

"Yes," cheered Coop, as he raced toward Vega. Firefighters joined them and helped Vega down the steps. With Coop's support and the assistance of a paramedic, Vega gently laid Deon on a blanket of green grass. "Get this man to the hospital."

Lonnie dropped to his knees by his brother. Coop pulled him back. "Give them room to work."

As Vega coughed, Deon grabbed his arm. "Max is under the bed."

"It's a beagle," shouted Lonnie.

Vega bolted back into the burning house.

Coop stared at the yawning hole that had been the doorway and caught a glimpse of Vega ducking.

Seconds later, he heard a loud crash that seemed to shake the house. Vega screamed as if in pain. Coop ignored the fire chief and charged up the stairs and through the doorway. The smoke had turned dense, oily, and black as it rolled in dark tumbling waves. The heat was unbearable. Smoke made it nearly impossible to breathe.

Firefighters skirted around a large section of ceiling that had fallen to the first floor. They continued moving through the structure, closing the doors as they cleared each room.

Coop got down low and crawled toward the front bedroom. The heat seared his skin. He squinted, held his breath, and scrambled into the room.

Six feet away he spotted Vega on his belly under the front window. Coop called out, "I got you. Hang on."

Vega did not respond. His body lay limp under a collapsed ceiling beam.

Coop kicked away debris and pulled a pocketknife from his duty belt. He gripped it tightly in his fist, ready to bash out the glass with the window punch, but a firefighter entered and pulled him back.

Behind the man's helmet, shield, and breathing apparatus, Coop focused on his big eyes. The firefighter pointed to the man on the porch who held up a tool that looked like a combined pickaxe and crowbar.

While the firefighter on the porch broke out the window with his Halligan, Coop in his bulletproof vest protected Vega from shards of falling glass.

Seconds later, Coop stuck his head outside. The fresh air helped, but it also fed the flames. He took a breath and ducked back inside where the firefighter had pushed the beam off Vega.

It felt as if Coop's face was about to melt. The carpet beneath his feet started to steam. His lungs ached for air.

Above them contorted fingers of fire writhed and squirmed in the black rolling haze as if the smoke itself were ablaze. A wall of flames approached. The firefighter in the room kicked the door closed.

Coop reached for Vega. Firefighters helped him lift Vega's limp body. Against the loud roar of the fire, the man outside in the soot-covered helmet yelled, "Hurry."

Coop and the firefighter next to him hoisted Vega's upper torso through the window and into the waiting arms of the crew on the porch. They yanked him out so fast it was as if he'd been sucked outside.

"You've got to get out," shouted the man in the soot-covered helmet. "It's too hot."

A whimper startled Coop. At his feet two big eyes stared up at him. Vega had found the dog.

Coop scooped up the beagle and handed him through the window.

The engine's horn sounded the alarm.

"Flashover!" The chief shouted over a megaphone. "Everyone out. Now! Let's go. Let's go."

The crew on the porch helped Coop and the firefighter with him climb out of the window. They handed Coop the dog. Together, they all jumped off the porch.

To his left, firefighters hustled out of the house while others continued to douse the flames to protect their escape route.

The moment Coop's feet hit the grass, he scrambled away from the house and heard the horrid *whoosh*. A wave of heat hit his back. Behind him, everything inside the living room had ignited at once. Ferocious flames and rivers of dense black smoke billowed from the broken windows and open doorway.

The man with the hose barely made it to safety.

Through the roof, flames shot up like booster rockets.

Coop rose to his feet in disbelief. The lethal ferocity of fire astonished him.

The whole house groaned as if in agony. The fire chief had been right. To those who understood, fire had a voice.

With sweat pouring from Coop's face, time and space seemed to have stopped, as he watched the paramedics lift Vega onto a gurney and wheel him toward the second ambulance.

Officers had cordoned off the roads and kept the crowd and press at bay.

Hoses covered the front yards like anacondas.

Coop watched Lonnie's home crumble and collapse. The firefighters took the only option left. Using a ladder truck, they continued sending high-powered arcs of water onto the roof. Others inundated the perimeter to protect the adjacent houses. They couldn't save Lonnie's home, but they could keep the blaze from spreading.

Coop's shirt clung to his skin.

Still cradling the dog in his arms, his boots stuck to the pavement. Part of the soles were gummy, as if melted.

As he tried to catch his breath, Coop rubbed his aching chest and stopped near the ambulances.

This time Coop's eyes watered for a different reason as he helplessly watched the medics working on Deon and dousing Vega's smoldering uniform. The smell of burnt hair and flesh poked at his worst fears.

DESPERATE HOURS

C OOP STOOD UNDER the refreshing mist from the fire hoses. The fine spray glistened in the staging lights. He closed his eyes and took in its cooling relief.

An EMT in a dark-blue uniform approached. He checked Coop's breathing and nodded toward Deon. "That cop pulled him out just in time. That took guts."

"Yes, it did," said Coop between coughs. "But, it wouldn't have happened without the firefighters, who knocked back the flames."

"Come with me," said the EMT. "I want to check your wounds. Bring the dog with you."

As patrol officers held back the gathering crowd, the ambulance carrying Lonnie and his brother sped down the street with lights and sirens blaring.

Fifteen feet away, the other ambulance sat near the curb with its double doors open. Inside was lit up like an emergency room. Coop sat on the curb comforting the trembling dog or maybe it was the other way around. The dog licked his hand.

"Good boy," he said softly.

Coop ignored his own wounds as he listened for any news about Vega's condition.

The EMT set up oxygen for both Coop and the dog. He hadn't expected that but appreciated it.

While the EMT quickly assessed the beagle, Coop continued talking to Max. "Hang in there, buddy." He licked Coop's fingers as he held the oxygen mask over the dog's nose.

Coop's jaw clenched. He hated seeing a helpless pooch caught up in this.

The EMT finished the exam. "The vet should take a look at his paws and check his lungs, but other than that and some singed fur, he looks pretty good."

"Thank you," said Coop. Even to himself, his voice sounded raspy. "Appreciate. Your help."

The EMT stroked the beagle. "I'm glad he is okay."

Coop continued to cough.

The EMT lifted an oxygen mask up to Coop's face. "Breathe nice and easy. Smell the roses, slowly blow out the candles."

Coop glanced up to see the captain approaching him. The man stood halfway between Coop and the ambulance.

With his arms crossed, the captain said, "Coop, you okay?"

"Yes, sir," said Coop.

The EMT cut off a large hunk of Coop's shirt to reveal the reddened skin on his forearm and part of his shoulder.

There goes another uniform.

Coop lifted his arm and inspected the inflamed skin that stung like a son of a gun.

"You will have some scars, but it'll heal," said the EMT. He pointed to the patch of blisters on Coop's left hand. "You need to take your ring off."

"No way," said Coop as he pulled his hand back. "That's my wedding ring."

"Listen," said the EMT. "Your hand is going to swell, which means your ring will act like a tourniquet. If you don't want it cut off, take it off now."

The captain nodded. "He's right."

Coop dropped the O2 mask and grumbled as he twisted off his ring and slipped it into his wallet. As Coop stood and stuffed his wallet back into his pocket, he found himself facing the open ambulance.

He and the captain stared at the gurney holding Vega. The medics leaned over him, pouring sterile water on Vega's uniform while an EMT cut it off. Meanwhile, someone else hung an IV bag.

Coop stared at his partner's burned boots.

Fearing the answer, Coop asked, "How is he?"

"They're doing all they can," said the EMT next to him.

Vega groaned.

Coop pushed past the captain and stepped up onto the back of the ambulance. The sight landed like a sucker punch.

Vega stared at Coop and reached out his hand.

"Just for a minute," the paramedic said as he helped Coop onboard. "Then we've gotta go."

The crew allowed Coop to sit by Vega's head while they secured the IV.

Coop wanted to grab Vega's hand or shoulder, but everything seemed raw and burned. "Hang in there, brother. It's gonna be okay."

He hoped his words weren't a lie.

Between the layers of black soot, odd patches of gray that didn't even look like skin, and the oxygen mask over Vega's nose and mouth, Coop barely recognized him.

The contrast between the whites of Vega's eyes and his blackened face were unnerving. Coop didn't know how much of it was soot and how much was burn.

Vega's voice sounded weak and muffled by the oxygen mask. His eyes turned red and watery. "Coop," said Vega. His chest heaved. "I screwed up. I've been wrong about everything."

His voice weakened. "Tell Deon I'm sorry."

———

COOP FOLLOWED THE AMBULANCE to the ER with the dog curled up in the passenger seat next to him. As he gripped the steering wheel, the swelling made the flesh over his knuckles feel tight. The EMT had been right.

Each time the dog sneezed Coop stroked its sooty fur. "We've had one helluva day, haven't we?"

The dog scooted closer and rested his muzzle on Coop's thigh.

"You're a good boy," said Coop as he gently stroked Max's shoulders.

Ten minutes later, Coop approached the crowded ER where he passed a K-9 officer helping an ambulance crew escort two young troublemakers inside. The one dressed as a pirate had bite marks on his leg, probably from her K-9. The other wore a black eye and a Batman costume. Coop nodded to the officer. She nodded back.

Inside, he passed a waiting area. On his way to the double doors, he brushed by a nurse. "You can't go—"

She hesitated. Her eyes went wide when she saw Coop's burns, bandaged hand, and ruined uniform.

"I'm looking for a fellow officer." The tone of his voice made it clear that this was not up for discussion.

The woman in blue scrubs opened the door and escorted him to the waiting room. "I'll tell them you're here."

A few minutes later, Coop took a seat in a bland gray room filled with uncomfortable chairs. In the aptly named room, large, framed prints of pink flowers hung on the walls and women's magazines filled the end tables as if that would forestall the anxious hours of waiting to know the condition of a loved one.

Four others in the room passed the time by playing with their phones. He stared at the ceiling and waited on news about Vega and Deon.

A nurse in white clogs came in and told him they had sedated Vega and were assessing his burns. "He's in critical condition. It will be awhile before we know anything else. I'm sorry. I know this is hard."

As she left, hope clung to him like a frightened child. Vega's apology and the pain in his face continued to haunt Coop.

How did things get this screwed up?

The time rolled by so slowly that an old man in a walker could've outrun it. Coop's burns stung and the bandage on his hand felt tight but sitting there feeling helpless was the worst. Images of the fire loomed in his mind. He couldn't help but wonder if Gunner would make good on his threat.

When he shifted in his seat, pieces of his boot fell off on the gray carpet. A middle-aged woman with flashy earrings and painted-on eyebrows stared at him. A younger man wearing a headset did a doubletake at Coop's ruined uniform. The others whispered to each other.

Coop sat forward. He'd had enough of this.

He ambled toward the door. Outside in the hallway, he found Lonnie leaning against a pale-blue wall.

"How's Deon?" asked Coop.

Lonnie shrugged and scuffed his feet against the polished linoleum floor. "He has smoke inhalation and a bad burn. Other than that, he's gonna be okay."

"Glad to hear it," said Coop.

Lonnie's voice was barely audible. "What's with Vega?"

"He's critical. Time will tell."

Lonnie nodded. "I'm still sorry for what I said to you."

"No hard feelings," said Coop. He inhaled, winced, and tried to stifle a cough.

Lonnie appeared lost. "Actually Coop, I'm sorry for everything. On the way here, Deon admitted that he hadn't listen to Vega's commands. Deon said he had been over at a house where a buddy of his was selling weed. When he left the house, Vega had stopped him. Deon said he panicked and ran into a house next door that was under construction. Said he had some weed in his pocket and was scared he'd be goin' to jail. So when Vega chased him down and grabbed his arm, Deon fought to get away. Vega thought he had a concealed gun. That's when Vega hit him with that stick."

Coop frowned. "His baton?"

"Yeah," said Lonnie. "Deon says that neither of them saw the drop off where Deon fell and broke his back."

"What a waste," said Coop. "We don't arrest people over a little pot. If he'd cooperated, he could've gone home with a warning."

Lonnie seemed at a loss. "Stupid kid."

"He's young," said Coop. "People do dumb things when they're scared. It took guts to be honest. However, there's still no reason for putting an unarmed kid in a wheelchair. Vega should've called for backup."

Lonnie's voice broke. "I tried to protect him, ya know? I tried to be the big brother he needed."

The words *big brother* hit Coop hard as he thought of his sister.

Lonnie struggled to contain his emotions. Coop had seen him indignant, self-righteous, and spitting mad, but he'd never seen him fighting to hold back tears.

"Shit, man," said Lonnie, "I couldn't even save the damned dog. Deon's been asking about Max. I couldn't tell him." Lonnie stared up at the ceiling. "He's gonna miss that dog."

"No, he isn't," said Coop.

Lonnie stared at him. "What?"

"Max has had a tough day," said Coop, "but he is safely sitting in my car."

Lonnie's eyes went wide as he busted into a laugh. "No shit. How'd that happen?"

"Vega went back in after him."

Lonnie stood there speechless.

"What he did was suicidal," said Coop. "You know that?"

Lonnie remained silent for a few seconds. "He saved my brother."

Coop nodded. "He did."

"I shoulda been the one runnin' in there to get him, but I couldn't. All that fire."

"Listen to me. What you felt is normal," said Coop. "If you'd gone in, you could've died."

"That didn't stop you or Vega. By the way, dude, you look like crap."

Coop chuckled at that.

"I'm such a dumbshit." Lonnie hung his head. "Even after what I said, you all showed up right when we needed help." Lonnie's voice dropped to a whisper. "I don't even know how to thank you."

They watched a man in green scrubs and stethoscope hustle toward a set of double doors.

"Lonnie," said Coop, "you need to know something. Before the ambulance took Vega away, he admitted he was wrong about Deon and all the things he'd done. He asked me to tell you that. My guess is that if..." he paused, "if he survives, he'll tell you himself." He cleared his throat and took a measured breath. "He asked me to tell Deon he's sorry."

Lonnie's chin quivered. "What he did tonight already told me that."

HARDEST WORDS

COOP COULDN'T REMEMBER ever having been this beat-up. The drive home had been a blur. The light in the living room meant Linda was still up, likely watching one of her movies.

He closed the garage door and went inside the house. Before him sat a blue basket overflowing with laundry waiting to be washed. In the kitchen, dishes filled the sink. In the living room his wife sat in the recliner eating ice cream and watching a romantic comedy. She didn't bother to get up.

As he headed down the hall, she said, "Be quiet. I just got Ellie to sleep." Her voice had a scolding tone.

After today and the fire, everything in him needed to see his little girl. He hurried past her school pictures on the wall and stopped at his daughter's bedroom door. He reached for the door-knob. The bandage and the black soot on his arms made him back away.

Instead, he went to his bedroom where he stood in front of the mirror on the closet door. Coop hardly recognized himself. With his face blackened by smoke and his uniform in ruins, he would have scared Ellie.

In the bathroom he stripped down, washed up, and put on shorts and a T-shirt. As he started to leave their bedroom, Linda blocked the doorway.

She flipped her long dark hair over her shoulder and glanced at his uniform in a heap next to the hamper.

"I told you not to put your dirty shit on the floor. Why can't you just put it in the hamper?"

He picked up his destroyed uniform and held it up so she could see the damage. "It's beyond washing."

She noticed his hand. "What happened?"

"I worked a fire."

"You okay?" she asked.

Coop felt a lump in his throat. "Will be, but I need to see Ellie for a few minutes."

"No." Linda wagged her finger in the air. "She needs consistency and regular bedtimes."

"I'll rock her back to sleep myself—"

"Coop! Just once, could you listen to me?"

Coop heard the distinctive squeak of the door to his daughter's bedroom. He brushed past his wife and cracked open Ellie's door just in time to see her dash back into bed and pull the covers over her head. He peeled down the sheet. With her eyes squeezed shut, her lids twitched. Coop stood over her and smiled.

He'd always been proud that she had his blue eyes and blonde hair. She even had his fair skin that sunburned easily. The day when she'd first come home from the hospital drifted through his thoughts. As a newborn, he'd watched over her while she slept. Part of him had been terrified. The other part had been in awe of her. Those feelings had never left.

Ellie opened her eyes. Immediately, she closed them so tight her little face scrunched up.

Coop laughed. "I think you're fooling me," he said in a playful tone.

She giggled and sat up. "Hi, Daddy."

He scooped her up and held her close. She smelled like jellybeans and baby shampoo. At almost six, it seemed as if she'd grown up overnight.

The baby décor in her room had been replaced with a pageant of pink sparkles and cartoon princess posters. Her soft arms wrapped around his neck. After tonight, he needed to bury himself in the presence of someone who still saw wonder in the world.

Coop sat in the rocking chair with Ellie on his lap.

Her giggle made his hand hurt less. She touched his bandage. "Did a bad guy hurt you?"

He pondered how to answer the question honestly, but without scaring her. "I helped save a dog. My hand got scraped up a little. It'll be fine."

She nodded, "What's the doggie's name?"

"Max." Coop gazed into her bright blue eyes. "Hey, how's my girl? Did you have a fun day?"

"Yeah," she said with her eyes open wide. "Today at school, Tyler had a birthday and we all got cupcakes."

Sugar high. Now he knew why she wasn't sleeping.

"That's cool," he said. The love he felt for his child engulfed him. He and Ellie were nearly eye to eye when he felt her warm little hands cup around his face.

Ellie then poked him in the nose and shook her finger. "You didn't come home for dinner."

"I'm sorry, sweetie," said Coop. "I had to work."

The expression on her face fell flat. She dropped her hands and stared at her lap. "I like my old daddy better."

Coop felt as if he'd been stabbed in the chest. "Wait. What do you mean?"

Ellie rested her head against his shoulder. "We used to play and have fun. Now you're mad all the time."

Coop wrapped his arms around her and rested his cheek against her silky soft hair. He wanted to say he was sorry, but the words wouldn't leave his throat. He kissed the top of her head and swallowed hard, hoping she didn't see the tears welling in his eyes. "I love you, sweet girl. I love you so much."

BROTHERS

TERROR HAD NEVER TOUCHED COOP as it did this morning. Sara had not shown up for her morning shift, confirming what his gut already told him.

It took everything he had to maintain his composure. "*Señor*," he said to the owner, "If you hear from her, please call me."

The owner seemed nearly as upset as Coop.

The sun barely cleared the horizon as he ran to his car. After searching a few beaches, he headed back to the station.

Inside the briefing room, patrol officers sat around the large conference table waiting for the lieutenant to assign orders. Coop stood near the doorway. His daughter's words haunted him. With Sara still missing and only a few fitful hours of sleep, sheer exhaustion beat against an urge to throw a chair against the wall and ditch the briefing altogether.

He had to find his sister. Coop scanned the faces of those at the table. It felt as if his entire world were collapsing as everyone else went on as usual.

He reluctantly pulled out a chair. Every seat cushion in the whole department bore the same distinctive curved line worn into the fabric from countless duty belts.

As Coop took a seat, several reached out to shake his right hand.

"Hey brother," said one.

"How ya doing?" asked another.

The word *brother* and the simple act of a handshake took off some of the edge. Outside of finding Sara, there wasn't anything they could have said that would have meant more.

After several seconds of silence, Coop's fellow officers went back to flipping wisecracks at each other in the ongoing banter between comrades. Those who were working doubles were downing coffee. Senior officer Trace cracked a joke that made everyone chuckle. His sense of humor had a way of lightening even the darkest days.

The scent of the coffee drew Coop's thoughts back to the coffee stand where Sara's boss had said, "Something is very wrong. Sara always comes early. No. This never happens."

Lost deep in thought, the chatter around the conference table drifted by him until everyone went silent.

He glanced up as the captain and the lieutenant marched in and everyone sat up straight.

The captain's terse greeting immediately segued into the matters at hand. He spoke in bullet-points. "Heads up," he said. "Fantasy Fest has us spread thin. Sheriff's office is helping out. Until you hear otherwise, everyone is working twelve-hour shifts."

Coop's fellow officers took the news without comment.

The captain nodded. "You all know about the fire. Call in if you see Gunner on the streets. We have a warrant out on him. ATF has stepped in to help with the arson investigation. The FBI office in D.C. called us about the bikers. Apparently, the Changós have become a rolling crimewave up and down the East Coast and have come here to lay low. The FBI has offered assistance."

He stopped and glanced at Coop. "As I'm sure you've heard, the fire last night injured a civilian and two of our officers. Vega is in rough shape. Beyond his burns, he has spinal damage. Apparently, a ceiling collapsed on him."

Coop stuck his bandaged fist under the table.

"We'll keep you apprised," said the captain.

Coop glanced up to find the captain staring down at him. "Coop, it's good to see you this morning."

"Thank you, sir."

The captain addressed everyone. "Do not approach these bikers without backup. They are armed and extremely dangerous."

The lieutenant reported on a shoplifting case and a domestic dispute at the same house they'd been called to many times before.

Coop's hopes of hearing about an effort to find Sara sank until the captain stood.

"Hear me clearly," said the captain. "I know you are stretched, but this is important. Coop's sister, Sara Cooper, is missing. Detective Rodgers has been assigned the case. I want you to go find this girl. Now." A photograph of Sara popped up on the overhead screen.

There were no words for the gratitude Coop felt. "Thank you, sir."

He chomped on his gum in an attempt to hold his emotions in check. Not knowing what had happened to her was the worst torture he could imagine.

The lieutenant sent a photo to everyone's phones. "While you're out on the streets, talk to people. Report to Rodgers and go find this girl."

Coop stood. "Thank you, sir."

The captain shook Coop's good hand. "You look like hell. Go home. We've got your back. We'll see you tomorrow."

"Thank you, sir," said Coop.

Coop left the briefing with no intention of going home.

OMINOUS HORIZON

BOWERS CALLED COOP, who picked up on the second ring. His voice sounded ragged.

"Coop," she said. "I found something you need to know about. While diving yesterday, I found a trench filled with bodies and bones offshore. It looks like a dumpsite."

Coop grunted as if she had punched the air out of his lungs. "Give me a minute."

"What's wrong?"

"Sounds like human trafficking," said Coop.

"I think so." She paused. "You all right?"

"Sara's missing."

"Jeez, Coop. I'm so sorry."

"Our briefing is just breaking up. Can I call you later?"

"Sure," said Bowers. She hung up and drove down Highway 1 with a white sack filled with croissants from the Old Town Bakery sitting in the passenger seat.

She looked forward to seeing Jay, but Coop sounded devastated. Knowing him, he'd turn the entire state upside down to find Sara.

The road snaked through a string of islands with names such as *Knockemdown*, *Ramrod*, and *Torch*. There had to be a story behind them.

The Spanish called Key West Cayo Hueso, meaning bone island. The irony wasn't funny.

Outside her car's windows, the landscape changed from towering palms and lush tropical vegetation to scruffy pines.

She'd always associated the Florida Keys with beaches and palm trees. She hadn't expected to see wooded areas.

Bowers spotted movement and slowed to a stop for a deer crossing the road. She marveled at its size. Never before had she seen adult deer only marginally larger than a big dog.

Five minutes later, she wound her way through Key Deer Boulevard and into a sparsely developed area where she found Jay's home.

Woods surrounded the one-story, gray stucco house with white trim. A new black Toyota Tundra sat in the circular drive.

She knocked at the door and smiled to herself. Not only had she spotted his surveillance cameras, the door was most certainly a high-security model. Bowers heard the deep growl of a large dog on the other side of the metal door. Jay had always loved dogs. Even back in the Army their bomb-sniffing K-9 had followed him everywhere.

"Lucas. Stand down," said a familiar voice that gave her butterflies. It had been so long since she'd seen him.

Moments later, locks clicked and the door cracked open. Jay sat before her in his wheelchair wearing a huge smile.

"Stryker! Welcome," he said.

Bowers handed him the sack of pastries. A rumble grew in the big German Shepherd's throat until Jay said, "Sit."

"Give me a sec," he said, as he shifted in his seat.

She watched in amazement as he rose to his feet with the help of a high-tech wheelchair fitted with a bracing mechanism.

He stood tall, but he was pale and thinner than she remembered. None of that mattered now.

They hugged each other. "Jeez, I've missed you," she said. "Look at you. This is amazing."

Luc wagged his tail and sniffed at the sack as Jay put a hand on her shoulder. "It gets better." He took a few stilted steps. "I'm not ready to go out dancing but living with this is getting easier."

"You drive that big truck out front?"

"I sure do." He beamed with pride. "Wait 'til you see how that baby is outfitted."

Bowers found herself laughing for the first time in a long while. Inside, his wheelchair skills were evident as he gave her a tour of his home.

The stunning polished oak flooring and woodwork, and signed photographs of NBA players were impressive.

Briefly, he showed her his office, which consisted of a massive wall of monitors and a vast array of computer equipment. "As you can probably tell, I work from home." That didn't surprise her. Riggs' comment that he was still active gave her a pretty good guess at what he did with all that high-tech, security equipment.

After passing through the kitchen to get some lemonade, they ended up in a living room that seemed an afterthought to a library where well-stocked bookshelves meant he still loved to read. One was filled with thrillers and biographies. The others held scientific journals, historical books on war, and technical manuals. Jay had always been wickedly smart and paid close attention to details. In the Army, his sergeant had often called him *the professor*.

Bowers sank into the soft maroon cushions of an overstuffed chair. Jay rolled up adjacent to her in his wheelchair with slanted wheels. It was clear that the beautifully finished interior, high-end electronics, and the brand-new customized truck meant Jay wasn't doing too badly.

After reminiscing about their time in the military, Jay hunched forward. "I heard you went to Metro PD in D.C."

Bowers smirked. "You heard or you did a little investigating?"

Jay's expression remained friendly, but his features were like a concrete wall. As an MP in Iraq, she'd ridden along as security with his convoys on missions to destroy caches of unexploded ordinances. As if it were a normal day at the office, he had destroyed bombs and fought beside her when under attack.

Bowers chuckled. "You do have skills, my friend."

Jay gave away no tells until he dropped the persona and allowed his eyes to hold a mischievous sparkle. "I might have done some looking around."

"You pain-in-the-ass," she said.

Jay's face lit up. "You're still badass. You've worked with the FBI and taken down some seriously evil dudes. I followed some of your cases."

Bowers enjoyed the novelty of feeling safe.

"Thanks," she said. "Looks like you're into more than web design."

He ignored her inquiry and scanned her bare arms. "Bowers, be straight with me." He gently lifted her hand to examine her defensive wounds. "Are you okay?"

She told him about the assault, Bo Somers, and her suspicions of human trafficking.

"Why didn't you come to me?" Jay's expression grew serious. "You could stay here. Luc wouldn't mind, would ya boy?"

The big brown and black dog wagged his tail.

"You've always had my back," she said.

Jay stretched. "You've done the same for me."

"It's what we do." She watched Luc roll on his back for a belly rub.

"You and Riggs still doing okay?"

"He wants to bring in the cavalry to rescue me, but his unit is up to its neck with some big cases."

"I expect Fowler and Hogan have something to do with that." Jay studied her reaction. "Did Riggs tell you they are planning to meet here in Key West, supposedly for a fishing trip?"

She nodded.

He leaned closer. "Bowers, Fowler doesn't fish. There's a bigger play about to go down."

"Like what?"

He stared at the floor with an expression she knew well. She figured he was deciding how much to reveal and how much to hold back.

"Come on, Jay. What's up?"

He took a deep breath. "I do computer security for sensitive industries. Several of my clients are communications companies under the parent organization, E-Connect."

Bowers stared into Jay's blue-gray eyes. "You know something."

"No shit!" he said. "Bowers, this deal with Sri Lanka is a fool's game. The company is small, outdated, and not up to the task. No way could they pull this off without major technical and financial backing. The deal makes no sense."

Bowers sipped her lemonade. "Who is backing them?"

Jay shrugged. "Indicators are it's North Korea, but that would be pretty ballsy with all the sanctions against them."

Bowers rubbed Luc's belly. "That's not happy news."

"Look at how they censor the internet in their country. They use it to spy on their own citizens. You think they wouldn't do that to us? Selling to them would put our entire communications system in jeopardy."

"That's what Riggs is worried about," she said.

Bowers thought of a frightening scenario. "Jay, what if we had an attack on the U.S., our power grid, or even a natural disaster and not coincidently lost our communication network at the same time?"

"That is a real threat," said Jay. "But if I'm right, there's even more at stake. This sale is about artificial intelligence and the weaponizing of computers."

Bowers reminded Jay about the daily attacks on the pentagon, major defense corporations, and technology industries and the hacking into water systems. "Even civilians are learning that online platforms are fraught with false or one-sided information distributed by those with political agendas, foreign forces, radical sects, and big business who want to sway public opinion. That's nothing new."

"This is," said Jay. "Washington doesn't grasp that our way of life is at stake. North Korea is itching for the power to hold their own against us, Russia, and neighboring China. They need a damned big stick to do it. Whoever gets it wins."

"What stick?"

"Think about it: E-Connect is on the edge of bankruptcy. They have no choice but to sell or go bust. Their biggest asset is a viable quantum chip. That's why there are so many vying for this deal."

Bowers bit at a hang nail. "All of this over a computer chip?"

"Yes, but not just any chip," said Jay. "This chip is the holy grail of AI. Google, Russia, UK, Germany, and China are in a cutthroat race to dominate artificial intelligence. It's all about who gets AI first. A viable quantum chip is the missing link and E-Connect has now put that jewel up for sale to the highest bidder."

Bowers felt uneasy. "How does one chip change the equation?"

"It would alter the global balance of power. Russia and China aren't going to stand for this sale, unless they are the recipient. I guarantee China will use all measures to ensure it doesn't fall into anyone's hands but their own."

Jay pulled a pad of paper from under the stack of computer magazines on the end table and began to scribble. "You know anything about quantum entanglement?"

"Some," she said. "Einstein called it 'spooky action at a distance' and didn't think it was real."

"Of course, he didn't. He understood the relationship between space and time. Quantum is different. Quantum mechanics proves that two particles can communicate almost instantaneously. If communication between two particles is hundreds of times faster than the speed of light, then hundreds or thousands or billions of bits of matter could work in unison, as if the space between them didn't exist. Harnessing that is a whole new kind of power."

Bowers set down her lemonade. "I get the fascination with this technology, but in real-world terms, what does that mean?"

Jay's brows went up. "What super computers can do in years or months can be done by quantum computers in a matter of minutes or seconds. It could make calculations that can't be done any other way."

Jay doodled on his notepad. "Quantum computers can easily unlock any code or encryption in a matter of seconds. That alone would make all passwords and security codes irrelevant. Top-Secret documents and proprietary technology would be jacked before anyone could stop it.

"From there, anything is possible. They could create genetically modified foods and pharmaceuticals or create plastics and water treatment additives that could kill, sicken, or disable an entire population or specifically go after one family, or even one person. The implications are staggering. China is already exploring how to use it to create new security systems."

Horrifying images ran through her thoughts.

Jay tapped his fingers on his notepad. "Developing a workable quantum chip with enough qubits that can operate above subzero temperatures, was the first step. Until E-Connect acquired it, no one had been able to do it.

Her mind raced through the implications.

Jay glanced up from his notepad. "If space can be manipulated like this, then potentially so could time. What if black holes are nothing more than collapsed space where quantum physics rules even time? The possibilities are mind-blowing."

"If we can control it," said Bowers.

Jay shrugged. "Even time travel could be possible."

She glanced at him as if he'd lost his mind. "Now that's over the top. Theory is one thing, but putting it into use is another."

"Then again," said Jay, pointing at his smart watch. "people once laughed at depictions of Dick Tracy talking to someone using a watch. What was once science fiction is now an everyday reality."

Jay adjusted his seat. "The biggest danger is that they could launch a cyber-attack that could use our computers against us to shut down our power grids, water supplies, transportation, and most importantly our communication—"

"So pharmaceutical companies," said Bowers, "could create and release genetically modified viruses to create a demand for their life saving but ridiculously overpriced drugs."

"Exactly," said Jay. "Pay or die."

"If they could use this chip to do all that," said Bowers, "what defenses would we or the rest of the world have against them?"

"Now you understand."

UNEASY ALLIANCE

DEEP IN THE BOWELS of the *Leisure Lee,* Bo Somers sucked down a Red Bull and shuffled over the grimy nonslip mat covering the narrow passageway. The activity onboard the ship had gone into high gear.

Each level on this stupid ship got progressively better or worse depending on whether he traveled above the main deck where the bigshots hung out or below deck where most of the crew and the girls were kept.

Next to him, two crewmen were busy packing supplies into the storage compartment as they prepared to depart for open waters. The fat one's trousers were slipping off his ass and giving everyone a show that no one wanted to see.

A ton of supplies had been loaded, including live lobsters imported from Maine. The crew would never get a bite of that. As usual, the good stuff was reserved for the VIPs coming aboard for their luxury fishing trip.

Assholes. They got everything. The luxury cabins, the fine foods, premium liquors, and fresh girls. Meanwhile he did all the work.

He watched Jung step out of the cabin where they kept the girls and zip up his fly. Jung swaggered away like he was somebody. That gave Bo one more reason to stay away from those girls. No telling what bugs that idiot carried.

A few minutes later, Jung and Scarface hustled down the passageway past Bo with their AK-47s.

Jung hesitated. "Better get your ass upstairs. Skipper wants a word." He stared at Bo with that smug smile.

Bo fantasized about grabbing the guy's assault rifle and bashing his head in with it. Taking his time to finish his Red Bull, Bo tossed his empty can into a trash bin and clomped up the starboard ladder.

On the main deck Bo found Jung, Scarface, and two deckhands in the mess where crewmen ate. The deckmen bolted for the door, leaving their chess game behind. Jung threw one of them against the wall and snarled.

As Bo sat next to the abandoned gameboard and waited for the go ahead, other crewmen poked their heads in and immediately left. Scarface snickered.

The crew mess had tables, an over-head TV, and a bookshelf in the back stocked with an assortment of books and games.

It wasn't as nice as the officer's dining room, but they had a microwave, sandwiches in a cooler, and often the chef would leave leftovers for the crew. This time three large cookies were left on a tray near the coffeepot. Jung snatched up all of them for himself.

What a pig.

Bo poured himself a cup of coffee and returned to his seat. He lit up a smoke and waited.

Two tables over, Scarface and another guard poked at their phones. They kept a close eye on each other. Security often hung out together, but it was an uneasy alliance. They were all crazy bastards, willing to do damn near anything—including violence.

Jung leaned against the wall next to the coffee station with his AK-47 over his shoulder. He set his coffee cup next to the empty tray and wolfed down the cookies.

I hope you choke on them, asshole.

The 3rd mate stuck his head into the room and signaled them to the forward cabin. On the way to the door, Bo dropped his cigarette into Jung's cup.

Jung glared at him.

Bo didn't give a crap. He wandered up the ladder and down the passageway to the forward cabin. The space gleamed like something out of a fancy magazine for millionaires. Despite its fine furnishings and warm lighting, Bo felt on edge.

He scanned the plush seating and took in the expansive view of the surrounding marina. The extravagant décor left no hint of the harsh realities below deck.

Preston sat on one of the white couches. The chief mate stood at attention.

Preston insisted on being surrounded by what he called "security." They were actually mercenaries. The crew feared them for good reason.

The 3rd mate, Dan Niko, was another douchebag whom Bo hated. He smirked as Niko sat down on one of the couches, stretched out his legs, and rested his dirty boots on the polished glass coffee table.

That won't fly.

When Preston glared at the man and then at his feet, Niko sheepishly returned to standing next to the chief mate.

All eyes were on Preston.

"I want your full attention," he said, as he paced before the crew. "We've finished fueling up and will be heading out to sea shortly. Make sure all staterooms are ready. Keep security tight. We'll stop at the usual spot to resupply."

As always, they would rendezvous off Cuba to pick up cigars and fresh girls. *Can't have bigshots going home with the clap.*

It also meant they had to clean out the used girls in the Hole.

Jung stood way too close. "Garbage boy," he hissed.

"Cocksucker," whispered Bo.

As he envisioned strapping Jung to the ship's anchor, Preston pointed at Bo. "Take care of the trash. We clear?"

Jung's smile widened.

AS BOWERS LEFT her meeting with Jay, the setting sun seemed like the dawn of a frightening new future.

Sunlight flickered through the trees, sending lacy gray shadows across the road. Reflecting on what she'd learned from Jay, Bowers wished such horrors were confined to fiction.

She stopped at the end of the driveway and sent Riggs a text: *Call me. Urgent.*

The time had come to rethink her next move.

She came to a stop at an intersection on Highway 1. Tugged in opposite directions, Bowers wanted to turn left and head for Riggs' office in Washington and yet, her car and belongings were back in Key West along with Lily, Coop, and a great many unanswered questions.

She couldn't put aside Lily and Coop's need for help or the open-mouthed skulls that seemed to plead for justice.

After talking with Jay, she now understood why Riggs had been so tied up.

Her fuel light came on. Bowers turned right toward Key West.

After pulling into a gas station, her phone buzzed with an incoming text from Coop: *I need your help.*

She called him back. "What's up?"

His voice sounded muffled and slurred. "I've been out all day, lookin' for Sara. I searched her apartment and talked with her friends and I went to all her favorite restaurants and stores and I walked the beach and went to the drug store where her roommate works." His husky voice quavered. "Bowers, I can't find her. What the hell am I supposed to do?"

She suspected Sara was in deep trouble.

"Where are you?" she asked Coop.

He gave her his address. GPS showed he was only a mile from her. "I'll be right there."

While filling her tank, Bowers scrolled through her phone for the local news.

What the hell? Her eyes landed on a story about Officer Vega rescuing Deon from a fire. The last time she saw Vega, he was about to punch Deon's lights out.

As she scrolled down, a picture came into view of Coop walking away from a burning house with a dog in his arms. Bowers grimaced at the tiny screen. She hated fire. Her little brother had been burned in a cooking accident when they were kids.

She scrolled down to a report on Coop's missing sister where the PD's public information officer asked for the public's help. He didn't say it, but his tone and careful wording told her they too suspected foul play.

A few minutes later, she parked in front of a modest beach house with a swing set in the yard. A wreath of seashells hung on the front door. She knocked. No one answered.

A teddy bear lay on the porch swing. A pair of women's flip-flops sat next to the doormat. A beach towel draped over the railing fluttered in the breeze.

Bowers went around the back and found Coop sitting on the steps, staring at the sea in a tattered plaid shirt and ragged cutoffs.

The empty beer cans in the flowerbed next to him explained why his speech had been impaired.

"Coop? You all right?" she asked.

He pointed to a white plastic chair. "Pull up a seat."

Coop gazed at her from under heavy lids. All the fight had been knocked out of him.

She noted his burns and that he didn't complain about them.

"The last two days," he said, "have been pure hell."

"Did I hear right? Vega rescued Deon? How the hell did that happen?"

Coop rubbed his neck. "I told you he had a good side. That damned blockhead really thought Deon was faking it. Makes me sick that it took a fire for him to realize he was wrong. He's paying for it now. He's in the hospital." Coop shook his head. "The pain must be unbearable. I'll never forget the smell and seein' him burned like that. The soles of his shoes were melted."

"What started the blaze?"

"If you mean who, it was Gunner." Coop gave her the short version of the exchange at the bar and Gunner being thrown out. "I rolled up just as he pitched an incendiary at the house. That animal needs to be in a cage where he belongs."

Coop started to take another sip of beer and stopped. He tossed the can aside as if it repulsed him. It landed in the flowerbed where the contents dribbled into the mulch.

The crickets chirped, as Bowers watched dusk turn the beach into a mural of oranges, golds, and reds. "I'm worried about Sara."

"Me too. That's why I called you." Coop reached out and gripped her hand. She couldn't help feeling for the guy.

Coop let go. "When we called Metro P.D., the chief said you were one of the finest investigators he'd ever met."

"Chief's a good man, but it's like football, it takes the whole team."

Coop stared at the ground as if the world had gone sideways.

"Bowers, I need to make a change," he said, staring at his empty hands. "With my job being what it is, I tell my family I love them every time I leave the house just in case. But my wife is pissed off at me all the time. I don't want her to leave."

It pained her to see a man tough as Coop, battling to hold his emotions in check.

His eyes reddened. His words caught in his throat when he told her about his little girl saying she liked her old daddy better. "I can't lose my little girl."

He swiped the cuff of his shirt over his face. "I can deal with busted knuckles and an idiot shootin' at me. But my little girl..." His voice failed him.

After a long silence, Coop began to ramble. She listened until he had nothing left to say.

"Come on, Coop. Get some rest. Let's talk more about this tomorrow."

"Yeah, okay," he said. She helped him to his feet and into the house.

Inside, the rooms were quiet. No TV or washing machine. No kids playing. No one cooking in the kitchen. She hoped his wife and daughter would return soon. He needed them.

When they entered his bedroom, Coop stumbled. Bowers kept him from falling and guided him to the edge of the bed. After taking a seat, his head nodded forward and pressed against her chest. She felt his hands on her waist and hip and promptly removed them and stepped back.

Coop grunted and flopped on the bed, landing on his side. He pointed to a photo of Sara on the nightstand. "Take it."

One of his sandy flip-flops fell to the floor.

She hoped he was too drunk to remember any of this in the morning.

As she tossed a blanket over him, he gripped her hand. "I'm not afraid of dying. But nothing scares me more than losing everything I care about. Please help me find Sara."

GRIM DISCOVERY

P ARKED NEAR THE COFFEE STAND, Bowers rolled down
her car window. She squinted at the last pink clouds as the sun
slipped below the horizon. Someone played a harmonica. Compared to
what she'd learned, the peaceful scene seemed a fragile deception.

Coop's photo of Sara sat in the seat next to her. The image showed
her wearing a sweet smile and the bracelet Coop had given her.

Bowers found Sara's Facebook page, but none of her posts indicated where she'd gone or with whom.

Coop's comment about losing everything resonated with Bowers
and made the insights she'd learned from Jay hit even harder.

The world had already come too close to nuclear destruction. She
prayed the sale of this chip would never happen. Such incredible
discoveries held so much promise for good and yet there were always
those with a lust for power who would subvert them to destroy others.
What else would humans create in the future that would further their
own demise?

The burden of this threat and not being able to do anything about
it brought back memories of being trapped in a building after a
bombing in Ramadi while her unit fought a desperate battle against
insurgents.

While waiting for Riggs's call, she approached the plaza. Without Sara smiling through the customer window, the coffee stand seemed a shadow of its former self.

As a homicide detective, she knew that people who walked away after an argument were eventually found once tempers settled. The ones who simply vanished for no apparent reason were usually found dead.

Bowers lined up at the stand's window, hoping the lull before dinner would allow her a few moments to speak with the man behind the counter.

When he handed her the coffee, she said, "Sir, I need to speak with you."

He stepped outside for a smoke while an older woman took charge of the window.

Bowers held up her cup. "Good coffee."

He smiled and nodded graciously. "*Gracias*. Thank you." The tip of his cigarette glowed bright red as he sucked in. A few seconds later, he blew out the harsh smoke.

"Sorry," he said as he dropped his cigarette and ground it into the pavement with the heel of his leather boot. "My wife say this habit is dirty."

"*Señor*. Is that your wife helping you?"

"*Si, señorita.*"

Bowers soon discovered his name was Santiago and he liked to talk.

The man, who now had to be in his late seventies, and his wife had immigrated from Cuba when they were newly married. That had been decades ago. He told Bowers all about the Cuban Missile Crisis.

"I wanted to raise a family and make a good life for my childrens." His trembling hand gripped a crumpled napkin. "Sara is like one of my own. I look after her."

Santiago appeared deeply worried as he swiped the napkin across his forehead. "I worry for her because she was seeing a boy, but she wouldn't bring him around to meet me."

He winked. "When a girl hides a boy, something is wrong. He is no good for her."

"Do you remember his name?" asked Bowers.

"No," said Santiago, "I see this man one time. He far. Long way. Down there." He pointed to the far end of the parking lot across the street.

His account of a tall man with brown hair was better than nothing, but it didn't give her much to work with. The description fit a large percentage of the men in the plaza in front of her.

After Santiago went back to work, Bowers stood at the edge of the crowd, studying the people on the street.

At the sound of movement behind her, Bowers whirled around to find Lily standing there. As if equally startled, Lily's eyes grew wide.

"Sorry," she said, "I didn't mean to scare nobody." Lily stared at the ground as if upset.

"No problem," said Bowers. "Are you all right?"

Lily nodded. "But I don't think the nice lady at the coffee stand is okay."

"You mean Sara?" asked Bowers.

"Yes'um." Lily appeared to be genuinely worried. "She was nice to me. You've been good to me too."

"Thank you for the article. It was about your sister, right?"

Lily nodded.

"I also got the coffee."

Lily smiled. "Was it good?"

"It was excellent. Thank you," said Bowers.

Lily beamed. "I wanted to say thank you."

"What did you mean by Sara not being okay?"

"I found this on the docks." Lily dug in her pocket and pulled out a silver bracelet, which she dropped into Bowers' palm.

The three tiny sea-turtle charms were covered in blood spatter.

UNDER THE DARKENING SKY, Bowers stared at Sara's bracelet and felt a knot in her gut. She took a slow deep breath. "Lily, can I get you a cup of coffee?"

Lily shook her head. "Thank you, but I didn't save that bracelet to git somethun for it. I just wanna help her, like she did me."

Bowers shrugged. "Maybe we could work together?"

Lily played with the hem of her shirt as she scanned the people around them.

"If we find Sara," said Bowers, "maybe we can find the others."

Bowers noticed something missing. Lily didn't smell of alcohol, but her hands trembled. "I want to help, but what can I do?"

"I need you to walk down the dock, stop where you found the bracelet, and act like you're tying your shoelaces. Then just walk away. Can you do that?"

"Yeah," said Lily, "like real smooth, too."

Once they reached the docks, Bowers settled into the shadows under a large royal poinciana tree. As people migrated toward the nearby restaurant, Bowers watched Lily shuffle down the wooden dock where boats gently rocked in their slips. The wind picked up and the rigging of a sailboat clanked against the mast.

Lily was no actor. However, the way she couldn't resist being distracted provided perfect cover.

As she meandered around the dock, she stopped to dig through trash bins. After pocketing whatever she found of value, she hesitated in front of an old Boston Whaler. After a few awkward seconds, Lily knelt down and fumbled with her shoelaces.

Bowers recognized the boat with a dive flag as Bo's.

She expected Lily to make a beeline for her, instead the woman surprised her. Lily continued to casually wander up and down the dock while perusing anything that appeared to be discarded.

Bowers found it interesting that Lily never stole anything. She only took what others deemed trash.

To avoid suspicion and blend in, Bowers moved into the crowd. A few minutes later, Lily came closer and stood about four feet away while inspecting a stack of discarded plastic buckets.

"Did I do okay?" she asked in a low, raspy voice.

"You did awesome," said Bowers as she dropped a twenty-dollar bill into one of the buckets. "Thank you."

Lily returned the bill and proudly wandered away with the bucket and a pleased grin.

Bowers chuckled. *Good for you.*

She knew better than to head straight for the boat. Instead, Bowers appeared to study posted restaurant menus and listened to a man playing a saxophone. All the while, she remained acutely aware of everyone around her.

One-hundred feet away at the end of the pier, lights on the *Leisure Lee* illuminated the action onboard where deckhands checked lines, polished rails, and made ready for something or someone.

As twilight dissolved to a black sky, Bowers strolled ahead as if she belonged there.

The boat with the dive flag rocked in the gentle swells. A well-worn wetsuit hung on a hook just outside the cabin. At the stern, a pair of flippers and two air tanks were locked and stowed under a bench along the starboard side. It appeared the owner lived onboard.

A few steps later, she passed a Hinkley cabin cruiser with the name *Off Grid* in a slip next to the gray skiff Bo had driven.

On the other side of the dock, a man scrubbed down his fishing boat with a long-handled brush. Except for the restaurant's customers and a handful of boaters, the crowds were modest.

With all her senses on alert, she drew closer to the boat. The windows were dark. Bowers spotted a brush on the stern.

She pulled her hair up under her ballcap, slipped on gloves from her vest pocket, and grabbed one of the five-gallon buckets that had caught Lily's attention. A few seconds later, Bowers stepped onto the fishing boat as if she owned it.

With the brush, she leaned over the gunnel and mimicked cleaning the hull. No one came running or demanded to know why she was onboard.

So far, so good.

As the stars came out, Bowers put down the brush and pulled a small kit out of the lining of her pocket. She jimmied the lock as quickly as possible and disappeared inside the cabin, hoping she hadn't been noticed.

Once inside, she took a few steps down into a messy galley and living space.

She clicked on her penlight. Toward the bow lay a berth for sleeping. A pillow and a rumpled blanket lay in a heap on a stained mattress.

Crushed beer cans and trash were strewn everywhere. Dirty bowls and spoons sat on the counter next to an empty soup can.

Bowers wondered how anyone could live like this. A clear plastic envelope taped to the wall held the boat's registration and other documents. With her phone, she took a photo of the official-looking papers that confirmed the boat belonged to Bo Somers.

In a storage closet, Bowers found clothing, including the dark-blue shirt Bo had worn when he'd attacked her on the beach. Spattered over the chest were stains that were probably her blood.

She snapped more pictures.

At the sound of laughter, Bowers clicked off her light. She crept toward the cabin door and heard a couple talking. They'd stopped on the dock next to the boat.

She peered between a slit in the window curtain. They had their hands all over each other. With the couple too preoccupied to notice, Bowers quietly locked the door.

After the couple left, Bowers clicked on her penlight and continued to examine the cabin. On a bench seat, she spotted a large duffle bag. With gloved hands, she examined the contents and found clothing and a brown package wrapped in cellophane that gave off the vinegary odor of heroin. Considering it was commonly mixed with fentanyl, she didn't dare take a closer sniff. Two or three grains of that could kill a person. She left the package in clear view on top of the duffle bag.

In the berth she found an orange life jacket in the corner and a woman's sandal wedged between the wall and the mattress.

Bowers pulled a metal box from a bin above the bed. After snapping open the lid, she dumped the contents on the mattress. A collection of jewelry, wallets, credit cards, panties, and a cellphone tumbled into a heap.

The trophies confirmed her suspicions.

Dried blood coated many of the items and the top of the metal box held two bloody fingerprints. The horrendous torture these women had suffered rocked her.

The hair rose on her arms when she spotted Sara Cooper's drivers' license.

IN PLAIN SIGHT

HENRY LOVED WALKING the docks at night. Sometimes it was peaceful, other times people did things they thought no one would see.

Buddy's tail wagged. He relished every opportunity to take in new sniffs. He would happily roll in dead crabs and pelican poop if Henry would've let him.

It wasn't uncommon to see drunks who couldn't help instigating a brawl. Henry suspected it was too early in the evening for much of that. And yet, up ahead near the entrance to the docks, the strobes from a patrol car were hard to miss.

At the open-air bar, he and Buddy passed two officers who had detained four college-age kids. The young hellraisers sat on the floor in a line with their hands secured behind their backs.

No doubt, the cops had broken up another fight.

"Amateurs," snorted Henry. "Buddy, trouble happens every time booze and emotions git all tangled up together."

When he and his dog reached the docks, it didn't surprise him to see the *Leisure Lee* preparing to leave, but the gunmen onboard caught his attention. Henry watched as one of them chased down a young woman in a skimpy outfit running toward the gangway. The way he manhandled her back inside left little doubt as to what they were up to.

As his heels scuffed over the rough wooden boards of the dock, three boats caught his interest: the Hinkley, Bo Somers' Boston Whaler, and the messed-up gray skiff. *This jerk couldn't take care of a tennis ball, much less a boat.*

As Buddy stopped to sniff at the base of a pole lamp, a soft glow shining through the cabin window of Bo's boat caught Henry's attention, especially when it moved.

Henry edged in for a closer look. When he stopped fifteen feet from the boat, the light went out.

This Bo fella was overdue to snag his tender parts in a ringer for all he'd done. It now appeared to Henry that someone had an interest in making that happen sooner rather than later.

Buddy tugged again on his leash. His paws scraped against the weathered wood in the direction of his favorite trashcan. "Nothin' like a good whiff of fish guts. Huh, Buddy?"

While Buddy's nose homed in on a dried-up strip of fish skin, Henry spotted Bo on the *Leisure Lee* arguing with a man Henry recognized as Jung Ji-hoon.

That snagged Henry's attention. He couldn't help wondering if Bo knew that the twenty-six-year-old Korean was a paid assassin.

Henry glanced back at Bo's boat. Whoever was onboard was in for a rude awakening, if he didn't high-tail it out of there—like now.

When Bo began to disembark from the super-yacht, Henry stood back to watch the show unfold. "Didn't know we'd get some entertainment tonight, did ya Buddy?"

Henry's chin dropped when Bowers stepped out of the cabin. She glanced toward the *Leisure Lee* and quickly back to the cops' bright lights down by the restaurant.

She jumped off the boat and crouched low on the dock next to the slip. Faster than Buddy could spot a cat, she pulled out a pistol and fired two double-taps into the water. Henry's brows went up. *Damn.*

Folks on the docks reacted with cheers and screaming, while she quickly buried the pistol under her shirt.

That was smart.

The bystanders did what people always do when confronted by gunfire. Most thought it was firecrackers and looked toward the sky. Some ducked and hurried away. Others gathered to watch.

As Bo sprinted toward his boat, Bowers played it smart. She screamed for help and hunkered down and covered her head as if she were as startled as everyone else.

"Buddy, that is one sharp lady," said Henry.

A knot of bystanders quickly assembled around him.

Henry hollered at Bowers, "Hey lady, you okay?"

He hustled forward with Buddy tagging along. A middle-aged man joined him. Together they escorted Bowers to the group of bystanders.

"Are you all right?" asked the middle-aged man.

"What was that?" she asked. Bowers stared past Henry without a hint of recognition.

He admired that kind of skill.

Henry held back a grin and said, "I reckon somebody lit off some firecrackers, ma'am. They do it every year at this time."

In less than a hot minute, cops from the bar came running toward them. In the opposite direction, Bo sprinted toward the ruckus. When he spotted the police, he did an about-face and wasted no time hot-footing it to the Hinkley.

A young man in camo pants pointed to Bo's boat and told officers, "Someone in that boat fired shots."

The tall officer asked, "Did you see what he looked like?"

"Nope. It was too dark. But I think he was probably six feet."

Bowers didn't even blink.

One of the officers set up a perimeter around the boat and directed everyone back.

Henry sunk behind the huddle of bystanders with Bowers at his side.

There's nothing better than gunfire to draw cops. If her intent had been to get them to search Bo's boat, she must have found something worth seeing. After watching Bo meet up with Gunner at Garrison Bight, Henry had a few thoughts on what she might have found.

Henry snorted. "Yup. Yup." Bo was in for a bad night.

His suspicions were confirmed when another officer arrived with a K-9, which usually meant a drug search.

Leaning closer to Bowers, Henry whispered, "Keep yur head down."

She appeared surprised when he draped his jacket over her shoulders and traded hats with her. The officers boarded the vessel with the K-9 and bright flashlights. As they searched the cabin, Bowers nodded at Henry and casually wandered away.

She entered the open-air bar and left his hat and jacket on a coat hook near the door, then vanished into the crowd.

BOMB SHELL

AT 8:00 P.M. RIGGS OPENED his office door to go home and found himself eye to eye with McDougall's scowling black eyebrows and Greg's pale face.

"Both of you," barked McDougall. "Conference room. Now. Let's go." The unflappable Patrick McDougall was in a knot over something.

Riggs stuffed his phone into his pocket and grabbed a notepad.

So much for going home.

McDougall marched away as quickly as he'd come.

On the way to the conference room, Riggs whispered to Greg, "What's this about?"

"You tell me." Greg shrugged. "Must be something important for him to pull us both in."

Once they entered the room, McDougall slumped into a chair. "You better sit down for this one."

Miller, a special agent from the FBI's Behavioral Analysis Unit, joined them at the table.

McDougall nodded to a woman wearing a dark suit and an expression set in concrete, a dead giveaway she was Secret Service.

As they took a seat, Riggs pulled out a notepad. "What have we got?"

McDougall peered over the top of his glasses at Riggs and rolled a No. 2 pencil between his fingers. "She is here to see you."

"Kory," the woman said, "tells me you have an uncanny ability to find missing teenagers."

"Okay," said Riggs, puzzled by all this dramatic posturing. "Is someone gonna tell me what's up or are we playing twenty questions?"

The agent appeared stressed. "Kory and our forward team are in Miami with POTUS. There's been a development."

She sat back in her chair. "The president's daughter and her friend are missing."

The ensuing silence made it feel as if the air had been sucked out of the room.

THE TICKING OF THE CLOCK was lost on no one. By 11:00 p.m. Roadrunner had been missing for five hours.

Riggs and Greg were already on their third cup of coffee. They had temporarily taken over a cluster of rooms at HQ to begin the enormous job of setting up the logistics required to organize a functional task force and a vigorous search.

The main room bustled with activity as the number of FBI agents and support staff grew by the minute. The tech crew had turned the vacant rooms into a hub for computers, phones, incoming news feeds, and secured space for meetings.

With a stone-faced scowl, McDougall intercepted higher ups, stopping in to hear the latest update.

Riggs and Greg had been on the phone for the last two hours making initial contacts with everyone from the field office in Miami and the resident office in Key West, to the Federal Marshalls and the Monroe County Sheriff's office.

Calling various agencies and rousting them into action this late wasn't the most pleasant task, but their grumbling stopped the instant they understood Roadrunner was missing.

Riggs sorted through pictures of the girls. Lauren grinned at the camera with a raucous head of light blonde curls. In his opinion, a glint in her expression exuded a little too much confidence. Molly's glasses, long brown hair, and cleft chin gave her a shy, studious vibe.

Riggs watched the huddle of Secret Service agents quietly conferring near the far corner. He expected they would take the lead. Things sometimes got interesting when agencies that were used to being in-charge were forced to work together.

Riggs sat next to Greg at a long white table. He waved over two Secret Service Agents and Miller, the Bureau's profiler from the BAU.

The female Secret Service agent took charge, making it clear that she was the senior agent. Riggs' focus remained solely on finding Lauren as quickly as possible and wasn't there to babysit anyone's ego. He cut to the chase. "Lauren has done this before. How long is she usually missing?"

"Two or three hours." The senior agent never flinched at his question, but her brown eyes studied him. "Longest she's ever been gone is four hours."

"What happened when you called her?" he asked.

"At first, both girls' phones went straight to voicemail, then they stopped pinging off cell towers."

That wasn't good.

"We have three scenarios," said Miller. "The girls ran away, a nut job grabbed them, or we have a terrorist on our hands."

Riggs routinely worked with the BAU and appreciated their analysis, particularly Miller's. Her welcoming smile and petite stature gave no hint she was an expert on analyzing the worst in criminal behavior.

"Miller," he said. "In D.C., I can see Lauren ditching her guard for a party with her buddies, but I can't see her running away in a strange city where she doesn't know anyone."

"I agree," said the senior agent. "A terrorist doesn't make much sense either."

Greg ran a hand through his black hair and stared at his notepad. "Her value as a target would be problematic. Any ransom demand would put so much heat on them, it wouldn't be worth the risks unless the intent was to strike back at the president. In that case, they wouldn't be after a ransom."

Everyone at the table knew what that meant.

A young agent with red hair crossed his arms and listened intently.

Riggs dropped his pen. "Greg is right. International terrorists know our surge capabilities would quickly overwhelm them. The fallout would buy them a shit-storm of grief."

"Even the domestic cells," said Greg, "like the hellraisers in Talla-hassee or the sovereign citizen groups in Alabama, are smart enough to know that much."

The young agent locked eyes with Riggs. "I understand you've been working a case involving the abduction of girls her age."

"I have, but I don't see any connection."

"What do you think happened?" he asked.

Riggs clicked his pen. "I think Lauren and Molly wandered off with the intent of exploring the waterfront or talking to a cute guy. It could be that a nut job stumbled across them, took advantage of two young girls, and is too stupid to know what kind of trouble he has gotten himself into."

Greg nodded. "That fits."

"Our best shot," said Riggs, "is to understand how Lauren and Molly think. What do they like to do? What are their favorite foods? Do they know anyone in the area?"

"Good plan," said the young agent. "We need to think like a teen. Look at malls or other attractions in the area that would draw girls this age. They'd like arcades, carnivals, hip clothing, and concerts with rap or boy bands."

"I know Lauren," said the senior agent, "she would be the one making the decisions."

"What is Lauren into?" asked Riggs. "Does she like the beach? Funnel cakes? Pet shops? Where would she likely hang out?"

"She loves ice cream," said the senior agent. "Kory reports that the staff keeps an extra gallon of it on hand just for her."

Riggs made a note. "What kind?"

"Rocky Road."

"One more thing," said the young agent. "Lauren has a credit card. She uses it a lot."

Greg caught Riggs' attention and nodded toward the doorway.

McDougall flicked his fingers, motioning them to step out into the hall.

Outside, McDougall's black brows drew into a ferocious frown as he stared at Greg. "I can give you Riggs to set up things, but he still works for me. We have several important cases that I can't let slide." McDougall's bulging eyeballs made it clear this wasn't a request.

13 HOURS MISSING

A T 6:45 A.M. RIGGS SPLASHED water on his face in the men's room. Watching in the mirror, he rolled up the frayed cuffs of his favorite blue shirt and remembered Bowers borrowing it. The memory of her long lean body in his shirt had woken him up faster than an espresso.

Damn I miss that woman.

With the breakroom's coffeepot empty and running on three hours sleep, Riggs hoped the rest of the day would cut him some slack. He returned with his empty cup and entered the Task Force Room and took a seat.

The young agent eyed Riggs empty cup. "Still no coffee? After putting up with these uncomfortable chairs and folding tables, the least they could do is have coffee available."

Riggs had never worried about the décor. When facing off with a terrorist bent on destruction, he'd rather have his top-of-the-line FBI gear and a fierce sub-machine gun than a pretty desk.

He quickly scanned the intel that had come in over the last few hours. It appeared that they were closing in on Lauren's location. As the young agent predicted, she had used her credit card at an arcade.

As Riggs worked the case, he wished Bowers could come to Miami to help. She was like a human bloodhound.

The last time they'd worked a big case together, she'd tracked down the killer. She and Riggs had both been shot. Riggs rubbed a hand over his thigh. Under his shirt and the gray fabric of his tactical pants lay scars that would forever remind him of that day. The wounds still ached. Hers probably did too.

Riggs owed his life to Bowers. One way or another, he would find his way to Key West, even if it meant butting heads with McDougall. Maybe Lauren's case would get him at least as far as Miami.

The tapping of fingers on keyboards and the low cadence of conversations continued even as shifts changed.

The task force now included Kory and the other FBI and Secret Service agents already in Miami, thirty or so staff members and agents in D.C., and another five agencies, including the PD in Downtown Miami.

They had the manpower. The trick now would be finding a large enough space on the fly for them to work together.

A map of Southern Florida and an enlargement of the Miami area were taped to a whiteboard, along with a timeline. Stacks of files and photographs were lined up on the table in front of him. Despite knowing teenagers inevitably left a digital footprint everywhere they went, he knew this wouldn't be that simple.

He studied the photos of Lauren and couldn't help thinking about Grace, the girl with the ponytail, who had been discarded in the woods. It bothered him that the ink on his palm where he'd written her name had begun to fade. Whether their parents were presidents or paupers, the lives of all these girls mattered.

As Riggs added *Lauren* and *Bowers* to his palm and re-inked *Grace*, Greg entered and slid a steaming cup of black coffee in front of Riggs.

"You're a true friend," said Riggs.

"You're welcome. Still no word on Lauren?"

Riggs shook his head. "It's been fourteen hours."

"That sucks." Greg yawned. "I'm stretched way too thin."

"Aren't we all," said Riggs as he gingerly sipped at the hot coffee. "We're in the deep end of the pool."

Greg rubbed his temples. "It feels more like the middle of the Atlantic. This bid for E-Connect is at a critical point and here we are chasing our tails over POTUS' rebellious teenager."

He appeared frustrated. "Who's handling the press? They're already going nuts on this one."

"Allan is on it," said Riggs. "He's a master at using the media and hopefully preventing this from spinning into a circus."

Greg yawned. "If you think this sucks, wait until the bogus leads start rolling in from every goofball out there."

He glanced across the room at the two Secret Service agents and lowered his voice. "Riggs, I've got something. Remember that little Sri Lankan company?"

"Yeah," said Riggs.

"It's owned by a conglomerate whose CEO is a North Korean businessman in tight with their supreme leader. SriCom is funded by and under the control of North Korea."

Riggs set down his coffee. "What the hell is Fowler thinking? Even for him, this is a new low."

Greg stared across the room. "We're still missing something. What is it?"

HAMMERED

BOWER'S PHONE BUZZED with a message from Coop: *Need to C U NOW. Higgs Beach.*

That sounded urgent.

She responded: *Be there in 7.*

Bowers typed the location into her phone's GPS.

After seeing how shattered Coop had been yesterday, she dreaded dropping more bad news about finding Sara's bracelet and drivers' license. At least, he'd be hearing it from her rather than seeing it on the News.

Bowers merged into traffic and rolled down the window to let the rushing air engulf her. Judging by the squawk of seagulls, the beach couldn't be far. Moments later, she pulled into a parking area just off Atlantic and stopped behind Coop's unit.

His patrol car sat at the curb. Its scraped fender and dented rear bumper meant Coop had drawn the short stick when it came to car assignments.

On the beach near a clump of palms, young men played volleyball. A couple strolled past Coop, who sat on a wooden picnic table with his feet on the bench. He quietly watched a man toss a green Frisbee into the surf for his barking black lab.

Coop's clean-scrubbed appearance and fresh uniform stood in stark contrast to the rumpled civilian clothes he'd worn yesterday.

The enticing aroma of tomatoes and garlic from a nearby Italian restaurant made her stomach grumble. She considered suggesting that they grab lunch, but his dark expression made it clear Coop had other matters on his mind.

Bowers took a seat next to him. The tabletop bore the usual adolescent carvings and scribbles.

Coop knocked sand off his polished boots and stared at the blue-green sea and postcard-perfect palms.

She waited.

The muscles of his jaw pumped as he chomped on his gum. "I heard about an incident on the docks last night."

Bowers blinked.

Coop sipped from a Yeti cup sporting a Key West PD patch. "Our K-9 found heroin on Bo's boat. He also found some oxycodone and several large wads of cash."

"What about the stained navy-blue shirt?"

He hesitated. "The lab has it."

"Good," said Bowers. "That's the shirt he wore when he attacked me. They should be able to match the blood to the DNA sample I gave them."

Coop cocked his head and frowned.

"The PD impounded the boat," he said, "but they won't tell me what else they found until they are finished processing it. Word is they responded because shots were fired."

His big shoulders rotated slightly toward her, but he kept his eyes on the young men playing volleyball. "They heard the shots," he said. "It's kind of weird that they didn't find any bullet holes or casings."

Bowers knew Coop would frown on firing a weapon within city limits, but he deserved a straight answer.

"They're in the water."

"How... Wait." He stared at her. "You fired the shots?"

Bowers drew a deep breath. "It was the only way to ensure the officers at the end of the pier would respond before the evidence disappeared."

He rubbed his neck as if exasperated.

"Coop," she said, "They needed probable cause. I gave it to them."

His blue eyes locked on her. "You were on his boat?"

She watched a man jog by and said nothing.

"Shit." He adjusted his duty belt. "You could have called me."

"You were out of commission."

"You mean drunk on my ass." He scrubbed a hand over his face. "I haven't been that hammered in years. Hope I didn't say anything stupid."

"Give yourself a break," she said. "You're not a robot." Bowers remembered when Riggs had poured shots for her after a brutal day on the job. "We've all been there."

"What else did you find?"

Bowers watched the man playing with his dog. "You sure you want to know?"

Coop's expression left no doubt.

She pulled the bracelet from her pocket and dropped it into the palm of his big, calloused hand. "I'm sorry, Coop. I know this stinks."

He frowned at the tiny silver sea turtles. The second he spotted the spatters of red, his jaw set and his fist tightened into such a hard knot that his knuckles blanched.

Coop slumped forward. He glared at the sand with an expression that tore her up.

"Coop, don't go there. Don't read into this until we know the facts. The bracelet's broken clasp tells me she fought back, vigorously."

Coop opened his hand and stared at the bracelet that appeared small in his big palm. "What else did you find?"

Bowers knew this question would come. "Her drivers' license."

He grimaced as if he'd been gut-punched. His expression seemed like a man trying to pull himself back from the edge. "Gunner threatened my family. I wonder if he had a hand in this."

"I left her license there," she said, "along with everything else for the PD to find. Besides, it was better that they found it, undisturbed."

After a long pause he frowned. "Then why did you take the bracelet?"

"I didn't," she said. "Lily found it on the dock in front of Bo's boat and gave it to me. It wasn't hard to figure out the rest."

"She didn't hawk it?" asked Coop. "She could have traded it in at the nearest pawnshop."

"Nope," said Bowers. "Lord knows she could've used the money. Instead, she said Sara had been nice to her and wanted to help her."

His eyes reddened. "There's more to Lily than most realize. Did you know she can sing? I heard her once. She was at the beach, mumbling to the sea, then out of nowhere she belted out this song. Her voice had that rasp. Reminded me of Steven Tyler or Janice..."

"Joplin?"

"Yeah. My mom liked Janice. Makes me wonder how Lily's life would've been if things had taken a different path."

His voice spoke of Lily and his mom, but his eyes remained focused on Sara's bracelet.

Coop picked up his cup and shook it. The ice inside rattled. "I'm empty."

She glanced over at the restaurant. "I'll get us something to drink. Stay put. I'll be right back."

Bowers hoped the break would give him a moment to pull his emotions together.

As she emerged from the noisy restaurant with two to-go cups, the rumble of motorcycle engines filled the air.

A man across the street ran for his car.

Something felt off.

She scanned the beach. Coop and his unit were gone. "Where the hell are you, Coop?"

His overturned Yeti cup lay on the table.

Oh, shit. "This is bad."

A dozen bikers roared past. Something had gone wrong.

Bowers dropped the cups and ran.

LEFT IN THE SAND

BOWERS SPRINTED ACROSS THE STREET and dodged two motorcycles zipping past. The beach had been vacated. The green Frisbee had been left in the sand.

She stared at Coop's Yeti. Her pulse began to pound. He wouldn't have forgotten that. Even worse, she found Coop's .40-cal Glock under the table. She felt a combination of dread and rage as she picked up his service pistol.

Bowers smelled the barrel. It had been fired recently. She tucked it under her waistband.

Cars honked as she raced into the street.

A few blocks away, she spotted Coop's mangled rear bumper as the unit turned right. The person at the wheel was too short to be Coop.

Worse, a band of bikers were in escort. They'd taken Coop.

Bowers' jaw set. Her focus hardened. Even if Coop were alive, that wouldn't last long. There was no time for emotion, only action. Career criminals like the Changós didn't highjack a police vehicle and a cop for noble purposes.

This only meant they were moving to a secluded spot to work their mayhem.

As Bowers grasped her car's door handle, a man on a motorcycle hesitated on the asphalt twenty-five feet away.

She and the biker locked eyes. With his eyebrows shaved off and a skull tattooed on his face, he appeared ominous.

He revved his engine and roared directly at her.

Bowers leapt out of the way and rolled over the warm hood of her car, landing near the front bumper.

The biker turned to come at her again. The diamond-shaped, yellow 1% patch on his vest told her all she needed to know.

When a patrol car coming up the street screeched to a stop, the skull-faced biker rolled his motorcycle behind a black SUV. He glared at the black-and-white cruiser where Officer Nolan sat behind the wheel.

The jittery biker tweaked as if he were on meth. This could go sideways in a hurry.

Bowers slipped Coop's Glock out of her waistband and took cover behind the engine block of her silver sedan.

Nolan opened his door with his weapon drawn. "Turn off your bike and show me your hands."

The biker reached for the cowboy-style revolver on his hip.

"Don't do it," shouted Bowers. She aimed for center mass.

"Drop it," ordered Nolan. "Don't make me—"

Two more units rolled in with sirens blaring.

That amped up the biker who appeared even more agitated.

"Put down your weapon," yelled the officers.

The biker ignored them.

As orders from the officers and the biker's expletives volleyed back and forth, Bowers retreated from his line of sight. While he focused on the police, she crept behind the skinny man and noted his baggy jeans. His skinny frame and sores on his arms told her the meth had messed this guy up good and that he was unlikely to go willingly.

The sidewalk was gritty with sand. She selected each step carefully to avoid making any noise.

Nolan and two other officers held defensive positions and attempted to talk him down.

Meanwhile, horns honked. Car doors slammed as annoyed drivers exited vehicles. Two officers began crowd control.

Bowers knew she was in the officers' line of fire. This could get dicey if shooting started.

"Crossfire," said Nolan.

"You're damn right you're in my crossfire," hollered the doped-up biker. The dumbass didn't have a clue that she stood right behind him.

Bowers pressed the Glock's muzzle against the back of his head. "Drop. Your weapon. Now."

The startled man froze.

"Hands on the car," she ordered. "Don't move."

She grabbed his gun, removed his ax from his belt and a knife from his pocket. She laid them on the trunk of the SUV, out of his reach.

Before the other officers moved in, Bowers forced him to his knees. "On the ground," she ordered.

"Shit, man. What's this about?"

"Get down or I will take you down."

The man laid on his stomach on the hot asphalt as a crowd gathered. Some took photos.

As Nolan secured the weapons, another officer warily approached Bowers. "Who are you?" she asked.

"The one who doesn't want you shot," said Bowers.

"Carver," said Nolan. "The captain says she's cool. She's a former cop from D.C."

"My name is Carver," said the officer. "Thanks for the help."

Bowers nodded as Carver knelt next to her and the other officers directed traffic away from the scene.

Bowers glanced down at Skullface. "What's your name?"

"They call me Crow."

"You'll be eating crow, if you don't tell me your real name."

The biker tried to wiggle away. Carver pinned his shoulder and arm to control his movement. He spat at her. It landed on her boot.

Carver ignored his vile behavior and stream of insults.

Nolan dug a spit mask out of his unit and placed it over the man's head. "Come on, dude. Dial it down. Incurring more charges won't help you."

"He's right," said Bowers. "If you're cool. We'll be cool."

"Fuck you, bitch."

Bowers ignored the blowing sand and the sweltering heat. She straddled him and used her weight to keep him pinned.

He bucked his hips. "Oh baby. Let's ride."

"Buddy, you're begging to be tased," said Bowers.

Carver pulled her Taser and dug it into his back. "Don't make me use this."

The biker stopped fidgeting.

Bowers held his hands behind his back, as Nolan slapped on the cuffs. She took a long-narrow key out of her vest, double-locked the cuffs, and enjoyed the surprised expression on Nolan's face.

"You're under arrest," said Carver.

"For what? I didn't do nothin'."

Bowers sat back. "Resisting, aggravated assault on a law-enforcement officer times three, second-degree assault on a police officer with bodily fluids, and failure to identify ought to cover it. For starters. Then again, if you are carrying that weapon unauthorized or it's stolen, you're in deep shit."

Carver smirked and wiped her boot off on the biker's shirt.

Skullface gave up. Nolan mirandized him and stuffed the man in the back of a unit for transport.

Bowers pulled Nolan and Carver aside.

"Gunner and his gang have Coop," she said. "You'll need your long guns and backup."

FRENZY

BOWERS JUMPED IN HER CAR and screamed down the street behind Carver. They passed a blur of palm trees, tourists, scooters, an ice-cream shop, and homes.

She hit the captain's number on speed dial.

He answered.

"Captain, this is Bowers. You told me I could call."

"Yeah, but I have—"

"Coop has been abducted," said Bowers. "Gunner and his gang have his unit and access to everything in it. I'm with Nolan and Carver. We are in pursuit. We need backup."

"Copy that." The line went dead.

Chickens ran from the road as Bowers continued following Carver and Nolan. Police vehicles had trackers. Bowers assumed dispatch and the captain would feed updates to the officers.

That was verified when Carver abruptly slammed on the brakes, made a U-turn, and screamed toward the airport.

A few miles later, Carver and Nolan turned off their lights and sirens and quietly wound their way onto a road that appeared long forgotten.

Knee-high weeds lined the broken, sunbaked asphalt. Gravel and broken pavement crunched as they crept around a series of potholes to find Coop's cruiser, sitting in the middle of a neglected parking lot with the doors open. A cluster of Harleys sat creaking in the sun near the woods at the far end of the lot.

Carver checked the interior of his vehicle and motioned to Nolan. "There's blood on the backseat."

Bowers ducked inside. "His rifle is missing."

Hooting and shouts came from the dense stand of trees.

"Stay back," whispered Bowers. "Let me see what's going on."

She approached the woods with one hand on Coop's pistol, hoping she wasn't too late. She passed the Harleys where heat radiated from their hot manifolds.

Bowers slipped into the woods and silently crept from the cover of one tree to the next. Empty beer cans, a bra, and a broken meth pipe were strewn over the wooded landscape.

Voices grew louder. Up ahead, she spotted a ruined one-story building. The sad structure had lost its roof, doors, and windows decades ago. What hurricanes hadn't destroyed, time and weather had. Only the masonry walls and some roof rafters remained intact.

Bowers ducked low and crept along the graffiti-covered wall where vines grew through the openings that once had been windows.

She heard jeering and peered around the corner. Twenty-feet away, over a dozen bikers were gathered around Gunner with their backs toward her.

Gunner's big black touring motorcycle sat along the side of the building near cans of spray paint.

He stood in front of his outlaw gang, pointing at Coop who had been tied to a tree.

Bowers felt a knot in her gut and the rough grip of Coop's pistol in her hand.

Gunner strutted between Coop and his expensive ride, ranting about his hatred of cops. It galled her to see this scumbag wearing Coop's bulletproof vest and mocking the police.

The bikers punched fists into the air. "Yeah," they roared.

Coop's face had taken some hard hits.

Cheers rose to Gunner's diatribe.

"Kill the pig. Kill the pig," they chanted.

Bowers retreated toward the parking lot. As soon as her feet hit the asphalt, she sprinted toward Carver. "They have Coop tied to a tree. Grab your long guns."

Nolan joined the huddle.

Carver's eyes went wide as the bikers continued chanting, "Kill the pig. Kill the pig."

"How many are we up against?" asked Nolan.

"A dozen or so," said Bowers. "How far out is backup?"

"Any second," said Carver.

"Good." Bowers opened her trunk, donned her bulletproof vest, and pulled out her AR-15.

Carver sounded worried. "Nolan. She's a civilian."

"She's a good Samaritan with skills. Bowers was an MP who has experience in combat."

Carver shook her head. "I don't think—"

"Listen," said Nolan. "Do you really want just the two of us to run in there and take on over a dozen violent bikers who are chanting 'kill the pig'? Or are you suggesting we just sit here and let them kill Coop?"

"Never mind," said Carver.

Bowers had expected some kickback but dropped the subject. "We need to move quickly. Do you have flash-bangs?"

"I do," said Nolan.

While he ran to his unit, Carver nodded at Bowers. "Sorry. It's not how we usually do this."

"No worries," said Bowers. "Let's just get to Coop."

Nolan returned and handed her two canisters.

"That'll work," said Bowers. "Now listen. We need to play this smart."

She stuffed loaded magazines into her pockets. "When the flash-bangs go off, hit your lights and sirens. Louder the better."

"How are we going to get Coop out?" asked Nolan.

Bowers flipped off the safety on her AR. "You stay here. Wait for backup."

Nolan frowned as a jet flew overhead. "Where are you going?"

"To do a little recon and interrupt their party. I'll flush them toward you."

Bowers slipped back into the woods and peered through the foliage. Gunner's crew was so busy howling like a pack of crazed wolves that they didn't notice her.

People don't see what they don't expect to see.

Bowers crouched behind the heavy bushes. Through a footpath to her right, she caught a glimpse of the parking lot where Nolan had taken a defensive position behind his unit with his long gun drawn. To her left, she spotted Coop. His arms bore fresh defensive wounds and blood ran down his face from a cut near his left eye.

She carefully eased closer to Coop. Surprise was everything. When Gunner turned his back, Bowers hurled the first flash-bang. It bounced into the undergrowth behind Gunner and exploded. Deafening pops, crackles, flashes, and smoke inundated the area. The shriek of sirens erupted from the parking lot.

Panicked bikers screaming and the howl of more sirens heightened the chaos. Birds took to the air as the cacophony of noise echoed in the woods.

Temporarily blinded, deaf, and disoriented, the bikers scrambled in all directions. Some crawled into the brush.

Bowers held her AR-15 ready and moved toward Coop.

Just as she thought the bikers had run away, one of them bolted toward Coop. The man's red face twisted into a knot of rage. Holding his ax high, he shrieked like a banshee. Bowers fired a double tap, hitting him in the chest. Carried by momentum, the man fell forward and planted his face into a tree before collapsing into a thorny bush.

Another biker emerged from the smoke and charged at her swinging a machete.

Knife to a gunfight. Idiot.

Bowers fired again. She popped him in each hip, zipped up the middle of his torso, and put a final shot in his forehead.

The man stopped and dropped.

Bowers confiscated the machete and ran to Coop.

"Get me out of here," he said, as he pulled at his restraints.

Bowers noted the damage to his face. "You okay?"

"I'll be a whole lot better when I have my AR back."

Two whacks on the rope with the machete freed Coops hands. She left the sharp blade embedded in the tree, as they hurried into the bushes for cover.

Despite his bruises, cuts, and his split lip, Coop wore that crooked smile.

"Good to see a friendly face," he whispered. "I feel naked. They also took my duty belt and vest."

"Hey. You're alive." Bowers knelt on the damp ground and handed him his Glock. "You'll be wanting this. Here are two more mags. We need to flush them to the parking lot. Backup is waiting."

Coop grabbed her arm. "I want Gunner in cuffs. He may know where my sister is."

"Roger, that."

The smoke provided cover. Gunner appeared from the dense cloud like an apparition with a semi-automatic rifle.

Coop shot high to warn him off. "Stop now. Next time. I won't miss."

Gunner darted behind a tree and aimed his rifle at Coop.

He raised his pistol to eye level and kept his voice low. "That asshole is trying to shoot me with my own damned rifle."

Coop peered between branches and shouted, "Don't do it."

"Drop the gun," shouted Bowers.

Branches snapped. Gunner shot and missed.

Coop returned fire. His round hit a tree trunk, sending a spray of bark and splinters into Gunner's face.

The biker shrieked, shielded his eyes, and stumbled into the smoky undergrowth.

Coop charged after him and stayed on his heels.

Bowers covered Coop's flank as they hustled through the scruffy undergrowth.

Even with the sun at high noon, the smoke made for low visibility. Coop pointed at the ground. Large boot prints in the dirt led to the ruined structure where she suspected Gunner was likely holdup. They gradually crept closer.

An arm holding an ax appeared in the doorway.

"Look out," shouted Bowers.

As he dropped and rolled next to a tree, the sharp blade flew above Coop's head and impaled a large branch.

From a prone position, Coop fired close to Gunner's location. Some of his shots plinked against the masonry block walls.

With Gunner hiding inside the ruined structure, Bowers laid down cover fire as they scrambled toward the building. Coop took a position on one side of the open doorway, she took the other.

Coop whispered, "Crossfire."

She nodded.

Coop aligned his sights, ready to take a shot. She showed him the last flash-bang canister.

He nodded.

She bent low and skirted under the open windows, careful to step around Gunner's bike and the cans of spray paint. She hurried toward the back of the structure.

A glance through a window showed Gunner hiding in the shadows in a corner twelve feet from the doorway. Directly above him an unstable beam appeared ready to fall.

Bowers aimed at the timber and fired.

She heard a loud *boom* and *crack* as it fell like a pendulum and whacked Gunner in the face and torso.

He staggered backward. "Son of a bitch."

"Give it up," shouted Coop. "You're surrounded."

With eyes still tearing from the blow, Gunner blindly fired the AR-15 in all directions.

Bowers ducked. Brass casings fell at Gunners feet. Chunks of the masonry blocks blew out of the window and spattered her neck and shoulder.

When the gunfire stopped, she heard a grunt and the thump of blows landing in rapid succession. She sprinted toward Coop. Just inside the doorway, she found him and Gunner in a desperate struggle for control of the AR. Gunner belted Coop with the stock of the rifle and rolled on top of him. Coop forced the barrel to the side. Fists flew.

When Bowers aimed the muzzle of her AR-15 at Gunner's right ear, Coop's eyes went wide as he shook his head.

She nodded. "Get off him and drop the weapon."

Gunner began to comply, then swung the butt of the AR into her knee. She stumbled sideways.

Gunner lunged to his feet with surprising power and raced outside. Coop went after him.

The two men squared off.

"I'm gonna enjoy seeing you bleed," said Gunner, as he started to swing the barrel of the AR toward Coop.

"Stop!" shouted Bowers. "Or I'll toast your bike."

The distraction gave Coop the few seconds he needed to tackle Gunner.

"Drop it," ordered Coop.

Gunner didn't comply.

With his knee on the AR, Coop continued to keep Gunner pinned to the ground.

Flanked by two other officers, Nolan stepped out of the shadows with his weapon drawn. "Last chance."

Gunner let go.

Bowers secured the AR and handed Coop a pair of handcuffs.

Once Gunner's hands were cuffed behind his back, she handed Coop his AR-15 and one of her magazines.

Coop examined his rifle. "I feel better already."

Nolan helped Gunner to his feet. He pulled his shoulders away and tried to kick Coop.

"Enough of this shit," shouted Bowers. She blasted away with her AR, riddling the bike with bullet holes. To add insult to injury, she plunked at the pile of paint cans. Multi-colored plumes of paint burst into the air. The yellow can twirled in a circle. A blue one flew sideways.

"Oops," she said with a wise-assed grin.

Gunner swore like a man possessed.

Bowers grinned at the holey Harley covered in green, yellow, and pink paint. "You asked for it."

Nolan chuckled. "Gunner, I thought you liked pink. Isn't that what you sprayed all over Coops car after you shot out his windows?"

"You're dead. All of you," screamed Gunner.

"Come on, now," said Coop. "That wasn't nice."

Nolan and Coop hauled Gunner into a clearing, where Coop retrieved his dirt-covered vest and put it on. He checked Gunner's abrasions.

"See, you can't kill me," said Gunner.

Coop stared at him. "Wasn't tryin' to. I'm looking forward to seeing you stand trial."

As Coop firmly escorted Gunner toward the parking lot, Bowers found it poetic that Coop would be the one to bring him in.

Gunner continued to bitch and moan.

A second later, the woods erupted in gunfire.

SURROUNDED

BOWERS TOOK COVER AS SLUGS whizzed over their heads and shredded the leafy branches.

Over a mic, the captain shouted orders from the parking lot. "You are surrounded. Come out with your hands up."

Gunner hooted. "Toast those fuckers."

Another volley of bullets echoed in the woods.

"Enough of this shit." Bowers lobbed the last flash-bang canister into the middle of the bikers.

The ear-shattering pandemonium made it sound as if a war had broken out in the woods.

Smoke drifted through the trees like a demon.

Coop immediately took charge of Gunner.

As they hustled toward the parking lot, Coop could've beat the shit out of Gunner, but didn't. Nor did he take any crap from him.

A bullet ricocheted and narrowly missed Gunner. Apparently not wanting to be shot in the ass, Gunner abruptly became cooperative.

When Coop, Bowers, and the other officers crashed out of the foliage and into the parking lot, they faced a wall of firepower. Long barrels stuck out like porcupine quills from the seven cruisers on site and a sheriff's unit.

When the waiting officers spotted Coop, they cheered. A frantic squirrel running from the noise dashed out of the woods behind them and beat-feet back into the bush.

Bowers sprinted across the parking lot and took cover behind a patrol car.

Once again Gunner signaled his crew with a whistle.

Bikers surrounded the beleaguered parking lot, one man behind a tree here, another there, two more kneeling in the brush.

Gunner ripped away from Nolan and began shouting, "Get your hands off me."

Coop grabbed Gunner's cuffed hands and pulled his arms up, forcing him to bend forward. "You're under arrest."

"Bullshit." Gunner shook his shaved head. His sweaty scalp and tattoo of a revolver glistened in the sunlight. "I don't recognize your laws."

Coop held his grip. "Tell it to the judge."

As he crammed Gunner into the back of a patrol car, the captain shouted over the mic. "Put down your weapons and come out. Now."

Bowers searched for any movement. "They're just inside the treeline."

From the woods, the bikers continued taking potshots at the patrol cars, blasting out several windows.

Next to Bowers, the officer carrying a yellow-and-black pepperball gun said, "Sir, I can get them to come out."

"Send it," said the captain.

The officer cut loose and launched a storm of pepperballs into the middle of the bikers.

Gunfire ceased immediately.

Red-faced men stumbled out of the woods, gasping. One careened right into a no-trespassing sign.

Seconds later, the air filled with moans and cursing.

"Oh God."

"Shit, I can't open my eyes."

"Son of a bitch."

All of them coughed and hacked and had similar complaints. Bowers chuckled and backed away from the patrol cars to avoid being downwind of the drifting pepper powder. She'd take a Taser over that crap any day.

The bikers were on their knees. Tears ran from their eyes, as they spit, coughed, and begged for water.

Bowers watched officers take the bikers into custody and escort them to a large transport vehicle near the mouth of the parking lot. One by one the bikers were patted down, cuffed, and loaded into the boxy unit.

Before the transport left for the jail, Nolan checked each biker for injuries. Coop brought a husky biker with a shot hand to the ambulance crew.

The captain joined them and glared at the greasy-haired biker's round face. "Why in the hell did you do this? Was taking on the entire PD going to get you anywhere?"

The biker glanced at his mangled hand and grimaced.

"Answer the captain," said Coop. "What were you thinking?"

The man shook his head. "Just bein' stupid, I guess."

"You got that right," said Bowers.

Gunner remained in the patrol unit. He continued kicking at the windows and ranting, "Hey assholes. You can't hold me."

Transporting him would now be the challenge.

24 HOURS MISSING

RIGGS GLANCED AT THE CLOCK in the Task Force Room until Ben, one of their seasoned staffers, became animated. He swiveled in his chair. "Riggs, I've got something."

Riggs hustled over to Ben's computer terminal.

Ben tapped the keyboard. "This just came in. Sheriffs and Miami PD have been checking areas near the beach where kids often hang out. They ran across this."

Riggs stood with arms crossed, squinting at the screen. Ben's monitor displayed footage from a bodycam showing Miami PD officers entering a convenience store. The clerk in the footage appeared startled. After a few questions, he told the officers about two teenagers, matching the girls' descriptions, who had just left.

Ben tapped on another file. "The officers helped the clerk save this footage from the store's surveillance system." Riggs watched a clip showing two girls approaching the checkout with a carton of ice cream, chips, and soda.

"That's Lauren," said Riggs.

"Yes sir," said Ben. "She used her credit card. If the PD had been fifteen minutes earlier, they would've run right into them."

"Call Miami now. Tell them *well done*."

"Riggs, there's more. The clerk reported that both girls had crammed into a yellow convertible and left." Ben's desk chair squeaked as he leaned back and showed Riggs footage from the security cameras that had captured images of a light-colored Corvette. Unfortunately, the image was grainy and sportscars were a dime a dozen in Miami.

Riggs knew that without a readable plate, they didn't have much to go on. "Did the clerk have anything else to say?"

"Yeah," said Ben. "He overheard them talking about going to a party on the beach. The PD and Sheriffs are searching, but Miami Beach is a huge amount of turf to cover."

"Maybe they'll get lucky," said Riggs. "Did they get a description of the driver?"

"He's described as a white guy wearing an expensive suit."

Riggs tossed down his notepad. "Crap. There are a million of them in Miami."

Ben leaned back in his chair. "But, how many of them have facial tatts?"

A new energy filled the room.

Riggs returned to his computer and stack of folders at the conference table. Just as he began reading the incoming reports and was about to make a call, he heard footsteps.

Greg and a woman from counterintelligence entered and came straight for Riggs.

RIGGS STOOD and walked toward Greg. "What's up?"

Normally, Greg's prominent jaw and penetrating blue eyes gave him an aura of confidence. However, this morning his wide-eyed expression seemed that of a man about to drown. Greg nodded for him to follow. "You need to see this."

A few doors down, they entered one of the task force's meeting rooms. After closing the door, chair legs scraped over the linoleum as Greg and the woman took a seat at a small wooden table.

Riggs respected her no-nonsense attitude that had come from a lot of time on the job.

She firmly shook Riggs' hand and dropped a thick brown packet in front of him. "Good to see you again."

Greg glanced at the agent. "Game changer. She's got something for us."

Everything from her western belt buckle to the stylish cut of her silver-gray hair drew his attention. Her confidence and slightly rebellious attire reminded him of Bowers.

She opened the envelope and spread documents, photos, and maps in front of them.

"What's all this?" asked Riggs.

Greg hunched over the table. "We had a case go sideways. Three days ago, a North Korean scientist who has been trying to defect was murdered. Cho, North Korea's supreme leader denies it, but the man was poisoned while trying to get out of the country. And get this, he was Cho's cousin."

That didn't surprise Riggs. "We already know he is a psychopath. What else is new?"

"This scientist had critical intel," said the agent.

Greg tapped the envelope. "Riggs, these documents spell out North Korea's plan to use quantum technology to weaponize computers. They're developing a new kind of cyberattack that would make today's computer viruses about as threatening as junk mail. A viable quantum computer could do everything from defeat NSA's security to opening the flood gates of the Hoover Dam, leaving thousands downstream to drown. They could turn our nuclear power plants into massive bombs or disrupt our military. This is serious."

"Do you trust the intel?"

"Absolutely," said Greg. He glanced at the woman.

She nodded. "We have a high-value asset that has been meeting with the scientist." She handed Riggs a photograph. "Fortunately, we were able to extract him moments after the murder."

"We just met with him," said Greg. "His story checks out and he has proof."

Unsettling images of the Pentagon being breached and *Air Force One* exploding in midflight raced through Riggs' mind. He didn't even want to think about subways and airports.

Greg stared at the wall. "They could target everything connected to computers and the internet. Smart TVs to the electrical grid. If this chip is what I think it is, it could cripple us."

"I've got the picture," said Riggs. "Clearly, we need to get down to Florida. We have little choice but to find the girls and then maybe a grateful president might help us stop the E-Connect sale."

"What about McDougall?"

Riggs set down his pen. "I'll deal with him."

His phone buzzed with an incoming call from Willie. They had been waiting on the results from Grace's rape kit.

"The lab just called," said Willie. "They ran the DNA."

Riggs hadn't expected such a prompt reply.

"We have a match," said Willie. "It's Gunner."

Riggs locked eyes with Greg. "I've got an outlaw biker in Key West wanted for rape and murder one. Let's go."

DEATH KNELL

A S THE SUN DIPPED BELOW the horizon, the *Leisure Lee* headed for open sea. Somewhere in the distance, a buoy bell clanked like a death knell.

Bo followed in the Hinkley. He glanced at the darkening sky. Instead of enjoying the stars, he stared at the black waters, knowing he had to find a way to win over Preston. If he didn't, odds were good he'd never see land again.

They drifted past the shadowy silhouette of Sunset Key where boats were returning after a day of fishing.

The super-yacht maxed out at a pathetic thirteen knots. Bo easily kept up in the Hinkley, as they headed toward the waters off Miami. Bo searched the horizon for pirates or worse—the Coast Guard. At least he could shoot pirates.

Once in a while, he caught sight of the *Leisure Lee's* guard boat, a heavily armed Fountain sport boat that had the advantage of tremendous speed.

After two hours at the helm, Bo grew weary of watching the *Leisure Lee* lumbering through the swells.

This wasn't how his life was supposed to turn out.

The cops taking his stuff and crawling all over his boat still chafed his hide. Not only had they taken his truck, they now had his boat. The worst had been losing his cash.

Up ahead and without warning, the *Leisure Lee* slowed.

That surprised him, considering how Preston had made such a big stink about making good time.

Bo squinted into the darkness, hoping he hadn't done something else to piss off Preston.

His radio crackled with a call from Niko. "Skipper wants to see you."

His stomach churned. *Now what?*

As much as he hated Preston, he didn't dare disobey him. Besides, he needed the fat wad of cash the skipper had promised him.

Unsure of what he'd find, Bo carefully docked at the stern and tromped up the steps toward the bridge. Niko blocked the passage.

As much as he hated the guy, this time Niko surprised him. He seemed genuinely upset. "We need you. There's a problem with the girls. Please help me fix it before Preston gets really pissed."

Bo's shoulders relaxed. It cracked him up that Niko had lied about the skipper wanting to see him. Of course, he could fix the problem. Girls were like dogs, instill enough fear and they'd do anything he wanted. Better still, doing something for Niko meant the guy would owe him.

"No worries. I got this," said Bo.

He reversed directions and descended into the ugly lower deck near the engine room. As he barreled down the passageway, crewmen in dark-blue shirts flatten themselves along the wall.

"Stand back," he shouted, knocking a young crewman into a fire extinguisher.

Farther down the passageway a couple of agitated guards slammed the door shut to the Hole where they kept the girls. Cooks from the main galley slipped on scattered food and other foul debris strewn over the floor.

Muffled shouts came from within the Hole. Fists pounded on the gray metal door. Sandwiches weren't the only thing that had been hurled at the crew. The space smelled like a toilet.

A deckman stood there covered in crap. He glanced up at Bo. "Screw this, man. They're your problem."

As he hurried toward the men's room, Jung appeared amused.

Obviously, a standoff had taken place when food had been delivered.

A voice from inside the Hole shouted, "We have rights. This is illegal!"

"*Por favor*," pleaded another. "Please, *señor*, let us go."

Bo clicked his radio. "Get the medic down here."

"Roger that," said a male voice.

Bo slapped a fresh magazine into his Beretta.

A few minutes later, Carson, a skinny fellow with long scraggly brown hair, arrived from sickbay.

After the raid on his boat, Bo only had one change of clothes left. He grimaced at the trashed uniforms of those who'd gone into the room. Carson's baggy, pale-blue pants looked as if they'd almost fit. "Take off your scrubs."

"No way, dude." Carson brushed a lock of his long wavy hair over his shoulder.

Bo pulled out his Beretta. "That wasn't a request. Do it!"

The medic glanced at Jung, who made no effort to help. "Sick fuck," said Carson as he slipped out of his scrubs.

Bo left his jeans and shirt wedged between the wall and a fire extinguisher and stepped into the blue pants that tied at the waist. They were tight and too short, but Bo didn't plan on being in them long. He didn't bother with the top.

The medic glared at him. "You're a sick bastard."

"So you keep telling me."

Deep within the lower decks, the Hole served as a holding cell, reminding Bo of lobster tanks at restaurants. In the dressing room next door, they cleaned up the girls before taking them to the clients.

Last time he'd been inside, mattresses were scattered over the floor and a bucket served as a toilet.

He'd grown used to their frightened stares, bite marks, and bruising around their wrists from clients who liked their sex served up rough.

As a crewman unlocked the door, Bo stood ready with his pistol in one hand and a food tray for a shield in the other.

As he entered the filthy room, all manner of crap flew at him until he fired a shot that hit one girl square in the forehead. She flopped onto the deck like a dead fish.

As shouting turned to panic, Bo waved a guard with a Taser into the room. Two women scooted away from the pool of dark red expanding over the deck.

While Bo kept them at gunpoint, guards zip-tied each girl's hands and ankles. Carson tiptoed around the debris, while cradling his medical kit like a beloved pet. Even Bo had to admit the guy looked pretty stupid, standing there in his big glasses, Hawaiian-print boxers, knobby knees, and clogs.

At the back wall, a girl with knotted black hair lay on the floor clutching her stomach and weeping. Like all the girls, she wore a skimpy bra and lace panties. Her pale face gave her the appearance of a ghost. Judging by her sweaty skin, Bo figured she had an infection. Eventually they all got something nasty.

Two others cowered near the sick one and kept silent.

He'd grown hardened to their pleas for help. Bo had no more compassion for them than he did the frozen corn in the walk-in cooler.

While Carson prepared syringes, he whispered, "Where's the H? You were supposed to bring me some."

Bo glared at the medic's squirrel eyes. "It was on my boat. The cops raided it. What do you expect me to do about that, asshole?"

"Jeez, dude. I'm just sayin' I'm short on goods."

It was only a matter of time before Preston figured out that the heroin from Gunner was now in police custody. Bo rummaged through the medical bag and pulled out a tiny vial of Fentanyl. "Boost it with this."

Rationing his supplies, Carson injected the fentanyl-laced heroin into the girls who'd been the most vocal. They became confused and lost muscle control. Their previous bravado melted into moans.

Once the room grew quiet, Carson stood. "You want us to cut-off the ties?"

"Nope," said Bo. "They can wallow in this mess. In fact, leave the body here. They can watch it bloat. That'll teach them."

Carson's shoulders quivered. "That's perverted."

Bo followed Carson into the corridor and called over one of the crewmen. "Clean this up before the captain sees it."

After peeling off the contaminated scrubs, he dropped them in a heap at the feet of the medic.

Carson glanced down. "Fuck me."

"No thanks," said Bo, as he dispensed a blob of sanitizer into his hands.

In the men's room, he cleaned up.

A few minutes later, he lumbered up the ladder and stopped just outside the bridge. From the open door, he heard Preston talking to Jung. "Where's Bowers?"

Jung wore his typical blank expression. "Finding her wasn't as easy as we thought. She constantly moves. If you want her taken quietly, I need a team who knows their shit."

"How many?"

"Me, plus four."

Preston wore a pained expression. "Ok. Pick your guys and let me know when you're ready. I want her back here, pronto."

Jung knocked into Bo as he shouldered past. "Shithead."

"Douchebag," Bo whispered.

Preston stood there in his immaculate white uniform. Even after washing up, Bo didn't feel clean. He wanted a long hot shower and to get something to eat.

He felt ridiculous, standing there while Preston ruminated. "Skipper, you wanted to see me?"

Preston flinched as if he'd forgotten about him. A scowl returned to the man's face. "How many times do I have to tell you not to fire your goddamned weapon onboard this ship?"

Apparently, our guns are decorative.

Bo leaned against the bridge's polished teak and brass railing.

Preston yammered on, "Do you have any clue what a stray bullet could do to all the equipment and pipes behind those bulkheads? Next time use pepper spray or a Taser. Hell, I don't care, use a cattle prod."

"Good idea." Bo would pay to use one on Jung.

Just when he thought he might smooth things over with Preston, he said, "I sent you for a fresh supply of H. Where is it?"

Shit. Bo exhaled. "It was in my bag."

"And?"

"It was on my boat when the cops raided it."

"Are you kidding me?" Preston threw his arms into the air. "So whose brilliant idea was it to store it on your shitty little chum-bucket with no security? Did it ever dawn on you that we have guards onboard for a reason?"

Bo felt his neck flush and temper rise.

Preston threw down his pen. "I can't believe this. It's always something with you."

"Hey," said Bo, "I was in the process of moving it to the ship, when your guys interrupted and hauled me off my boat. Remember? You can put this on Jung and Scarface. Not me."

Preston reminded Bo of his father, the one man he hated most.

His Daddy's face—dead, frozen, and silent—hung in his mind like a Christmas card. He'd gladly do the same to Preston, if given the slightest opportunity.

A freckled young man with blond eyelashes and deep-blue eyes appeared in the doorway. Preston glanced up at the chief mate. "What do you what?"

The young officer wore a pained expression. He spoke quickly and quietly to Preston.

Veins in the skipper's forehead bulged. "On top of all your horseshit, a faulty circuit board just took down our main cooler with all the goddamned food onboard."

Bo shrugged. "I could go to the mainland and get the parts to fix it."

Preston glared at him and smiled. "Ok. I'll call in an order for the new circuit board. You take the Hinkley to Miami and pick it up. While you're there, go find us some goddamned H."

Preston pointed at him. "Don't come back without them, or you're a dead man."

HAIR TRIGGER

PRESTON'S WORDS—*DEAD MAN*—hammered through Bo's mind, not as a warning but as a match igniting the rage he'd known most of his life.

He'd always had a soft trigger. In high school he'd received a failing grade on a biology test and had torched the teacher's car. Bo remembered those years, but in truth his anger started much earlier with his mother's screams, the leather belt, the shed, and the abuse he could never forget, especially now when Preston kept dancing on his hot buttons.

On the way to Miami, part of him wanted to head south until he reached Mexico. At least there he could live on the beach and get by on his photography and selling a little dope. As much as he liked the idea, their support boats had tracking devices. He could outrun the *Leisure Lee*, but not the gunmen who would come after him on the Fountain.

As Bo approached Miami, he viewed the festive coastline with his scope. Palm trees and tall hotels were bathed in bright colors reflected in the sea.

Twenty minutes later, he dodged increased boat traffic and tied up to a dock near a ramshackle building.

In a tourist mecca like Miami, boat slips were hard to come by and expensive. Preston had an agreement with a local charter fishing operation that was willing to share their dock space for extra cash. Judging by the condition of their boats and office, they needed the income.

Bo tied up and muttered, "You'd think getting heroin was as easy as picking up a burger."

After a cab ride and ten-minutes in a HVAC supply store, Bo had the components to fix the cooler.

Now came the tough part. His former contacts were either in jail or had died of an overdose. He texted Roy, a man whom he didn't trust any more than he did Jung, but odds were good he'd have a supply on hand.

He and Roy had been cellmates. After getting out, they'd done some business before Bo had gone on the run.

Roy responded by texting an address, which meant he had product to sell.

Bo caught a cab to a fancy hotel on the beach not far from his boat. Finding Roy hosting a gig at the hotel's seaside bar didn't surprise him, but the number of cops on the beach made him uneasy.

Bo pulled his ballcap down low and thought about leaving but returning without the heroin would be suicide.

He joined the partygoers in the open-air bar. Under its thatch roof, booze and beer flowed freely. A band jammed on with a combination of pop and reggae. Those looking for a good time wandered in wearing flip-flops, while others from the hotel were dressed to the nines.

Bo knew Roy had a thing for fancy clothes and being the center of attention, especially with women.

As usual, Bo found Roy in the middle of the party, wearing one of those designer jackets.

It was hard to miss a white boy with red cornrows.

Bo kept an eye on the beach and wanted to get this done before the cops became curious.

As Bo shouldered through the crowd, he found Roy up into a tall gorgeous black woman. Bo wished he had time to get into some of that business.

"Hey, Roy!" shouted Bo.

Roy continued dancing to the funky beat.

Bo shouted, "Roy!"

The thin man searched the dancefloor. The strobing lights made Roy's blond eyelashes appear to change color. When they locked eyes, he didn't seem to recognize Bo.

He pulled off his hat. "I told you I was coming. Remember?"

Roy inched closer. "Bo? You look like shit, dude."

His face still ached, but he made a joke of it. "The other guy looks worse."

He scanned the bar for the cops. "Listen, I'm in a jam."

"I can see that." Roy's smile revealed a new gold tooth. He pointed to Bo's face. "Other than that mess, how ya doin'?"

"Let's do some business."

Roy glanced at the beach. "Come to my room."

As they strolled toward the hotel entrance, Bo noticed a sweet yellow Corvette sitting in the parking lot. They went upstairs to the twelfth floor. As soon as Bo entered the suite, he couldn't help being jealous of the full bar, bay windows with a stunning view of the water, and the huge soft bed where two girls lay sprawled out on a soft comforter.

"Hey, Roy," said the blonde. She had the dreamy voice and tousled hair of someone who'd been asleep. "I must have crashed."

"No problem *chiquita*," said Roy. "I got you." He swayed his hips and made a few dance moves. "Listen, I got some business I need to attend to. You ladies make yourselves comfortable. There are drinks in the fridge." He kissed the blonde on the forehead.

Bo watched the blonde girl comb her fingers through her tangled curls and began to suspect she and her friend were too young to be legal. Not that that would stop Roy.

With problems mounting with the skipper, Bo didn't need to add to them. More immediate, he didn't want any surprises.

He cautiously followed Roy and kept a keen eye on the rest of the suite. Drug deals were notorious for going bad. The last thing he needed was to be robbed. That would end it with Preston.

After the girls went back to the bedroom, Roy opened a closet safe. As they were about to settle into the sitting area, the blonde poked her head out of the bedroom door. She caught Bo's eye and giggled.

He couldn't help staring. Roy chuckled. "Nice. Huh? I found them on the beach and gave them a place to crash."

"Be careful, man," said Bo. "They're a little on the young side."

Roy leaned forward and slapped Bo's arm as if they were best friends. "Yeah. I noticed. I prefer a skilled woman, if you get my drift."

Bo played along and hoped the deal would go smoothly. He wanted the H and to get the hell out of there. Roy had a reputation as a wild card, which meant anything could happen.

"Dawg, let's get to it," said Roy. "You got the sugar?"

Bo's pulse pounded as he took off his backpack and set it on the floor. The zipper made a ripping sound as he opened a pouch and pulled out the plastic bag full of bills Preston had given him.

Roy could be generous or violent. No telling which way he would swing. Bo tried to appear relaxed, knowing Roy could use his pistol to take the money, keep the drugs, and toast him before all was said and done.

When Roy snatched up the packet of bills, Bo flinched.

"Easy dude," said Roy, "Just checkin' my pay. That's all. Nothin' personal."

He thumbed through the cash, as if satisfied.

Bo had helped Roy out of a jam a few years back and hoped he remembered it. He handed Bo a package a little smaller than the one he'd purchased from Gunner.

"Thanks, man," said Bo. He checked out the mirrored ceilings, the huge TV screens, and the bar. "Shit man, I could get used to this."

Roy held his arms out in grand style. "Come work for me, dude."

Before Bo could even ponder the offer, the blonde came around the corner from the bedroom pulling her dark-haired friend behind her. "You boys wanna party?"

"I'm buying the first round," said Roy. He slapped the blonde on the ass and the four of them returned to the beach bar.

Bo hung around for a bit, watching the girls dancing with each other and ogling men. Roy plied them with apple martinis. The girls quickly became giggly.

With a lot of miles still to cover, Bo drank sweet tea. This wasn't the night to get hammered. Sweat ran down his back, but he didn't dare take off the backpack. Losing another shipment would mean a bullet to the brain.

Although, he wouldn't mind some of that blonde girl. It annoyed him that she and her dark-haired friend in the glasses came as a set.

Bo eased over close to the blonde, who put her hand on his arm. Her friend laid her head on the table and began to snore.

"What's your name?" he asked.

Roy joined them and leaned over the table and locked eyes with Bo. "Listen, I ain't forgot how you did me a solid. How about I return the favor?"

"Like what?"

Roy slapped two one-hundred-dollar bills on the table. "How about you take these ladies and show them a real nice time? Debt paid?"

Bo needed the cash and nodded.

"Cool," said the blonde. "Let's go par-tay." This time she ran a hand up his thigh. That woke him up. Bo saw his luck changing.

After a little kissing, he hailed a cab. The brief ride dropped them off at the dock near the Hinkley.

The tipsy brunette had her arm around the blonde who captured his attention by swaying her hips as she strolled in front of him.

Tonight, offered an unexpected opportunity for some fun.

Fifty feet from the boat reality set in. His tender parts were still too sore to perform. Besides, getting back in Preston's good graces meant more to his survival than getting laid.

A couple of sweet young things like this would be a treat for Preston's special clients. Two fresh girls at no cost would offset the expense of the lost H. Even hard-assed Preston would appreciate that.

IN DEEP

THE LOCK ON THE HINKLEY'S BERTH would soon come in handy. At the dock, the bow gently rocked in the swells. Bo's eyes surveyed each girl. Being so young, they had soft skin, firm thighs, and bright-eyed trust.

While the attendant at the charter fishing place went inside to answer a call, the brunette watched Bo filling the boat's fuel tank. She pushed up her glasses to study his face. The small crinkle between her brows told him she felt uneasy about his busted nose. To explain the cuts and bruises, he told them a bullshit story about fighting off three thugs to protect a biker chick. Even the blonde bought it.

Their hesitation turned to smiles as he passed around some beer. He made it look as if they were simply there for a good time.

To ensured they felt safe, he said, "If you girls get tired and want to go back to the hotel, I'll cover the cab."

They didn't know that wouldn't be happening.

They chatted like teenagers do. All excited and wide-eyed, they yapped about wanting to travel and live well. Bo flirted, pretended to put shots in his iced tea, and played along until the girls were hammered. It didn't take much after the shots started to flow. They thought they were tough, especially the blonde, but they were just young and naive.

Bo wondered if he'd ever been like that. If he had, his daddy had beaten it out of him long before he'd even reached twelve.

Bo kept an eye on the attendant. While he had his cellphone up to his ear, Bo quietly untied his boat and drifted away from the dock.

The attendant nearly dropped his phone and ran toward the gas pump. "Hey," he yelled. "Come back. You have to pay."

Bo pushed the throttle forward and headed out to sea until the shoreline was little more than a glittering bobble of lights behind him.

While the girls were sprawled on the mattress in a drunken stupor, he turned off the engines and listened to the peaceful sea. He took his time and made sure no one had followed. The moonlight shimmered on the swells.

His time on the *Leisure Lee* had not gone as planned. He'd also grown tired of running. He had hoped to avoid the cops by remaining at sea and skippering a ship. Bo vowed at all costs never to return to prison.

His calendars and photographs were the one thing he'd done right in his life. Every one of those photos had been the real deal, not photoshopped. That meant something.

Preston stood as a link to something bigger or the man who could ruin everything. Bo watched the rolling sea and expected the girls would gain the skipper's approval.

Snoring came from the bunk and reminded him of the work ahead. He zip-tied the girls' wrists and ankles and locked the door.

Hours later, the *Leisure Lee* loomed ahead like a beacon against the black sea.

He steered into its wake and imagined Preston's greedy delight when presented with the girls. Bo envisioned the skipper thanking him and shaking his hand. That would piss off Jung.

Bo tied up and checked on the girls. The long ride back had given them time to shake off some of the buzz. The blonde nagged at him. "Hey. You can't do this. Take me back to the hotel."

Cutting the zip-ties off the brunette's ankles was easy compared to the blonde, who tried to kick him. A good hard backhand shut that down.

Waves slapped against the hull as Bo led the girls to the rear platform. The tipsy brunette stumbled and lost her glasses. Bo thought they made her look nerdy and left them on the Hinkley.

Jung appeared on the stern of the *Leisure Lee*. He did a doubletake as Bo offloaded his prize catches.

"What the hell is this?" asked Jung.

"Brownie points."

Getting the woozy girls up the steps proved to be a challenge. A few minutes later, Bo entered the passageway and paraded the girls in their lowcut tops toward the forward cabin.

Armed men whistled as they groped at the girls' short skirts. When Jung reached for the blonde, she slapped his hand away, "Don't touch me, asshole."

Jung and two guards followed. One had a hard face with slits for eyes; the other wore a full beard and bandana. Bo found Preston relaxing on a plush couch, watching the news on TV. He clicked the mute button and tossed the remote onto the coffee table.

Bo's anticipation built as he forced the girls to stand before the skipper, but the man surprised him by showing no reaction.

Preston squinted at Bo. "What's this?"

"A gift."

"Where'd you find them?" Preston waved over Jung and Niko.

Bo grinned as if he'd just handed the skipper the keys to a brand-new yacht. "You might say I made a package deal with an old friend." He dug in his backpack and pulled out the bundle of heroin and the circuit board, which he laid on the coffee table.

"I got you everything you asked for and a little extra to make up for the lost H."

The skipper rose to his feet. "You didn't ask me first."

Bo still felt a little cocky about scoring two hot chicks. "You're welcome."

Preston smacked him. "Did it ever dawn in your muddled pea brain that they might be missed? That their families could have called the cops? That's why we switched from taking local girls for more secure supplies offshore. Are you stupid?"

Stunned and confused, Bo rubbed his stinging cheek. Just like his dad, nothing was ever good enough.

"What the hell, man. I'm trying to help. I did everything you asked. I picked up your damned circuit board and got your fucking H, which was not easy on the fly. Unlike H, you can use girls more than once. I thought you'd appreciate that."

The 3rd mate hadn't taken his eyes off the blonde and stepped forward for a closer view. When Niko reached for her breasts, she crossed her arms and pulled away.

The brunette trembled. "I want to go home."

The blonde glared at Bo with smeared streaks of black makeup around her eyes. They hardly looked like the same girls at the bar.

Jung spoke up, "You want us to take 'em back?"

"It's too late," said Preston. "They've seen the ship and our faces." He pointed his stub of a finger at Bo. "Next time, I do the thinking, not you."

Bo clenched his jaw. *Asshole.*

Preston waved Jung closer. "Take them below."

Jung, with his usual flat expression, grabbed the blonde by her hair and hustled her below deck. Scarface followed with the brunette.

Preston stormed off to his adjoining office, leaving Bo standing there. He watched the skipper through the open door, shuffling through papers on his desk.

The silent television mounted on the wall showed a Breaking News banner. They flashed a bulletin about two missing girls across the screen. Bo picked up the remote to turn it off until he spotted the pictures of the girls. He recognized them immediately. The closed captioning identified the blonde as the president's missing daughter and the dark-hair girl as her friend, Molly. Bo's chest tightened.

He clicked off the TV. *I'm totally fucked.*

BO TRIED NOT TO PANIC as he headed toward the doorway with a suffocating sense of dread.

"Sit down," ordered Preston. "You are not dismissed."

Bo's mouth went dry. His palms began to sweat. Getting rid of those girls before anyone recognized them just became priority one.

He sat on the edge of a couch just feet from the passageway, as Preston jotted a few notes.

Time passed, as Bo's anxiety continued to ramp up.

The skipper continued to focus on his notes. As soon as Bo thought he might have dodged the bullet, Jung marched in with the big German guy they called Knuckles, who didn't go anywhere without his AK-47. Bo had seen him sleep with the damned thing.

"Skipper," said Jung, "you need to see this. Someone just posted a video on social media."

Bo's fingers tightened around the edges of the couch cushion. The news about the girls must have hit the internet.

I'm a dead man.

Bo cringed as Preston grabbed the phone from Jung. As he squinted at the small screen, his jaw clenched and his face reddened.

With his fingers tingling, Bo wondered if he could reach the Hinkley before being shot. He stood and edged toward the door, but Knuckles blocked his path.

Bo ducked when Preston marched toward the couch and threw the phone at him. "You care to explain this?"

With trembling hands, Bo picked up Jung's phone. Any second, he expected the business end of Knuckles' AK-47 to blow a hole right through him.

Bo tried to focus on the grainy video.

Someone in Key West had posted footage of his boat being raided. The clip caught a glimpse of Bowers amid the bystanders. The relief nearly made him giddy.

Bo tossed the phone onto the couch. "She hangs out at the docks. So what?"

Jung wore his usual smug expression.

"I told you she was trouble," shouted Preston. "You let her lead the cops right to us."

"I didn't let her do anything," said Bo. "Jung was supposed to go find her. Remember? This is on him."

Jung pulled his knife from its sheath and stepped toward Bo.

"Put it away," ordered Preston. He paced back and forth, while running a hand over his beard. "We need to clean out the Hole. Tonight."

Bo waited.

"That's an order." Preston glared at him. "Do it now."

Bo left the room and fell back against the nearest wall. While attempting to collect himself, he heard Preston yelling at Jung. "I told you to go get her."

"I gathered the guys," said Jung, "like you asked. They're loading up the Fountain right now."

"We need to expedite this." Preston spoke to someone on the phone. "Come see me, now."

The skipper paced the floor. "When you find Bowers, make absolutely certain the guys don't touch her. I want a word with her first."

Bo stayed just outside the door to listen. A few minutes later, a guy in a flight suit passed him and entered the forward cabin.

"Yes, sir?" asked their helicopter pilot.

"Slight change in plans," said Preston.

"We're all set," said the pilot, "the bird is ready to go pick up your guests anytime you want."

"I'm in a hurry," said Preston. "I need you to drop Jung and his crew off in Key West tonight. After you shuffle them back, head up to Miami and wait there for our guests."

"Roger that," the pilot said. "I'll warm her up right now."

Preston pointed at Jung with that creepy finger.

"Go get her."

FIREWORKS

UNABLE TO SLEEP, BOWERS STARED at the ceiling where lights from passing cars sent yellow flashes across the room. The firefight in the woods replayed in her mind. After the beating Coop had taken from the bikers, he had to be sore as hell.

Her phone buzzed with a text from Riggs: *SS. Call you soon.*

His abbreviation could mean anything from *shit show* or *stay safe* or he was involved with the Secret Service and couldn't talk. His fragmented message meant he was strapped into another long night with something big.

After talking with Jay and hearing on the News that the president's daughter was missing, she could understand why.

She sent Riggs a text: *Gunner in custody. HD*

HD was their code for *keep your head down.*

The old walls of her hotel did little to buffer the booming music and air horns. By 3:00 a.m. she gave up, got dressed, and slipped through her hotel room's window to the fire escape.

Sitting there on the landing with her pistol and phone, the air smelled fresh after a brief squall. The rain dampened the streets, but not the high-spirited crowds below.

Nothing deterred Key West from a good time. Even the shops advertised being open until 4 a.m. when the bars closed.

She sat on a towel and laughed as women with painted breasts shimmied to the music and people dressed as zombies tossed beads to the crowd. The crackle of fireworks drew her attention to the sky over the marina.

Officers on bikes searched for signs of trouble. Bowers knew their demeanor well and had never understood exactly why she and officers such as the ones below inevitably ran toward mayhem while everyone else ran away or stood to watch.

A middle-aged couple wandered up the street in face paint and white shirts covered in fake blood. As the couple danced to the music, it hit her that horror to them was pretend. Nothing more than a Halloween costume for fun.

A puzzle piece fell into place. Being a soldier, a cop, and a detective had never been about bad guys. Rather, it had been about protecting ordinary people from them. She faced real horror, so they didn't have to. Perhaps her uncle Marvin had never asked her why she ran into danger because he understood and had done the same.

After the firefight in the woods, she'd written out a statement for the captain and stayed with Coop until the ambulance crew had checked the wounds on his face and arms.

Bowers thought about the evidence in Bo's boat that the PD would find damning. Combining that with the prints and hair she'd left in the driver's seat of Bo's truck would give them all they needed to file charges. However, that would only be the beginning. She had an uneasy feeling Bo had his hands into something far worse.

Bowers rested against the painted wood siding. The gunpowder from the fireworks filled the air with the pungent smoky odor of sulfur. She took in the sounds of a steel-pan band. When they stopped for a break, she heard a *thump* from inside her room.

Bowers sat forward and listened.

Slowly, she stood against the wall with her hand on the cool grip of her Glock. Another *clunk* came from inside.

Adrenaline drove up her pulse.

Someone with a low voice asked, "Where is she?"

"You sure this is the right room?" asked another.

That put a new wrinkle in her evening.

Bowers lowered the ladder.

It made a horrendous racket as the sliding metal *clunked* to a stop. She rapidly descended toward the sidewalk.

As she hung from the last rung, a tank of a man with an AK-47 poked his head out her window and glared down at her.

She dropped to the pavement and sprinted away. He came after her, followed by a smaller man with black hair and Asian features.

Bowers ducked into a tent, where a man with a ponytail and paint brushes said, "Take off your shirt. It's fifty bucks."

"No thanks," she said as she exited.

Bowers blended into the crowd where she dodged a man playing a harmonica and a cloud of cigar smoke that smelled like a horse barn. A block later, a crowd cheered for couples dressed in flashy costumes dancing to furious drumbeats. People on scooters decorated with flags puttered up the street. Paper streamers, strings of beads, and empty beer bottles littered the damp sidewalk.

As she scanned the crush of partygoers, the scent of savory street foods and funnel cakes hung in the air. To her right, she spotted three men running toward her.

She ducked into a vape shop. The odd fruity odor made it smell more like a candy shop than a smokers' emporium, except that the display cabinets were filled with vape pens and vials with exotic names.

Her sudden entrance startled the older gentleman manning the cash register. He frowned, as she hid behind the counter.

Bowers put her finger up to her lips, hoping he'd get the message and keep his mouth shut. As the old guy pointed to his T-shirt to show her the Marine emblem on the chest, the front door flew open.

"Where is she," a male voice demanded.

Bowers held her pistol ready as two customers fled.

"Young man, git out of my store," said the shopkeeper.

The gunman stepped closer.

"I said, back off. Now," hollered the old man.

Bowers peered between displays of bongs on the counter. The big guy with the AK-47 was almost on top of her.

When he shoved the old man out of the way, Bowers bolted for the rear exit. As she shouldered the door open, she glanced back at the old man in time to see him shove a big flashlight at the gunman's torso. When the older Marine pressed a button, it emitted a crackling sound Bowers knew well. The colorful string of expletives that followed confirmed that the old guy had tasered the gunman, who keeled forward like a plank of wood.

The gutsy old Marine winked at her and waved for her to leave.

Bowers bolted out the back door, knowing the gunman would soon recover and would likely come after her. She picked up the pace and sprinted into a dark alley.

After ducking behind a dumpster, Bowers nearly ran into a fellow in a kilt, taking a whiz. Beyond them, the silhouette of a dark figure carrying a long gun blocked the alley.

Shit.

"Go inside. Now," she ordered the startled man in the kilt. He scrambled toward the bar's backdoor. She heard the door slam as the man in the alley began to fire. His muzzle flashed. As the assault rifle fired on full auto, the deafening sounds echoed down the alley.

This dude is nuts.

The sound triggered people on the adjacent street to run or search the sky for fireworks.

Bowers held her position, knowing a Glock was no match for a rifle.

The gunman fired another burst. The loud music in the bar stopped abruptly. She heard a lone siren and hoped the PD had heard the shots. They wouldn't mistake it for fireworks.

The gunman fired another barrage. Like the spray-and-pray action in movies, this guy didn't appear to care what he hit. Glass broke. Lead plinked against the dumpster and the exterior walls of a bar where the sounds of a party and music meant a lot of people were inside. Bullets from his high-powered rifle could easily rip through the wood. She heard a woman screaming. A bleeding man burst out the rear door.

This stops now.

Before the gunman could hurt anyone else, Bowers pulled a pizza box from the dumpster's access door and flung it into the air, Frisbee style. When he fired at it, she leapt from cover, aimed, and fired two rounds at center mass. The man dropped to the pavement.

Bowers sprinted out of the alley, climbed over a chain-link fence, dodged stands of banana trees, jumped over a small retaining wall, and ended up on an adjacent street. The flashing strobes from patrol cars and an ambulance raced toward the alley.

Several blocks away, the party continued. A crowd of revelers on the main road cheered for a man on a unicycle as he performed a juggling act.

Standing in an alcove long enough to catch her breath, she watched two inebriated mermaids stumble past.

Bowers wondered how many men were after her and why.

In case this went really bad, she shifted her extra burner phone to her pocket where it would be easily found and hid her good phone in her bra.

When she stepped out to leave, another man appeared across the street. In the middle of the road, a frightening clown with yellow fangs and an evil grin twirled a baseball bat covered in bright stickers.

Bowers backed away.

The gunman cut around the clown and charged at her.

She tossed a metal trashcan in his path and sprinted away. The sound of running feet drew closer until she heard a grunt.

Bowers glanced over her shoulder. Behind her the gunman lay face-first on the pavement. The clown stood over him with his baseball bat and that diabolical grin.

Another whack with the bat put the guy out of commission.

Bowers nodded to the clown and ran.

As police units headed toward the alley, Bowers backtracked. She searched for cover away from civilians and quickly realized she'd made a mistake.

A car roared up the street and came straight at her. Brakes squealed. The big man with the AK-47 hopped out of the passenger seat. She sprinted away and ducked through an archway as he took a shot. Two men grabbed her from both sides. One held a sharp blade to her throat. The other pressed a large caliber pistol into her side.

The guy, who'd been tasered at the vape shop, aimed his AK-47 at her chest.

YOUR FUNERAL

BO HAD NO DOUBTS that what lay behind the Hole's rusted metal door could end his life. If Preston were to learn he'd brought the president's daughter onboard, it would be the point of no return.

Lauren knew his name and his face. If the feds showed up or she went home, he'd be a dead man.

She and her friend needed to disappear.

Bo took a breath and opened the lock. His eyes watered from the stench.

"Hey, jerk!" yelled Lauren.

Bo pulled back his hand as if he intended to belt her. "Shut. The. Fuck. Up."

She threw her arm up in defense. Her friend with the brown hair sat with her face in her hands.

There were six girls in the room: five alive and one dead.

He forced two deckhands with masks and gloves to haul away the corpse. The shaken men moved with surprising speed, as if eager to get this over with.

A frail voice pleaded. "*Señor*. Please let me go home."

Bo ignored her. She and the sick one were the last two from the old stock. Once they were gone, that would leave Lauren, Molly, and the one in the corner Bo didn't dare tell Preston about.

Carson sprayed some pine-scented shit in the air. It didn't help. The medic stood ready to use drugs to control those who didn't cooperate. His glasses fogged from the mask over his nose and mouth. "Which ones go?"

Bo pointed to the sick one and the girl who'd pleaded with him. "That one too."

The deckhands returned. One took out the wobbly sick girl. The other grabbed the one who continued to plead for help.

The three remaining girls stared at him.

Carson pointed to the one in the corner.

"What about her?" he asked.

"Leave her," said Bo. "No reason to dump fresh goods. I'm not a total shit-bag."

Carson snorted. "Wanna bet?"

"Hey! I have standards," said Bo.

"Yeah, right." Carson tugged at his stethoscope. "Does the skipper even know she's here?"

"What do you care?" asked Bo. "Just leave her."

Carson threw up his hands. "It's your funeral."

After he left, Bo pulled the blonde to her feet. Their eyes locked. Defiant as ever, she kicked him.

Bo slapped her. Her soft skin felt like that of a child's against his rough hands. He pointed his pistol at her temple. "You make one more fucking sound and I will gut your friend like a fish and make you watch."

The brunette whimpered.

He forced Lauren and Molly out of the Hole, hoping no one would notice. Bo hurried down the passageway toward the stern. The girls' slow pace annoyed him.

"Hurry up," he hissed.

Just as he reached the steps to the stern, he heard footsteps.

"Hey, Bo," shouted Niko. "Hold on."

Bo stopped. *Dammit.*

The 3rd mate hustled closer. "What are you doing?" he asked.

"Following orders."

Niko ogled the slender blonde. "Where are you taking them?"

Bo wished the man would keep his damned nose out of Bo's business.

"The skipper told me to clean out the Hole," said Bo, hoping this asshole would just go away.

"But we just got them. Besides, I kind of like this one."

As Niko reached out to touch the blonde, she slapped his hand away.

"See," said Bo, faking a smile. "That's why Preston doesn't like them."

"He doesn't like anybody. One thing for sure, he hates wasting assets, and this little *chiquita* has a nice ass-ette. Put them back. Now."

OVER THE EDGE

R IGGS KNEW THERE WOULD BE HELL to pay when McDougall discovered he had departed for Miami.

As the sun peered above the horizon, Riggs sat in a window seat next to Greg as their jet headed south. He stared out at the white clouds in the distance.

Waiting for them, the Miami Coast Guard had a helicopter, a flight crew, and a rapid response cutter on standby. They had also setup a large room at the station they could use as a command center.

Pleased to be heading closer to Bowers, Riggs kicked his bag under his seat.

Greg stood in the aisle and stretched. "I'll grab some water." While he went to the rear, Riggs sent a text: *Update?*

A few minutes later, Greg dropped heavily into his seat on the aisle and handed one of the cold bottles of water to Riggs.

"Thanks."

Greg glanced at Riggs' phone as he put it away.

Riggs cracked open his water bottle. "I had an interesting phone conversation with a guy in Miami."

Greg stretched one leg out into the aisle.

"You'll love this one," said Riggs. "Remember me telling you about

Bo Somers, the fugitive who assaulted Bowers? Same guy showed up at a dock last night in Miami. The witness sells fuel and rents out dock space to supplement his charter-fishing business."

Greg closed his eyes. "I'm listening."

"Somers filled the boat's fuel tank and left without paying. Really pissed off the guy who'd let him use the dock."

Greg pulled his ballcap over his face. "Riggs, why do I care?"

"Because Somers left Miami with two teenage girls."

Greg lifted the brim of his hat.

"The witness is being interviewed as we speak. He claims the girls match the description of Roadrunner and Molly."

———

WHILE WAITING FOR the jet's doors to open, Riggs' phone buzzed with the call he'd been dreading.

"Where the hell are you?" demanded McDougall.

"Miami," said Riggs, hoping this wasn't a career-altering blunder.

"Shit," said McDougall. The line went dead.

Calling him back would do no good. Besides, it was too late for his boss to do anything about it. Riggs would have to settle that score later.

As he stepped off the jet, the morning sun winked off the shiny, white exterior of the plane. His belly grumbled for breakfast.

Confronted by heat and humidity, his sunglasses fogged. He stuffed his jacket into his bag and hoisted his rifle over his shoulder.

Station Miami's accommodations were as expected: large and functional with polished tile floors and white walls.

Kory greeted Riggs with a vigorous handshake and a cup of coffee. Riggs then took a seat next to Greg at a sturdy folding table. He marveled at how Kory and the forward team had already transformed the space into an effective command center. While waiting for the posting of the latest reports, Riggs continued to fill Greg in on Somers.

"The Hinkley was docked within walking distance to the party where the girls were last seen."

Greg frowned. "How do you know this?"

"A taxi driver reported picking up a man at the dock standing near a Hinkley cabin cruiser. The cabbie claimed the man's blackened eyes caught his attention. He took the man to a HVAC supply store and then gave him a ride to a bar on the beach. His story fits with what the dock attendant said. Then the bartender recognized the girls. When they left with Bo, he called the police."

"Nice find," said Greg.

"Bowers had seen Somers driving a Hinkley cabin cruiser, but he doesn't own one, which means he is working with or for someone." His reported income showed a smattering of paychecks from a bar and a printing shop. It wasn't enough to live on, which confirmed he must be taking cash payments from someone.

Greg studied a report on the computer screen.

Riggs told him about Key West PD finding drugs on Bo's old Boston Whaler.

"Don't like the sound of that," said Greg. "Human trafficking and drugs go hand-in-hand. I sure hope our girls aren't mixed up in that. POTUS would come unglued."

Riggs stretched. "Coast Guard Key West tells me that this Hinkley has been shadowing a super-yacht named the *Leisure Lee*. It all fits. Somers bought drinks at this same bar on Miami Beach with a company credit card."

Greg clicked his pen. "Let me guess, the card is from the *Leisure Lee*?"

"Indeed," said Riggs, "Bowers has been watching the docks. She says hired guns routinely go back and forth between the Hinkley and the *Leisure Lee*. She'd also told me about a Fountain speed boat with a heavily armed crew."

"Who owns them?" asked Greg.

"They are part of a fleet of luxury super-yachts owned by a corporation in Miami that caters to wealthy travelers. Our vessels of interest have been operating out of a marina in Key West for approximately eight months."

Greg watched Kory and other Secret Service agents across the room. "Maybe they have a trafficking operation like that celebrity pimp that committed suicide." Greg glanced between the computer and his notepad. "Has Bowers noticed anything else?"

Riggs shrugged. "I don't know. I sent her a text around five this morning, but she hasn't answered."

"Then who were you texting on the plane?" asked Greg.

Riggs kept his eyes on his phone. "I have sources."

"Pain in the ass." Greg scratched down some notes. "I'll work with the Miami team and search for Lauren and Molly."

As he continued writing notes, Riggs noticed Greg watching him.

"We need someone," said Greg, "to go down to Key West to hunt down that Hinkley. You wouldn't happen to be interested, would you?"

Riggs chuckled. "Hell, yes."

As he started to set up transport, his phone buzzed with an incoming message: *URGENT. Bowers abducted at zero three-thirty. Can't locate. Action needed.*

IN THE LINE OF DUTY

C OOP'S BOOT HEELS THUDDED against the station's linoleum floor. When his lieutenant had called him to his office, Coop knew something was up.

He entered a room that held five workstations filled with officers doing paperwork.

Wondering what this was about, Coop took a seat.

He watched the LT take apart his cellphone. "I dropped it in the toilet."

Coop knew he hadn't called him in to discuss a wet phone.

The LT set his phone aside and gave Coop his full attention. "I've got some bad news."

"What?" Coop prayed this wasn't about his sister being found in a ditch.

"Gunner got away."

"You've got to be shittin' me," said Coop. "How the hell did that happen?"

"Coop, we're not happy about this either," said the LT. "Gunner didn't go with transport. He tried to kick out the window of the patrol unit and officers had to hog-tie him. In the process he continued to resist and was tasered. They transported him in an ambulance. Officer

Drake rode with them. On the way to the hospital a swarm of bikers forced them off the road. They shot out the tires and the windows and took Gunner."

Coop stared at the floor. "How's Drake?"

With no warning, the Chief of Police stepped into the room. Everyone stood.

"Coop, I need a word," said the chief. He motioned for everyone to clear the space. "Take a break, fellas."

Coop figured he was in deep shit.

After everyone left, the chief closed the door and dropped Coop's missing duty belt on the desk. "We found this in the woods."

Coop immediately tried to explain himself. "Chief, I—"

The chief took a seat and held up a hand to silence him. "Relax. You were outmanned and outgunned. No need to apologize, but Brian, I want you to listen to me."

The chief never used Coop's first name.

They locked eyes.

"First, you're beat up. You okay?"

"It's been a long week, sir," said Coop, "but I'll be fine."

The chief glanced at Coop's bandages. "No easy way to say this. Officer Drake died in the line of duty."

Coop slumped forward. "He was a good officer." Disbelief rocked him. "Five years ago, I took pictures of his dad pinning on his badge. His poor family."

The chief listened.

Coop felt at a loss. "I should've ridden with him."

"This isn't your fault," said the chief.

"What about the ambulance crew?" asked Coop.

"They're in the hospital," said the chief. "One is critical, but it sounds like they'll pull through. Drake fought hard. If he hadn't, they'd all be gone."

"I'm glad the EMTs are okay," said Coop, "but... damn."

The chief watched him closely. "The captain says Bowers played a role."

"Yes, sir," said Coop. "I know we don't usually accept civilians into the mix, but Nolan and Carver said Bowers saw the odds were against us and stepped in. No hesitation. The three of us wouldn't be here, if it weren't for her."

The chief nodded. "Nolan said she made a difference."

Coop picked at his bandage. "She had our backs, sir."

The chief tilted his head. "My FTO used to tell me that actions speak louder than words. You did good. And, if I'm listening right, this woman's actions are telling us something important."

Coop nodded. "She is, sir. Bowers is on our side. Wish you could've seen her in action. Lordy, does she have skills. I wouldn't want that woman pissed at me."

The chief studied Coop's face. "I'd like to speak with her and hear her take on what happened."

"I'm sure she'd like that, sir," said Coop.

The chief put a hand on Coop's shoulder. "I need your report. Then go home and get some rest. You've been through the ringer lately."

Coop didn't like the orders, but he appreciated the chief's concern. "Yes, sir. Thank you."

The chief didn't walk away as Coop expected. He lowered his voice. "I just got off the phone with the FBI. They've offered to assist in capturing Gunner. They found his DNA on the remains of a girl they recovered from the woods in Virginia."

"But what about our cases?" asked Coop. "The torched house? The assaults on our officers? Drake is dead because of him."

"Coop, federal charges mean Gunner will be looking at a much harsher sentence. He's done. We'll get him."

The chief's brown eyes homed in on him like a laser.

"Sir?"

The chief took a deep breath. "Now. About your sister."

DARK DEEDS

BO STOOD AT THE HELM of the Hinkley, scanning the horizon and searching for Coast Guard vessels. Their distinctive white ships with the huge slanted red stripe near the bow and tall radar tower made them easy to spot. If they were to get an eyeful of the mess on this deck, they'd lock him up for sure.

Last night had been messier than usual. He dreaded the cleanup ahead of him.

After this, they owed him a promotion and command of his own ship.

Bo washed a tooth and a hunk of hair overboard and scrubbed the decks with bleach. The dried blood didn't come off as easily.

The events from last night tumbled through his thoughts. The dead one's bloated body had repulsed him. He'd used the sheet to drag her to the stern, tied an old anchor from a salvage yard around her ankles, and slid the body into the sea.

The other two had tried to fight back. The guards onboard were useless. They did little more than watch.

As Bo hosed down the boat, he thought of his daddy, who used to tell Bo "say your prayers" right before he beat him. Bo had learned that the old saying about dead weight had been true. Daddy had been a big man. Bo had used a hack saw and a pully strung up over the rafters to get all of Pop's parts into the freezer.

Bo enjoyed reminiscing about his dad until he heard Niko's voice. "Hey, Bo. Preston's looking for you."

Now what? Bo kicked a scrub brush across the deck. He wanted chow, a shower, and some shuteye.

After drying his hands, he clomped up the stairs and took off his soggy shoes before entering the forward cabin.

Preston rose from behind his oak desk and waved him into the office. In his pristine uniform, he stared down at Bo's bare feet and damp jeans.

"Everything go okay?"

"Yes, sir," said Bo as he stuck his pruned hands into his pockets.

"Any problems?"

Bo didn't answer. After dumping the trash, they'd met up with a supply boat to get cigars, booze, and fresh girls. Preston didn't need to know that it hadn't gone entirely as planned.

One girl from the fresh supply still stuck in his mind. She had stared at him with big pleading eyes. Her body had seemed way too young for this. The supplier claimed she was eighteen. That was bullshit.

It still bothered him. *I must be getting soft.*

"Bo," barked Preston. "You gonna stand there or answer my question?"

"Sorry, sir. It's been a long night."

"You picked up five girls. Right?" asked Preston.

Bo folded his arms. "We got three."

"Why?"

"We reached the supply boat. Picked up the cigars, then it went sideways. They claimed they only got part of the payment from Gunner and he hadn't returned their calls."

Preston took a seat and tossed his pen aside. "Shit. I gave Gunner the funds and his cut. What the hell did he do with it?"

"You'd have to ask him, sir."

"How many girls did you get?"

"They were only going to give us one, but our AK-47s changed their minds. They coughed up two more."

Bo heard footsteps. The 3rd mate showed up in the doorway.

Preston scribbled on a notepad. "With the three Bo brought onboard, we'll be okay."

Bo's face flushed. Apparently, Preston knew all about the extra girl, which meant someone had ratted on him.

Niko's smug expression meant he had to be the one who'd squealed.

Preston rocked back in his chair. "Save the blonde and her friend for our senators."

Niko stood before the skipper with his feet apart and his arms folded like he was somebody.

Preston stood. "Our chopper will pick-up the senators in Miami." He locked eyes with Bo. "We cannot afford anymore screwups."

"Yes, sir."

Preston stepped closer. "I'm putting you on security where I can keep an eye on you." He glanced at Bo's bleach-stained jeans. "Go clean up. You look like shit."

Bo sucked it up and didn't say a word.

"You and Knuckles will guard the senators when they arrive. Make sure they have time to unwind with the girls. And, as soon as our guests leave the ship, I want the Hole cleaned out. All of them. You read me?"

"Yes, sir."

He left to get a shower and shave. Sleep would have to wait.

His head pounded. Knowing the senators were bound to recognize the blonde, this was like waiting for a firing squad to pull the trigger.

STARING DOWN AT THE EARTH from the open bay of a Coast Guard MH-65 Dolphin helicopter was exhilarating or terrifying, depending on a person's point of view.

With a 400-mile range, Riggs wasn't worried about fuel, but everything about choppers unnerved him. Gliding with wings made sense

but beating the air into submission had always seemed tenuous at best.

A pilot had once pointed out a giant nut that kept rotor blades attached. "We call it *the Jesus nut* because—"

Riggs had gotten the picture.

He headed for Key West, knowing this trip would be a longshot. Bo and the girls could be anywhere by now.

The cramped interior certainly didn't coddle to comfort. Due to the *whomping* of the rotor blades, any interaction with the crew required shouting.

Greg had stayed behind in Miami to coordinate with the Secret Service on the local search for Lauren and Molly. Meanwhile, Riggs had other things on his mind.

Once on the ground, priority one entailed following the lead about Bo and the Hinkley. Hopefully that would point them toward the girls.

Riggs thought about the bikers, Bo, and their connections to human trafficking. If finding Lauren hadn't been urgent, he would have asked the pilot to do a flyover on the coordinates Bowers had given him for the dumpsite to get a feel for the area. No doubt, the dive team will have their hands full doing evidence recovery on such a large site.

He couldn't imagine a trafficker being dumb enough to pick up POTUS' kid. *But then again, ya can't fix stupid with duct tape.*

He also intended to find Bowers. Riggs took a deep breath and tried to ignore the bumpy ride.

His phone buzzed with an incoming text from Greg that read: *Good Luck. Hope you find her.*

Riggs chuckled. *Thanks,* he replied.

After working together for so long, it felt as if he and Greg had been through a war together. Brotherly bonds were often forged in the trenches of pandemonium. If he had to go into battle with someone, there were few he trusted more than Greg and Bowers.

He checked his phone for recent messages. One provided Bowers' last-known location and a series of photographs. The sense of alarm he felt grab him like a vise.

Riggs vividly remembered the feel of her skin and the way she wouldn't leave his side when he'd been shot. He vaguely recalled going in and out of consciousness, and yet each time lucidity found him, so did the feel of her holding his hand. He chided himself for not getting down here sooner.

The winds picked up as they began their descent. In response to the turbulence, Riggs held on and pressed back into his seat until the wheels touched down. The bird landed so gently it made him feel a little foolish for being apprehensive.

Once on the ground, he checked in with the Coast Guard command who had put out an alert to all of their vessels to be on the lookout for the Hinkley and the *Leisure Lee*.

"We've got a fleet of vessels all over these waters," said the captain. "We should get something soon. We'll find them."

While the Coast Guard executed the search, Riggs had another search in mind.

RED FLAGS

R IGGS PROWLED THE STREETS of Key West in a car borrowed from the Coast Guard. While searching for Bowers, he found huge crowds celebrating Fantasy Fest.

Key West certainly knew how to put on a bash, but he wasn't there to party.

Even with the description, pinpointing her last location proved challenging.

He examined the pictures on his phone showing the cross streets near where she'd been abducted.

He drove another two blocks and parked by the broken fence that matched the picture. Riggs left the car and found himself facing the pale-blue archway where she'd been taken.

At the stucco structure, he could see how they'd ambushed her. The bloodstains and scuffs in the dirt told him she'd put up a fight.

Riggs returned to the car and hustled toward her hotel.

Along the way, he spotted two patrolmen guarding an alley blocked off with yellow crime-scene tape. The coroner's van and the brass shell casings littering the pavement told him he'd found the scene of a firefight.

Riggs became more unsettled.

When he found Bowers' hotel, he glanced up at the renovated Victorian house. The third-floor windows had a decent view of the streets. Knowing Bowers, he'd bet a steak dinner that she'd chosen it for that reason.

Next to the gated pool, he opened a red door under a sign that read: *Office*. At the check-in desk a girl with purple hair looked up from her phone.

"Hey. Welcome," she said. "You here for Fantasy Fest?"

Riggs pulled out his FBI creds and a photo of Bowers. "I'm looking for this woman."

"Oh." The girl froze for a moment.

Riggs got that a lot.

"Yeah," she said. "She's really cool. Her room is 304." The young woman played with a lock of her purple hair. "She must be popular. Lots of people are lookin' for her."

That sent up a red flag.

Riggs took the stairs two at a time until he got a call from Greg. He leaned on the white railing and stared down at the pool below.

"Hey, Riggs," said Greg. "E-Connect's CEO and the MIT guy who built the chip are in Miami or at least they were. We just missed them. But there is no sign of them leaving on any commercial bus, train, cab, or plane. And get this. The head of SriCom and an entourage from North Korea have just arrived in Nassau. Customs says they're on vacation."

"That fishing trip is bullshit," said Riggs. He gave Greg an update on the Coast Guard's response and ended the call.

Knowing Greg, a covert team would already be deployed to keep an eye on the North Koreans.

Riggs approached Bowers' room. The door stood ajar. He carefully mounted the last few steps to avoid making any noise. He hesitated as a light flashed inside the room. Bowers would never have left her door open like that.

Riggs drew his weapon and took a position next to the doorframe.

When he heard movement inside, he kicked the door wide open.

RIGGS QUICKLY GLANCED inside at the man in Bowers hotel room. The doorframe provided cover.

"Drop your weapon," they both yelled simultaneously.

That surprised Riggs. The guy sounded like a cop. He jerked his head just enough to snatch another glimpse of the bull of a man who had also taken cover.

Crap. The tall blond man in civilian clothes had the shoulders and biceps of a committed bodybuilder. With his weapon aimed, Riggs stood ready to take him on.

"Police," yelled the man inside the room. "Drop your weapon."

"FBI," shouted Riggs in a voice that could rattle the walls. "You drop it!"

Without backing down, Riggs pulled out his wallet with one hand and flipped it open to show his Bureau ID.

"Who are you?" asked the big man.

"Special Agent Steven Riggs. You?" He waited for a few more seconds and heard footsteps. Riggs backed away as the man came outside with his weapon lowered.

"What are you doing here?" the big man asked.

"Where's Bowers?" asked Riggs. "Why are you in her room?"

"It was unlocked." The man shoved his pistol into his holster. "Sorry. You startled me. I'm Officer Cooper. Key West Police Department."

Riggs lowered his weapon. "You're Coop?"

"Yeah." Coop seemed surprised. "How do you know my name?"

"Bowers told me about you," said Riggs.

The two men eyed each other for a few tense moments.

Riggs noted the red lump on the side of his face and bandages. "Where is she?"

"Wish I knew. I've been looking for her." Coop's voice trailed off. "But then lately, my skills at locating people have sucked."

Riggs remembered Bowers telling him about her search for Coop's missing sister. "She was helping you."

"She was." Coop rubbed his side. "I'm afraid that's what got her in trouble."

"Don't blame yourself. There's more to it," said Riggs.

Coop's expression shifted to a hard focus. "I've got a damned good guess as to who took her."

He showed Riggs the open window.

Riggs stuck his head outside. "I'm guessing Bo Somers had something to do with it?"

Coop nodded. "He isn't in this alone. He's into some nasty shit. Bowers was right about him all along. We should've brought that bastard in sooner."

THE RUSE

CARRYING LUGGAGE AND A BRIEFCASE for some monkey in a suit rubbed against Bo's temperament.

The man who'd been introduced as the CEO strutted down the passageway with perfectly groomed, silver hair and fine leather shoes as if he owned the damned ship. The tycoon had landed in his own company's chopper.

Must be nice.

Bo didn't know much about briefcases, but he bet this one cost more than he could afford.

Doug, the round-faced guy with the CEO, reminded Bo of a gamer. He wore an oversized T-shirt and red shoes with thick white soles. The fellow didn't talk much until the door to the CEO's stateroom closed. Then he and the CEO got into it.

Bo stood guard in the hall.

"You can't do this," yelled Doug. "You'll compromise our whole communications network. Your selling out our country."

"Lower your voice," said the CEO. "If I hadn't bought your damned chip in the first place, my company wouldn't be broke. You owe me. Everything I own is on the line here. Show me some courtesy and help me get this done."

"Don't put this on me," argued Doug. "I warned you about people giving up their landlines for cellphones. With cable going the way of videotapes, I told you that to be competitive, you needed to invest in internet streaming, direct-to-consumer subscriptions to hot channels, apps, and the huge digital advertising market. You wouldn't listen."

As their angry voices echoed in the hall, crewmen hurried to finish last-minute preparations. One delivered a fancy box of Cuban cigars and a brand-new bottle of Glenlivet to the room down the hall, their largest stateroom, which overlooked the sundeck. Preston's guests got the best.

Bo imagined himself in that room someday.

As a crewman walked past Bo, the fight inside the CEO's quarters intensified. The crewman's eyes grew wide.

Preston wanted a nice quiet meeting.

Good luck with that.

SEVERAL HOURS LATER, Bo stood near the helipad, watching the setting sun paint the blue sky in ribbons of purple and gold. The ship's red helicopter circled the ship. The pilot made sure the passengers had one hell of a view from the open bay doors before landing.

Bo shielded his eyes from the rotor wash.

A man in a dark-blue suit and red tie disembarked and ran a hand through his windblown hair. "That was exhilarating."

When the man spotted Preston, he put-on a smile as phony as his dyed hair.

Preston shook the man's hand. "Senator Fowler, welcome."

With pale skin and obvious discomfort on a rolling ship, Fowler didn't appear to be the type who would enjoy fishing.

Bo spotted a flying fish gliding inches above the deep-blue waters. A dolphin surfaced and snapped up the fish before it knew what hit him.

Preston greeted the next man exiting the chopper. "Welcome aboard, Senator Hogan."

Hogan took particular interest in their security team.

As Preston escorted the senators inside, Niko tagged along, grinning like he'd just been elected class president.

Bo didn't share his joy. With congressmen onboard, the odds of the blonde being recognized became a certainty.

As he lugged the senator's baggage down the stairs, Bo mulled over his options: get rid of her or get off this ship before it was too late.

Hogan took a room on the starboard side. Fowler scored the big stateroom with the view off the stern and the bottle of fine scotch.

Fifteen minutes later, Preston and the two senators gathered in the forward cabin for a meeting.

Bo stood guard, wishing he could've grabbed his camera and gone diving instead. Knowing that the shopkeeper wouldn't get his photos on time, made Bo hate Preston even more.

Bo stood near the bar, while a deckhand mixed drinks and elevator music played in the background.

Preston signaled to the 3rd mate. "Tell the chef we're ready for appetizers."

"Yes, sir," said Niko.

Bo watched the 3rd mate scurry away.

Hogan, a tall black man, carried himself like a man of confidence, but in a likeable way. He definitely wasn't like the arrogant bastards they usually entertained.

Fowler kept checking his watch, as if something were about to happen. Unlike Hogan, Fowler's smug attitude quickly got on Bo's nerves.

When Hogan left for the men's room, Fowler leaned back into the soft cushions of the white couch and started in on Preston.

"Let's cut the crap," said the senator. "I expect full cooperation. Nothing happens on this ship without my approval. Capiche?"

Seeing the tables turned on Preston made standing duty suddenly a lot more interesting. Bo thought it hilarious to see Fowler full of swag and Preston red in the face with nothing he could do about it.

Fowler left Preston and wandered over to the bar where he handed a wad of bills to the bartender.

Moments later, Hogan returned.

As the crew delivered drinks and colorful trays of finger food, the senators and Preston sat in a circle on the white couches shootin' the shit.

Fowler put his feet up on the coffee table. "The CEO and Doug are here, right?"

"Yes, sir," said the skipper. "They're in their staterooms relaxing after their journey." Preston glared at Fowler's shoes on the glass coffee table.

Yes, sir! Bo bit his lip to keep from laughing.

Fowler selected a big fat Cuban cigar from a fancy wooden humidor and took his time lighting it.

The smell reminded Bo of burnt hay.

After a few drinks and conversations about deep-sea fishing, Hogan grimaced.

Fowler tilted his head and paid close attention as Hogan leaned forward, rubbed his neck, and started to sweat.

Fowler sipped his scotch and casually watched Hogan.

"Senator," said Fowler, "you don't look so good."

Hogan sagged forward. "Something's wrong."

Preston acted unusually calm. "Are you seasick? I can get someone from sickbay to bring you some medicine."

Hogan stood. "I need to go to my room. Sorry."

His balance seemed off. Fowler snapped his fingers and pointed to the bearded guard in the bandana. "Escort the senator to his quarters."

Preston sat there like a couch cushion. He didn't utter a peep about someone else ordering his men around.

That's a first.

Hogan leaned on the guard to steady himself.

Fowler's brows rose as he grinned at Preston and took another puff on his cigar.

Preston watched Hogan leave. "Why did you even bring him?"

"Leverage," said Fowler. "Politics is a chess game. I need his vote to get this done."

The two yammered on for another hour. Fowler squinted through the cigar smoke. "I've got a lot riding on this deal. When that little Korean shit gets here, treat him like his ass is made of gold."

Fowler picked up a tiny piece of toast piled high with caviar. "The president is too worried about his stupid kid to get CFIUS off their asses. No matter how this shakes out, I want to close the deal on that damned chip."

"What about the CEO and Doug?" asked Preston.

"Keep them in their rooms until dinner." Fowler flicked his ashes into an ashtray.

"Give them a little time to enjoy the amenities." He winked at Preston and stuffed another piece of toast and caviar in his trap. "Mind you, I expect impeccable service tonight. A gourmet meal to cajole our E-Connect boys. Then when they're all mellowed out, we'll get down to brass tacks."

Preston looked nervous. "What if Hogan doesn't cooperate?"

Fowler grinned with a piece of parsley stuck to his front tooth. "Oh, he will. He can't afford not to."

FEARLESS CARGO

A S FOWLER LEFT FOR HIS STATEROOM, Preston pulled
Bo aside like they were suddenly old pals. "We've got incoming.
We're running late. Jung should've been here hours ago. Make sure he
moves his ass and the bird is back in the air pronto."

The helipad sat on the top of the ship next to the bridge. Bo
lumbered up the ladder just in time to see Jung and Knuckles hauling
Bowers away from the chopper.

That was something worth seeing, but the idiots had zip-tied her
hands in front. *That was stupid.*

Bo had already learned his lesson with her. For someone like
Bowers, he would've hog tied her using chains and duct tape. Jung
pulled her forward by her shirt and held her there like a fishing trophy.

Dude you are asking for it.

Without warning, Bowers lurched sideways. She interlocked her
fingers and abruptly snapped her wrists apart. The wire-ties fell to the
deck in pieces.

As Jung reached to grab her, she shoved him sideways. Before he
regained his balance, she grabbed his hair and drove his head down,
slamming his face into her knee.

Knuckles blinked. It all happened so fast.

Jung stumbled over the stool used for boarding passengers and pulled an evil-looking Condor knife. He lunged, slashing its hooked blade at Bowers, but her reflexes were faster.

She dodged left as the ship rolled. The knife fell from Jung's grip. He helplessly watched as it skidded over the deck and plunged overboard. Bowers crashed the wooden stool over Jung's head.

Bo fully enjoyed seeing Jung eat the deck.

While he lay sprawled face down, their security team swarmed in. It took three guys to wrestle Bowers toward the stairs.

While Preston glared through the tinted windows on the bridge, Bo shouted, "Let's go. Hurry it up."

Bo heard the whine and felt the downdraft of the chopper taking off as they hurried aft and descended the stairs.

He hoped that Jung's face would soon look at least as bad as his own. That would be righteous.

Seeing Preston schooled by Fowler, Jung with a busted face, and watching Bowers tossed into the Hole by three goons made his day.

BOWERS BRACED HERSELF AGAINST a metal wall in the dark room and heard breathing and a moan.

"Please, *señorita,*" said a woman. "Help me."

When Bowers' eyes had adjusted to the dim light, she counted four young women lying on mats, including the one with the Cuban accent. She reminded Bowers of the woman in the red dress who'd been rescued by the fishermen.

Bowers took a seat on one of the mats.

Two underage girls sat next to her. The one with long brown hair whimpered as she rocked back and forth.

The other stared at Bowers as if bewildered. Despite her smeared black makeup, Bowers recognized her immediately.

She leaned closer. "Do they know who you are?" she asked quietly.

The blonde girl shook her head. "No."

"Good," said Bowers, "Keep it that way."

BLACKMAIL

BO HEADED TOWARD THE GALLEY. Seeing Bowers trapped like a rat made his day.

As ordered, he'd come to check in with the cooks. The odor of garlic and butter hung in the air before he reached the kitchen. The clanking of pots and the chef's agitated voice filled the narrow passageway.

"Throw that out. Start over. This time keep the temperature lower and don't forget the salt."

The harried assistant chef raced past Bo with a large pan that smelled burnt.

The red-faced chef threw a spoon across the room. "Why are three of my lobsters dead? Somebody get me some shrimp out of the goddamned freezer."

Bo backed away.

The chef spotted him. "Tell Preston dinner is delayed by an hour."

"Roger that," said Bo. He radioed Niko. *He can be the chump that delivers that news.*

Bo figured he was better off laying low. Retreating to the state-rooms, he circled through passageways to ensure all was quiet. Doug and the CEO had apparently called a truce. Sounds of a television came from Doug's room.

Two of their guys stood guard in front of the *Horizon* stateroom, glancing at each other and smirking.

One raised his brows and whispered, "I'd take some of that any day."

The other snickered.

Hogan's door stood open a crack, inside he lay passed out and naked on the bed, while Jung directed one of the girls from the Hole into a series of provocative poses.

Hogan lay there limp and didn't flinch as the photos were taken. The naked woman attempted to cover herself with a sheet.

"*No, señor*." She pleaded. "Stop."

Her voice startled Hogan, who held his head up and glared at her with glazed eyes. "What the hell are you doing in my room?"

As Hogan spotted the guards and struggled to sit up, the girl jumped back and scampered away.

As if all was well, Jung lowered his phone. "Sir, let me get you some coffee."

———

BOWERS SCANNED THE DARK spaces and shadows. Around her young women in thong lace panties and skimpy bras sat on mats on the floor. She'd seen this before.

As a way of controlling their victims, traffickers often take their clothing away, leaving them naked or in revealing lingerie. For women who are unwilling to run away undressed, the ploy often worked.

Bowers noticed a young woman with dark blonde hair curled up on a filthy mattress in the far corner of the room. She faced the wall and used her arms to cover herself.

Bowers leaned toward Lauren and whispered, "How long has she been here?"

"Don't know," said Lauren. "She's been in that corner since those wankers stuffed us in here."

"It's hideous to do this to anyone. I'll do all I can to get you out of here."

"Yah, right." Lauren rolled her eyes. "Why would you care? You still have clothes."

Clearly, this teen's reputation in D.C. as having an attitude had been well founded.

"I will get you out of here."

As Lauren turned her back on Bowers, Molly reached out her hand. "Thank you."

Bowers crept toward the woman in the corner and knelt for a better view.

She bit down hard when she recognized the sweet girl from the coffee stand. "Sara?"

The woman turned to face Bowers. "Oh my God. It's you."

Sara's hug nearly knocked Bowers over.

"Are you all right?" asked Bowers. "Coop has been looking everywhere for you."

Tears welled in Sara's eyes. "Where is he? I need him, Bowers. I need my brother."

BACKFIRE

THE LAST FEW DAYS had given Bo an in-your-face view of Preston's depraved mind. The man would cross any line and exploit anyone to get what he wanted.

The skipper had his sights set on a big payoff that depended on wealthy clientele willing to pay top dollar for services they didn't dare acquire at home. The risks to their reputations guaranteed they would keep their mouths shut.

Bo had heard Preston telling guests that the girls were willing participants, well paid for their "hospitality," who wouldn't cause them problems. As he stopped at each stateroom to notify their guests about the delayed dinner, Bo wondered what these men would say if they knew these girls would be killed to ensure their silence.

Bo's plan to avoid going back to prison had included spending as much time at sea as possible. He had hoped to do more diving and develop his photography business, but when they offered to advance him through the ranks to commanding his own ship, he'd jumped at the opportunity.

Despite his best plans and all the promises, being stuck on the *Leisure Lee* under the command of a nutjob like Preston had screwed up everything. Even his hopes of promotion were looking grim.

Passing Hogan's room, Bo knew he'd done a lot of crazy shit but Preston and Fowler's attempt to drug and blackmail a senator was begging for trouble. The girls wouldn't be missed, but Hogan would be a different story.

When the man had disembarked from the chopper, he'd had an air about him, which left Bo suspecting they'd picked the wrong guy to mess with.

Bo wanted no part of that crap.

Moving to Mexico was looking better by the minute.

Continuing his rounds, Bo slipped cards under the doors to inform guests that dinner would be delayed. When he slipped a card under the CEO's door, the door creaked open. The CEO stood there wearing one of the VIP robes with the ship's logo. Behind him, the youngest girl sat on the bed in tears.

"Sir," said Bo, "dinner will be served in about an hour. Sorry to interrupt."

The girl began to sob for her mother. Clearly frustrated, the CEO ran a hand through his tousled hair. "I'm done. Get her out of here."

Bo pulled the girl from the room. "Can we bring you another girl?"

"No," said the CEO, as he slammed the door.

As Bo escorted the young girl below deck, his curiosity got the better of him. "How old are you?"

"*Doce.*"

He frowned and stared down at her. "Twelve?"

"*Sí, señor,*" she said. "I have brother, same age. We have our birthday three months from now." She bent forward and began to cry. "I want to go home."

Even for Bo, who saw himself as a hard ass, this was bullshit. Up ahead he spotted the 3rd mate returning with the girl from Hogan's room. He pushed her, using more force than needed.

"Easy, dude. Don't bruise the peaches," said Bo. He handed the twelve-year-old over to him. "Preston wants me to watch the staterooms. Can you take her back to the Hole?"

"Sure," said Niko. As he walked away, his radio crackled with an incoming message: "Take the blonde to Fowler's room. Now."

That brought Bo to an abrupt halt as his mouth went dry.

TRIPWIRE

B OWERS HAD HEARD THE CREW refer to this room as *The Hole*. She could see why. As a former homicide detective, Bowers knew the black matter pooled in the corners and crevices of the floor was probably dried blood. The odor of decomp seemed to cling to the walls.

Under the dim light from a bulb at the peeling ceiling, she scanned the oppressive surroundings and the frightened faces staring at her. None of them fit Lily's description of her sister. The grim reality was that Lily's twin probably lay at the bottom of the sea with the others.

These girls needed to be rescued before they were gone too.

Bowers leaned against the rusted-metal wall and felt the ship rocking. Her options were clear.

Near the engine room, a neat row of lifejackets with rescue beacons hung on the wall. The Coast Guard couldn't be more than an hour away. The water was warm enough. She could call Riggs, pick the lock, grab a vest, jump off the stern, and wait for a rescue. That would mean abandoning these women to Bo Somers and the other shitbags on this boat. She couldn't do that.

The faces of these terrorized women set her off like a tripwire.

Bowers paced the grimy floor, remembering every hall, exit, and person she'd seen on the ship.

Sara watched her. "You look pissed."

"I am."

Sara stood. "That's the best thing I've heard all day."

"What?"

Sara crossed her arms. "Coop says you're at your best when you're mad."

Bowers hid a smirk. "If your brother were here, what would he do?"

The dim overhead lamp highlighted the smattering of freckles over Sara's nose. "He'd tear this ship apart and put Bo and the rest of them in jail."

"Exactly," said Bowers. "It's time to put a wrench in their plans."

Sara managed a smile that faded quickly.

"You okay?"

"I will be," said Sara, "when Bo is behind bars. He's the one that brought me here. I thought we were dating. Obviously, that was a lie."

"Doesn't surprise me," said Bowers. If they survived this, perhaps someday she would tell Sara about jabbing Bo's junk with rebar.

Bowers put her ear to the door and closed her eyes to listen for movement outside. She needed to find reception and call Riggs.

As planned, Jung had frisked her and found her burner phone. He didn't bother to look any further after finding her Glock. The idiot had missed the phone in her bra and the array of other helpful items hidden in her underwear and seams. With all the weapons she'd seen onboard, replacing her pistol was the least of her worries.

Bowers heard footsteps and the clink of a metal door opening. It sounded as if it were next door.

She crept along the wall toward the door between the two rooms and jumped aside as it flew open.

The muffled voice of a child cried out, "I want my mama."

Bowers peered into what was clearly a dressing room where the man who'd unlocked the door grabbed a young woman and a girl by the arm.

"No," screamed the younger one.

Bowers entered the dressing room. "Let them go."

When the child pulled away, Bowers guided her toward the women in the other room. The remaining woman grabbed a cocktail dress and held it up to cover herself.

"Put it down," he ordered, "or I'll slit your damn throat."

"No, you won't," said Bowers.

"Mind your own business."

The tearful Cuban woman dropped the dress and bolted through the door to join the rest of the women.

The man pushed Bowers into the Hole. She stood as a barrier between him and the women.

He pointed at Lauren. "You're next. Get in here."

Lauren didn't budge. This man obviously didn't know Lauren's identity.

"Leave her be," said Bowers in a firm voice.

He attempted to slap Bowers, but she diverted his swing with one hand and punched him with the other.

When Sara tried to help, he shoved her aside and grabbed Lauren's arm. "You're coming with me."

Lauren pulled away. "Listen, asswipe, if you don't let me go I'm gonna tell—"

The man belted her so hard she would've fallen if Bowers hadn't caught her.

"I'm the 3rd mate," the man yelled. "I'm in charge here. I own your ass."

"Wrong answer," said Bowers. "Get your hands off her."

When she ripped Lauren out of his grip, the man pulled a knife and swung. The blade narrowly missed Bowers' arm.

Lauren screamed.

Bowers deflected his next few swipes until he pulled out his Ruger 1911 and fired at one of the mattresses. The deafening *boom* left everyone stunned.

The 3rd mate pointed the gun at Lauren's head. "Back away or the next round will blow her brains all over this shithole."

ONE TO REMEMBER

F OR SENATOR LARRY FOWLER, nothing had ever been so
  erotic as leveraging power and making a shitload of money while
doing so.

He took a break in his stateroom named *Grandeur*. It wasn't as
spacious as the Four Seasons, but it had fine silk sheets, a nice view of
the ocean, his favorite Cuban cigars, and a bottle of Glenlivet, which
sat next to a crystal glass and an insulated bucket of fresh ice.

He peered through the bifocals of his aviator-style glasses to read
the label of the eighteen-year-old scotch.

After pouring a glass, he stretched out on the bed with his glass of
amber liquor on the nightstand. The mellow scotch rolled over his
tongue. Its oaky flavors carried a hint of vanilla.

He opened his laptop and busted out laughing as he flipped
through the pictures of Hogan caught with his pants down.

These were priceless. The righteous, holier-than-thou SOB, who
had always challenged him on ethics and integrity, was buck naked
with a woman who wasn't his wife.

Fowler had paid Preston handsomely for these and didn't regret a
nickel of it. This was great stuff. He especially liked the close up of

Hogan being kissed with his eyes closed. No one needed to know the man was unconscious.

Early on Hogan had been offered a girl but declined. Fowler couldn't understand why a man wouldn't willingly take advantage of such amenities. Hell, he would've, especially after his wife had taken to wearing flannel pajamas and sleeping in another room over ten years ago.

The warmth of the alcohol provided a heady sense of ease, as Fowler studied the provocative pictures. His eyes skied down the soft sloping curves of the naked woman's body.

He felt the stirring in parts of him that hadn't seen action in a long time. Fowler tossed his trousers aside and put on silk boxers and the VIP robe. His aching hunger would soon be satisfied. Traveling without the wife had its advantages.

Fowler studied his reflection in the bathroom mirror and tossed his bottle of Viagra back in the drawer. His early morning workouts had paid off. He flexed his arms, checked his teeth, and combed back his charcoal-black hair.

The knock on the door filled him with anticipation. Fowler smiled and drained his glass of scotch.

He graciously welcomed Niko and the pretty young thing into the room and stuffed a wad of cash into Niko's greedy palm.

"Thank you, sir."

Before leaving, the 3rd mate handed Fowler a small white card with the ship's logo and a phone number. "Call me when you're finished," said Niko.

Fowler locked the door and flipped the latch.

Before him a gorgeous blonde stood in the middle of his room. The bottle of scotch was probably older than this girl, but what the hell—no one would ever know. Besides, he liked them young.

He reached out to touch her, but she slapped his hand and jumped back. He smiled. A feisty one. He could play this game.

When she bolted for the door, he enjoyed the chase but quickly tired of the game when she attempted to lock herself in the bathroom.

He walloped her good and threw her on the bed. His juices were flowing now. He hadn't been this excited since that time in Vegas when two chorus girls had done him good.

He straddled the girl and ran a hand up her firm thighs. Her skin was soft and smooth. With her blonde curls still slightly damp from a shower, her fresh clean scent engulfed him.

When she tried to wiggle away, he tore off her black lace panties. As his excitement grew, he fumbled with his boxers. This was going to be one to remember.

While breathing heavily, he began to position himself. Fowler glanced down at her face and froze.

His heart seemed to skip a beat.

Fowler swiped the soft blonde curls from her face and stared in abject horror at the wide eyes glaring up at him.

"Shit." He sat back as if he'd been kicked by a mule.

What in God's name is she doing here?

His chest tightened. His knees felt weak. Fowler hoped against hope that she hadn't recognize him.

Lauren's hands trembled, as she tried to cover herself with the pale-blue sheet.

"You are so busted," she said. "My dad is gonna kill you, if the Secret Service doesn't do it first."

WETWORK

S HOCK AND DISBELIEF ROCKETED through Fowler as he stared at Lauren. His mind raced as he fumbled to wrap the robe around himself as quickly as possible.

He paced the room, trying to reign in waves of panic. Preston had promised to be discreet and to procure girls from reliable sources. Fowler stopped in the middle of the room and wondered if the guy had set him up.

Her words, *Dad is gonna kill you,* nearly bowled him over.

She was right.

Anyone who'd been behind the scenes in the Oval Office knew the president had connections known as gray contacts, people who saw themselves as patriots, willing to do covert missions, wetwork, or whatever it took to maintain the balance of power.

Fowler paced the floor. Preston must be setting him up.

Lauren still glared at him.

Kids loved pushing the edge. Access to alcohol was a big deal for a teen. Maybe a scotch or a beer would calm her down. "You want a drink?"

"Hell no," she said. "What do you think got me here?"

He knew the president was aggressively protective of his family and wouldn't hesitate to use every resource at his disposal.

He finds out and I'm fucked.

When Fowler sat on the edge of the king-size mattress, she crawled away.

"Lauren, I didn't know it was you. I was expecting my... date."

"You mean hooker." She wrapped her arms around her torso. "I'm not stupid."

Fowler wondered what it would take to keep her quiet. Giving her money and playing the part of a trusted uncle was worth a shot.

"Dear girl, are you okay?"

She rubbed her arms and stared at the torn underwear lying on the bed. "This is so screwed up. I wanna go home."

"Sweetie, how did this happen? How did you wind up on this ship?"

Her chin quivered. "We just wanted to see the beach and party like everyone else. Then everything went nuts."

She told him about a man named Bo, who'd forced her and Molly onto the ship. Lauren talked about being tied up, beaten, and grabbed by the men onboard, and the stinky room where a girl had been shot. "Can you call my dad?"

She watched Fowler closely.

He combed a hand through his hair. "Sure, sweetie."

Lauren stared at his face. "You're lying, aren't you?"

BATTLE HARDENED

RIGGS AND COOP SEARCHED Bowers' room. The open window and the deployed fire-escape ladder told Riggs some of the story.

Coop pointed at the bathroom. "Look at this."

Riggs stared at a pile of cigarette butts lying in an ashtray. "Bowers doesn't smoke."

His chest tightened when he saw a strip of used duct tape stuck to the mirror. "It has blood on it."

Dammit, Bowers. Where the hell are you?

"I feel your pain," said Coop.

Riggs took a deep breath. "Any word about your sister?"

Coop shook his head.

Riggs felt his phone vibrate. When he spotted a new message from Bowers, his pulse skipped a beat.

The message read: *SOS - onboard* Leisure Lee – *offshore Miami 35 mi - RR and Molly here.*

Riggs knew RR meant Roadrunner. He raced for the door and signaled Coop. "Let's go! Now."

"What's up?" asked Coop.

"Tell you in the car." Riggs raced out of the hotel room and down the stairs to his vehicle. They jumped in and he peeled toward Coast Guard Station Key West.

Riggs briefed Coop and called Greg.

"Hey," said Greg. "How's—"

"Bowers found Roadrunner. They are on the *Leisure Lee*."

"Holy shit. Where?" asked Greg.

"International waters," said Riggs, "Thirty-some miles off Miami. Hold on."

The buzzing of his phone meant another incoming message.

"Greg. I got another text. Mercenaries are onboard and Lauren and Molly are being held with trafficked women."

Greg shouted to someone. A moment later he came back on the line. "Riggs, I need you back here. ASAP."

"I have a better idea," said Riggs. "Find that damned ship and get me on it."

"Let me call you back."

Coop directed Riggs through side streets and around the crowds. With trumpets and steelpan drums rocking in the background, Riggs floored it.

A half-mile later, they reached the Coast Guard Station where a guard let them in. At the building, Riggs took the first available parking stall. He and Coop jogged toward the Command Suite. Instead of stopping them, security anxiously hustled them inside.

The space consisted of a reception desk encircled by offices. Through one of the glass panels, Riggs spotted the four stripes of gold braid on a man's shoulders marking him as a captain. He emerged from behind a huge desk and waved them into an adjacent conference room.

The dark-haired, clean-cut captain directed them toward the big wooden table as if he were accustomed to facing problems head on. "I understand we have a situation."

As they set up the conference call, a muscular young petty officer with a big pistol strapped to his thigh approached Coop with a wide smile. "Hey, brother. How yah doin'?"

The captain reached over the table and shook Coop's hand. "Good to see you, son."

Riggs glanced at Coop and back at the captain, who appeared to notice Riggs' surprise.

"It's a small town," said the captain. "We all know Coop. Besides, I served with his late brother at Station Kodiak, Alaska. He was one of our best swimmers."

"Thank you, sir," said Coop. "He thought highly of you too."

Within minutes they were on the line with FBI Miami. The tense conference call included voices shouting in the background on both sides. Radios squawked with incoming intel from multiple sources. In Miami, it sounded as if Greg had pulled in everyone from admirals to dog catchers.

Riggs stood over the table near the phone to make his voice heard. "We need to get on that ship and recover Lauren."

The Coast Guard captain spoke up. "We've got ships in the area, and choppers available. But the wind has picked up and there's a line of storms coming in."

When Secret Service attempted to give the captain orders, he appeared unflappable. With seven rows of ribbons on his chest, the captain was no pushover and made it damn clear he knew his sector.

"With all due respect," he said. "Laws have been broken at sea. Maritime crime is our jurisdiction. You are welcome to join us, but we have the ships, personnel, and resources to do the job on these waters."

"What about the storm?" Greg asked.

"We're always ready," said the captain. "We go when no one else will."

Riggs' phone buzzed with an incoming call from Bowers. He took it and signaled for everyone to hush. "Bowers, I'm putting you on speaker. We're at Coast Guard Station Key West and are on the line with FBI Miami."

Everyone leaned in to listen, especially Coop.

"First," said Bowers, "according to the GPS on my phone this is our location."

As she provided the longitude and latitude coordinates, Riggs and the petty officer scribbled down the data. The petty officer went straight to a computer terminal.

"Things are going to hell, fast," she whispered. "Molly is here with me and the other women. Well, most of them."

Bowers paused. The conference room went dead silent. All ears were fixed on her voice.

"Riggs, they took Lauren."

He dropped his pen. "How many women do they have?"

"Six. Among them is a twelve-year-old child."

Riggs grimaced.

"We need to get them off this boat," said Bowers.

Riggs leaned forward. "We will. Anything else?"

"Yeah, Coop are you there?"

Coop leaned over the phone. "Yes, ma'am."

"Standby," said Bowers. Soft voices murmured in the background.

"Coop? It's Sara. Are you there?"

At the pleading sound of Sara's voice, trembling with fear, Coop gripped the table as if his knees were about to buckle. His bandaged hand tightened into a fist. "Please tell me you're okay."

"I love you," she said. "Please help us."

The line went dead.

GRAVITY

B OWERS' CALL ENDED WHEN the door to the Hole flew
open and they found themselves staring at the 3rd mate.

A swathe of light from the passageway flooded the floor as he
shoved the twelve-year-old out of his way.

Jung and Bo followed him inside.

The heavy metal door *clanked* when they kicked it shut.

Oh, shit.

Bo did not seem his usual cocky self. Instead, he appeared frayed
and nervous as he searched the women's faces.

"If you're looking for her," said Bowers, "she isn't here."

Bo blanched and glanced at the door.

That hit a nerve.

"Shut up," he snarled. Bo stood behind Jung as if wary.

You should be, asshole.

Bowers pocketed her phone. The encounter at the helipad had left
Jung's sallow face swollen and stippled with abrasions.

Couldn't happen to a nicer guy.

His arrogance, mixed with a fierce violent streak, made him
capable of far worse than the typical hired gun. Jung pushed up the
sleeves of his dark shirt.

Showing fear would be a mistake.

"This won't end well," she said, "for either of you."

They glowered at her and stepped forward.

"That's enough," said the 3rd mate, "Jung, she has a phone. Get it."

Jung watched her with those soulless black eyes. She might as well have been staring directly at the business end of a double-barrel shotgun.

Bowers didn't flinch.

Appealing to his non-existent conscience would be a waste of time. She needed a distraction to draw these thugs away from Sara and the girl.

Bowers pointed at Jung's face. "Love the new look."

He lunged at her.

"No," screamed the twelve-year-old.

Jung began reaching for his knife.

Before his hand touched the sheath, she drove her elbow at his neck. Jung ducked just enough that the blow smacked into his nose with exceptional force. She heard a crack. He stumbled backward. Stunned by the impact, his eyes watered as blood gushed from his snout.

Bo smirked.

"Quit horsing around," ordered the 3rd mate, "and get the damned phone."

Not wanting them in her pockets, she pulled out her phone.

Bo ripped it out of her hand and threw it on the deck where Jung crushed it with his boot and threw it out into the passageway.

As Jung started toward her, Bo gripped his AK-47.

"Both of you, knock it off," shouted the 3rd mate. "You heard the skipper's orders: do not touch her."

Bowers wondered what Preston wanted from her.

Bo and Jung stood guard near the connecting door. She couldn't overpower more than three-hundred pounds of muscle and the AK-47.

The 3rd mate nodded to Jung. "Just keep her back until I lock the door. And mark my word." He jabbed a finger into Jung's shoulder. "If she has so much as a hair messed up, I'll make sure neither of you see sunrise. I'm sick of your shit."

The 3rd mate scanned the women.

"And you," he yelled at Bowers. "If you cause me anymore problems, I will cut her." He pointed at the twelve-year-old.

Jung and Bo blocked Bowers from the doorway, as the 3rd mate wrestled a kicking, screaming Sara into the adjoining dressing room. Bowers' jaw tightened as the tumblers of the lock clicked.

Bo slammed Bowers against the rusted metal wall almost as if to provoke her into a fight. She didn't take the bait. "Piss off Preston at your own risk."

Jung nudged Bo's arm. "I need fresh air. Let's go."

Jung stopped at the door, staring at her with those dark eyes. "We aren't done."

Bo held up the AK-47. "Say your prayers."

JUSTICE COMES CALLING

B OWERS HEARD SARA SHRIEK, "Get off me, pervert!"
The sound came from the dressing room.

From the hem of her vest, Bowers quickly pulled out four slender tools with hooked ends, then rapidly picked the lock.

Sara's screams grew louder as a woman in the Hole pleaded, "Help her."

She threw open the door and found the 3rd mate on top of Sara who tried to push him away. The man's pants were down to his knees.

"Get off her," ordered Bowers.

He glanced over his shoulder just as she jumped him from behind and put him in a headlock.

Sara elbowed him in the face, crawled out from under his weight, and scurried away.

Bowers refused to let go.

The 3rd mate twisted and drew his Ruger pistol. His awkward attempt to aim over his shoulder gave him no leverage.

Bowers used that to her advantage and her weight to pin him to the deck. To further limit his range of motion, she pressed his face into the abrasive floor and drove her knee into his hand and wrist.

While bearing down with all her weight, she pulled back his trigger finger until she heard the bone *snap*.

The man howled and violently pulled his hand away, losing control of the pistol. It skidded across the floor between the scattered pieces of clothing and shoes.

He howled in pain. As the 3rd mate stared at his deformed finger, Bowers quickly grabbed his knife.

"What the hell do you want?" he asked between gritted teeth.

"Lauren. Where is she?"

"Who the hell is Lauren?"

"The blonde teenager you took from this room is the president's missing daughter."

His eyes went wide. "Shit. I gotta tell Preston."

The 3rd mate flipped over and threw a punch.

Bowers took a hard hit as the man rolled on top of her, but his broken finger made for an easy and painful target.

He clasped onto her throat, but Bowers was already in full-combat mode. She wrapped her legs around his shoulder, entrapping his arm. Bowers arched her back and threw him off.

Still holding his wrist, Bowers summoned an incredible burst of force. She drove his wrist down and her hips up against his elbow until it snapped.

The man screamed and rolled away. He rose to one knee. "I'll kill you and every one of those bitches for this."

"No, you won't," said Bowers.

The 3rd mate lunged for the Ruger but stumbled over his low-riding drawers and fell.

Bowers jumped on his back, forcing him face-first into the deck.

When he fought to pry the knife out of her hand, the blade cut deeply into his palm.

She grabbed him by the hair.

"Sara, look away. Now," she ordered. Bowers yanked his head back.

"I will kill you," he snarled.

"I don't think so," she said as she ripped the sharp blade across his trachea.

His white fingers pulled at her hand as panic set in. When his movements became weaker and spastic, she backed away.

Shocked and unable to speak, the man rolled on his back. He stared up at her in a futile effort to breathe.

A terrorist in Iraq had reacted the same way when she'd severed his windpipe. While traveling through a small town, her convoy had come upon a female body in the middle of the road. A terrorist had raped and murdered a mother in front of her family and then decapitated her small son and infant. When he charged at Bowers, she'd ended the struggle. Saving the woman's mother, six-year-old daughter, and distraught husband was some consolation, but it couldn't undo the family's life-long pain and loss.

With this man, she couldn't undo what he'd done either, but she could stop him from killing anyone else.

As the dying man stared up at Bowers, she searched the pockets of his trousers and recovered his phone. "You could've helped these women. Instead, you preyed upon them."

His eyes lost their focus. His body grew still. As his sightless eyes fixed on the ceiling, she lifted his limp hand and used his thumb to unlock the phone screen. Bowers quickly changed the passcode and pocketed the phone. She relieved him of his keys, radio, and spare ammo.

Bowers heard a gasp.

Sara sat against the wall with her hands over her mouth, staring at the growing pool of red as gravity pulled the puddle toward the floor drain.

"I'm sorry you had to see that," said Bowers, wishing she could've spared Sara from such a sight. "Are you okay?"

Sara picked up the Ruger and shot the dead man. Twice.

Bowers nodded. "Answers that question."

BO SPOTTED FOWLER in a navy-blue blazer, barreling toward the forward cabin with his jaw set. After hearing Niko's orders to take the blonde to Fowler's room, Bo feared his luck had just run out.

He quickly backed away from the double-doors and headed for the far wall near the bar. It was all he could do not to run.

If this were about Lauren, he was cooked.

From across the room, Fowler stood by the white couch, glaring at him. Bo began to sweat as he inched closer to the door.

With his mouth pursed into a grimace, Fowler made a beeline across the soft carpet for the bartender. He took a seat on the fancy leather barstool next to Preston. As he sipped his drink, he kept a wary eye on the skipper.

Preston seemed to have problems of his own. "Where the hell is my 3rd mate?"

Fowler's hands trembled slightly as he nursed his scotch.

"What's up with you?" asked Preston. "You look like someone pissed on your pancakes."

"We got a problem," said Fowler.

"Which one?" snorted Preston.

"I think Doug is going to be a problem."

"Speak of the devil," said Preston.

The CEO and Doug arrived, clearly not speaking to one another. The CEO ordered a drink, while Doug stood squinting out the window at the sea with his arms folded.

As Bo scanned the windows that offered a panoramic view of the ocean, he tried to act as if all was well. And yet, on the horizon, dark clouds approached like a bad omen. Lightning flashed, causing him to flinch.

Bo felt some consolation when Jung entered the forward cabin with white tape over his nose. As he drew closer, Jung glanced at Bo and flipped him off. He returned the gesture until Preston scowled at them.

The dining table had been decked out in fine white linens. Flickering candles and the recessed lighting made the fancy gold-rimmed plates glimmer.

Bo felt a little better after Fowler through back a few drinks and appeared to calm down.

Bo didn't care about all the fancy stuff on the table, but he did enjoy watching the CEO, Fowler, and Preston vying for positions of power at either end of the table. Preston lost out and seemed none too pleased.

Platters piled high with lobsters and other delicacies were presented to the bigshots in a lavish display.

Bo saw himself as a grab and growl kind of guy when it came to food. He didn't have much patience for linen napkins or that prissy shit about which fork to use. The only thing worse than standing guard at a dinner party was doing it on an empty belly.

Doug stared at his plate with a sour expression.

Fowler continued acting like the man in charge, as he spoke with the CEO.

Meanwhile, Doug hadn't touched his food. He began to drum his fingers on the table when the CEO and Fowler talked about tonight's meeting with someone named Gim.

The dour-faced Doug didn't say a word as a crewman took his full plate away and replaced it with a crystal dish topped with whipped cream and tropical fruit.

Expecting Lauren would soon be a hot topic, Bo kept a close ear on Fowler and Preston's conversation.

A few minutes later, it became clear they had other problems on their plates.

Fowler had just ordered another drink when Hogan stormed into the room. "What the hell is going on?"

He pointed to the CEO and Doug. "Why are they here? This is no goddamned fishing trip."

ENEMY TERRITORY

BOWERS HAD TO FIND LAUREN and fast, but these women needed help too.

When the twelve-year-old peered into the dressing room, Bowers distracted the girl away from the body. She called over Elena, the Cuban woman with long black hair, and directed them toward the shower.

Bowers asked the young girl, "What is your name?"

"Novia," she said, eyeing the towels and shampoo.

The innocence of this child made Bowers even more determined to turn this ship upside down.

"Your name means *sweetheart*."

"Yes," she said. "My papa chose it. He say I was a sweet surprise."

"That you are," said Bowers.

The girl hugged her. "Someday, I want to be strong like you."

Elena handed Novia a towel and pointed her toward the shower.

Sara quickly draped a shower curtain over the 3rd mate's body.

"Well done," said Bowers.

"They don't need to see this," said Sara.

Bowers nodded. They watched the women enter the dressing room, which was a lot cleaner than the Hole.

Elena returned. *"Uno momento,"* she said, "one minute." She ripped back the makeshift tarp and spat on the corpse.

"Imbécil," she snarled. "Die in hell for you."

Elena hurried back toward Novia and the showers.

Molly squinted at the bright light as she entered with the Cuban woman known as Yadra.

When Yadra saw the body, she put a fist in the air and declared, *"Justicia!"*

Their reaction to the dead man surprised Bowers. She looked down at the body. "Pal, you certainly didn't win any popularity contests."

While the women eagerly took to the shower and grooming supplies, Sara and Bowers dragged the wrapped body into the Hole.

Back in the dressing room, the women each selected pieces of skimpy clothing from large plastic baskets. The items didn't offer much coverage, but they were significantly more than the bras and underwear they were used to.

With the dead man's master key, Bowers locked the door connecting the two rooms.

Sara nodded toward the Hole. "He's the one who belongs in there."

As Sara hosed the mess into the floor drain, Bowers contemplated her next move.

"Keep everyone in here. I'll be back."

NOW IN ENEMY territory outside the Hole, Bowers prepared to face off with their captors. She ripped an evacuation map off the wall and carefully slipped past the engine room.

As she approached the ladder to the upper deck, a man came out of the men's restroom. He stopped zipping up his fly and caught her on the first step. With a pistol shoved into her back, he grabbed her waistband and pulled her into the men's room.

"You shouldn't be here," he said.

"You got that right."

Without warning Bowers flipped around to face him, entrapping his right arm under her left arm so tightly he couldn't aim the pistol at her. The startled man pulled the trigger. The shot ricocheted off the metal wall and shattered his ankle.

"Clever," said Bowers.

As he bent forward, she coldcocked him with a blow to the temple.

The man went down hard, hitting his head on a urinal. She relieved him of his pistol, AR-15, and dumped his radio into a toilet. It seemed poetic to use his handcuffs to secure him to the piping under the urinal.

With two down, she ascended to the upper decks. Unlike the rusted walls and minimal accommodations below, the main deck shone with polished brass, beveled glass windows, and plush carpeting.

Bowers passed staterooms with names such as *Oasis* and *Marlin* that had been engraved on brass plates and mounted on the doors. Other than the muffled echo of an angry voice, the long passageways were surprisingly empty.

The ship had to be over 150-feet long. Like the rungs in a ladder the two long passageways on either side of the ship were connected by a series of short halls.

Bowers stopped at a corner. Through walls that were half wood paneling and half glass, she discovered a huge forward cabin at the bow. She crawled around the corner on her knees and slipped behind a navy-blue curtain into an alcove within the connecting passageway. The entrance to the big room stood seven feet away.

The dark alcove stored a broom and cleaning supplies. A rolling cart heaped with tableware and ice buckets sat outside in the hall.

Bowers peered between the heavy curtains. Luxurious didn't begin to define the spacious room's full bar, huge television screens, lush couches, a table big enough for a large dinner party, and an eye-popping, panoramic view of the ocean.

It didn't surprise her to see Bo Somers standing guard at the far wall. However, finding Senator Fowler and the CEO of E-Connect in an intense conversation confirmed this was no fishing trip.

Human trafficking and the president's daughter were only a small part of the bigger picture. It infuriated her that Fowler had gone so far beyond the bounds of his authority and thumbed his nose at CFIUS to push forward with this deal.

This was the worst possible scenario.

Bowers' mission shifted into a completely different strategy. *Riggs needs to see this.*

She bit back her temper to focus on Fowler, who wore his usual navy-blue suit and sucked on a cigar as if he were the master of ceremonies.

Their dinner had just broken up. The CEO went to the bar and appeared to be celebrating with champagne.

Bowers heard the sound of heavy steps coming closer. Three worked-up guards stormed past the alcove and entered the forward cabin where they reported to Fowler.

Seconds later, the doors banged open. Voices filled the corridor. Bowers quietly stepped away from the curtain.

A few feet from the alcove, Fowler bumped into the cart as he met with the three guards. She heard the flicking of a lighter and Fowler puffing to relight his cigar.

"Everything okay?" he asked.

"Yes, sir," said one man. "Hogan wasn't happy when we locked him in his room. Carson will administer the drugs while Derrick makes sure Hogan doesn't cause a problem. They'll take it from here."

"Good," said Fowler, "I hate like hell havin' to do this. I expected him to cooperate, but since he has refused, he is giving us no other option but to keep him out of the way. Permanently, if necessary."

His words rocked Bowers.

She heard Fowler drop his lighter on the cart and eyed the young men. "Gentlemen, we are about to make history. I'm counting on you boys to keep things under control. When the meeting is over, I'll make sure there is a hefty payoff in this for you."

"Thank you, sir," said the lead guard. His radio squawked. He stepped backward to stand against the curtain covering the alcove. Inches away, Bowers stood perfectly still.

She couldn't decipher much of the static transmission but heard "incoming" and "North Korean" clearly.

"Roger that," said the guard. When he moved closer to Fowler, Bowers returned to peering through the curtain.

The guard lowered his voice. "Gim should be landing in about fifteen minutes."

Fowler nodded and blew out a stream of white smoke. "I think we need to go greet the bastard."

Knowing North Koreans were arriving ratcheted the stakes up even higher.

Fowler leaned against the corner with his back to the alcove. She noted his hands had a slight tremor.

A young man with a round face bolted out of the forward cabin and stormed down the hall. "I'm not doin' this," he grumbled. "Ya'll are stupid."

"Hold on, son," said Fowler. "A word, please."

The young man had disdain written all over him.

"Let's take a walk," said Fowler.

In the reflection of the glass, she watched the man follow Fowler down the passageway until they were out of earshot.

GAME CHANGER

BOWERS SLIPPED AWAY FROM the forward cabin, hoping to remain undetected. Moments later she entered the starboard passageway where the radio she carried crackled with a startling message about Ron Hogan. Footsteps came closer.

A laundry closet provided the only cover. Outside, she heard voices. Through the slats she saw the legs of two men who'd stopped in front of the louvered door.

"Hogan isn't buying it," said a deep male voice. "If blackmail photos didn't faze him, how are we supposed to control him?"

"Easy," said the other man. "I'll unlock his door. You hold him at gunpoint. I'll give him a little H. That'll stall his jets."

"Carson, are you nuts? We need more guys. He's a big dude. What if he fights us?"

"Shoot his ass." We'll throw the stiff into the sea and tell everyone there was a tragic accident. He fell overboard while fishing off the stern."

Having worked in D.C., Hogan was more than Fowler's archrival. He was a big man, well trained by the Marine Corps, and well known for his integrity. She knew he would never put up with this bullshit.

She sent Riggs a text warning him that this was quickly evolving into a soup sandwich and needed help fast.

"Come on, Derrick," said Carson. "Let's get this done. When we're finished, we'll go do the girls."

Bowers couldn't believe what she'd heard.

It takes nuclear-grade stupidity to hold a U.S. senator hostage.

RIGGS AND COOP boarded the bright orange and white helicopter at Station Key West. Lifting off in a chopper would be an adrenaline rush for anyone but doing so in a U.S. Coast Guard MH-65 Dolphin with a M240 machine gun and a precision .50-cal rifle designed for airborne use of force definitely upped the ante.

With two huge engines they ripped over the sparkling lights of the Keys and out toward the deep black waters at a cruising speed of 130 mph.

Riggs noted the HITRON patch on the right sleeve of one crewman.

"Gunner?" asked Riggs.

The man smirked. "Precision Marksman."

Just as Riggs thought this couldn't get any uglier, the pilot said, "Riggs, we just got word that a cruise ship heading back from the Caribbean spotted a suspicious vessel. At first, they thought it was an old fishing boat from Cuba doing night trawling, but the captain of the cruise ship says they were deploying heavily armed men into black inflatables."

LANDING ON A MOVING SHIP ranked as a high-risk operation in the best of circumstances. Doing so in the dark with high winds moving in shot up the pucker-factor more than Riggs wanted to ponder. He white-knuckled his harness as the bird tentatively eased down onto a ship's deck. It surprised him to see a USN lieutenant commander waiting for them.

He'd expected to land on a Coast Guard cutter, instead they'd just set down on the stern of a Zumwalt, the largest and most technologically advanced surface combatant class of multi-mission destroyers on the planet.

They don't call them destroyers for nothing.

"Shit. This just got real," said Coop as they disembarked.

The officer who'd been waiting ducked and shouted. "Welcome aboard. Keep your heads down."

The officer escorted Riggs and Coop across the rough deck where Riggs did a doubletake at seeing Coast Guard colors flying on a Naval vessel.

A few minutes later they entered a cramped cabin known as CIC, the Combat Information Center. Riggs spotted Greg's wavy black hair.

He shook Riggs' hand. "Welcome aboard. You have no idea how good it is to see you."

"What's our situation?" asked Riggs.

"Admiral Gray up at SOCOM is reviewing the situation. Intel is coming in from all sources."

"That's reassuring," said Riggs. The admiral had an impeccable reputation for getting the job done, which meant the SEALs were likely gearing up.

In the cramped quarters, banks of computers, radar equipment, secure communication lines, and a map table were typical. However, Riggs had rarely seen this much brass in one room.

As two radar operators monitored the sweeps, Riggs leaned toward Greg. "Everyone with a missile to a peashooter is engaged, let's hope this doesn't turn into a cluster."

Greg glanced around the room. "I'm with you, bro. We're all on edge. You heard about the armed men deploying from a fishing vessel?"

Riggs nodded. "Do we know who they are?"

"We'll know soon. The Coast Guard is searching for them as we speak."

The fervor inside CIC seemed a controlled dance on the rim of panic. Intel streamed in from multiple sources. Like clashing cymbals, radios and transmissions crackled at the same time. Real-time updates on asset locations and information about the players aboard the *Leisure*

Lee forced constant adjustments and re-evaluations. Every soul in that room grasped the seriousness of their mission.

Riggs helped the commander provide SOCOM and Homeland Security with info on the friendlies onboard, including Bowers, Lauren, and Molly.

Assets were streaming into place. Like a lion in tall grass, the Coast Guard's fast cutters waited in the dark near the reported location of the *Leisure Lee*, far enough away to look normal, but close enough to interdict at a moment's notice.

An aircraft carrier had made its presence known off Cuba and the frigates and destroyers with five-inch artillery stood ready. All eyes and ears were on these waters, as they waited for news.

"It would suck to be a drug runner tonight," said Coop, "with these assets in the water."

Greg chuckled. "You got that right."

Riggs stood in awe of the stunning response. The unsheathed sharp end of the stick stood ready. Tensions soared above anything Riggs had ever witnessed short of a war. Overwhelming forces were about to be deployed.

Riggs chomped on gum as he listened to correspondence with Naval ships out of Mayport. After a discussion with two Coast Guard officers about the tactical approach to securing Roadrunner, the man with the HITRON patch entered the room.

"Captain, sir," he said. "We just heard from Jacksonville. HITRON has choppers on two of your Coast Guard cutters. We can have them in the air in minutes."

"Thank you," said Captain Dickson.

Riggs knew HITRON stood for Helicopter Interdiction Tactical Squadron, an elite group from the Coast Guard that included highly trained snipers, adept at airborne use of force.

U.S. Navy Captain Dickson motioned to Riggs and Greg to join him at the map table. "We lucked out," said the captain. "In addition to HITRON, DEVGRU is in the area. We're in contact with AUTEC." He pointed at the map. His finger landed on the far side of Andros Island, near a deep-ocean basin.

"They've been testing a new SEAL Delivery Vehicle and are ready to rock and roll with six-man teams. Two Black Hawks are on standby to transport as many special ops on site as needed."

Coast Guard Captain Ayers joined them at the map table. "For now," said Ayers, "Naval assets are on standby. The Coast Guard is under the authority of Homeland Security and we're damned determined to shut this down."

The search was on to find the men in the inflatables.

Riggs now understood why the flags had been flipped. Military stood ready to act, but they needed the Coast Guard for law enforcement. With captains from both branches on the same command vessel they had options, which could prove critical, if the report on the armed men deploying from a Cuban vessel turned out to be more than drug runners.

It seemed that every asset they had within 200-miles was streaming for the waters between Miami, Cuba, and the Bahamas.

"Mark! Mark! Mark!" shouted a man at a radar terminal. Officers squinted over his shoulder at the screen. "The *Leisure Lee* is forty nautical miles from Miami."

"Now find the inflatables," said Dickson. "Check in with the pilot of the P-3. Let's see if he has a handle on who they are and where they're headed."

Riggs listened as Ayers and Dickson conferred with Admiral Gray about disabling the *Leisure Lee*. With friendlies onboard, including the president's daughter and two senators, they didn't want to cause a fire or risk sinking it, but bringing it to a halt would contain the situation.

A few minutes later, while Greg took a call, Riggs checked his phone and realized he'd missed an incoming message. He didn't recognize the number, but there was no doubt who sent it: *Bowers here. Hogan held hostage. E-Connect CEO onboard. North Koreans arriving soon.*

Riggs glanced up to see Greg had gone pale. "Hogan just sent out a call for help. You won't believe this but—"

"I know," said Riggs, as he showed Greg the message from Bowers.

FULLY LOADED

TORN BETWEEN HELPING HOGAN and returning to protect the girls, Bowers quickly realized that helping Hogan might do both.

After the men headed toward Hogan's room, she slipped out of the closet and followed far enough behind to avoid detection. From around a corner, she studied Carson. The slender man clearly wasn't law enforcement material, which made him the softer target. She couldn't say the same for the other guy.

The two men stood before a stateroom named *Horizon*. The door had been locked from the outside using a chain through the brass door pulls and a padlock. Derrick drew his AK-47 and stood ready.

Carson popped open the lock, stepped back, and followed Derrick inside. Bowers crept forward. Near the doorway, she held her AR-15 ready and kept an eye on the passageway.

Hogan's deep voice was unmistakable. "What the hell do you think you're doing?"

"Just chill, man," said Carson. "This will only take a sec. I brought you some medicine to help you feel better."

"I'll feel better when I'm off this damned ship and you are all behind bars."

Bowers took a quick peek. Hogan had his fist around the hanging rod from his closet. She smirked. *Once a Marine, always a Marine.*

Derrick made his intentions clear as he aimed his rifle at the senator's chest.

"I've already called the FBI for help," said Hogan. "They will find you."

Hogan glared at Derrick. "How can you justify doing this to a fellow veteran?"

Derrick appeared uneasy. "Carson, maybe—"

"Shut up," said the medic. "Shoot him, if he even blinks."

Bowers moved in. "I wouldn't do that," she said with the AR-15 pointed at Derrick's back.

The guard froze and put up his hands.

Carson faced her with the loaded syringe.

"Drop your weapons," she ordered and took a step back. "Put the syringe down. Now."

Hogan took his first swing. Derrick went down like a dropped mic.

Carson began to back away. "Hold on, bro," he said, as he abruptly lunged at Hogan with the syringe.

Hogan swung like a batter going for a homerun. Carson's head snapped to the side. He hit the deck with a thump.

"I'm not your bro, asshole," said Hogan.

Carson's sightless eyes stared at nothing. Bowers felt his neck to confirm what she already knew. "No pulse."

"I warned him," said Hogan.

Derrick moaned until Hogan pried the syringe out of the dead man's hand and jabbed the needle into Derrick's thigh. The heroin would put him out of commission.

Bowers took a seat on the bed, while Hogan watched her closely.

"Now what?" he asked.

As she filled Hogan in on all that had happened, Bowers grabbed Derrick's weapons and made sure they were fully loaded.

"Even for Fowler," he said, "this is over the top. He's always been a polarizing factor, but I never thought he'd go rogue."

"Power and greed," said Bowers.

He pointed at the men on the floor. "We've got to do something with them."

"There's a laundry closet across the hall."

"Perfect," said Hogan.

Hearing footsteps outside their door, Bowers signaled Hogan to be quiet. They locked eyes and listened until the chatter faded.

A few minutes later, she and Hogan carried Carson and Derrick across the passageway and left them in the laundry closet.

They quickly returned to Hogan's stateroom where they hid Carson's medical kit.

"Washington misses you," said Hogan. "It's good working with you again."

"Thank you, sir. Let's bring the women up to your stateroom."

Transferring Molly, Yadra, and Elena up to Hogan's room was frightening but ultimately uneventful. Once in the room, the women took large bath towels from his bathroom to cover themselves and seemed thrilled to stretch out on a clean bed.

Bowers put Molly in charge. "Keep quiet. Do not answer the door or go outside. Clear?"

Molly nodded. "Yes ma'am."

Hogan tucked the pistol in his waistband and held the AK-47 ready. "Let's go."

Bowers hoisted her rifle over her shoulder and followed Hogan from the room.

Below deck, they joined Sara and Novia. On the way back to the room, Hogan ran cover as Bowers searched for Lauren.

When they reached the stateroom, Molly draped a blanket over Novia. Like a lost child, the twelve-year-old had gone mute.

"Hey, sweet girl. Are you okay?" asked Bowers. Novia didn't answer. Instead, she curled up in the corner with her arms wrapped around her legs.

Bowers watched Hogan pull T-shirts and a large sweatshirt from his bag and tossed them on the bed. "Ladies, help yourself."

Hogan leaned toward Bowers. "We need to get them home to their families."

He respectfully turned away as the women wrapped their towels around their waists and put on the shirts. All except Novia who stayed in the corner staring at the wall.

Bowers knelt next to her and handed her a soft T-shirt. "Your mama will be very proud of you. You've been very brave."

Novia's eyes filled with tears. Her chin quivered. "I want to go home."

"You will. Remember, you are stronger than you think."

The girl hugged Bowers with surprising force.

Novia nodded and wiped her eyes. "*Gracias.*"

"*De nada,*" said Bowers. *De nada* meant your welcome or *it's nothing.* This wasn't nothing, but it was a promise she intended to keep even if it meant sinking this damned ship.

When Novia curled up on the bed. Hogan put a blanket over her.

Molly had been watching. "Thank you for helping us. I hope you find Lauren. I'm afraid of what they'll do to her."

It was the first time the girl had spoken more than two words.

A few minutes later, Bowers sent Riggs a text: *Hogan free. Lauren still missing.*

He replied immediately: *Help on the way. Can you disable the ship?*

Her text back included a thumbs up and read: *Sounds like fun.*

Hogan picked up the AR-15. "Bowers, you up for wreaking a little havoc on their party?"

"Absolutely."

NEW INTEL HAD STARTED BREAKING so fast that the radar operator's excited tenor caught Riggs attention.

"Sir," he said. "An LSF is approaching our target."

That wasn't happy news. The last thing they needed was another party involved in this mess. Riggs had his eyes on Ayers, whose square jaw and crewcut fit with his tough-as-nails attitude.

"Who's on the low slow flyer?" asked the captain.

Greg studied the map. "Our assets in Nassau confirmed that the Sri Lankan businessman and two North Koreans just left Nassau in a chopper. In all probability, they're the ones heading toward the *Leisure Lee*."

"What do we have on them?" asked Riggs.

Ayers mirrored Riggs concern as he locked eyes with Greg.

"The Sri Lankan is a puppet," said Greg, "likely bought and paid for by North Korea. The real player here is the North Korean business-man. We've identified him as Gim Kwang-su. He is married to the supreme leader's niece, which is kind of gross considering he is forty some years her senior. And the man with him may look like an assistant, but in all likelihood, he's an armed government operative there to ensure Gim does as he's told."

Because of the deadlock between CFIUS and congress over the E-Connect deal, neither Riggs nor Greg had expected any action on that front for another few weeks.

"Let's go," said Coop, who appeared ready to jump in the water and swim.

Riggs pulled Greg aside. "I want on that boat. Now."

UNHINGED

WHEN THE BIGSHOTS TOOK their break, Bo knew he had a target on his back and snuck away with plans of his own.

The port passageway led him toward the staterooms where he found a guard making his rounds. "Hey, man," said the guard. "How's it goin'?"

"Listen," said Bo. "Did Fowler ever get his girl?"

"The blonde?"

Bo nodded.

"Oh yeah," said the stocky guard. "Niko gave him the pretty one. She's still in there. Fowler is gonna be a happy boy tonight."

"Thanks," said Bo. "Gotta keep the guests entertained."

Bo hid his relief when the guard on duty checked his watch and said, "My shift is done. Time for chow."

Once the guard had left the passageway, Bo headed for the stern, hoping to get inside Fowler's suite.

Just as Bo thought he could do this without a witness to rat him out to Preston, a deckhand appeared from an adjacent passageway, carrying a bottle of brandy and two crystal glasses.

The deckhand jumped as a loud voice shouted, "This is stupid. You are out of your mind."

"I'm the one in charge here," yelled the other. "You will do what I tell you to do."

Their argument echoed in the passageway.

The deckhand's eyebrows went up. He did an about-face. "I'll come back later."

Bo recognized both voices. He peered around the corner where the passageway ran between Fowler's stateroom and the CEO's. Bo watched Fowler follow Doug into the CEO's room.

Moments later, Doug bolted out of the room with a brown leather briefcase and scurried toward the stern. Both men were absorbed in their argument and didn't appear to notice Bo standing against the wall in the passageway.

Hot on Doug's heels, Fowler lunged for the briefcase and missed. "Get your ass back here."

Doug didn't listen. "Screw you." When he shouldered the door open a blast of ocean air flooded the passageway.

Fowler charged after Doug. "Give me that, dammit."

Doug went outside, hugging the briefcase as if his life depended on it. Fowler followed.

Fascinated, Bo eased into a corner by the open door and peered through the tinted window.

"This was a mistake," shrieked Doug. "It's toxic. I wish I'd never designed it."

Fowler wore a ferocious snarl with that cigar wedge in his teeth. The tussle over the briefcase spilled onto the aft deck designed for sunbathers.

With the door still cracked open, Bo heard the senator barking orders.

When Doug refused to give in, Fowler tossed aside his cigar. "Give me that damned briefcase. Now."

As Doug backed toward the railing and began to swing it as if to toss it overboard, Fowler shoved Doug against the railing and glommed onto the briefcase.

The stern rose in a swell. A string of decorative white lights along the canopy lit up both men. Fowler kicked aside a lounge chair to get a better grip on the briefcase. Bo watched Doug struggle to keep his balance and hold on with both hands.

Fowler pivoted sideways under the lights.

"You can't do this," argued Doug.

"Like hell I can't," said Fowler.

Bo's eyes widened as Fowler drew a pistol, buried the muzzle into Doug's chest, and pulled the trigger.

Muffled by direct contact and the wind, Bo heard little more than a *thud.*

As Doug stumbled backward, Fowler shoved his pistol back into a concealed holster and set the briefcase on a lounge chair.

Doug slumped forward, clutching his chest.

Bo hadn't seen this one coming. He shifted his position and watched as Fowler muscled the injured man toward the steps. Bo lost sight of them as they descended toward the platform where the Hinkley and the Fountain were tied up.

Doug didn't stand a chance. Seconds later, Bo heard the splash and knew Doug was gone.

Fowler trudged up the steps alone and took a seat on a lounge chair with the briefcase on his lap. He pulled out a fresh cigar and patted his pockets. "Where the hell is my lighter?"

Taking the cue, Bo strolled outside as if he hadn't noticed Fowler and lit up a cigarette. The surprised senator studied him.

"Good evening, sir," said Bo. "Everything okay?"

Fowler gestured at Bo's pocket. "You got a light?"

Bo handed his lighter to Fowler, who leaned forward and lit his cigar. "Thank you."

It pissed Bo off when the man pocketed his lighter.

"You going up to the helipad, sir?" ask Bo. He didn't give a crap what Fowler did. Only that he stayed out of his room long enough to allow Bo the opportunity to nab Lauren.

"I'll be there in a bit. I'm going to have myself a smoke first."

"Yes, sir." Bo scanned the horizon. "Looks like we'll get a few squalls tonight. Hope you have a nice evening."

Bo went inside, intending to make a fast track to Fowler's room. Instead, he found Preston heading his way. *Shit. Now what?*

"Where's Fowler?" demanded Preston.

Bo pointed a thumb over his shoulder. "Outside on the deck, sir."

"Get upstairs to the helipad," said Preston. He glanced back at Bo as he went outside. "That's an order."

BOWERS STOOD GUARD inside Hogan's room. She flinched when a fist pounded on the door.

As Hogan directed the women to the safety of the bathroom, Bowers asked, "Who is it?"

"Crewman Keller, ma'am," he said. "Please help me."

Hogan stepped in front of Bowers and answered with his pistol drawn. A wide-eyed crewman in a blue shirt stood in the passageway. Bowers pulled him inside.

The shaken young man bent forward to catch his breath. "There's crazy shit going on in the engine room. A guard is threatening to shoot us. He hit my shipmate so hard the guy is unconscious. Please help us."

"Show me," said Hogan.

Fearing an ambush, Bowers followed Hogan and the crewman below deck toward the engine room. On the way, she probed for information. "What do you do?"

"I'm an engineer. I work on the machinery."

The man appeared young and genuinely scared.

As they drew closer, Bowers recognized Jung's voice. His screaming could be heard down the passageway.

She peered around the corner where Jung had a crewman on the ground, punching the guy in the face.

Jung pointed to the unconscious man lying in the hall. "I'm ordering you to dump this sack of shit overboard."

"No way," yelled a crewman. "What's your problem, dude?"

Bowers silently crept up and aimed the barrel of her AR at Jung. "Stand down," she ordered.

Jung glared at them as Hogan disarmed him.

"On your face," ordered Bowers. "Hands out to the side. Do it now."

With the help of the crew, they gagged and wire-tied Jung's wrists, and stripped him of his radio, keys, and phone. Their steps echoed in the narrow passageway as she and Hogan marched Jung past the rusted walls to the Hole, where they forced him inside with the dead 3rd mate.

When Bowers returned to the area outside the engine room, the crew gathered around her.

"Thank you," said a crewman, "but there will be hell to pay for this."

"The Coast Guard is en route," said Bowers. "Until they get here, we need to keep you safe." She hesitated. "Do any of you know what happened to the sixteen-year-old blonde who was in the Hole?"

"Yes, ma'am," said a stocky crewman in a blue shirt. "They took her to Fowler's room. She never came back."

Hogan glanced at Bowers with concern and went back to watching the passageway.

A distinguished Hispanic man stepped forward. "My name is Torres. I'm the ship's chief engineer. "Thank you for your help.

"We need to stop this," she said, "before anyone else gets hurt."

"Take care of my crew," said Torres, "and I'll do whatever you want."

"We need to disable the ship," said Bowers, "and get your men to a safe location."

Torres immediately went into action. He pointed to the man who'd been knocked out. "Mason, go help Colton to his feet. Owens, get some chains and wire-ties from the equipment locker. We're going to hole up in the crew mess. Johnson, gather everyone you can trust together and get up there, pronto. Be sure housekeeping staff and the chef and his crew are secured too."

"Yes, sir," they said in unison.

Torres motioned to Bowers. "Come with me."

She expected the engine room to be hot and greasy. Nothing was further from the truth. Inside was like a different world. Beyond the loud vibrations and noise, the immaculate engine room sparkled under bright lights.

"Look at that," said Hogan. "You've got two MTU V16 diesels."

"Yes, sir," shouted the chief engineer above the rumble. He seemed perfectly at home among the huge engines and equipment.

"We'll need power to the ship," he said. "We'll want to preserve lights, communications, and most importantly, the bilge pumps."

"How?" asked Bowers.

"I'll disconnect the linkage to the props. No worries. I'll take care of it."

"Thank you," said Bowers.

"I appreciate your help," said Torres. He waved her outside and lowered his voice to a whisper. "What they are doing on this ship is criminal. Some crewmembers are guilty as sin. Others are not. Be very careful."

"Are you willing to testify?" asked Bowers.

"Yes ma'am. But watch out for Preston and Fowler. They are dangerous. So are their henchmen, especially Bo."

CORNERED

S TANDING ON DISPLAY around the helipad so Preston could feel like a big man left Bo feeling like a trapped coyote.

Every survival instinct he had screamed at him to go to Fowler's room and rid himself of the Lauren problem before Preston got wind of it.

With everyone gathered to greet the chopper, this would be the perfect time to slip away, if it weren't for Preston eyeballing him.

Wearing his captain's hat, Preston stood near Fowler who pulled out a small flask and took a swig.

Seconds later, two short men with black hair disembarked from the chopper. One looked like an older businessman. The other man was a different breed entirely. Bo noted the bulge at his hip and ankle, which meant he was packing heat.

The pilot helped a wobbly third passenger off the chopper. The small, black-haired man wore a goatee and a shiny blue-gray suit. The pilot handed him off to Preston.

The skipper left the sick man clinging to a railing and pulled Bo aside. "He has motion sickness. Don't let him puke on the carpets."

Bo shrugged. "Carson should come up here and take him to sick bay."

"I radioed him," said Preston, "but he's not answering. Take our guest to his stateroom. Then go find Carson and tell him to check in on him."

Bo approached their sick guest still clinging to the railing.

"I'll help you, sir," said Bo. He reluctantly held the ill man's arm and let the other guests leave first. As he guided the man toward the bridge, Bo spotted Fowler near the chopper, handing a thick envelope to the pilot.

The pilot quickly stuffed it into his pocket. "I'll be ready, sir."

Bo pretended to be helping their sick guest. "Breathe easy and look at the horizon."

Fowler passed Bo, who acted as if he hadn't noticed the senator or the pilot.

While heading below deck, Bo wondered what Fowler was up to.

A few minutes later, he unlocked the door to the sick Sri Lankan's stateroom. The man bolted for the bathroom but didn't make it.

Bo grimaced and went to look for a deckhand to clean up the mess.

On the way, he passed Fowler's door and was sorely tempted to enter, but not knowing the senator's location stopped him. He had no intention of ending up like Doug.

Finding a deckhand should have been easy, but the passageways were oddly empty. That annoyed Bo.

He entered the laundry closet and began to rummage for cleaning supplies. He nearly jumped out of his skin when he heard a moan.

"They're coming," said a strained voice.

Bo did an about face and found himself staring at Derrick.

The man's eyes were wild and crazy. He pulled off his shirt and mumbled a bunch of paranoid shit that didn't make sense. "We gotta get out of here and tell the sergeant."

Everyone onboard knew that Derrick and a bunch of their guards had PTSD, but Derrick had never been this far gone.

"Chill, man," said Bo. "We got this."

"No," said Derrick. "Find cover. Insurgents are a hundred yards out with RPGs." He crashed through the door and stumbled into the passageway.

Bo picked up a can of carpet cleaner and peered inside the laundry bin looking for rags. Instead, he found Carson's body. "Shit."

He left the closet to find Niko. Bo needed his help. Besides, Niko owed him one for helping with the girls' rebellion.

A few minutes later Bo ran into the bearded guard near the crew quarters. "Hey, man. Have you seen Niko?"

"Pal, I ain't seen anyone." The guard smirked and leaned closer. He smelled of chewing tobacco. "Niko likes to visit the ladies. Maybe he's in the Hole amusing himself, but you didn't hear it from me."

"Thanks," said Bo as he hurried below deck.

Just as the guard had said, the passageway was unusually quiet. *They must be prepping for Fowler's next meeting.*

Bo stopped near the Hole, opened the door to the dressing room, and found the place a wreck. Towels, a bottle of shampoo, and women's outfits were scattered over the floor. He stopped at the drain and spotted a ring of pink around the grate. "Niko? You here?"

Pulling out his keys, he opened the lock to the Hole.

Without warning, the door flew open. Jung charged at him in a rage. His wrists were bloody and bruised.

"What the hell?" asked Bo.

The man slammed Bo against the wall, then shoved him into the Hole. He pointed at a body. "That's Niko. Preston will be furious."

"What happened?" asked Bo.

"Your girlfriend, Bowers, is what happened, asshole."

Jung belted Bo and launched into a tirade. "This is all on you. If you hadn't messed with Bowers, none of this shit would've happened. You screwed up everything."

Bo took a fist to the gut.

"One more thing," sputtered Jung with a finger pointed at Bo's face. "You're a dead man when Preston hears your blonde girlie is the president's missing kid. And I'll be the one to tell him. I'm done with your bullshit."

Raw fury coursed through Bo as Jung stormed toward Preston's office.

"Stop," yelled Bo.

Jung didn't listen.

Bo tackled him. Jung tried to fight back but was no match for the sharpness of Bo's knife and the unleashing of the Urge. His inner beast. The hatred. Bo's frenzied blitz attack only took five seconds.

AFTER DUMPING JUNG'S body inside the Hole, Bo washed up and locked both rooms.

A minute later, he stood in the passageway to catch his breath. It felt as if the walls were closing in on him.

With his pulse still pounding, his radio crackled with orders from Preston. "Report to the forward cabin."

Bo reversed direction, stopped by the berth for a change of clothes.

The soft sound of jazz music enveloped Bo as he entered the luxurious room, hoping he'd gotten all the blood off of his shoes.

Preston seemed annoyed as usual. "I'm getting reports of a fight below deck. You know anything about that?"

"No, sir."

Preston eyed him closely. "Have you seen Carson?"

Bo shook his head. "He's probably at the stern, smoking weed again."

"What about our sick guest?"

Bo shrugged. "I couldn't find Carson, so I gave the man a bottle of water and suggested he rest."

Preston waved over Knuckles. "Our Sir Lankan guest is seasick. We need to get him on his feet. Go find Carson and have him give the guy some meds."

"Yes, sir," said the big guard.

As he left, Preston scanned the room. "Bo, we're about to have a meeting that can't be interrupted. I need you to be on your toes."

"Yes, sir," said Bo.

As guests began to gather, Bo tried to calm his pounding pulse. Mr. Gim's assistant caught his attention. No way was this guy a pencil-pushing, desk-jockey. The man wore that same flat expression as Jung and at least two concealed weapons. Bo had been around enough mercenaries to realize the guy was a bodyguard or something more lethal.

To Bo's left, Fowler had his ear to his phone and seemed even more worked up. As he pulled Preston aside, Bo tried to blend into the woodwork.

Still amped up, each heartbeat felt like the pounding hooves of wild horses. His quickest exit lay to his right.

Desperate to get off this ship, he tried to remember how much fuel the Hinkley had onboard.

DEAD IN THE WATER

A S FOWLER BENT PRESTON'S EAR, Bo stood a few feet
away and listened. "I've got some bad news," said the senator.

Bo nearly choked.

Fowler's voice became raspy. "CFIUS just killed the bid for E-Connect. Gim and our CEO will be furious when they find out."

"Dammit," said Preston. "We can't let twelve-billion dollars go down the drain. Not after all this. What do we do?"

"I don't give a shit what they say. We can still sell the chip. Let's get this done and get out of here." He pointed a finger at Preston. "As soon as the money transfer is complete, shut down your internet before anything hits the news."

Preston rubbed his beard and called over the chief mate. "Wait for my signal and then turn off SeaMobile."

The red-haired man stood there frowning as if puzzled.

"That's an order," Preston snarled. "Go."

The chief mate hurried toward the bridge.

Fowler continued fuming. "When I get back to Washington, they'll regret this." He shook a finger in the air. "Funding for their campaigns and pet projects are going to dry up faster than California during a drought." Fowler clutched the brown briefcase with white knuckles.

"I'm getting this done. Make sure you keep Hogan and the CEO in their rooms for now."

Preston radioed Jung, but he didn't answer. He called over Scarface. The big gnarly scar that ran through the middle of the man's face spoke of a ferocious fight, but the creepiest part was the white scar covering his left eyeball.

"Something is screwy," said Preston, "I can't raise Jung, Niko, or our medic. Go check it out."

As Bo waited for an opportunity to slip away, Fowler straightened his tie and took a seat on the white couch next to Gim.

Preston pulled Bo aside. "Keep your eye on Fowler. I don't trust that bastard. Have my back and I'll double your paycheck. Got it?"

"Yes, sir," said Bo. He'd never seen Preston show fear before.

With his rifle cradled in his arms, Bo took a position against the wall within ear shot of Fowler and pretended to be watching the doorway.

Fowler greeted Gim as if everything were running perfectly. The North Korean businessman appeared to be in his mid-sixties, old school, and fearful of the man sitting next to him.

The small businessman glanced over the top of his glasses. "I am Gim Kwang-su, you call me Gim. My greatest pleasure to meet you."

Bo wondered what Gim would do when he discovered his big deal had tanked.

All eyes were on the briefcase in Fowler's lap. Bo recognized it as the one he'd taken from Doug. Fowler rubbed his hand over the soft brown leather. "The documents for the sale of E-Connect should arrive soon. In the meantime, we can finalize the transfer of the chip."

The way Mr. Gim locked eyes with Fowler wasn't a complement.

To Americans, looking someone in the eye was a sign of honesty. However, Jung had taught him that when a North Korean has direct eye contact, it was meant as a challenge or an insult.

Gim glanced at his bodyguard, as if seeking approval. The bodyguard stared at the briefcase and nodded for him to continue.

"I will examine the chip," said Gim. "If all is good, we are prepared to make the first transfer of funds."

Fowler sat forward and gently placed the briefcase on the glass coffee table. When he opened it, Gim's bodyguard pulled the briefcase closer and began to inspect the contents.

As he dug into his pocket for a lens, Bo caught a glimpse of the pistol on his left hip.

Gim sat straight in his seat like a dutiful schoolboy while his bodyguard studied the chip under magnification and the thick file of documentation.

Moments later, the man made a phone call. Bo didn't speak Korean and had no clue what he'd said.

After hanging up, the bodyguard nodded to Gim, whose smile was as phony as Fowler's.

The senator grabbed his phone and wandered over next to Bo. As he looked out the window, it sounded as if Fowler were talking to a banker or accountant who didn't speak English.

"Yes, my Cayman account," he said quietly. "Right. Nine billion. It has been approved for transfer? Ok."

Such a large sum nearly bowled Bo over. No wonder Fowler had been so tense.

When the senator made another call, Bo imagined what he could do with that kind of money.

Meanwhile, tensions in the room rose until Fowler ended his calls with a hearty laugh and big smile. "Gentlemen it's been a pleasure working with you. Your payment has been received."

As Fowler handed over the briefcase containing the chip, he cleared his throat. "There is still the matter of paying the skipper."

The bodyguard eyed Fowler closely as he set a black briefcase next to the senator. Fowler briefly popped it open and smiled. "Thank you, I'm sure Preston will appreciate your kind gesture."

The senator stood. "Let's take a break." He called over Preston. "As soon as I get the paperwork, we'll meet back here with the CEO of E-Connect and our SriCom executive to sign papers and make the last transfer. Please inform them."

HAYWIRE

F OWLER MARCHED out of the forward cabin to find Preston waiting for him in the hall. The little chicken-shit had Bo guarding his back.

"What are you doing?" hissed Preston. "You know the deal with E-Connect won't go through and they'll retrieve those funds."

The air around Fowler felt uncomfortably warm. He loosened his tie and wiped the sweat from his forehead with a handkerchief.

Play the game, Fowler reminded himself.

"Not to worry," he said, putting on a smile. "I always have a plan B."

Preston didn't need to know the number of friends Fowler had in high places nor that he had a retreat waiting for him in Belize. He squinted at Preston. "Don't get your panties in a wad. I suggest you keep in mind that your paycheck is contingent upon my success."

Shit seemed to be flying at him from all directions. It still irked Fowler that Hogan hadn't cooperated. Gim was waiting for papers that would never be signed. This was not the time for Preston's bull crap.

Fowler had to get back to his stateroom and Lauren, whom he'd left tied up and drugged in the closet. He needed to get rid of her, just like he had with Doug.

As he started to return to his room, he felt the ship roll sideways hard enough that it forced him to put a hand on the wall to keep his balance.

That surprised him. He stared down at the plush, dark-blue carpet and wondered what had happened.

"We need to get something clear—" Preston stopped mid-sentence as if he too had noticed the ship's odd movement.

His radio squawked.

"Skipper," said the chief mate. "Something is wrong. We're dead in the water."

Fowler's survival instincts launched into high gear, sending a prickle down his spine. He could feel this whole situation slide south. His window of opportunity to get off this ship was closing fast.

It felt as if the broad passageway with its paneled walls were now no more than a trap. It was time to get off this damned ship before anything else went haywire.

Preston tugged on Bo's shirt. "Come with me," he barked. They headed toward the bridge.

Fowler sent a text to the pilot: *warm up the bird. Now.*

Within seconds, he replied: *Roger that.*

Time was dwindling fast. Fowler didn't even bother to grab his personal effects. When he got done with his plan, nothing would be left anyway.

He followed Preston and Bo as they hurried up the white metal steps to the bridge.

Being convinced that Preston had set him up gave Fowler even more incentive to get to that chopper before Preston did.

On the bridge, the chief mate stood at the helm where the classic ship's wheel seemed in stark contrast to the array of high-tech navigation, computerized radar, and modern steering equipment.

While Bo retreated toward the ladder, Fowler watched his every move. He never had liked that guy.

Fowler glanced outside, pretending to watch the light rain spattering the windows and helipad, when in reality he was keeping a close eye on the pilot and the chopper that would take him off this ship.

When Preston's back was turned, Fowler nodded to the pilot, who nodded back.

At the sound of the *whomping* rotor blades, Preston abruptly turned to stare at Fowler and then the helipad. He left the monitors, and screamed at Fowler, "Why is my bird warming up?"

Fowler took a step back behind a row of seats. Preston's eyes bulged as if they would pop out of his head.

The first mate flinched as he glanced between digital displays. The little punk looked nervously at Bo, standing by the steps.

Fowler had a hard grip on the black briefcase and put on his politician's smile. "Everything is fine."

"No, it's not," said the chief mate, who pulled off his headset. "Our steering is offline."

The row of windows, which usually provided a spectacular view of the sea, were now dark. The moon had vanished behind a line of clouds.

As the bow rose in the swells, Fowler thought he saw something in the water flare in their starboard lights but lost it in the chop.

As the ship rocked sideways in a large wave, the chief mate's expression turned to alarm. Fowler heard clicking as the chief mate frantically tapped on a keyboard. "I don't know why this is happening."

"Get Torres on the phone," ordered Preston. "Tell him to get his ass up here. Pronto."

"I can't, sir. You ordered me to shut down the service."

"Then use the damned radio," barked Preston.

The chief mate pointed to the radar. "Sir, there is something else. There are a number of vessels circling us."

That caught Fowler's attention. The hair went up on his neck.

Preston frowned at the monitors and pointed to the pulsing dots on the screen. "Who the hell are they?"

"Coast Guard, I think," said the chief mate, "and what looks like a destroyer." He glanced nervously at Fowler. "And I thought I saw two small vessels heading straight for us. Now I can't find them."

Preston stared down at the bow.

Fowler gripped the black briefcase and headed for the door to the helipad. "I'm out of here."

Preston came unglued and rushed toward Fowler. "Where the hell do you think you're going? We made a deal."

"And you broke it," shouted Fowler. "You set me up."

"What the fuck are you talking about?"

Fowler pushed Preston back. "That blonde you sent to my room was the president's missing kid. Did you really think I wouldn't recognize her?"

Preston frowned, then his chin dropped. His eyes widened as his head snapped left. He glared at Bo who vanished like a ghost down the steps, leaving behind nothing more than the sound of his fading footsteps.

Preston grabbed the briefcase. "This is mine and so is that damned chopper."

Fowler refused to let go. "Not anymore," he shouted. The senator drew his pistol. "Let go or eat a bullet."

Preston stared at the gun and released his grip.

As he and the chief mate scurried toward the steps like a couple of rats abandoning ship, Preston glanced over his shoulder. "I will get you for this."

As the yacht rolled sideways, Fowler grabbed the brass handrail and glanced at the unmanned helm. Outside at the helipad, the landing lights flashed on and the rotor blades picked up speed.

Before taking off, Fowler took out his pocketknife and ripped through the fabric of the seat cushions. He pulled out his flask of scotch and drenched the exposed stuffing.

Flicking his lighter, he lowered the flame to the alcohol-soaked cushions. They burst into a fireball.

Fowler bolted out the door toward the chopper.

TERROR

RIGGS IGNORED THE TENSING of his gut as he took a seat inside the MH-65 and stared out of the open door. He'd do whatever it took to get onboard that ship.

Riggs' headset dampened the noise and allowed him to hear communications. He'd sent a text to Bowers but hadn't received a reply.

Next to him, Coop scanned the scenery below with his elbows resting on his knees. "Hey, Riggs, you should sign up for being a Coast Guard swimmer."

"Pain in the ass." Riggs pivoted toward Coop. "Is it that obvious?"

Coop's blond eyebrows went up. "You weren't this tightly wound when you found me in Bowers' hotel room."

As the chopper flew toward the *Leisure Lee*, they passed over two Coast Guard vessels heading the same direction.

"Riggs," said the pilot. "The *Leisure Lee* is no longer under power."

Riggs pulled against his harness to peer over the shoulder of the co-pilot at his digital avionics and screens tracking the super-yacht, which showed it bobbing in the swells like a buoy. Their lights meant they had power, but they weren't going anywhere.

The pilot leveled out and swooped into a turn as it circled the ship.

The landing lights illuminated the helipad, but it was occupied by a small red chopper.

Riggs white-knuckled his harness as they veered in the opposite direction.

"Where are we going?" asked Riggs.

"We've been diverted," said the pilot. "The crew sent out an SOS. They said there's gunfire onboard and the skipper is trying to escape in a Fountain speedboat. We've been ordered to intercept."

As they raced over the water, Riggs put back on his headset and felt the pilot descending faster than Riggs would've preferred.

Channel 16 crackled with a message from the Coast Guard's thirty-three-foot, fast boat. "Be advised. We're four minutes out."

"Roger," said the pilot. "We'll slow 'em down."

When the HITRON marksman settled in behind the machine gun, Riggs had a clear picture of their intended method.

"Riggs. Hold on," said the pilot.

They swooped in low and ripped over the dark waters.

"Hooyah!" said Coop as he pumped his fist in the air.

"Mark, Mark, Mark," shouted AMT Mozzi. "Vessel of interest is at two o'clock."

The chopper circled the red Fountain Thunder Cat. "One male onboard," said a crewman. "Let's lay down check fire about thirty feet in front of his bow."

The pilot came in hot. Their marksman cut loose with the machine gun and laid down a line on the water.

The Fountain didn't stop. While they chased the go-fast boat, the pilot called command to obtain permission to disable the boat.

"You are authorized to engage," said the voice on the com.

"Roger," said the pilot.

He shouted to the HITRON marksman, "Put rounds on target."

"Yes, sir." With the barrel of his .50-cal precision rifle supported by a strap, he carefully lined up his sights on the twin Mercury outboard engines.

Riggs couldn't help himself. He held on and stared down at the speeding boat. The wind whipped through his hair and pummeled his face. The resounding rapid-fire *BOOMS* echoed in the cabin.

The armor-piercing bullets took out both of the Fountain's outboard engines.

The boat swerved to port where a big swell lifted the vessel and submarined the bow into the trough between waves. The man onboard was jettisoned into the drink.

"Nice work," said Coop.

The chopper positioned a floodlight over the wreck and the man in the water.

"One PIW," said the pilot. "Repeat one person in the water."

Riggs cheered when the Coast Guard's fast boat arrived on scene.

The man struggling to stay afloat stared up at the chopper with a pale face. "That's Preston," said Riggs. "He's responsible for the human trafficking on his ship."

Preston didn't argue with the armed seamen who pulled him out of the water and detained him.

"You got him," said Riggs. Drowning would be too easy for that bastard. A monster like him deserved to face a judge and the rest of his life behind bars.

"Thanks for your help," said the commander of the Coast Guard vessel. "We'll take it from here. You're clear to depart."

The celebratory moment vanished when the radio crackled. "Occupants in the inflatables are confirmed as Chinese Black Dragons. They're about to board the *Leisure Lee*. DEVGRU is seven minutes out. Authorized to engage."

"Buckle up, guys," said the pilot.

NOT ON MY WATCH

B OWERS AND HOGAN HID in the alcove outside the forward cabin and watched the North Korean businessman and his bodyguard grow more edgy by the minute.

Their occasional whispers to each other evolved into a running tense dialog.

Across the room, the guard called Scarface appeared ready to doze off.

"Something is wrong," whispered Bowers. "Where is Preston and Fowler?"

Hogan peeked over her shoulder. They both watched as the CEO threw open the double-doors and charged into the room as if hellbent on tearing someone's face off. "Where the hell is Fowler?"

At first, Mr. Gim seemed startled. He stood and bowed. "I wait for him as well. He said we would sign papers."

The CEO scowled at the businessman as if the guy were stupid. "Don't you get it? The deal is a bust."

The businessman glanced at his bodyguard as if confused. "What is bust?"

"It means we're done," said the agitated CEO. Fowler screwed us. I swear I'll sue that bastard into the ground."

The Sri Lankan entered. As the CEO's shouts increased in volume, the Sri Lankan man retreated toward the door.

While the men fumed about Fowler's deception, Scarface strolled over to the couches as if to calm the situation. "Hold on. The skipper will be here in—"

Scarface stopped and stared out the windows.

At the same time Bowers spotted shadowy figures moving over the deck outside. The hair went up on her neck as she recognized what their body language meant.

The guard warily backed away from the white couches and raised his rifle.

Gim's bodyguard jumped to his feet. With his pistol drawn, he squinted at the dark scene outside as if he'd heard something. His eyes went wide and he immediately began pushing Gim toward the exit.

A terrified Mr. Gim ran for the door with the briefcase clutched against his chest.

"Hogan," whispered Bowers. "We've got company."

He peered over her shoulder and through the curtain.

"Shit," said Bowers. "Duck!"

Within a split second, the silence in the forward cabin was obliterated by a barrage of bullets, shattering the windows.

As she and Hogan took cover, Bowers caught a glimpse of the guards, including Scarface, diving for the floor. Streaks of red splattered the white couches.

The sound of gunfire was deafening. Glass exploded in a torrent of flying shards. The mirror behind the bar fractured into a bazillion pieces. Bottles of booze burst.

Screaming guests ran for the door.

Bullets sprayed all four corners and shattered the glass panels between Bowers and the forward cabin.

She peered between the curtain as the CEO went down. Scarface covered his head and screamed, "Don't shoot."

Amid the chaos, men in black uniforms kicked in the remaining broken glass and swarmed into the room.

Bowers and Hogan stayed concealed behind the curtain.

"They're Black Dragons," she whispered. "Look at the patch on their sleeves."

"Chinese black ops. That ain't good."

She nodded.

"Help me," pleaded the CEO.

A Dragon fired one shot, point blank. "Quiet," he said, standing over the CEO's body. Then he aimed his AK-47 at Scarface. "No weapon. Put down," he yelled in broken English.

Scarface dropped his rifle and held up his hands.

Two shots rang out as the operative executed him.

———

BOWERS FELT HOGAN GRAB her arm. "Let's go," he whispered. They crouched low and scrambled around the corner. He stopped and winced. "Bowers, I'm hit."

She could see blood oozing from his right shoulder. They hurried down the passageway to Hogan's stateroom.

As they entered, Bowers signaled the women to keep quiet.

Sara grabbed a hand towel, while Molly hustled the women into the bathroom.

Bowers grabbed Carson's medical kit from the closet. She quickly examined Hogan's wound and pulled a packet of Quick Clot out of the kit and applied the powder. The bleeding slowed.

"You're lucky it missed your lung," said Bowers. "How do you feel?"

"Pissed off," said Hogan. "The Marine in me doesn't like being sidelined."

"Trust me. We still need you," she said. "This boat is like a convention for scumbags. They're thick as fleas on a stray dog."

"You've got a point," said Hogan.

"How about you protect the women while I take a walk?"

Hogan winced. "I can do that, but where are you going?"

"To find Lauren."

After leaving him additional ammo, Bowers cautiously headed down the long corridor toward Fowler's stateroom.

Minutes later, she found his door standing wide open. With his personal effects still on the bed and in the closet, it appeared Fowler had left in a hurry.

She heard a yelp from the sundeck and ran outside. Below, she spotted Bo dragging Lauren down the steps toward the Hinkley.

Bowers raced toward the ladder. She heard gunfire, leapt over a lounge chair, and took cover behind a service bar. The Dragons were advancing quickly.

Lauren continued to struggle until Bo grabbed her by the hair and threw her onto the Hinkley.

Bowers heard Lauren cry out in pain.

Bo untied the lines and fumbled with the ignition key.

The engine sputtered. The delay was all Bowers needed. She sprinted toward the boat and made the leap of a lifetime. As the engines revved, she landed on the deck and rolled to her feet.

Before Bo could react, she smacked the side of his head with the butt of her rifle. Bo swung and hit Bowers hard, causing her to stumble over a push broom. He jumped on top of her. Fists flew. It was like the assault on the beach all over again. That pissed her off.

As his hands squeezed down on her throat, his hideous smile returned. "You have no idea how much I've looked forward to watching you die."

Bowers felt her airway close and the pressure in her face. She kneed him in the crotch, hard.

Bo's face twisted into agony as he gasped.

Lauren picked up the broom and started wailing on him with the wooden handle.

"Let her go," she screamed.

"Dammit," shouted Bo. He lunged to his feet. Angry and in obvious pain, he guarded his head with one arm and protected his crotch with the other.

Lauren continued to wildly swing the broom.

After being smacked in the ear, Bo stumbled sideways and turned away from Bowers.

Lauren screamed, "I hate you, asshole."

He tried to grab her, but the deck tilted in the swells.

As Lauren continued to beat him with the broom, Bowers rolled to one knee and stood. With one hand, she pulled Lauren behind her and aimed her AR-15 at Bo. "Give it up."

Bo started to raise his Beretta.

Bowers squeezed off two rounds, hitting him in the chest. "Say your prayers, asshole."

Bo fell to one knee, then collapsed onto the deck.

The sudden silence seemed deafening. Lauren hadn't uttered a word. Bowers found her slumped against a wall, staring out the door as the boat rocked on the swells.

Her eyes were glassy and dilated. It appeared that either Bo or Fowler had drugged her.

Bowers briefly considered taking off in the Hinkley with Lauren, but the gas gauge indicated the tank was almost empty. She only had one more magazine and no immediate backup. They would be sitting ducks.

Bowers refused to allow foreign operatives to capture the president's daughter. *Not on my watch.*

She steered toward the *Leisure Lee* with great caution.

Bowers listened for a chopper and searched the sea for the Coast Guard but saw nothing. In the dark, the crack of gunfire and hot yellow muzzle flashes continued to flare onboard the super-yacht.

A minute later, she cut the engines and let the swells push the Hinkley into the platform at the back of the ship. Bowers tied up to the stern and helped Lauren onboard.

Smoke poured from the top deck near the bridge. The ship's fire alarm blared in a pulsing wail.

With the Chinese killing squad still roaming the decks, this battle was far from over.

BOWERS CREPT OVER the swim platform at the back of the super-yacht with Lauren close. The *whomping* of the choppers circling them offered a distraction and some relief knowing that help was coming.

At one o'clock, Bowers spotted a hostile in black on the upper deck pointing at the Hinkley. They'd seen her.

Bowers aimed her AR-15 and fired off two rounds. As if in slow motion, the man's heavy gear rocked him forward and pulled him over the rail, where he bounced against the tinted windows and flopped into the sea.

Protecting Lauren became Bowers immediate priority.

As she crept toward the steps, with Lauren behind her, a Chinese operative cleared the deck. He stood on the sundeck with his back to her, searching the sky for choppers.

His silhouette against the landing lights revealed a helmet, AK-47, and a bulky armored vest.

Like a leopard homing in on prey, she moved forward slowly and deliberately. Her pulse pounded in her ears.

She balanced her stance at the bottom of the steps, listened to his breathing, and shot him in the ass.

He yelped something in Chinese and attempted to return fire. When he rotated to face her, he opened up more targets, especially from her line of fire.

Bowers popped off a shot that hit his belly below the vest, and another one a little lower. He fell limp to the deck.

"Don't look," she said to Lauren, as they scrambled up the stairs and ducked into Fowlers room. "Sit down and don't move."

Bowers went back to the sundeck and removed the man's helmet, vest, and rifle. She returned to Fowler's stateroom and put the vest and helmet on Lauren.

Seconds later, Bowers silently crept down the passageway with Lauren behind her.

"Squeeze my shoulder if you see anyone," whispered Bowers.

Five steps later, Lauren squeezed.

"*Tíng.* Halt!" The shout came from around the corner.

Bowers pushed Lauren back into Fowlers' room and handed her the AK-47. Lauren's blue eyes went wide.

From the doorway Bowers knelt with her AR-15 ready.

The hostile entered the passageway near the fire extinguisher mounted on the wall. She cut loose with a short burst, hitting the red canister. She didn't expect it to explode, but it did spray a large plume of white into the air. The sound and blast startled the hell out of the gunman. The white haze allowed Bowers to take a better angle. She fired two rapid rounds, nailing him in the neck and side.

Returning to Lauren, Bowers grabbed her by the arm. "Come with me. Stay close."

Lauren hurried to keep up.

As Bowers hustled her toward Hogan's stateroom, he appeared at the door.

Again, Lauren squeezed down hard on Bowers' shoulder.

Derrick stumbled into the passageway and rammed into the wall. Dazed and covered in blood, he called out, "Sarge. Where is everybody?"

Another one of Preston's guards peered around the corner, wearing a red bandana. He reached out and tried to corral Derrick, who pulled away and shrieked about RPGs. Fueled by delusions and genuine fear, Derrick came unhinged and began screaming.

Gunfire broke out from the adjacent hall. Both Derrick and the guard in the bandana went down. The Dragons were excellent marksmen.

Hogan fired at one of the hostiles, but the man kept coming. Bowers swiveled, aimed, and made a head shot. Lauren buried her face in Bowers' back.

"You're ok," said Bowers. "Just stick with me."

Bowers and Lauren ran the last ten feet and disappeared into Hogan's room. Molly was so overjoyed to see her friend, she doubled over and burst into tears.

Lauren hugged her. "I'm so sorry I got you into this."

"No one," said Bowers, "could've anticipated this."

Hogan approached her as if something were wrong. "Bowers," he said. "You've been shot."

"I know. It burns."

"No shit," said Hogan as Molly handed him the medical kit and another envelope of Quick Clot.

Bowers pulled up her vest and shirt. "Hurry."

"Jeez," he said, staring at the wound. "You ok?"

"I've been through worse."

Hogan applied the powder to her wound. "Looks like the bullet grazed your lower back and went through the fleshy part at your waist."

"Thank you for doing this," she said.

"What's with the fire alarms?" he asked.

She grabbed her rifle. "I'm about to go find out."

INFERNO

FOWLER SCRAMBLED TOWARD the chopper with the bridge on fire behind him. He heard more gunfire as he jumped onboard the small red helicopter. His clothing smelled of smoke.

Even with all the shit that had gone wrong, he could still outwit these assholes and looked forward to starting anew somewhere tropical. Through the door he watched the flames. He'd left Lauren drugged and tied up in his closet. Ships were highly flammable. He expected the super-yacht would soon explode into a raging inferno. The ship, Lauren, and any evidence would soon be gone.

Fowler spotted dark figures approaching that were backlit by the fire.

He screamed at the pilot, "Get me off this damn ship!"

As the rotor blades picked up speed, Gim rushed toward them and dove into the seat next to Fowler.

"They're shooting," shouted Gim. "Fly us away."

Gim still hugged the briefcase holding the chip. As Fowler was about to tell him to get off, he realized the opportunity. He could sell that chip on the dark web for a fortune.

The dark figures in the shadows were men in black military-style uniforms and they were advancing quickly.

As the rotors turned faster, Fowler screamed. "Get us in the air! Now."

The chopper shuddered as the pilot began liftoff. Gim's bodyguard bolted out of the darkness. He jumped onto the landing skid. With both hands he clung to the metal handle next to the door.

Fowler noted how his hair blew into his face from the rotor wash. When the man glared at him, Fowler glanced away.

Incoming fire made Fowler jump.

"Hold on," shouted the pilot.

Fowler's pulse pounded as the pilot demonstrated his combat training and swooped away from the incoming bullets.

Lead plinked against the exterior as they gained altitude. The bodyguard clung on with one hand and fired back with the other. Moments later they swung over the water. The blood on the bodyguard's shirt and pants meant he'd been hit in the exchange.

In the blinking lights from the cockpit, Fowler stared at the man's face. Seemingly in slow motion, his stance wobbled, and his eyes lost focus. The man struggled to hold on, but his arms went limp. He fell backward and plunged into the sea.

Gim had curled his body around the briefcase and didn't seem to notice the wound on his hip. Clearly, the man would protect that chip at all costs.

As the chopper flared away from the ship, Fowler gaped through the open door in utter dismay. The blaze he'd set had withered to little more than wisps of white steam.

"Where to?" shouted the pilot as a light rain hit the windows.

"Bahamas," yelled Fowler. "And close the damned doors. I'm getting wet."

The pilot didn't reply.

"When we land. You find big trouble," said Gim, as he grimaced. "Your word is no good."

Fowler glared at the man. "What the fuck are you babbling about? You got your damned chip."

"You did not honor our deal. You promise to sell whole company. I cannot go home. You put big shame on me and my family. You must make fix and honor our deal."

Fowler's hair blew in the wind as he twisted in his seat to glare at Gim. "Don't you dare school me, asshole."

Gim did that stupid thing where he crossed his arms on his chest. "This means we are finished," he said.

"You got that right." Fowler grabbed the brown briefcase, but Gim refused to let go. The senator pulled the small North Korean man out of his seat, still clutching that damned briefcase.

Gim struggled to hold on. "You have money. I buy fair and square. This now mine. Let go."

"Okay." Fowler pushed the man backward toward the open door. Much to his horror, Gim hugged him as he lost his footing.

OVERWHELMING FORCE

RIGGS AND COOP BRACED themselves for the worst-case scenario. Riggs imagined the horrors they must be facing on the decks below.

Every minute counted as he shouted over the cockpit noise to the pilot. "We can't wait for backup."

He stared out the door with his gut rolling. From what he could see the Dragons were showing no mercy and weren't taking any prisoners. He hoped Bowers and Roadrunner were still alive.

As the pilot reported in with sector Key West and Homeland Security, the rain shower came to an end.

"We have visual confirmation," said the pilot. "Foreign operatives have boarded the *Leisure Lee*."

"Understood, lieutenant," said the Commandant at Homeland. "Do everything you can to hold them off until DEVGRU arrives on scene. They will contact you on channel 16."

"Sir?" asked the pilot. "Do we need to raise DEFCON?"

There was a pause. "No need. They were never here."

The pilot's brows went up as he focused on his instrument panel. "Roger that."

The global balance of power reminded Riggs of a convoluted chess game. The Dragons sealed their fate by boarding an American ship. Military assets wouldn't leave any of them alive, which would put China in a dicey situation. If they inquired about their missing men, they'd be forced to acknowledge attacking an American ship so close to our coast. China was pretty ballsy, but even they wouldn't go that far.

The chatter on the radio made it sound as if every American military asset were itching to descend on the scene. Even the 160th SOAR, a.k.a. Night Stalkers, stood ready. They were well known for their mission into Abbottabad, Pakistan where they joined DEVGRU in the takedown of Osama bin Laden.

Despite his apprehension, Riggs edged toward the door. The flight mechanic grabbed his harness and clipped on a tether. "Safety, sir."

The helipad glistened in the landing lights as their MH-65 circled the *Leisure Lee*. Riggs recognized Fowler below as he climbed into a little red chopper. A moment later a small man ran across the helipad and jumped inside with the senator.

Riggs anxiously waited for them to take off so they could get down to business and protect the friendlies onboard.

"Riggs," shouted Coop. "Checkout the guys below on deck."

Men in black were advancing. Gunfire broke out. The pilot veered away and tracked the little red chopper as it gained altitude. Amid the gunfire something fell from the chopper.

Their SARs night vision monitors showed a heat signature consistent with three on board. The way the chopper swayed and the bodies jerked seemed to indicate some sort of disturbance onboard.

Coop hailed the co-pilot. "Can you get a picture of that?"

"It's automatic, sir. We'll give you a copy of the footage."

When the pilot made a wide circle and passed the red chopper, Riggs saw two men at the door, locked in a deadly embrace.

He gasped when they fell.

"Holy shit," said Coop. "Did you see that?"

Riggs could not believe what they'd witnessed. The only remaining heat signature had to be the pilot. "Holy crap, Larry Fowler just did a 1,000-foot nosedive into the sea."

"Do you want to go after them?" asked the swimmer.

"Negative," said the pilot. "They're dead. We have live souls to protect."

As they returned to the helipad, Riggs could see the fire had been extinguished, but another battle raged on the decks of the *Leisure Lee*. The two inflatables were big enough to hold six or more men each.

"Riggs," said the pilot. "Blackhawks are three minutes out."

At the open door, Riggs firmly gripped his MP5. He lay on his belly and scooted up to the edge of the opening. Riggs took a deep breath and poked his head out of the door. "Let's hold these clowns off until DEVGRU gets here," he shouted.

"Hell, yes," said HITRON'S precision marksman.

As the chopper swooped in, Riggs could smell the smoke. The chopper avoided the white steam bellowing from the bridge. Riggs and the marksman laid down fire along the port side, forcing one of the inflatables to back off.

"Riggs," shouted Coop, "Hold your fire! Bowers is lying in wait at the stern."

Two Black Dragons swarmed straight for her. Riggs' jaw set as he heard them fire. His mouth went dry. The crew cheered as she took them out.

When she backed under cover, the flight mechanic directed the pilot to the bow of the ship. It tore at Riggs as she drifted out of sight.

As they circled the bow, Riggs spotted the second inflatable offloading another wave of Dragons on the starboard side. These elite forces could only be matched by the SEALs, who couldn't get there fast enough.

"Look out," shouted Coop.

Two Dragons fired on their chopper. Riggs and the HITRON marksman returned fire. They took them both out.

Everyone onboard searched for any flicker of movement below. With so much at stake, the stress factor was off the scale. His heart felt as if it were about to explode.

Two more Dragons executed one of Preston's guards and continued their search. Riggs suspected they were hunting for Lauren and targets of value. Their marksman shot one of them. Riggs nailed the other one. As they continued to circle the ship, Riggs realized Bowers had moved to the upper deck near the bridge.

"Hold your fire," ordered the pilot. "Blackhawks are here."

A message came over channel 16. "Coast Guard airborne 6515, this is Blackhawk One. Please advise who's the female near the helipad?"

"A friendly," responded the pilot. "Former MP and she's one hell of a shot."

"Roger that."

Riggs and Coop watched the SEALs fast-rope in. Riggs, with his background within the FBI's SWAT team, would've given anything to be on that deck with them.

Three of the Black Dragons scrambled to the port side where they leapt onto an inflatable and took off. The second Blackhawk chased them down. In the distance Riggs spotted the muzzle flare of a machine gun obliterating the invaders.

The flight mechanic nudged Riggs. "That'll teach them."

SEALs lined up on deck and pushed forward like a rolling arsenal. The firefight went inside where the tinted windows on the upper two decks shattered.

The deafening rotor wash of the second Blackhawk returned as more SEALs fast-roped in.

Riggs glanced at the ink on his palm where he'd written *Bowers* and closed his hand into a tight fist.

BOWERS HAD TAKEN OUT six Dragons and stood ready to eradicate more if they dared to approach Hogan's stateroom.

The bodies of Preston's guards lay scattered throughout the corridors. The Dragons had killed Scarface and the bearded guard in the forward cabin. Knuckles' body lay on the deck not far from Fowler's room.

As she held the passageway, she heard a soft shuffle. Taking cover and having no idea how many hostiles were still onboard, she prepared for the worst.

Bowers spotted big men in full battle rattle clearing the passageway.

Helmets fitted with cameras, faces darkened by camo paint, night-vision goggles, huge armored vests loaded with ammo, lethal weaponry, their sheer mass, and the way they moved were terrifying until she saw U.S. Navy embroidered on their vests. The men were Navy SEALs.

Bowers silently changed positions and watched. Fast and quiet, the SEALs rushed in. She felt confident they would put an end to this, but it wouldn't be easy. The Black Dragons were equally aggressive and trained to the point of fanaticism.

As the wall of muscle and firepower approached her, Bowers set down her AR and held up her hands.

A SEAL pulled her hands behind her back until the team leader gesture for him to let go.

"What's your name?" asked the team leader.

"Bowers."

"Good," he said. "I've been looking for you. I'm Mike."

The SEALs split into two groups. One rapidly went to clear the port passageway.

Mike glanced at her back. "You're injured. You need a medic."

"It's more important that we secure Roadrunner and Senator Hogan."

Mike nodded as if he appreciated her dedication to mission.

"Follow me." Bowers picked up the AR-15 and led them down the bullet-riddled passageway and around a shot-up fire extinguisher and two bodies.

Bowers heard a shuffle. She spotted movement up ahead and signaled Mike. The black muzzle of a rifle was slowly protruding from the laundry closet not five feet away. Bowers slammed her body into the paneled door, knocking the occupant backward. She flung open the door. A Black Dragon raised his AK-47. She shot first and ended it.

The SEALs stared at her and Mike.

"Are you coming?" she asked as she hustled down the passageway.

"Ladies first," said Mike.

A few minutes later, she waved for Mike to find cover and pointed to a sliver of a black sleeve barely visible around the corner. The SEALs engaged in a short but deadly salvo. One of their own fell.

As they assisted their injured man, another gunman in black

charged around the corner, screaming as he raised his rifle. Bowers and two SEALs beat him to the trigger. A rapid *Bam-Bam-Bam* echoed in the passageway. His battle cry stopped when he careened into the wall with dark holes in his forehead and neck.

The SEALs guarded her on both sides as Bowers led them to the door labeled *Horizon*. She whispered, "Hogan. It's Bowers."

She heard nothing but silence. A moment later Hogan opened the door. His chin dropped when he saw the men behind her.

"Senator Hogan meet SEAL Team Six."

They hustled into the room where Ron Hogan stood shirtless with a bandage taped to his shoulder. He seemed exhausted but had done the job and had kept the women safe.

Two men carried their wounded teammate into the room where Bowers helped lay him on the bed. He had been shot in the thigh. A medic immediately took off his pack and began applying a tourniquet.

As the SEALs marched into the room and took over, Bowers introduced Mike to Lauren and the others.

Lauren rubbed her eyes. "I'm still a little foggy. Fowler forced me to take Valium." Her speech was slightly slurred, and her pupils were dilated.

The arrival of these huge men in serious military gear was intimidating. Mike would be an imposing figure all by himself, even without tactical gear.

As he approached Lauren, she backed toward the bathroom and began to tremble as if terrified. "Look, I'm really sorry." Her eyes grew teary. "I'm in so much trouble."

"Lauren," said Mike. "We're here to keep you safe."

He stopped and studied the girl's face. "I'm a dad and I guarantee there are a lot of people who will be thrilled to see you, but we need to get you off this ship."

"Do what he says," said Bowers.

Lauren nodded.

SEALs blocked both ends of the passageway. Anyone who dared to attempt to breach that room would pay dearly for their stupidity.

Another SEAL approached the doorway. "Hey Bowers," he said. "Who is this?"

She went to the door. "He's the Sri Lankan who's under North Korea's thumb."

"Detain him," said Mike.

Everyone ducked as the sound of gunshots drew closer. The sporadic gunfire ended quickly. In the room, radios squawked as each sector was cleared. The medic caught Mike's attention and nodded toward Bowers.

Mike leaned in close. "How about you let him take a quick look?"

"Later," she said. "I've survived worse. Right now, we need to ensure that Lauren and Molly get off this ship and that the others are safe."

Mike coordinated the extraction with the Blackhawk pilots. In another transmission he hailed the pilot of the MH-65 Dolphin.

"Go ahead, team leader," said the pilot.

"We have precious cargo and need paramedics and transport for eight survivors, plus one of our own. We'll take five in Blackhawk One. Can you take four?"

"Roger that," said the Coast Guard pilot.

She suspected Riggs would be onboard the Coast Guard's chopper, probably ripping the pilot a new one for not getting him onboard. She hoped the word *survivors* would help ease his worries.

Mike sent another transmission. "Be advised. Bowers is injured but refuses care until the women and Hogan are away and safe. Let's step it up."

Bowers smirked when she heard Riggs voice.

"That's Bowers for ya."

THE ASSET

RIGGS STARED AT THE DARK, smoldering grand ship rocking in the gloom, a ghost of its former self. Ribbons of steam drifted away from the upper deck in the wind and were caught in the lights of choppers and searchlights from two Coast Guard cutters.

The lights cast an eerie glow on the ship's battle scars. Bullet holes and bodies dotted the deck below. Water spewing from a broken pipe was tinted pink by blood as it dripped from the gunnels. The ship stood as a crime scene, a grim testament to all that had happened.

Two Blackhawks circled the ship. One guarded the perimeter, while the other hovered, waiting to pick up survivors.

Coast Guard cutters had moved in with surprising speed. Within minutes their teams began boarding the ship.

Riggs expected the Blackhawks would go in first, but the Coast Guard pilot surprised him and began their descent. Hurricane-force winds from their rotor wash blew water and shell casings off the heli-pad, as they eased down onto the deck.

The teams guarded every inch of the landing area.

Surrounded by SEALs, women began funneling through the shattered doors of the bridge.

Riggs' spotted Bowers. The sight of her left a lump in his throat.

Somehow, it didn't surprise him to see that the women were as fiercely protective of her as were the Navy SEALs. Bowers had one arm firmly around Lauren and the other around a young Cuban girl.

As the SEALs attempted to pull Lauren away, she and the women clung to Bowers' side.

Riggs couldn't hear what Bowers said, but she spoke to each of them. Lauren stayed close.

Senator Hogan stood behind Bowers. To her right a Navy SEAL held Bowers by the arm for support. Riggs suspected it was Mike, the man he'd spoken with over the COM.

"Sara," shouted Coop. He jumped onto the deck, ducked, and ran to a young woman who leapt into his arms. He scooped her up and ran, carrying her to the chopper.

Riggs jumped off and took a few steps. Even with exhaustion etched on her face and covered in the grime of battle, Bowers stood strong until they locked eyes. Her expression softened and took his breath away.

The blood on her shirt made his jaw clench.

His legs couldn't move fast enough.

The women stepped back.

The feel of Bowers in his arms nearly had him undone. The warmth of her skin and odor of her hair engulfed him. With his callused thumb he gently wiped the sweat from her temple. He felt the weight of her head on his shoulder and her soft breath against his neck. He wanted to hold her like this forever. Riggs rested his chin against her forehead, but his eyes stared blankly into space. Muzzle flashes and the fear that had nearly swallowed him still raced in his thoughts.

She winced as he hugged her too tightly.

"Easy," said Mike in a deep voice.

With one arm cradling Bowers, Riggs clasped hands with Mike and mouthed *thank you*.

Mike patted his shoulder and gave them a moment.

The world seemed right again.

Two SEALs guarded Molly and Hogan. When they came for

Lauren, Bowers called out to her. "Lauren, let them take care of you. I'll see you soon. I promise."

Lauren nodded and waved as she wrapped her arm around Molly.

Riggs could feel Bowers tremble from the exhaustion and the adrenaline dump and yet she insisted the women and Hogan were helped first.

Bowers cocked her head and grinned at him. "It's about time you showed up."

Riggs laughed.

Mike leaned in. "Riggs, you were wrong. She wasn't just a friendly. She is one hell of an asset. Hogan razzed us for being late to the party. By the time we arrived, she'd already taken care of business."

Bowers reached out and patted Mike's shoulder. "Riggs, don't listen to him. We made it out because of these men."

Mike shook her hand. "You can be on my team anytime."

ABOVE AND BEYOND

BOWERS AWOKE IN A STRANGE bunk in the Zumwalt's medical unit known as sickbay. The air smelled like disinfectant and alcohol wipes. A fan somewhere softly hummed. The first thing she felt was Riggs holding her hand like she had held his when he'd been shot.

She opened her eyes to find Riggs watching over her.

"Morning," he said. The gravelly sound in his voice and the lines at the corners of his eyes meant he was beyond tired and worried.

She started to move. "Oh, jeez. Damn, I'm stiff."

He scooped his big arm under her shoulders and helped her sit up. She swung her legs over the edge of the bunk and leaned forward, pressing her head into his shoulder.

Riggs curled forward and exhaled. The warmth of his face next to hers felt like heaven. "I missed you."

He closed his eyes and gripped her hand. Riggs then raised his head and stared deeply into her eyes. "I was afraid I'd lose you." His hand tightened harder. "I love you."

Bowers reached up and hugged him. "Now you know how I feel when you're in the line of fire."

"I get it."

She kissed his face. "We did it."

"Lauren's safe," he said. "She's asking for you."

She took a deep breath and grimaced. "What about the ones at the bottom of the sea?"

"You did all you could. That's all anyone can do."

She glanced down and realized she had on a patient gown and nothing else. "Well this is attractive."

He gently inspected the bruises and scrapes on her knuckles, then locked eyes with her. "You look great to me."

For a long moment, they sat there in silence, enjoying the closeness.

"Did you find what you needed in Key West?"

"I did." She shrugged. "It was never about thugs and criminals. It's about protecting the innocent."

BOWERS SAT AT A dark-blue table in the wardroom watching Lauren poke at her scrambled eggs, as if she were about to face a firing squad.

The dining area was small, tables on one side and the chow line and coffee pot on the other. Mounted on the cream-colored walls were a large screen TV and a collection of photos from Naval history.

Lauren picked up her dropped napkin from the polished wood floor. Lieutenant Haley had gathered up donated sweatpants and T-shirts for Lauren and the women to wear, which meant the shaking of her hands wasn't from feeling cold.

Bowers sipped at her coffee and was thankful for the crew who'd washed her clothes for her. "You nervous?"

Lauren smeared jam on her toast. "Yeah. My dad is gonna kill me. I'll be grounded until I'm forty-two."

"Cut him a break," said Bowers. "He cares. He was so worried about you that he tormented the crap out of the FBI, Secret Service, and everyone else until they found you."

"You mean until *you* found me." Lauren bit at her lower lip. "I never thought my dad cared that much."

"This was way beyond what most people ever have to deal with, but you did it. I'm proud of you."

Lauren glanced away. Tears trickled down her cheeks. "Thank you."

Bowers waited until Lauren had finished her breakfast. "Come on. Let's do this."

Lauren wiped her eyes on a napkin and tried to smile. Together they walked into the fresh morning air on the stern of the Zumwalt.

The SEALs stood overwatch along the ship's railing. Mike nodded to Bowers in his dress blues.

"You clean up nicely," she whispered. He pulled back his shoulders and stood taller.

Lauren stayed at Bowers side like a puppy as Mike escorted them to the hanger, where they stood next to Molly. Riggs joined Bowers. They glanced up at the sound of rotor blades. The gray Naval ship made the clear blue sky seem even bluer by contrast.

A rumble of excitement grew as *Marine One* landed on the helipad. The captain and crew saluted.

Secret Service agents wearing earpieces and dark suits had kept them in the hanger until the president's chopper had safely landed. Moments later, they were escorted to the helipad.

The salty breeze off the ocean felt invigorating. Bowers scanned the waters. With the Miami coastline on the horizon, they were surrounded by a flotilla of warships and USCG cutters.

Molly's parents disembarked the big chopper and immediately began to search the crowd of faces.

"Mom! Dad," shrieked Molly, as she ran to her parents. Lauren squeezed Bowers' hand so tightly it almost went numb.

Bowers glanced to her right and spotted Hogan, who had his arm in a sling. He smiled and nodded. Riggs greeted a gruff man with ferocious black eyebrows. "Special Agent McDougall. Good morning, sir," said Riggs.

McDougall grunted. His black hair fluttered in the wind. "I don't know whether to fire your ass or promote you."

Riggs squinted at the chopper. "I'd prefer the latter."

"With a bust like this, I expect you'll get your wish." A slow smile spread across McDougall's face. "It's a fine day."

"Yes, it is, sir."

The captain and Hogan saluted the president and escorted him and the first lady toward Lauren. The president wore his usual stern face and dark-blue suit. Lauren's mother wore a white wool pantsuit with a collarless Navy-blue shirt.

POTUS stopped mid-deck, surrounded by Secret Service. He focused on his daughter as if no one else were there. He seemed a different man. His brows rose above watery eyes.

Lauren took a hesitant step forward and stopped. The crowd on deck fell silent. All eyes watched as she whirled around and buried her head in Bowers' shoulder. "I'm scared."

Her arms held on so tightly, it felt as if she would crush Bowers' ribcage. Her fresh wound stung, but Bowers sucked it up. This was an important moment. When she'd left for a simple vacation, Bowers had never dreamed she'd end up holding the president's trembling daughter.

Bowers whispered in Lauren's ear. "Listen, after what you've just faced, this is a piece of cake. You've got this. Just picture him in bunny slippers."

Lauren giggled and turned to face her father. He opened his arms. After a few hesitant steps, Lauren ran into her parents' embrace.

Bowers swallowed the lump in her throat.

Lauren surprised her when she grabbed her father's hand and dragged him over to meet her.

"Dad," said Lauren. "I'd like you to meet Kate Bowers."

The president kindly shook her hand and gratefully smiled at the officers and crew. "Thank you all."

"Dad. Wait." Lauren demanded her father's full attention. "Bowers is the one who found me. She..." Lauren's voice quivered. Tears ran down her cheeks. "Dad, she took a bullet for me. She's the one who saved me."

Never before had Bowers seen this hardline president display any kind of emotion. He wrapped his arms around Lauren and stared at Bowers as if lost for words.

The president cleared his throat. "Ms. Bowers, I am beyond grateful." His voice cracked. "Mere words aren't enough."

"Sir," said Bowers. "Many put their lives on the line for this day. The FBI, the Secret Service, the Coast Guard, the U.S. Navy, and many others saw this through."

She introduced Riggs, Greg, and Mike to the president.

Mike saluted. "We have a fine team, sir, but this woman went above and beyond the call. I was there. Bowers was in the fight all the way. Everything your daughter said is true."

Bowers felt the weight of Riggs hand on her shoulder.

The president eyed McDougall closely and shifted his gaze to Bowers. "It seems to me the FBI could use someone like you. You interested?"

Riggs' grip tightened.

"Yes, sir," said Bowers.

"McDougall," said the president, "I want your fine agents rewarded for their exceptional service. They are an honor to our country."

"Thank you, sir." McDougall shook his hand. "I will make certain that happens."

POTUS glanced toward the chopper. "One more thing: Hire this woman. That's an order."

As the first family was about to board *Marine One*, Lauren bolted toward Bowers and hugged her again. "Don't forget me. Okay?"

"That won't happen."

Lauren giggled. "Good. Call me. Promise?"

"Promise."

Lauren handed Bowers her phone number scribbled on a scrap of paper and ran back to her family.

After lunch with Riggs and the command staff, Bowers and Riggs waited for the Coast Guard chopper that would take them back to Key West.

Riggs glanced at the gun on her hip. "I see Captain Ayers went out of his way for you."

Bowers rested a hand on her Glock. "I can't believe he made sure they returned my service pistol."

She stood next to Riggs on deck, listening to the sounds of the sea.

She leaned on the railing and enjoyed the warmth of the sun on her back. She pointed at a flying fish as it skimmed the waves.

Riggs quietly squinted at the horizon. "Looks like we're both getting a promotion."

He opened his hand and showed Bowers her name written in faded ink on his palm. "Maybe I should have this tattooed here?"

NO WHERE TO HIDE

F ROM AN ARMORED VEHICLE, Bowers watched the FBI execute the takedown of Gunner and his gang. They had shut down a section of Highway 1, a 113-mile stretch of road over the waters between Key West and the mainland. Based on intel, the joint task force had picked this moment to put an end to the Changós reign of terror.

Their well-planned interdiction had been executed with speed and precision. Thirty motorcycles were now barricaded between FBI agents from Miami on one side and the Key West PD and Sheriffs on the other. This section of the bridge between Duck Key and Long Key had no exits, no nearby land, just a road elevated above the water. It had been selected because it gave Gunner and his crew nowhere to hide and nowhere to run. It also protected any bystanders in the event shooting erupted.

On this beautiful sunny day, it appeared that Gunner's luck would finally run out. The remaining question was whether he and his crew would give up or fight to the bitter end.

The Changós had already demonstrated their willingness to kill law enforcement. This time police and agents weren't taking any chances.

They all came prepared with armored vests and high-powered, automatic rifles and the FBI's HRT, Hostage Rescue Team.

Bowers stood close to Riggs. They'd taken cover behind the armored vehicle known as The Bear. Tensions rose as the bikers scattered and Gunner and his crew realized they were trapped.

The FBI's warning and HRT's calls for calm and compliance were repeated again and again.

When the announcement came over the mic that the bikers were surrounded and ordered to comply, one of the bikers dumped his bike, ran to the railing, and leapt off the bridge. He landed with a splash in the blue waters. When the man spotted a dorsal fin, he panicked and pleaded for rescue and was more than happy to be apprehended. The Coast Guard never told the guy that the animal he saw was a dolphin.

The wet biker was so thrilled to be out of the water that he didn't fight being taken into custody. The man's two outstanding felony warrants likely had something to do with why he'd jumped.

A MH-65 chopper from Station Key West flew overhead. After seeing the shape of the bird's nose, she could see why they called it a dolphin. They expected the encounter to be brief. Overwhelming force had that effect on most people.

Gunner was the exception. Most of his crew circled their bikes around him as if their counter-barricade was any match for the huge armored vehicles and concrete barriers that the FBI had moved in with front end loaders.

The bikers' axes were worthless against the SWAT team.

"This is stupid," whispered Bowers, "They can't win this. What are they thinking?"

"Suicide by Cop," said Riggs.

When the Coast Guard's MH-65 buzzed the bridge to ward off a News chopper, Gunner began firing at the MH-65 with a semiautomatic pistol. His gang cut loose and wildly shot at the officers and agents with every pistol, rifle, and shotgun they had.

SWAT and the marksman in the Bear's turret returned fire.

The bikers' bravado was astonishingly brief. The moment gunfire ceased, a brief silence was followed by moans and cries for help.

The next wave of response came from the SWAT Team that swarmed in and disarmed the bikers, dead or alive.

Coop, the Key West PD, and Sheriffs joined the medical crews on standby and moved in to deal with the mass casualty situation.

Some of the bikers wandered aimlessly, staring at the responders as if lost.

"If you can walk," shouted Coop through a mic, "go to the side of the road. Sit on the pavement with your back to the concrete barrier. Do it now."

Bowers heard the wail of more medical services rushing to the scene.

She followed Riggs toward Coop. They passed the concrete barriers where The *Changós* were lined up on their butts with their feet out in front of them. Nolan nodded to her as he zip-tied the bikers' hands behind their backs.

Bowers scanned the scene. Most of the bikers had survived and were sitting by the barriers as ordered. The rest were either severely injured or dead.

EMTs filtered through the wounded left on the pavement and rendered care to the most seriously injured first and the others as needed. An injured officer was busy performing CPR on a limp biker. As quickly as possible, the injured were escorted by law enforcement to nearby hospitals for emergency services before going to jail.

Bowers found Coop in the center of the melee. At his feet lay Gunner's body.

"I didn't want it to end this way," said Coop. "I wanted him to face justice in a court of law."

It was obvious that Gunner's condition was incompatible with life. Multiple rounds had ripped through his chest, neck, and abdomen.

"Riggs, is this the man?" asked a sheriff wearing a big black hat.

"Glad you could come," said Riggs as he shook the sheriff's hand. "This is him. The DNA found on Grace and in her rape kit is a match to him."

The sheriff stared at Gunner's body and glanced at Coop. "Anyone who saw what he did to Grace, wouldn't find this such a bad outcome."

Coop appeared puzzled.

"Riggs," said the sheriff. "Thank you for giving me a call."

"I promised I would."

The sheriff nodded and walked away.

"Who was that?" asked Coop.

"He was at the murder scene where Gunner had killed a fourteen-year-old girl with an ax. Her name was Grace. Her head was five feet from her body. We think they transported her there in a van."

Riggs turned and squinted at a white van parked on the shoulder behind the bikers. He shouted at Coop and another officer. "Come with me."

Bowers recognized the white van and watched as Riggs, Coop, and agents surrounded it.

Muffled sounds came from inside. Bowers heard kicking against the back doors. Riggs stood ready with his pistol drawn. Coop and an agent opened the van's rear, double doors.

Riggs lowered his gun immediately. In the back were two terrified women. One appeared to be around eighteen to twenty. The other was closer to twenty-five. Both were bound and gagged.

Riggs called over an agent with HRT. She immediately brought in their Evidence Recovery Team, a paramedic, and other officers to clear the area.

The sight of these terrified women instantly took Bowers' mind back to the Hole. Riggs stood next to her and gripped her hand as if he understood. A moment later, he glanced up and spotted the sheriff in a black hat who'd been watching. He tipped his hat and signaled Riggs with a thumbs up.

Coop stood staring into the back of the van as the women were untied and escorted to a waiting ambulance.

"You just saved those women," said Bowers.

———

THE FOLLOWING DAY, Bowers and Riggs entered the Key West Police Station at 6:00 p.m. The last time she'd been up that elevator seemed a lifetime ago.

Greg had returned to Miami. Riggs had stayed in Key West to

work with the FBI's Evidence Recovery Team and the Coast Guard to begin the processing of multiple crime scenes, including the dumpsite. Bowers had taken a break to heal, enjoy the sun, and do more diving.

Today, they assembled in a large room for the promotion of Officer Brian Cooper. Rows of chairs faced a podium adorned in the bright blue and gold emblem of the department. On the wall behind it hung a white screen where a short video of Coop's time on the Rock played to rounds of hoots, heckles, and cheers. The chief of police and the captain called Coop up front. Sara sat in the audience, clapping.

Coop's wife arrived with their daughter, who wore a tiara that matched a doll in her arms. Coop seemed the happiest she'd ever seen him. The chief offered praise and recapped what had happened over the last two weeks, including yesterday's takedown of Gunner and his outlaw biker gang.

While Coop's wife pinned on his new insignias, his daughter Ellie reached up. With his little girl in his arms, Coop thanked the chief, the captain, his fellow officers, and his wife and family. As Sara joined him, officers came up to congratulate Coop.

Bowers enjoyed seeing him holding hands with his wife. It appeared they were on the mend. Ellie, still in his arms, eyed Coop's police cap and impishly pulled it off his head. She giggled and replaced it with her tiara. As laughter rose from the audience, Coop took his cap and put it on Ellie's head. The crowd roared and cheered.

The captain whispered to Bowers. "His kid stole the show."

"Yes, sir."

"Thank you," he said, "for everything. I thought you might like to know that we recovered evidence that confirmed your statements."

She had to ask, "Did you find the origins of the hand?"

"We are still working on it," he said. "Riggs is helping us. It's at the FBI lab as we speak."

"What about the stainless-steel bracelet?"

The captain nodded. "We found it and we also found the finger-prints and hair you left all over the driver's seat and windows of Bo's truck. That was quick thinking."

"Thank you, sir," said Bowers.

The big captain shook her hand. "If you ever want a job, we've got one for you."

Riggs playfully put his arm in front of Bowers. "Hey, we finally got her to agree to join the FBI. Don't you go stealing her."

The captain laughed. "Well, Riggs, you've got yourselves a real asset."

Riggs shook his hand.

On the way down the aisle, Coop stopped in front of Bowers. Still holding his daughter, he scanned the faces of all those gathered, especially his little girl, who threw her arms around his neck and said, "Daddy, you did good."

A few minutes later, Linda took Ellie off to get a piece of cake. Coop gazed at his wife and child, and then back at Bowers. "I don't know where to begin." He cleared his throat. "Thank you for having my back."

THREE WEEKS LATER, Bowers took the short walk from the police station to Bayview Park. She took a seat on a bench next to Deon's wheelchair.

Meanwhile, Lonnie paced the basketball court as Deon gripped Max's leash and watched children playing in the grass.

The park's lush green lawn, pavilion, and basketball court seemed the perfect spot to re-connect Deon to the things he loved and show him his life wasn't over. However, the longer they waited, the more edgy he became.

"You nervous?" ask Bowers.

"Yeah, big time."

Bowers leaned forward. "Deon, stop for a minute and look at what you've survived. That says a lot about who you are. Besides, my friend Jay will understand like no one else can."

Deon nodded until he heard the engine of a big black truck arrive. His chin dropped when the driver's door swung open and a lift lowered Jay in his wheelchair to the ground.

When Jay waved them over, Lonnie took charge of Max while Bowers rolled Deon to Jay's truck.

Deon was speechless as he stared up at the shiny black truck.

"Deon," said Bowers, "this is Jay. We served together in Iraq."

Deon appeared fascinated. "You drive this? By yourself?"

"Absolutely," said Jay. "Bowers, give us a hand."

She wheeled Deon onto the lift. Jay secured the wheelchair and put the controls in his hand. "Press the green button."

Deon's face lit up as he rode up and into the cab and back down.

With the ice broken, Bowers stood back with Lonnie as Jay and Deon tossed a basketball back and forth. They played for a bit. Jay showed Deon how his wheelchair's bracing mechanism allowed him to stand and shoot baskets.

"Hey, I got you," said Deon. He tossed the ball and made a basket.

Bowers heard Deon laugh for the first time.

As the two men gave each other high-fives, Lonnie sat next to Bowers. "This is exactly what he needed. Thank you."

"We aren't done yet."

The action on the court stopped as a medical transport arrived. A figure in a wheelchair was lowered to the ground.

Deon stopped playing. He couldn't take his eyes off the man in the wheelchair as a woman in scrubs wheeled him closer. A rigid back brace encircled the man's torso. Bandages covered much of his head and arms.

The man was nearly unrecognizable as the nurse wheeled him up next to Deon.

He silently stared at the man for several seconds. "Vega?"

Max barked and tugged on his leash.

The two men stared at each other until Lonnie dropped Max's leash and the dog gently approached Vega with a wagging tail and sat next to his foot.

Vega's eyes filled with tears as the dog leaned into his leg. He reached for the little beagle, but the brace and bandages restricted his movement.

Deon grabbed Vega's extended hand. They locked eyes.

"I wish we could've done this all different," said Deon. His chest heaved as he nodded toward Max. "Thank you for saving us."

Vega lost it. "You should never have been in that chair." Tears streamed down both their faces.

"I'm so sorry," said Vega.

BOWERS GREETED SANTIAGO at the coffee stand. He insisted on giving her a cup of coffee on the house. "Life is now good. Sara is back."

Riggs pulled up at the curb and waved Bowers over. "Get in."

He did a U-turn in the parking lot. "There's something you need to see."

They exited the car at the marina and stood on the docks. "We found Novia's parents," said Riggs. "All of the Cuban women have been reunited with their families."

"That's great news," said Bowers.

"We also found the Cuban boat that supplied the women. The crew was offered a deal to give up their ringleader, which they did. Yesterday morning before dawn, the FBI raided his compound. They arrested him, a bunch of traffickers, and a drug lord."

Riggs' grin appeared irrepressible. "They also found a boatload of enslaved workers forced to provide grounds keeping and maid services for the kingpin, including one you'll find of particular interest."

Two patrol units pulled in with strobes flashing. A curious crowd gathered. Coop stepped out of one of the cruisers and opened the door of the passenger seat.

Out stepped Lily in clean jeans and a yellow shirt. Her hair had been freshly cut. She appeared nervous and a bit confused, but Coop escorted her to the dock and stood next to her as if to assure her. She waved at Bowers and looked up at Coop. "Why am I here?" asked Lily.

"You'll see," said Coop as an orange and white Coast Guard boat pulled up to the dock. Seaman secured the lines and Lily appeared even more confused as additional officers surrounded her.

A blonde woman stepped off the boat.

Lily gasped and doubled over. Coop kept her from falling.

"Oh my God! Oh my God," chanted Lily. She screamed, "Lana," and sprinted for the blonde-headed woman.

Officers cheered as the two sisters embraced. They stared at each other and held on to one another as if in disbelief. Both sobbed for joy.

Bowers lost it.

BOWERS AND RIGGS enjoyed their last day in Key West by soaking up some sun on the beach before heading back to D.C. in the morning.

Out of nowhere came a voice, "Tamales. Anyone want tamales? Nice hot tamales. Good price."

The man pulled a cart with an insulated container behind him and stopped right in front of Bowers. She sighed and wished the bald guy with day-old stubble and a gold tooth would move on down the path.

Just as she was about to tell him to leave, something familiar caught her eye. A baseball bat covered in stickers and a clown mask with yellow teeth sat in his cart.

Images of the evil clown who'd helped her careened through her thoughts. Bowers stood, lifted her sunglasses, and squinted at the man.

After stepping closer she asked, "Henry?"

He donned a dark-blue ballcap, with a red-and-white dive flag embroidered on the front, and tapped the brim.

"That's my hat!"

Henry took it off and handed it to her. "I thought you'd like it back."

He sounded so different. The stilted speech and *yup-yups* were gone.

"Hey man," said Riggs. They gripped fists and gave each other a brotherly slap on the back.

"She's something else," said Henry. "I don't know how you keep up with her. She lost me so many times. She made me work for it, that's for sure."

Riggs was clearly enjoying this.

Henry lowered his voice. "I'm just glad you got Gunner before I had to mess him up."

Riggs chuckled. "He's the one who alerted me that you'd been abducted. We had him tracking Gunner too."

Henry shrugged.

Bowers was stunned. "Thank you."

He shook her hand. "You're welcome. It's been a pleasure. Hey Riggs, let me know about next time."

Henry, if that was even his name, wandered away, pulling his cart with him. He whistled. Seconds later, Buddy stopped sniffing at a trashcan and trotted back to his side.

She glared at Riggs, who was still chuckling. "Besides you, he's the best undercover guy I've ever worked with. He even pulled off pretending to be an informant."

Bowers roared with laughter. "You got me."

CLOSURE

B OWERS EXHALED HEAVILY as she sat in a rented vehicle with Riggs. They had returned to Key West for a ceremony on the beach for the victims and their families.

It had taken over a year for the FBI, in partnership with the U.S. Coast Guard, to recover and test the remains found at the dumpsite and track down those responsible. This operation turned out to be the largest trafficking case in Coast Guard history.

Even without the recovery of the president's missing daughter, this was a career-making bust for Riggs and one that would forever be part of FBI history.

So far, over 85 people had been arrested, 257 victims were recovered, and the FBI seized 3 submarines, 2 boats, 1 small plane, 24 drones, and 68,000 pounds of cocaine valued at $2.3 billion.

The dumpsite held the remains of 141 souls: 93 women, 10 men, and 38 children between the ages of 10 and 17. The hand found on the beach was matched to a woman at the dumpsite.

More than the outlaw bikers' gang, they had shut down an international human trafficking and illicit drug operation.

Bowers smiled every time she thought about Preston awaiting trial in a federal prison. He'd been deemed such a flight risk that the judge refused to bond him out.

She sat in the passenger seat, reflecting on the successful mission and watching people as they gathered on the beach. She teased Riggs about his promotion.

He wore a satisfied smile. "Don't tease your superiors, agent Bowers."

Bowers put a hand on his thigh.

"Easy girl."

Bowers smirked and twisted in her seat. "Where do you think they'll send us next?"

"We should find out soon." Riggs stared out at the beach.

She felt his big hand wrap around hers. He tilted his head back and closed his eyes. "I'll never forget what ran through me when I saw you on the bridge of that ship."

"You have no idea how glad I was to see you." She tried not to think about the Hole. "This has been one for the record books. I'm just glad that the deal for E-Connect never went through and that damned chip disappeared."

"I'm told," said Riggs, "DTSA stepped in to assess the case and is partnering with government agencies and industry leaders to prevent the diversion of technologies that could prove detrimental to U.S. national security."

"Good. I hope it works. We came far too close to the edge."

Riggs focused on her. "You ready to jump into the global playing field?"

She nodded.

Riggs squeezed her hand. "The Chief of Police and Coop just arrived. Time to go."

They left the car and joined the peaceful crowd gathered on the white sandy shore for the somber ceremony. The Coast Guard deployed two ships with fire hoses that shot two graceful arcs of water into the air.

City officials and the Chief of Police called Riggs, Bowers, USN Captain Dickson, and USCG Captain Ayers to the podium and thanked the Coast Guard, U.S. Navy, and FBI for their tremendous service.

Bowers looked out at the sea of faces. Some held photographs. Some wore T-shirts printed with images of their lost friend or relative. Way in the back stood a petite Cuban woman with long black hair, surrounded by what appeared to be her family. Bowers recognized her immediately as the woman the fishermen had found clinging to a cooler and had rescued. Seeing her surrounded by family made Bowers' day.

She still ached for the victims and their families, who now tossed wreaths into the water in their memory. The damage could never be undone, but there was some justice in holding the perpetrators accountable. Images ran through her mind of Bo, Gunner, Jung, Niko, and Fowler whose body was never found. The thought of their corpses decomposing to bones as they had done to their victims seemed only fair. People were safer with them no longer stalking the Earth.

Bowers squinted up at the bright-blue sky as Lily and Lana sang a clear sweet song of strength and hope and the Key West Wildlife Center released rehabilitated gulls, skimmers, and three brown pelicans that quickly took to the air.

After the ceremony, silence hung over the crowd until people began to mingle. They reached out to greet each other. Many shook hands, hugged, and shared stories. A sense of peace radiated from Lily's expression as she came closer.

"Bowers, this is my sister Lana."

Bowers reached to shake Lana's hand and found herself engulfed in a hug from both women.

"Thank you," said Lily. "Thank you so much."

Both Lana and Lily were overcome with emotion. Even Bowers shed a few tears.

Riggs put a hand on Bowers' shoulder. "We need to go."

When he and Bowers began walking back to the car, he stopped by a picnic table and said, "Wait here for me. This will just take a sec."

Riggs joined the tall police captain.

As she waited, her curiosity was piqued when the captain glanced up at her just as Coop and a group of officers surrounded her.

Bowers expected they'd come to say good-bye, but Coop surprised her. He set a shallow box on the picnic table. With a mischievous glint in his eyes, he glanced at Nolan, Carver, and Rodgers, who began to snicker.

The captain wore a big smile as he folded his arms and watched. Even Riggs grinned at her.

Bowers scanned their faces. "Okay, what are you guys up to?"

"We want," said Coop, "to thank you for having our backs." He handed her the box. "In addition to Bo's bracelet, our divers also found this."

Nolan put a hand over his mouth.

Bowers frowned at the gold and blue package and lifted the lid.

"No way," she said. Nolan and Carver began to chuckle.

Bowers pulled out a piece of rebar mounted on a wooden plaque and glared at Coop.

The officers' giggling rolled into waves of laughter.

The captain smiled.

"Thought you might like..." Coop laughed so hard he had to stop to catch his breath. "Keep it as a memento."

Bowers cracked up. "I can't believe you guys."

The captain strolled over to shake her hand.

Coop hugged her. "Trust me, this is one we'll never forget."

"You guys are the best. Thank you."

After talking with them for a bit, Bowers slid into the waiting SUV to return to D.C., but instead of leaving right away, they rolled down the car windows and listened to the ocean's lapping waves and kid's playing on the beach.

Bowers glanced down at the rebar plaque in her lap and shook her head. "You have to love this place."

They watched the crowd break up and a man tossing a ball to a golden retriever. Henry glanced over his shoulder at their car and winked. Riggs gave him a thumps-up, then his phone buzzed.

After the call, Riggs said, "We need to get back to D.C. We've got orders and a new case. You ready?"

She nodded. "I've had all the time off I can stand, but this time, let's try not to get shot."

WHAT'S NEXT?

I hope you enjoyed ISLAND OF BONES.
Please consider leaving a review.

YOU ARE WELCOME to visit my website martasprout.com and signup for my no-spam-ever mailing list, which will soon include membership in Marta's VIP Readers Group, occasional newsletters where you'll be the first to hear about upcoming events, new releases, and fun giveaways.

Check out KILL NOTICE, the 1st book in the *Bowers Thriller Series.* "Devious, fast-paced. Highly Recommended." - JONATHAN MABERRY, NEW YORK TIMES BESTSELLING AUTHOR

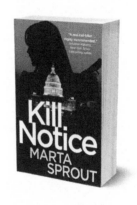

COMING SOON! Within the wrenching chaos of war, Bowers will blow your mind in 31 BRAVO, the 3rd BOOK of *The Bowers Thriller Series*.

Books in The Bowers Thriller Series:
 Kill Notice
 Island of Bones
 Fetish for Murder - coming soon
 31 Bravo - coming soon
 For updates: Go to martasprout.com

ACKNOWLEDGMENTS

A GREAT DEBT OF GRATITUDE goes to those who offered insights based on their extensive careers in the military and law enforcement; and for the humbling encouragement from my fellow writers.

David Farland is my valued friend, mentor, and extraordinary editor. One cannot help but respect this remarkable man who tirelessly shares his insights and wisdom with other writers. A huge thank you is due to the Key West Police Department, its officers who were so welcoming, the Chief of Police Donald J. Lee, Jr., Public Information Officer Alyson Crean, and especially Officer Michael Andruzzi for their tremendous service and for introducing me to Duval Street and this vibrant community.

The assistance of the FBI's Office of Public Affairs is greatly appreciated. A heart-felt thank you goes out to retired FBI Special Agent Mitch Stern and retired FBI Special Agent Gary Noesner.

As always, I must thank my best friend, co-adventurer, and husband Dennis and my family and friends for putting up with my latte-driven obsession to write.

ABOUT MARTA SPROUT

THAT I WRITE THRILLERS IS NO SURPRISE for those who know me. When not writing, I relish skiing big mountains, scuba diving with everything from sea horses to manta rays, and snorkeling with gentle giants like whale sharks and manta rays.

I teach at the police academy and have done training scenarios with SWAT. In addition to the pursuit of an accurate and credible story, the bond I have with law enforcement, military, and firefighters comes from a deep respect for those who put themselves in harm's way to protect total strangers. For me, being an advocate for others came as a result of one incident that rocked my world. As a teen, I drove to Hollywood long before sunrise. After becoming hopelessly lost, I parked near a driveway in a gated community to read a map. Arriving home later that night, I spotted that driveway on the news. It was Sharon Tate's home. I'd been there just before the bodies were discovered. Today, writing thrillers gives us all a safe way to unravel why some are violent, to honor victims and the bravery of those who protect others, and to wonder: What would you or I would do in the shoes of a hero?

facebook.com/MartaSproutAuthor
instagram.com/marta_sprout

Made in the USA
Coppell, TX
30 September 2022